R. F Winch

**The Life and Writings of Addison**

R. F Winch

**The Life and Writings of Addison**

ISBN/EAN: 9783337055677

Printed in Europe, USA, Canada, Australia, Japan

Cover: Foto ©Raphael Reischuk / pixelio.de

More available books at **www.hansebooks.com**

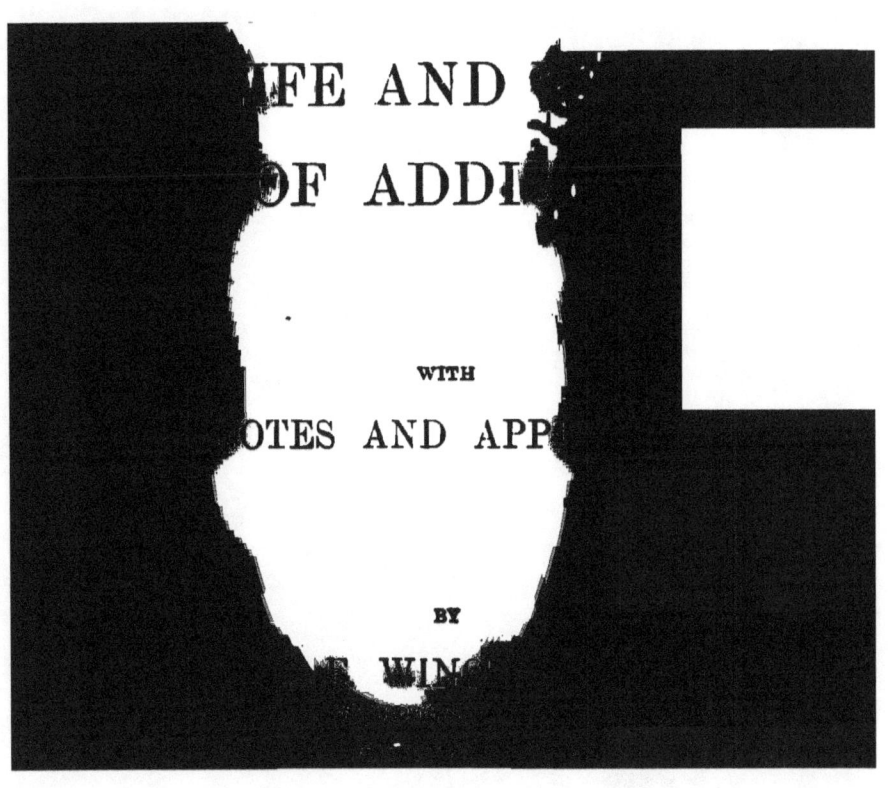

IFE AND

OF ADDI

WITH

OTES AND APP

BY

WIN

London
MACMILLAN AND CO., L
NEW YORK: THE MACMILLAN CO
1898

# PREFACE.

No one can read Macaulay's Essays without being struck by his fascinating ease of style, his vast erudition and prodigious memory. So strong was his memory that he seldom forgot anything that he either read or heard; he had therefore vast stores of knowledge from which to illustrate his meaning, enforce his argument, and delight his reader.

Some of his illustrations and allusions, however, are rather abstruse and not easily understood by all readers. The cursory reader indeed is often carried away by the style of his author and is content to run on from page to page without understanding every allusion: to such a reader this edition may or may not be useful. To the painstaking student, who has the time, the inclination, and the library at command to do for himself the work that has been done by the editor, this little book will be worse than useless; and the editor assures all such students that they cannot do better than work out their difficulties in their own way. But to the careful reader that has only a limited supply of books and not very much time to spare on abstruse allusions, this annotated edition will perhaps prove helpful and be more or less welcome.

1 desire to acknowledge, with many thanks, help of various kinds from my old friend and colleague, Mr. R. P. Brereton, M.A., Jesus College, Cambridge, and formerly Second Master of Oundle School, from Rev. J. F. Bethune Baker, M.A., Fellow and Dean of Pembroke College, Cambridge, from Mr. H. N. Tedder, Librarian of the Athenaeum, and from Messrs. Macmillan.

R. F. W.

TILSDEN, CRANBROOK,
    *July*, 1898.

# CONTENTS.

# THE
# LIFE AND WRITINGS OF ADDISON.

*The Life of Joseph Addison.* By LUCY AIKIN, 2 vols. 8vo. London, 1843.

SOME reviewers are of opinion that a lady who dares to publish a book renounces by that act the franchises appertaining to her sex, and can claim no exemption from the utmost rigour of critical procedure. From that opinion we dissent. We admit, indeed, that in a country which boasts of many female writers, eminently qualified by their talents and acquirements to influence the public mind, it would be of most pernicious consequence that inaccurate history or unsound philosophy should be suffered to pass uncensured, merely because the offender chanced to be a lady. But we 10 conceive that, on such occasions, a critic would do well to imitate the courteous Knight who found himself compelled by duty to keep the lists against Bradamante. He, we are told, defended successfully the cause of which he was the champion ; but, before the fight began, exchanged Balisarda for a less deadly sword, of which he carefully blunted the point and edge.

Nor are the immunities of sex the only immunities which Miss Aikin may rightfully plead. Several of her works, and especially the very pleasing Memoirs of the Reign of James 20 the First, have fully entitled her to the privileges enjoyed by Addison information.

by good writers.  One of those privileges we hold to be this,
that such writers, when, either from the unlucky choice of a
subject, or from the indolence too often produced by success,
they happen to fail, shall not be subjected to the severe discipline which it is sometimes necessary to inflict upon dunces
and impostors, but shall merely be reminded by a gentle
touch, like that with which the Laputan flapper roused his
dreaming lord, that it is high time to wake.

Our readers will probably infer from what we have said
10 that Miss Aikin's book has disappointed us.  The truth is,
that she is not well acquainted with her subject.  No person
who is not familiar with the political and literary history of
England during the reigns of William the Third, of Anne,
and of George the First, can possibly write a good life of
Addison.  Now, we mean no reproach to Miss Aikin, and
many will think that we pay her a compliment, when we
say that her studies have taken a different direction.  She is
better acquainted with Shakspeare and Raleigh, than with
Congreve and Prior ; and is far more at home among the
20 ruffs and peaked beards of Theobald's, than among the
Steenkirks and flowing periwigs which surrounded Queen
Anne's tea table at Hampton.  She seems to have written
about the Elizabethan age, because she had read much about
it ; she seems, on the other hand, to have read a little about
the age of Addison, because she had determined to write
about it.  The consequence is that she has had to describe
men and things without having either a correct or a vivid
idea of them, and that she has often fallen into errors of a
very serious kind.  The reputation which Miss Aikin has
30 justly earned stands so high, and the charm of Addison's
letters is so great, that a second edition of this work may
probably be required.  If so, we hope that every paragraph
will be revised, and that every date and fact about which
there can be the smallest doubt will be carefully verified.

To Addison himself we are bound by a sentiment as much
as any sentiment can be which is inspired by

one who has been sleeping a hundred and twenty years in Westminster Abbey. We trust, however, that this feeling will not betray us into that abject idolatry which we have often had occasion to reprehend in others, and which seldom fails to make both the idolator and the idol ridiculous. A man of genius and virtue is but a man. All his powers cannot be equally developed ; nor can we expect from him perfect selfknowledge. We need not, therefore, hesitate to admit that Addison has left us some compositions which do not rise above mediocrity, some heroic poems hardly equal to 10 Parnell's, some criticism as superficial as Dr. Blair's, and a tragedy not very much better than Dr. Johnson's. It is praise enough to say of a writer that, in a high department of literature, in which many eminent writers have distinguished themselves, he has had no equal ; and this may with strict justice be said of Addison.

As a man, he may not have deserved the adoration which he received from those who, bewitched by his fascinating society, and indebted for all the comforts of life to his generous and delicate friendship, worshipped him nightly, in his 20 favourite temple at Button's. But, after full inquiry and impartial reflection, we have long been convinced that he deserved as much love and esteem as can be justly claimed by any of our infirm and erring race. Some blemishes may undoubtedly be detected in his character ; but the more carefully it is examined, the more will it appear, to use the phrase of the old anatomists, sound in the noble parts, free from all taint of perfidy, of cowardice, of cruelty, of ingratitude, of envy. Men may easily be named, in whom some particular good disposition has been more conspicuous than 30 in Addison. But the just harmony of qualities, the exact temper between the stern and the humane virtues, the habitual observance of every law, not only of moral rectitude, but of moral grace and dignity, distinguish him from all men who have been tried by equally strong temptations, and about whose conduct we possess equally full information.

His father was the Reverend Lancelot Addison, who, though eclipsed by his more celebrated son, made some figure in the world, and occupies with credit two folio pages in the Biographia Britannica. Lancelot was sent up, as a poor scholar, from Westmoreland to Queen's College, Oxford, in the time of the Commonwealth, made some progress in learning, became, like most of his fellow students, a violent Royalist, lampooned the heads of the University, and was forced to ask pardon on his bended knees. When he had left 10 college, he earned a humble subsistence by reading the liturgy of the fallen Church to the families of those sturdy squires whose manor houses were scattered over the Wild of Sussex. After the Restoration, his loyalty was rewarded with the post of chaplain to the garrison of Dunkirk. When Dunkirk was sold to France, he lost his employment. But Tangier had been ceded by Portugal to England as part of the marriage portion of the Infanta Catharine ; and to Tangier Lancelot Addison was sent. A more miserable situation can hardly be conceived. It was difficult to say whether the 20 unfortunate settlers were more tormented by the heats or by the rains, by the soldiers within the wall or by the Moors without it. One advantage the chaplain had. He enjoyed an excellent opportunity of studying the history and manners of Jews and Mahometans ; and of this opportunity he appears to have made excellent use. On his return to England, after some years of banishment, he published an interesting volume on the Polity and Religion of Barbary, and another on the Hebrew Customs and the State of Rabbinical Learning. He rose to eminence in his profession, and became one 30 of the royal chaplains, a Doctor of Divinity, Archdeacon of Salisbury, and Dean of Lichfield. It is said that he would have been made a bishop after the Revolution, if he had not given offence to the government by strenuously opposing, in the Convocation of 1689, the liberal policy of William and Tillotson.

In 1672, not long after Dr. Addison's return from

Tangier, his son Joseph was born. Of Joseph's childhood we know little. He learned his rudiments at schools in his father's neighbourhood, and was then sent to the Charter House. The anecdotes which are popularly related about his boyish tricks do not harmonize very well with what we know of his riper years. There remains a tradition that he was the ringleader in a barring out, and another tradition that he ran away from school and hid himself in a wood, where he fed on berries and slept in a hollow tree, till after a long search he was discovered 10 and brought home. If these stories be true, it would be curious to know by what moral discipline so mutinous and enterprising a lad was transformed into the gentlest and most modest of men.

We have abundant proof that, whatever Joseph's pranks may have been, he pursued his studies vigorously and successfully. At fifteen he was not only fit for the university, but carried thither a classical taste and a stock of learning which would have done honour to a Master of Arts. He was entered at Queen's College, Oxford ; but 20 he had not been many months there, when some of his Latin verses fell by accident into the hands of Dr. Lancaster, Dean of Magdalene College. The young scholar's diction and versification were already such as veteran professors might envy. Dr. Lancaster was desirous to serve a boy of such promise ; nor was an opportunity long wanting. The Revolution had just taken place ; and nowhere had it been hailed with more delight than at Magdalene College. That great and opulent corporation had been treated by James, and by his Chancellor, with 30 an insolence and injustice which, even in such a Prince and in such a Minister, may justly excite amazement, and which had done more than even the prosecution of the Bishops to alienate the Church of England from the throne. A president, duly elected, had been violently expelled from his dwelling : a Papist had been set over

the society by a royal mandate : the Fellows who, in
conformity with their oaths, had refused to submit to
this usurper, had been driven forth from their quiet
cloisters and gardens, to die of want or to live on charity.
But the day of redress and retribution speedily came.
The intruders were ejected : the venerable House was
again inhabited by its old inmates : learning flourished
under the rule of the wise and virtuous Hough ; and
with learning was united a mild and liberal spirit too
10 often wanting in the princely colleges of Oxford.    In
consequence of the troubles through which the society
had passed, there had been no valid election of new
members during the year 1688.    In 1689, therefore,
there was twice the ordinary number of vacancies ; and
thus Dr. Lancaster found it easy to procure for his young
friend admittance to the advantages of a foundation then
generally esteemed the wealthiest in Europe.

At Magdalene Addison resided during ten years.    He
was, at first, one of those scholars who are called Demies,
20 but was subsequently elected a fellow.    His college is
still proud of his name : his portrait still hangs in the
hall ; and strangers are still told that his favourite walk
was under the elms which fringe the meadow on the
banks of the Cherwell.    It is said, and is highly probable,
that he was distinguished among his fellow students by
the delicacy of his feelings, by the shyness of his manners,
and by the assiduity with which he often prolonged his
studies far into the night.    It is certain that his reputation for ability and learning stood high.    Many years
30 later, the ancient Doctors of Magdalene continued to talk
in their common room of his boyish compositions, and
expressed their sorrow that no copy of exercises so remarkable had been preserved.

It is proper, however, to remark that Miss Aikin has
committed the error, very pardonable in a lady, of over-
rating Addison's classical attainments.    In one department

of learning, indeed, his proficiency was such as it is hardly possible to overrate. His knowledge of the Latin poets, from Lucretius and Catullus down to Claudian and Prudentius, was singularly exact and profound. He understood them thoroughly, entered into their spirit, and had the finest and most discriminating perception of all their peculiarities of style and melody ; nay, he copied their manner with admirable skill, and surpassed, we think, all their British imitators who had preceded him, Buchanan and Milton alone excepted. This is high 10 praise ; and beyond this we cannot with justice go. It is clear that Addison's serious attention during his residence at the university, was almost entirely concentrated on Latin poetry, and that, if he did not wholly neglect other provinces of ancient literature, he vouchsafed to them only a cursory glance. He does not appear to have attained more than an ordinary acquaintance with the political and moral writers of Rome ; nor was his own Latin prose by any means equal to his Latin verse. His knowledge of Greek, though doubtless such as was, in his 20 time, thought respectable at Oxford, was evidently less than that which many lads now carry away every year from Eton and Rugby. A minute examination of his works, if we had time to make such an examination, would fully bear out these remarks. We will briefly advert to a few of the facts on which our judgment is grounded.

Great praise is due to the Notes which Addison appended to his version of the second and third books of the Metamorphoses. Yet those notes, while they show him to have 30 been, in his own domain, an accomplished scholar, show also how confined that domain was. They are rich in apposite references to Virgil, Statius, and Claudian ; but they contain not a single illustration drawn from the Greek poets. Now, if, in the whole compass of Latin literature, there be a passage which stands in need of

illustration drawn from the Greek poets, it is the story
of Pentheus in the third book of the Metamorphoses.
Ovid was indebted for that story to Euripides and Theocritus, both of whom he has sometimes followed minutely.
But neither to Euripides nor to Theocritus does Addison
make the faintest allusion ; and we, therefore, believe
that we do not wrong him by supposing that he had
little or no knowledge of their works.

His travels in Italy, again, abound with classical quo-
10 tations happily introduced ; but scarcely one of those
quotations is in prose.  He draws more illustrations from
Ausonius and Manilius than from Cicero.  Even his notions of
the political and military affairs of the Romans seem to be
derived from poets and poetasters.  Spots made memorable
by events which have changed the destinies of the world, and
which have been worthily recorded by great historians, bring
to his mind only scraps of some ancient versifier.  In the
gorge of the Apennines he naturally remembers the hardships which Hannibal's army endured, and proceeds to
20 cite, not the authentic narrative of Polybius, not the
picturesque narrative of Livy, but the languid hexameters
of Silius Italicus.  On the banks of the Rubicon he never
thinks of Plutarch's lively description, or of the stern
conciseness of the Commentaries, or of those letters to
Atticus which so forcibly express the alternations of hope
and fear in a sensitive mind at a great crisis.  His only
authority for the events of the civil war is Lucan.

All the best ancient works of art at Rome and Florence
are Greek.  Addison saw them, however, without recalling
30 one single verse of Pindar, of Callimachus, or of the Attic
dramatists ; but they brought to his recollection innumerable passages of Horace, Juvenal, Statius, and Ovid.

The same may be said of the Treatise on Medals.  In
that pleasing work we find about three hundred passages
extracted with great judgment from the Roman poets ;
but we do not recollect a single passage taken from any

Roman orator or historian ; and we are confident that not a line is quoted from any Greek writer. No person, who had derived all his information on the subject of medals from Addison, would suspect that the Greek coins were in historical interest equal, and in beauty of execution far superior to those of Rome.

If it were necessary to find any further proof that Addison's classical knowledge was confined within narrow limits, that proof would be furnished by his Essay on the Evidences of Christianity. The Roman poets throw little 10 or no light on the literary and historical questions which he is under the necessity of examining in that Essay. He is, therefore, left completely in the dark ; and it is melancholy to see how helplessly he gropes his way from blunder to blunder. He assigns, as grounds for his religious belief, stories as absurd as that of the Cock-Lane ghost, and forgeries as rank as Ireland's Vortigern, puts faith in the lie about the Thundering Legion, is convinced that Tiberius moved the senate to admit Jesus among the gods, and pronounces the letter of Agbarus King of 20 Edessa to be a record of great authority. Nor were these errors the effects of superstition ; for to superstition Addison was by no means prone. The truth is that he was writing about what he did not understand.

Miss Aikin has discovered a letter, from which it appears that, while Addison resided at Oxford, he was one of several writers whom the booksellers engaged to make an English version of Herodotus ; and she infers that he must have been a good Greek scholar. We can allow very little weight to this argument, when we con- 30 sider that his fellow-labourers were to have been Boyle and Blackmore. Boyle is remembered chiefly as the nominal author of the worst book on Greek history and philology that ever was printed ; and this book, bad as it is, Boyle was unable to produce without help. Of Blackmore's attainments in the ancient tongues, it may

be sufficient to say that, in his prose, he has confounded
an aphorism with an apophthegm, and that when, in his
verse, he treats of classical subjects, his habit is to regale
his readers with four false quantities to a page.

It is probable that the classical acquirements of Addison
were of as much service to him as if they had been more
extensive.  The world generally gives its admiration, not
to the man who does what nobody else even attempts to
do, but to the man who does best what multitudes do
10 well.   Bentley was so immeasurably superior to all the
other scholars of his time that few among them could
discover his superiority.   But the accomplishment in
which Addison excelled his contemporaries was then, as
it is now, highly valued and assiduously cultivated at all
English seats of learning.   Every body who had been at
a public school had written Latin verses ; many had
written such verses with tolerable success, and were quite
able to appreciate, though by no means able to rival, the
skill with which Addison imitated Virgil.   His lines on the
20 Barometer and the Bowling Green were applauded by hundreds, to whom the Dissertation on the Epistles of Phalaris
was as unintelligible as the hieroglyphics on an obelisk.

Purity of style, and an easy flow of numbers, are
common to all Addison's Latin poems.  Our favourite
piece is the Battle of the Cranes and Pygmies ; for in
that piece we discern a gleam of the fancy and humour
which many years later enlivened thousands of breakfast
tables.  Swift boasted that he was never known to steal
a hint ; and he certainly owed as little to his predecessors
30 as any modern writer.   Yet we cannot help suspecting
that he borrowed, perhaps unconsciously, one of the
happiest touches in his Voyage to Lilliput from Addison's
verses.   Let our readers judge.

"The Emperor," says Gulliver, "is taller by about the
breadth of my nail than any of his court, which alone is
enough to strike an awe into the beholders."

About thirty years before Gulliver's Travels appeared Addison wrote these lines:

" Jamque acies inter medias sese arduus infert
Pygmeadum ductor, qui, majestate verendus,
Incessuque gravis, reliquos supereminet omnes
Mole gigantea, mediamque exsurgit in ulnam. "

The Latin poems of Addison were greatly and justly admired both at Oxford and Cambridge, before his name had ever been heard by the wits who thronged the coffee-houses round Drury-Lane theatre.  In his twenty-second year, he ventured to appear before the public as a writer of English verse.  He addressed some complimentary lines to Dryden, who, after many triumphs and many reverses, had at length reached a secure and lonely eminence among the literary men of that age.  Dryden appears to have been much gratified by the young scholar's praise : and an interchange of civilities and good offices followed.  Addison was probably introduced by Dryden to Congreve, and was certainly presented by Congreve to Charles Montague, who was then Chancellor of the Exchequer, and leader of the Whig party in the House of Commons.

At this time Addison seemed inclined to devote himself to poetry.  He published a translation of part of the fourth Georgic, Lines to King William, and other performances of equal value, that is to say, of no value at all.  But in those days, the public was in the habit of receiving with applause pieces which would now have little chance of obtaining the Newdigate prize or the Seatonian prize.  And the reason is obvious.  The heroic couplet was then the favourite measure.  The art of arranging words in that measure, so that the lines may flow smoothly, that the accents may fall correctly, that the rhymes may strike the ear strongly, and that there may be a pause at the end of every distich, is an art as mechanical as that of mending a kettle or shoeing

a horse, and may be learned by any human being who
has sense enough to learn any thing.   But, like other
mechanical arts, it was gradually improved by means of
many experiments and many failures.   It was reserved
for Pope to discover the trick, to make himself complete
master of it, and to teach it to every body else.   From
the time when his Pastorals appeared, heroic versification
became matter of rule and compass; and, before long, all
artists were on a level.   Hundreds of dunces who never
10 blundered on one happy thought or expression were able
to write reams of couplets which, as far as euphony was
concerned, could not be distinguished from those of Pope
himself, and which very clever writers of the reign of
Charles the Second, Rochester, for example, or Marvel, or
Oldham, would have contemplated with admiring despair.

   Ben Jonson was a great man, Hoole a very small man.
But Hoole, coming after Pope, had learned how to
manufacture decasyllable verses, and poured them forth
by thousands and tens of thousands, all as well turned,
20 as smooth, and as like each other as the blocks which
have passed through Mr. Brunel's mill in the dockyard
at Portsmouth.   Ben's heroic couplets resemble blocks
rudely hewn out by an unpractised hand, with a blunt
hatchet.   Take as a specimen his translation of a celebrated passage in the Æneid:

> " This child our parent earth, stirr'd up with spite
>     Of all the gods, brought forth, and, as some write,
>   She was last sister of that giant race
>   That sought to scale Jove's court, right swift of pace,
> 30    And swifter far of wing, a monster vast
>   And dreadful.  Look, how many plumes are placed
>   On her huge corpse, so many waking eyes
>   Stick underneath, and, which may stranger rise
>   In the report, as many tongues she wears.

Compare with these jagged misshapen distichs the
neat fabric which Hoole's machine produces in unlimited

abundance. We take the first lines on which we open in
his version of Tasso. They are neither better nor worse
than the rest:

> " O thou, whoe'er thou art, whose steps are led,
> By choice or fate, these lonely shores to tread,
> No greater wonders east or west can boast
> Than yon small island on the pleasing coast.
> If e'er thy sight would blissful scenes explore,
> The current pass, and seek the further shore."

Ever since the time of Pope there has been a glut of 10
lines of this sort; and we are now as little disposed to
admire a man for being able to write them, as for being
able to write his name. But in the days of William the
Third such versification was rare; and a rhymer who
had any skill in it passed for a great poet, just as in the
dark ages a person who could write his name passed for
a great clerk. Accordingly, Duke, Stepney, Granville,
Walsh, and others whose only title to fame was that they
said in tolerable metre what might have been as well
said in prose, or what was not worth saying at all, were 20
honoured with marks of distinction which ought to be
reserved for genius. With these Addison must have
ranked, if he had not earned true and lasting glory by
performances which very little resembled his juvenile
poems.

Dryden was now busied with Virgil, and obtained from
Addison a critical preface to the Georgics. In return for
this service, and for other services of the same kind, the
veteran poet, in the postscript to the translation of the
Æneid, complimented his young friend with great liberality, 30
and indeed with more liberality than sincerity. He affected
to be afraid that his own performance would not sustain a
comparison with the version of the fourth Georgic, by "the
most ingenious Mr. Addison of Oxford." "After his bees,"
added Dryden, "my latter swarm is scarcely worth the
hiving.

The time had now arrived when it was necessary for Addison to choose a calling. Every thing seemed to point his course towards the clerical profession. His habits were regular, his opinions orthodox. His college had large ecclesiastical preferment in its gift, and boasts that it has given at least one bishop to almost every see in England. Dr. Lancelot Addison held an honourable place in the Church, and had set his heart on seeing his son a clergyman. It is clear, from some expressions in the young man's
10 rhymes, that his intention was to take orders. But Charles Montague interfered. Montague had first brought himself into notice by verses, well timed and not contemptibly written, but never, we think, rising above mediocrity. Fortunately for himself and for his country, he early quitted poetry, in which he could never have attained a rank as high as that of Dorset or Rochester, and turned his mind to official and parliamentary business. It is written that the ingenious person who undertook to instruct Rasselas, prince of Abyssinia, in the art of flying, ascended
20 an eminence, waved his wings, sprang into the air, and instantly dropped into the lake. But it is added that the wings, which were unable to support him through the sky, bore him up effectually as soon as he was in the water. This is no bad type of the fate of Charles Montague, and of men like him. When he attempted to soar into the regions of poetical invention, he altogether failed ; but, as soon as he had descended from that ethereal elevation into a lower and grosser element, his talents instantly raised him above the mass. He became a distinguished financier, debater, cour-
30 tier, and party leader. He still retained his fondness for the pursuits of his early days ; but he showed that fondness not by wearying the public with his own feeble performances, but by discovering and encouraging literary excellence in others. A crowd of wits and poets, who would easily have vanquished him as a competitor, revered him as a judge and a patron. In his plans for the encourage-

ceeded to Paris, and was received there with great kindness
and politeness by a kinsman of his friend Montague, Charles
Earl of Manchester, who had just been appointed Ambassador to the Court of France. The Countess, a Whig
and a toast, was probably as gracious as her lord ; for
Addison long retained an agreeable recollection of the
impression which she at this time made on him, and, in
some lively lines written on the glasses of the Kit Cat Club,
described the envy which her cheeks, glowing with the
genuine bloom of England, had excited among the painted 10
beauties of Versailles.

Lewis the Fourteenth was at this time expiating the
vices of his youth by a devotion which had no root in
reason, and bore no fruit of charity. The servile literature
of France had changed its character to suit the changed
character of the prince. No book appeared that had not an
air of sanctity. Racine, who was just dead, had passed the
close of his life in writing sacred dramas ; and Dacier was
seeking for the Athanasian mysteries in Plato. Addison
described this state of things in a short but lively and 20
graceful letter to Montague. Another letter, written about
the same time to the Lord Chancellor, conveyed the strongest
assurances of gratitude and attachment. "The only return
I can make to your Lordship," said Addison, "will be to
apply myself entirely to my business." With this view he
quitted Paris and repaired to Blois, a place where it was
supposed that the French language was spoken in its highest
purity, and where not a single Englishman could be found.
Here he passed some months pleasantly and profitably. Of
his way of life at Blois, one of his associates, an Abbé named 30
Philippeaux, gave an account to Joseph Spence. If this
account is to be trusted, Addison studied much, mused much,
talked little, had fits of absence, and either had no love
affairs, or was too discreet to confide them to the Abbé. A
man who, even when surrounded by fellow countrymen and
fellow students, had always been remarkably shy and silent,

B

was not likely to be loquacious in a foreign tongue, and among foreign companions.  But it is clear from Addison's letters, some of which were long after published in the Guardian, that, while he appeared to be absorbed in his own meditations, he was really observing French society with that keen and sly, yet not illnatured side glance, which was peculiarly his own.

From Blois he returned to Paris ; and, having now mastered the French language, found great pleasure in the
10 society of French philosophers and poets.  He gave an account, in a letter to Bishop Hough, of two highly interesting conversations, one with Malbranche, the other with Boileau.  Malbranche expressed great partiality for the English, and extolled the genius of Newton, but shook his head when Hobbes was mentioned, and was indeed so unjust as to call the author of the Leviathan a poor silly creature.  Addison's modesty restrained him from fully relating, in his letter, the circumstances of his introduction to Boileau.  Boileau, having survived the friends and rivals
20 of his youth, old, deaf, and melancholy, lived in retirement, seldom went either to Court or to the Academy, and was almost inaccessible to strangers.  Of the English and of English literature he knew nothing.  He had hardly heard the name of Dryden.  Some of our countrymen, in the warmth of their patriotism, have asserted that this ignorance must have been affected.  We own that we see no ground for such a supposition.  English literature was to the French of the age of Lewis the Fourteenth what German literature was to our own grandfathers.  Very few, we suspect, of the accom-
30 plished men who, sixty or seventy years ago, used to dine in Leicester Square with Sir Joshua, or at Streatham with Mrs. Thrale, had the slightest notion that Wieland was one of the first wits and poets, and Lessing, beyond all dispute, the first critic in Europe.  Boileau knew just as little about the Paradise Lost, and about Absalom and Ahitophel ; but he had read Addison's Latin poems, and admired them

greatly. They had given him, he said, quite a new notion
of the state of learning and taste among the English.
Johnson will have it that these praises were insincere.
"Nothing," says he, "is better known of Boileau than that
he had an injudicious and peevish contempt of modern
Latin; and therefore his profession of regard was probably
the effect of his civility rather than approbation." Now,
nothing is better known of Boileau than that he was singularly sparing of compliments. We do not remember that
either friendship or fear ever induced him to bestow 10
praise on any composition which he did not approve. On
literary questions, his caustic, disdainful, and self-confident
spirit rebelled against that authority to which every thing
else in France bowed down. He had the spirit to tell
Lewis the Fourteenth firmly and even rudely, that his
Majesty knew nothing about poetry, and admired verses
which were detestable. What was there in Addison's
position that could induce the satirist, whose stern and
fastidious temper had been the dread of two generations, to
turn sycophant for the first and last time? Nor was 20
Boileau's contempt of modern Latin either injudicious or
peevish. He thought, indeed, that no poem of the first order
would ever be written in a dead language. And did he
think amiss? Has not the experience of centuries confirmed
his opinion? Boileau also thought it probable that, in the
best modern Latin, a writer of the Augustan age would have
detected ludicrous improprieties. And who can think otherwise? What modern scholar can honestly declare that he
sees the smallest impurity in the style of Livy? Yet is it
not certain that, in the style of Livy, Pollio, whose taste 30
had been formed on the banks of the Tiber, detected the
inelegant idiom of the Po? Has any modern scholar understood Latin better than Frederic the Great understood
French? Yet is it not notorious that Frederic the Great,
after reading, speaking, writing French, and nothing but
French, during more than half a century, after unlearning

his mother tongue in order to learn French, after living
familiarly during may years with French associates, could
not, to the last, compose in French, without imminent risk
of committing some mistake which would have moved a
smile in the literary circles of Paris? Do we believe that
Erasmus and Fracastorius wrote Latin as well as Dr.
Robertson and Sir Walter Scott wrote English? And are
there not in the Dissertation on India, the last of Dr.
Robertson's works, in Waverley, in Marmion, Scotticisms at
10 which a London apprentice would laugh? But does it
follow, because we think thus, that we can find nothing to
admire in the noble alcaics of Gray, or in the playful
elegiacs of Vincent Bourne? Surely not. Nor was Boileau
so ignorant or tasteless as to be incapable of appreciating
good modern Latin. In the very letter to which Johnson
alludes, Boileau says—"Ne croyez pas pourtant que je
veuille par là blâmer les vers Latins que vous m'avez envoyés
d'un de vos illustres académiciens. Je les ai trouvés fort
beaux, et dignes de Vida et de Sannazar, mais non pas
20 d'Horace et de Virgile." Several poems, in modern Latin,
have been praised by Boileau quite as liberally as it was his
habit to praise any thing. He says, for example, of the Père
Fraguier's epigrams, that Catullus seems to have come to
life again. But the best proof that Boileau did not feel the
undiscerning contempt for modern Latin verses which has
been imputed to him, is, that he wrote and published Latin
verses in several metres. Indeed it happens, curiously
enough, that the most severe censure ever pronounced by
him on modern Latin is conveyed in Latin hexameters. We
30 allude to the fragment which begins—

> " Quid numeris iterum me balbutire Latinis,
> Longe Alpes citra natum de patre Sicambro,
> Musa, jubes?"

For these reasons we feel assured that the praise which
Boileau bestowed on the *Machinæ Gesticulantes*, and the

*Gerano-Pygmæomachia*, was sincere. He certainly opened
himself to Addison with a freedom which was a sure indica-
tion of esteem. Literature was the chief subject of conversation. The old man talked on his favourite theme much
and well, indeed, as his young hearer thought, incomparably
well. Boileau had undoubtedly some of the qualities of a
great critic. He wanted imagination ; but he had strong
sense. His literary code was formed on narrow principles ;
but in applying it, he showed great judgment and penetration.
In mere style, abstracted from the ideas of which style is 10
the garb, his taste was excellent. He was well acquainted
with the great Greek writers ; and, though unable fully to
appreciate their creative genius, admired the majestic simplicity of their manner, and had learned from them to
despise bombast and tinsel. It is easy, we think, to discover
in the Spectator and the Guardian, traces of the influence, in
part salutary and in part pernicious, which the mind of
Boileau had on the mind of Addison.

While Addison was at Paris, an event took place which
made that capital a disagreeable residence for an Englishman 20
and a Whig. Charles, second of the name, King of Spain,
died ; and bequeathed his dominions to Philip, Duke of
Anjou, a younger son of the Dauphin. The King of France,
in direct violation of his engagements both with Great
Britain and with the States General, accepted the bequest
on behalf of his grandson. The house of Bourbon was at
the summit of human grandeur. England had been out-
witted, and found herself in a situation at once degrading
and perilous. The people of France, not presaging the
calamities by which they were destined to expiate the perfidy 30
of their sovereign, went mad with pride and delight. Every
man looked as if a great estate had just been left him.
"The French conversation," said Addison, "begins to grow
insupportable ; that which was before the vainest nation in
the world is now worse than ever." Sick of the arrogant exultation of the Parisians, and probably foreseeing that the

peace between France and England could not be of long duration, he set off for Italy.

In December 1700 he embarked at Marseilles. As he glided along the Ligurian coast, he was delighted by the sight of myrtles and olive trees, which retained their verdure under the winter solstice. Soon, however, he encountered one of the black storms of the Mediterranean. The captain of the ship gave up all for lost, and confessed himself to a capuchin who happened to be on board. The English 10 heretic, in the mean time, fortified himself against the terrors of death with devotions of a very different kind. How strong an impression this perilous voyage made on him, appears from the ode, "How are thy servants blest, O Lord !" which was long after published in the Spectator. After some days of discomfort and danger, Addison was glad to land at Savona, and to make his way, over mountains where no road had yet been hewn out by art, to the city of Genoa.

At Genoa, still ruled by her own Doge, and by the nobles whose names were inscribed on her Book of Gold, 20 Addison made a short stay. He admired the narrow streets overhung by long lines of towering palaces, the walls rich with frescoes, the gorgeous temple of the Annunciation, and the tapestries whereon were recorded the long glories of the house of Doria. Thence he hastened to Milan, where he contemplated the Gothic magnificence of the cathedral with more wonder than pleasure. He passed Lake Benacus while a gale was blowing, and saw the waves raging as they raged when Virgil looked upon them. At Venice, then the gayest spot in Europe, the traveller spent the 30 Carnival, the gayest season of the year, in the midst of masques, dances, and serenades. Here he was at once diverted and provoked, by the absurd dramatic pieces which then disgraced the Italian stage. To one of those pieces, however, he was indebted for a valuable hint. He was present when a ridiculous play on the death of Cato was performed. Cato, it seems, was in love with a daughter of Scipio. The lady

had given her heart to Cæsar.  The rejected lover determined to destroy himself.  He appeared seated in his library,
a dagger in his hand, a Plutarch and a Tasso before him ;
and, in this position, he pronounced a soliloquy before he
struck the blow.  We are surprised that so remarkable a
circumstance as this should have escaped the notice of all
Addison's biographers.  There cannot, we conceive, be the
smallest doubt that this scene, in spite of its absurdities and
anachronisms, struck the traveller's imagination, and suggested to him the thought of bringing Cato on the English 10
stage.  It is well known that about this time he began his
tragedy, and that he finished the first four acts before he
returned to England.

On his way from Venice to Rome, he was drawn some
miles out of the beaten road, by a wish to see the smallest
independent state in Europe.  On a rock where the snow
still lay, though the Italian spring was now far advanced,
was perched the little fortress of San Marino.  The roads
which led to the secluded town were so bad that few travellers had ever visited it, and none had ever published an 20
account of it.  Addison could not suppress a goodnatured
smile at the simple manners and institutions of this singular
community.  But he observed, with the exultation of a
Whig, that the rude mountain tract which formed the territory of the republic swarmed with an honest, healthy, and
contented peasantry, while the rich plain which surrounded
the metropolis of civil and spiritual tyranny was scarcely
less desolate than the uncleared wilds of America.

At Rome Addison remained on his first visit only long
enough to catch a glimpse of St. Peter's and of the Pantheon. 30
His haste is the more extraordinary because the Holy Week
was close at hand.  He has given no hint which can enable
us to pronounce why he chose to fly from a spectacle which
every year allures from distant regions persons of far less
taste and sensibility than his.  Possibly, travelling, as he
did, at the charge of a Government distinguished by its

enmity to the Church of Rome, he may have thought that
it would be imprudent in him to assist at the most magnificent rite of that Church. Many eyes would be upon him ;
and he might find it difficult to behave in such a manner as
to give offence neither to his patrons in England, nor to
those among whom he resided. Whatever his motives may
have been, he turned his back on the most august and affect-
ing ceremony which is known among men, and posted along
the Appian way to Naples.

10    Naples was then destitute of what are now, perhaps, its
chief attractions. The lovely bay and the awful mountain
were indeed there. But a farmhouse stood on the theatre
of Herculaneum, and rows of vines grew over the streets of
Pompeii. The temples of Pæstum had not indeed been
hidden from the eye of man by any great convulsion of
nature ; but, strange to say, their existence was a secret
even to artists and antiquaries. Though situated within a
few hours' journey of a great capital, where Salvator had not
long before painted, and where Vico was then lecturing,
20 those noble remains were as little known to Europe as the
ruined cities overgrown by the forests of Yucatan. What
was to be seen at Naples, Addison saw. He climbed Vesuvius, explored the tunnel of Posilipo, and wandered among
the vines and almond trees of Capreæ. But neither the
wonders of nature, nor those of art, could so occupy his
attention as to prevent him from noticing, though cursorily,
the abuses of the government and the misery of the people.
The great kingdom which had just descended to Philip the
Fifth, was in a state of paralytic dotage. Even Castile and
30 Aragon were sunk in wretchedness. Yet, compared with the
Italian dependencies of the Spanish crown, Castile and Aragon might be called prosperous. It is clear that all the
observations which Addison made in Italy tended to con-
firm him in the political opinions which he had adopted at
home. To the last, he always spoke of foreign travel as
the best cure for Jacobitism. In his Freeholder, the Tory

foxhunter asks what travelling is good for, except to teach a man to jabber French, and to talk against passive obedience.

From Naples, Addison returned to Rome by sea, along the coast which his favourite Virgil had celebrated. The felucca passed the headland where the oar and trumpet were placed by the Trojan adventurers on the tomb of Misenus, and anchored at night under the shelter of the fabled promontory of Circe. The voyage ended in the Tiber, still overhung with dark verdure, and still turbid with yellow sand, as 10 when it met the eyes of Æneas. From the ruined port of Ostia, the stranger hurried to Rome: and at Rome he remained during those hot and sickly months when, even in the Augustan age, all who could make their escape fled from mad dogs and from streets black with funerals, to gather the first figs of the season in the country. It is probable that, when he, long after, poured forth in verse his gratitude to the Providence which had enabled him to breathe unhurt in tainted air, he was thinking of the August and September which he passed at Rome.     20

It was not till the latter end of October that he tore himself away from the masterpieces of ancient and modern art which are collected in the city so long the mistress of the world. He then journeyed northward, passed through Sienna, and for a moment forgot his prejudices in favour of classic architecture as he looked on the magnificent cathedral. At Florence he spent some days with the Duke of Shrewsbury, who, cloyed with the pleasures of ambition, and impatient of its pains, fearing both parties, and loving neither, had determined to hide 30 in an Italian retreat talents and accomplishments which, if they had been united with fixed principles and civil courage, might have made him the foremost man of his age. These days, we are told, passed pleasantly; and we can easily believe it. For Addison was a delightful companion when he was at his ease; and the Duke, though he seldom forgot that he was a Talbot, had the invaluable art of putting at ease all who came near him.

Addison gave some time to Florence, and especially to the sculptures in the Museum, which he preferred even to those of the Vatican. He then pursued his journey through a country in which the ravages of the last war were still discernible, and in which all men were looking forward with dread to a still fiercer conflict. Eugene had already descended from the Rhœtian Alps, to dispute with Catinat the rich plain 10 of Lombardy. The faithless ruler of Savoy was still reckoned among the allies of Lewis. England had not yet actually declared war against France : but Manchester had left Paris ; and the negotiations which produced the Grand Alliance against the House of Bourbon were in progress. Under such circumstances, it was desirable for an English traveller to reach neutral ground without delay. Addison resolved to cross Mont Cenis. It was December ; and the road was very different from that which now reminds the stranger of the power and genius of Napoleon. The winter, 20 however, was mild ; and the passage was, for those times, easy. To this journey Addison alluded when, in the ode which we have already quoted, he said that for him the Divine goodness had warmed the hoary Alpine hills.

It was in the midst of the eternal snow that he composed his Epistle to his friend Montague, now Lord Halifax. That Epistle, once widely renowned, is now known only to curious readers, and will hardly be considered by those to whom it is known as in any perceptible degree heightening Addison's fame. It is, however, decidedly superior to 30 any English composition which he had previously published. Nay, we think it quite as good as any poem in heroic metre which appeared during the interval between the death of Dryden and the publication of the Essay on Criticism. — *r* It contains passages as good as the second-rate passages of Pope, and would have added to the reputation of Parnell or Prior.

But, whatever be the literary merits or defects of the Epistle, it undoubtedly does honour to the principles and spirit of the author. Halifax had now nothing to give. He had fallen from power, had been held up to obloquy, had been impeached by the House of Commons, and, though his Peers had dismissed the impeachment, had, as it seemed, little chance of ever again filling high office. The Epistle, written at such a time, is one among many proofs that there was no mixture of cowardice or meanness in the suavity and moderation which distinguished Addison from all the other 10 public men of those stormy times.

At Geneva, the traveller learned that a partial change of ministry had taken place in England, and that the Earl of Manchester had become Secretary of State. Manchester exerted himself to serve his young friend. It was thought advisable that an English agent should be near the person of Eugene in Italy; and Addison, whose diplomatic education was now finished, was the man selected. He was preparing to enter on his honourable functions, when all his prospects were for a time darkened by the death of William the Third. 20

Anne had long felt a strong aversion, personal, political, and religious, to the Whig party. That aversion appeared in the first measures of her reign. Manchester was deprived of the seals, after he had held them only a few weeks. Neither Somers nor Halifax was sworn of the Privy Council. Addison shared the fate of his three patrons. His hopes of employment in the public service were at an end; his pension was stopped; and it was necessary for him to support himself by his own exertions. He became tutor to a young English traveller, and appears to have rambled with 30 his pupil over great part of Switzerland and Germany. At this time he wrote his pleasing treatise on Medals. It was not published till after his death; but several distinguished scholars saw the manuscript, and gave just praise to the grace of the style, and to the learning and ingenuity evinced by the quotations.

From Germany Addison repaired to Holland, where he learned the melancholy news of his father's death. After passing some months in the United Provinces, he returned about the close of the year 1703 to England. He was there cordially received by his friends, and introduced by them into the Kit Cat Club, a society in which were collected all the various talents and accomplishments which then gave lustre to the Whig party.

Addison was, during some months after his return from 10 the Continent, hard pressed by pecuniary difficulties. But it was soon in the power of his noble patrons to serve him effectually. A political change, silent and gradual, but of the highest importance, was in daily progress. The accession of Anne had been hailed by the Tories with transports of joy and hope ; and for a time it seemed that the Whigs had fallen never to rise again. The throne was surrounded by men supposed to be attached to the prerogative and to the Church ; and among these none stood so high in the favour of the sovereign as the Lord Treasurer Godolphin 20 and the Captain General Marlborough.

The country gentlemen and country clergymen had fully expected that the policy of these ministers would be directly opposed to that which had been almost constantly followed by William ; that the landed interest would be favoured at the expense of trade ; that no addition would be made to the funded debt ; that the privileges conceded to Dissenters by the late King would be curtailed, if not withdrawn ; that the war with France, if there must be such a war, would, on our part, be almost entirely naval ; and that the Government 30 would avoid close connections with foreign powers, and, above all, with Holland.

But the country gentlemen and country clergymen were fated to be deceived, not for the last time. The prejudices and passions which raged without control in vicarages, in cathedral closes, and in the manor-houses of fox-hunting squires, were not shared by the chiefs of the ministry.

Those statesmen saw that it was both for the public interest, and for their own interest, to adopt a Whig policy, at least as respected the alliances of the country and the conduct of the war. But, if the foreign policy of the Whigs were adopted, it was impossible to abstain from adopting also their financial policy. The natural conse- quences follow :d. The rigid Tories were alienated from the Government. The votes of the Whigs became necessary to it. The votes of the Whigs could be secured only by further concessions; and further concessions the Queen was 10 induced to make.

At the beginning of the year 1704, the state of parties bore a close analogy to the state of parties in 1826. In 1826, as in 1704, there was a Tory ministry divided into two hostile sections. The position of Mr. Canning and his friends in 1826 corresponded to that which Marlborough and Godolphin occupied in 1704. Nottingham and Jersey were, in 1704, what Lord Eldon and Lord Westmoreland were in 1826. The Whigs of 1704 were in a situation resembling that in which the Whigs of 1826 stood. In 20 1704, Somers, Halifax, Sunderland, Cowper, were not in office. There was no avowed coalition between them and the moderate Tories. It is probable that no direct com- munication tending to such a coalition had yet taken place ; yet all men saw that such a coalition was inevitable, nay, that it was already half formed. Such, or nearly such, was the state of things when tidings arrived of the great battle fought at Blenheim on the 13th August, 1704. By the Whigs the news was hailed with transports of joy and pride. No fault, no cause of quarrel, could be remembered by them 30 against the Commander whose genius had, in one day, changed the face of Europe, saved the Imperial throne, humbled the house of Bourbon, and secured the Act of Settlement against foreign hostility. The feeling of the Tories was very different. They could not indeed, without imprudence, openly express regret at an event so glorious

to their country ; but their congratulations were so cold and
sullen as to give deep disgust to the victorious general and
his friends.

Godolphin was not a reading man. Whatever time
he could spare from business he was in the habit of
spending at Newmarket or at the card table. But he
was not absolutely indifferent to poetry ; and he was too
intelligent an observer not to perceive that literature was
a formidable engine of political warfare, and that the
10 great Whig leaders had strengthened their party, and
raised their character, by extending a liberal and judicious
patronage to good writers. He was mortified, and not
without reason, by the exceeding badness of the poems
which appeared in honour of the battle of Blenheim.
One of these poems has been rescued from oblivion by
the exquisite absurdity of three lines.

> " Think of two thousand gentlemen at least,
> And each man mounted on his capering beast;
> Into the Danube they were pushed by shoals."

20    Where to procure better verses the treasurer did not
know. He understood how to negotiate a loan, or remit
a subsidy : he was also well versed in the history of
running horses and fighting cocks ; but his acquaintance
among the poets was very small. He consulted Halifax ;
but Halifax affected to decline the office of adviser. He
had, he said, done his best, when he had power, to
encourage men whose abilities and acquirements might
do honour to their country. Those times were over.
Other maxims had prevailed. Merit was suffered to
30 pine in obscurity ; and the public money was squandered
on the undeserving. "I do know," he added, "a gentleman who would celebrate the battle in a manner worthy
of the subject : but I will not name him." Godolphin,
who was expert at the soft answer which turneth away
wrath, and who was under the necessity of paying court

to the Whigs, gently replied that there was too much
ground for Halifax's complaints, but that what was amiss
should in time be rectified, and that in the mean time
the services of a man such as Halifax had described
should be liberally rewarded. Halifax then mentioned
Addison, but, mindful of the dignity as well as of the
pecuniary interest of his friend, insisted that the Minister
should apply in the most courteous manner to Addison
himself ; and this Godolphin promised to do.

Addison then occupied a garret up three pair of stairs, 10
over a small shop in the Haymarket. In this humble
lodging he was surprised, on the morning which followed
the conversation between Godolphin and Halifax, by a
visit from no less a person than the Right Honourable
Henry Boyle, then Chancellor of the Exchequer, and
afterwards Lord Carleton. This highborn minister had
been sent by the Lord Treasurer as ambassador to the
needy poet. Addison readily undertook the proposed
task, a task which, to so good a Whig, was probably a
pleasure. When the poem was little more than half 20
finished, he showed it to Godolphin, who was delighted
with it, and particularly with the famous similitude of
the Angel. Addison was instantly appointed to a Commissionership worth about two hundred pounds a year,
and was assured that this appointment was only an
earnest of greater favours.

The Campaign came forth, and was as much admired
by the public as by the Minister. It pleases us less on
the whole than the Epistle to Halifax. Yet it undoubtedly ranks high among the poems which appeared 30
during the interval between the death of Dryden and
the dawn of Pope's genius. The chief merit of the
Campaign, we think, is that which was noticed by
Johnson, the manly and rational rejection of fiction. The
first great poet whose works have come down to us sang
of war long before war became a science or a trade. If,

in his time, there was enmity between two little Greek
towns, each poured forth its crowd of citizens, ignorant
of discipline, and armed with implements of labour rudely
turned into weapons.  On each side appeared conspicuous
a few chiefs, whose wealth had enabled them to procure
good armour, horses, and chariots, and whose leisure had
enabled them to practise military exercises.  One such
chief, if he were a man of great strength, agility, and
courage, would probably be more formidable than twenty
10 common men ; and the force and dexterity with which
he flung his spear might have no inconsiderable share in
deciding the event of the day.  Such were probably the
battles with which Homer was familiar.  But Homer
related the actions of men of a former generation, of men
who sprang from the Gods, and communed with the
Gods face to face, of men, one of whom could with ease
hurl rocks which two sturdy hinds of a later period
would be unable even to lift.  He therefore naturally
represented their martial exploits as resembling in kind,
20 but far surpassing in magnitude, those of the stoutest
and most expert combatants of his own age.  Achilles,
clad in celestial armour, drawn by celestial coursers,
grasping the spear which none but himself could raise,
driving all Troy and Lycia before him, and choking
Scamander with dead, was only a magnificent exaggeration of the real hero, who, strong, fearless, accustomed
to the use of weapons, guarded by a shield and helmet
of the best Sidonian fabric, and whirled along by horses
of Thessalian breed, struck down with his own right
30 arm foe after foe.  In all rude societies similar notions
are found.  There are at this day countries where the Life-
guardsman Shaw would be considered as a much greater
warrior than the Duke of Wellington.  Buonaparte loved
to describe the astonishment with which the Mamelukes
looked at his diminutive figure.  Mourad Bey, distinguished above all his fellows by his bodily strength, and

by the skill with which he managed his horse and his
sabre, could not believe that a man who was scarcely
five feet high, and rode like a butcher, could be the
greatest soldier in Europe.

Homer's descriptions of war had therefore as much
truth as poetry requires.  But truth was altogether
wanting to the performances of those who, writing about
battles which had scarcely anything in common with the
battles of his times, servilely imitated his manner.  The
folly of Silius Italicus, in particular, is positively nauseous. 10
He undertook to record in verse the vicissitudes of a
great struggle between generals of the first order : and
his narrative is made up of the hideous wounds which
these generals inflicted with their own hands.  Asdrubal
flings a spear which grazes the shoulder of the consul
Nero ; but Nero sends his spear into Asdrubal's side.
Fabius slays Thuris and Butes and Maris and Arses, and
the longhaired Adherbes, and the gigantic Thylis, and
Sapharus and Monœsus, and the trumpeter Morinus.
Hannibal runs Perusinus through the groin with a stake, 20
and breaks the backbone of Telesinus with a huge stone.
This detestable fashion was copied in modern times, and
continued to prevail down to the age of Addison.
Several versifiers had described William turning thousands
to flight by his single prowess, and dyeing the Boyne
with Irish blood.  Nay, so estimable a writer as John
Philips, the author of the Splendid Shilling, represented
Marlborough as having won the battle of Blenheim
merely by strength of muscle and skill in fence.  The
following lines may serve as an example :      30

> " Churchill, viewing where
> The violence of Tallard most prevailed,
> Came to oppose his slaughtering arm.  With speed
> Precipitate he rode, urging his way
> O'er hills of gasping heroes, and fallen steeds
> Rolling in death.  Destruction, grim with blood,

> Attends his furious course.  Around his head
> The glowing balls play innocent, while he
> With dire impetuous sway deals fatal blows
> Among the flying Gauls.  In Gallic blood
> He dyes his reeking sword, and strews the ground
> With headless ranks.  What can they do?  Or how
> Withstand his wide-destroying sword?"

Addison, with excellent sense and taste, departed from this ridiculous fashion.  He reserved his praise for the
10 qualities which made Marlborough truly great, energy, sagacity, military science.  But, above all, the poet extolled the firmness of that mind which, in the midst of confusion, uproar, and slaughter, examined and disposed every thing with the serene wisdom of a higher intelligence.

Here it was that he introduced the famous comparison of Marlborough to an Angel guiding the whirlwind.  We will not dispute the general justice of Johnson's remarks on this passage.  But we must point out one circumstance which appears to have escaped all the critics.  The extraordinary
20 effect which this simile produced when it first appeared, and which to the following generation seemed inexplicable, is doubtless to be chiefly attributed to a line which most readers now regard as a feeble parenthesis,

> "Such as, of late, o'er pale Britannia pass'd."

Addison spoke, not of a storm, but of the storm.  The great tempest of November 1703, the only tempest which in our latitude has equalled the rage of a tropical hurricane, had left a dreadful recollection in the minds of all men.  No other tempest was ever in this country the occasion of a parlia-
30 mentary address or of a public fast.  Whole fleets had been cast away.  Large mansions had been blown down.  One Prelate had been buried beneath the ruins of his Palace. London and Bristol had presented the appearance of cities just sacked.  Hundreds of families were still in mourning. The prostrate trunks of large trees, and the ruins of houses, still attested, in all the southern counties, the fury of the blast.

The popularity which the simile of the angel enjoyed among
Addison's contemporaries, has always seemed to us to be a
remarkable instance of the advantage which, in rhetoric and
poetry, the particular has over the general.

Soon after the Campaign, was published Addison's Narrative of his Travels in Italy.  The first effect produced by this
Narrative was disappointment.  The crowd of readers who
expected politics and scandal, speculations on the projects
of Victor Amadeus, and anecdotes about the jollities of
convents and the amours of cardinals and nuns, were con- 10
founded by finding that the writer's mind was much more
occupied by the war between the Trojans and Rutulians
than by the war between France and Austria ; and that he
seemed to have heard no scandal of later date than the
gallantries of the Empress Faustina.  In time, however, the
judgment of the many was over-ruled by that of the few ;
and, before the book was reprinted, it was so eagerly sought
that it sold for five times the original price.  It is still read
with pleasure : the style is pure and flowing ; the classical
quotations and allusions are numerous and happy ; and we 20
are now and then charmed by that singularly humane and
delicate humour in which Addison excelled all men.  Yet
this agreeable work, even when considered merely as the
history of a literary tour, may justly be censured on account
of its faults of omission.  We have already said that, though
rich in extracts from the Latin poets, it contains scarcely
any references to the Latin orators and historians.  We
must add that it contains little, or rather no information,
respecting the history and literature of modern Italy.  To
the best of our remembrance, Addison does not mention 30
Dante, Petrarch, Boccaccio, Boiardo, Berni, Lorenzo de'
Medici, or Machiavelli.  He coldly tells us, that at Ferrara
he saw the tomb of Ariosto, and that at Venice he heard the
gondoliers sing verses of Tasso.  But for Tasso and Ariosto
he cared far less than for Valerius Flaccus and Sidonius
Apollinaris.  The gentle flow of the Ticin brings a line of

Silius to his mind.   The sulphurous steam of Albula suggests
to him several passages of Martial.   But he has not a word
to say of the illustrious dead of Santa Croce ; he crosses the
wood of Ravenna without recollecting the Spectre Huntsman,
and wanders up and down Rimini without one thought of
Francesca.   At Paris, he had eagerly sought an introduction
to Boileau ; but he seems not to have been at all aware that
at Florence he was in the vicinity of a poet with whom
Boileau could not sustain a comparison, of the greatest lyric
10 poet of modern times, Vincenzio Filicaja.   This is the more
remarkable, because Filicaja was the favourite poet of the
accomplished Somers, under whose protection Addison
travelled, and to whom the account of the Travels is
dedicated.   The truth is, that Addison knew little, and
cared less, about the literature of modern Italy.   His
favourite models were Latin.   His favourite critics were
French.   Half the Tuscan poetry that he had read seemed
to him monstrous, and the other half tawdry.

His Travels were followed by the lively Opera of Rosamond.
20 This piece was ill set to music, and therefore failed on the
stage, but it completely succeeded in print, and is indeed
excellent in its kind.   The smoothness with which the
verses glide, and the elasticity with which they bound, is,
to our ears at least, very pleasing.   We are inclined to think
that if Addison had left heroic couplets to Pope, and blank
verse to Rowe, and had employed himself in writing airy
and spirited songs, his reputation as a poet would have
stood far higher than it now does.   Some years after his
death, Rosamond was set to new music by Doctor Arne ;
30 and was performed with complete success.   Several passages
long retained their popularity, and were daily sung, during
the latter part of George the Second's reign, at all the
harpsichords in England.

While Addison thus amused himself, his prospects, and
the prospects of his party, were constantly becoming brighter
and brighter.   In the spring of 1705, the ministers were

freed from the restraint imposed by a House of Commons, in which Tories of the most perverse class had the ascendency. The elections were favourable to the Whigs. The coalition which had been tacitly and gradually formed was now openly avowed. The Great Seal was given to Cowper. Somers and Halifax were sworn of the Council. Halifax was sent in the following year to carry the decorations of the order of the garter to the Electoral Prince of Hanover, and was accompanied on this honourable mission by Addison, who had just been made Undersecretary of State. The Secretary of State under whom Addison first served was Sir Charles Hedges, a Tory. But Hedges was soon dismissed to make room for the most vehement of Whigs, Charles, Earl of Sunderland. In every department of the state, indeed, the High Churchmen were compelled to give place to their opponents. At the close of 1707, the Tories who still remained in office strove to rally, with Harley at their head. But the attempt, though favoured by the Queen, who had always been a Tory at heart, and who had now quarrelled with the Duchess of Marlborough, was unsuccessful. The time was not yet. The Captain General was at the height of popularity and glory. The Low Church party had a majority in Parliament. The country squires and rectors, though occasionally uttering a savage growl, were for the most part in a state of torpor, which lasted till they were roused into activity, and indeed into madness, by the prosecution of Sacheverell. Harley and his adherents were compelled to retire. The victory of the Whigs was complete. At the general election of 1708, their strength in the House of Commons became irresistible ; and, before the end of that year, Somers was made Lord President of the Council, and Wharton Lord Lieutenant of Ireland.

Addison sat for Malmsbury in the House of Commons which was elected in 1708. But the House of Commons was not the field for him. The bashfulness of his nature made his wit and eloquence useless in debate. He once rose, but

could not overcome his diffidence, and ever after remained
silent. Nobody can think it strange that a great writer
should fail as a speaker. But many, probably, will think
it strange that Addison's failure as a speaker should have
had no unfavourable effect on his success as a politician. In
our time, a man of high rank and great fortune might,
though speaking very little and very ill, hold a considerable
post. But it would·now be inconceivable that a mere adven-
turer, a man who, when out of office, must live by his pen,
10 should in a few years become successively Undersecretary of
State, chief Secretary for Ireland, and Secretary of State,
without some oratorical talent. Addison, without high birth,
and with little property, rose to a post which Dukes, the
heads of the great houses of Talbot, Russell, and Bentinck,
have thought it an honour to fill. Without opening his lips
in debate, he rose to a post, the highest that Chatham or Fox
ever reached. And this he did before he had been nine years
in Parliament. We must look for the explanation of this
seeming miracle to the peculiar circumstances in which that
20 generation was placed. During the interval which elapsed
between the time when the Censorship of the Press ceased,
and the time when parliamentary proceedings began to be
freely reported, literary talents were, to a public man, of
much more importance,.and oratorical talents of much less
importance, than in our time. At present, the best way of
giving rapid and wide publicity to a fact or an argument is
to introduce that fact or argument into a speech made in
Parliament. If a political tract were to appear superior to
the Conduct of the Allies, or to the best numbers of the
30 Freeholder, the circulation of such a tract would be languid
indeed when compared with the circulation of every remarkable word uttered in the deliberations of the legislature. A
speech made in the House of Commons at four in the morning is on thirty thousand tables before ten. A speech made
on the Monday is read on the Wednesday by multitudes in
Antrim and Aberdeenshire. The orator, by the help of the

shorthand writer, has to a great extent superseded the pamphleteer. It was not so in the reign of Anne. The best speech could then produce no effect except on those who heard it. It was only by means of the press that the opinion of the public without doors could be influenced ; and the opinion of the public without doors could not but be of the highest importance in a country governed by parliaments, and indeed at that time governed by triennial parliaments. The pen was therefore a more formidable political engine than the tongue. Mr. Pitt and Mr. Fox contended only in 10 Parliament. But Walpole and Pulteney, the Pitt and Fox of an earlier period, had not done half of what was necessary, when they sat down amidst the acclamations of the House of Commons. They had still to plead their cause before the country, and this they could do only by means of the press. Their works are now forgotten. But it is certain that there were in Grub Street few more assiduous scribblers of Thoughts, Letters, Answers, Remarks, than these two great chiefs of parties. Pulteney, when leader of the Opposition, and possessed of thirty thousand a year, edited the Crafts- 20 man. Walpole, though not a man of literary habits, was the author of at least ten pamphlets, and retouched and corrected many more. These facts sufficiently show of how great importance literary assistance then was to the contending parties. St. John was, certainly, in Anne's reign, the best Tory speaker ; Cowper was probably the best Whig speaker. But it may well be doubted whether St. John did so much for the Tories as Swift, and whether Cowper did so much for the Whigs as Addison. When these things are duly considered, it will not be thought strange that Addison should 30 have climbed higher in the state than any other Englishman has ever, by means merely of literary talents, been able to climb. Swift would, in all probability, have climbed as high, if he had not been encumbered by his cassock and his pudding sleeves. As far as the homage of the great went, Swift had as much of it as if he had been Lord Treasurer.

To the influence which Addison derived from his literary talents was added all the influence which arises from character. The world, always ready to think the worst of needy political adventurers, was forced to make one exception. Restlessness, violence, audacity, laxity of principle, are the vices ordinarily attributed to that class of men. But faction itself could not deny that Addison had, through all changes of fortune, been strictly faithful to his early opinions, and to his early friends ; that his integrity was without stain ; that 10 his whole deportment indicated a fine sense of the becoming ; that, in the utmost heat of controversy, his zeal was tempered by a regard for truth, humanity, and social decorum ; that no outrage could ever provoke him to retaliation unworthy of a Christian and a gentleman ; and that his only faults were a too sensitive delicacy, and a modesty which amounted to bashfulness.

He was undoubtedly one of the most popular men of his time ; and much of his popularity he owed, we believe, to that very timidity which his friends lamented. That timidity 20 often prevented him from exhibiting his talents to the best advantage. But it propitiated Nemesis. It averted that envy which would otherwise have been excited by fame so splendid, and by so rapid an elevation. No man is so great a favourite with the public as he who is at once an object of admiration, of respect, and of pity ; and such were the feelings which Addison inspired. Those who enjoyed the privilege of hearing his familiar conversation, declared with one voice that it was superior even to his writings. The brilliant Mary Montague said, that she had known all the 30 wits, and that Addison was the best company in the world. The malignant Pope was forced to own, that there was a charm in Addison's talk, which could be found nowhere else. Swift, when burning with animosity against the Whigs, could not but confess to Stella that, after all, he had never known any associate so agreeable as Addison. Steele, an excellent judge of lively conversation, said, that the conversation of Addison was at once the most polite, and the most mirthful, that could be imagined ; that it was Terence and Catullus in one, heightened by an exquisite something which was neither Terence nor Catullus, but Addison alone. Young, an excellent judge of serious conversation, said, that when Addison was at his ease, he went on in a noble strain of thought and language, so as to chain the attention of every hearer. Nor were Addison's great colloquial powers more admirable than the courtesy and softness of heart which appeared in his conversation. At the same time, it would be 10 too much to say that he was wholly devoid of the malice which is, perhaps, inseparable from a keen sense of the ludicrous. He had one habit which both Swift and Stella applauded, and which we hardly know how to blame. If his first attempts to set a presuming dunce right were ill received, he changed his tone, " assented with civil leer," and lured the flattered coxcomb deeper and deeper into absurdity. That such was his practice we should, we think, have guessed from his works. The Tatler's criticisms on Mr. Softly's sonnet, and the Spectator's dialogue with the politician who is 20 so zealous for the honour of Lady Q—p—t—s, are excellent specimens of this innocent mischief.

Such were Addison's talents for conversation. But his rare gifts were not exhibited to crowds or to strangers. As soon as he entered a large company, as soon as he saw an unknown face, his lips were sealed, and his manners became constrained. None who met him only in great assemblies would have been able to believe that he was the same man who had often kept a few friends listening and laughing round a table, from the time when the play ended, till the 30 clock of St. Paul's in Covent Garden struck four. Yet, even at such a table, he was not seen to the best advantage. To enjoy his conversation in the highest perfection, it was necessary to be alone with him, and to hear him, in his own phrase, think aloud. "There is no such thing," he used to say, "as real conversation, but between two persons."

This timidity, a timidity surely neither ungraceful nor unamiable, led Addison into the two most serious faults which can with justice be imputed to him. He found that wine broke the spell which lay on his fine intellect, and was therefore too easily seduced into convivial excess. Such excess was in that age regarded, even by grave men, as the most venial of all peccadilloes, and was so far from being a mark of illbreeding that it was almost essential to the character of a fine gentleman. But the smallest speck is 10 seen on a white ground ; and almost all the biographers of Addison have said something about this failing. Of any other statesman or writer of Queen Anne's reign, we should no more think of saying that he sometimes took too much wine, than that he wore a long wig and a sword.

To the excessive modesty of Addison's nature, we must ascribe another fault which generally arises from a very different cause. He became a little too fond of seeing himself surrounded by a small circle of admirers, to whom he was as a King or rather as a God. All these men were 20 far inferior to him in ability, and some of them had very serious faults. Nor did those faults escape his observation ; for, if ever there was an eye which saw through and through men, it was the eye of Addison. But, with the keenest observation, and the finest sense of the ridiculous, he had a large charity. The feeling with which he looked on most of his humble companions was one of benevolence, slightly tinctured with contempt. He was at perfect ease in their company ; he was grateful for their devoted attachment ; and he loaded them with benefits. Their veneration for him 30 appears to have exceeded that with which Johnson was regarded by Boswell, or Warburton by Hurd. It was not in the power of adulation to turn such a head, or deprave such a heart, as Addison's. But it must in candour be admitted that he contracted some of the faults which can scarcely be avoided by any person who is so unfortunate as to be the oracle of a small literary coterie.

One member of this little society was Eustace Budgell, a young Templar of some literature, and a distant relation of Addison. There was at this time no stain on the character of Budgell, and it is not improbable that his career would have been prosperous and honourable, if the life of his cousin had been prolonged. But, when the master was laid in the grave, the disciple broke loose from all restraint, descended rapidly from one degree of vice and misery to another, ruined his fortune by follies, attempted to repair it by crimes, and at length closed a wicked and unhappy life 10 by selfmurder. Yet, to the last, the wretched man, gambler, lampooner, cheat, forger, as he was, retained his affection and veneration for Addison, and recorded those feelings in the last lines which he traced before he hid himself from infamy under London Bridge.

Another of Addison's favourite companions was Ambrose Phillipps, a good Whig and a middling poet, who had the honour of bringing into fashion a species of composition which has been called, after his name, Namby Pamby. But the most remarkable members of the little senate, as Pope 20 long afterwards called it, were Richard Steele and Thomas Tickell.

Steele had known Addison from childhood. They had been together at the Charter House and at Oxford ; but circumstances had then, for a time, separated them widely. Steele had left college without taking a degree, had been disinherited by a rich relation, had led a vagrant life, had served in the army, had tried to find the philosopher's stone, and had written a religious treatise and several comedies. He was one of those people whom it is impossible either to 30 hate or to respect. His temper was sweet, his affections warm, his spirits lively, his passions strong, and his principles weak. His life was spent in sinning and repenting ; in inculcating what was right, and doing what was wrong. In speculation, he was a man of piety and honour ; in practice he was much of the rake and a little of the swindler. He

was, however, so goodnatured that it was not easy to be
seriously angry with him, and that even rigid moralists felt
more inclined to pity than to blame him, when he diced
himself into a spunging house or drank himself into a fever.
Addison regarded Steele with kindness not unmingled with
scorn, tried, with little success, to keep him out of scrapes,
introduced him to the great, procured a good place for him,
corrected his plays, and, though by no means rich, lent him
large sums of money. One of these loans appears, from a
10 letter dated in August 1708, to have amounted to a thousand
pounds. These pecuniary transactions probably led to frequent bickerings. It is said that, on one occasion, Steele's
negligence, or dishonesty, provoked Addison to repay himself
by the help of a bailiff. We cannot join with Miss Aikin in
rejecting this story. Johnson heard it from Savage, who
heard it from Steele. Few private transactions which took
place a hundred and twenty years ago, are proved by stronger
evidence than this. But we can by no means agree with
those who condemn Addison's severity. The most amiable
20 of mankind may well be moved to indignation, when what
he has earned hardly, and lent with great inconvenience to
himself, for the purpose of relieving a friend in distress, is
squandered with insane profusion. We will illustrate our
meaning by an example, which is not the less striking
because it is taken from fiction. Dr. Harrison, in Fielding's
Amelia, is represented as the most benevolent of human
beings; yet he takes in execution, not only the goods, but
the person of his friend Booth. Dr. Harrison resorts to this
strong measure because he has been informed that Booth,
30 while pleading poverty as an excuse for not paying just
debts, has been buying fine jewellery, and setting up a coach.
No person who is well acquainted with Steele's life and
correspondence can doubt that he behaved quite as ill to
Addison as Booth was accused of behaving to Dr. Harrison.
The real history, we have little doubt, was something like
this:—A letter comes to Addison, imploring help in pathetic

terms, and promising reformation and speedy repayment.
Poor Dick declares that he has not an inch of candle, or a
bushel of coals, or credit with the butcher for a shoulder of
mutton. Addison is moved. He determines to deny himself some medals which are wanting to his series of the
Twelve Cæsars ; to put off buying the new edition of Bayle's
Dictionary ; and to wear his old sword and buckles another
year. In this way he manages to send a hundred pounds
to his friend. The next day he calls on Steele, and finds
scores of gentlemen and ladies assembled. The fiddles are 10
playing. The table is groaning under Champagne, Burgundy,
and pyramids of sweetmeats. Is it strange that a man
whose kindness is thus abused, should send sheriff's officers
to reclaim what is due to him ?

Tickell was a young man, fresh from Oxford, who had
introduced himself to public notice by writing a most
ingenious and graceful little poem in praise of the opera of
Rosamond. He deserved, and at length attained, the first
place in Addison's friendship. For a time Steele and Tickell
were on good terms. But they loved Addison too much to 20
love each other, and at length became as bitter enemies as
the rival bulls in Virgil.

At the close of 1708 Wharton became Lord Lieutenant of
Ireland, and appointed Addison Chief Secretary. Addison
was consequently under the necessity of quitting London for
Dublin. Besides the chief secretaryship, which was then
worth about two thousand pounds a year, he obtained a
patent appointing him keeper of the Irish Records for life,
with a salary of three or four hundred a year. Budgell
accompanied his cousin in the capacity of private Secretary. 30

Wharton and Addison had nothing in common but
Whiggism. The Lord Lieutenant was not only licentious
and corrupt, but was distinguished from other libertines
and jobbers by a callous impudence which presented the
strongest contrast to the Secretary's gentleness and delicacy.
Many parts of the Irish administration at this time appear

to have deserved serious blame.  But against Addison there
was not a murmur.  He long afterwards asserted, what all
the evidence which we have ever seen tends to prove, that
his diligence and integrity gained the friendship of all the
most considerable persons in Ireland.

The parliamentary career of Addison in Ireland has, we
think, wholly escaped the notice of all his biographers.  He
was elected member for the borough of Cavan in the
summer of 1709 ; and in the journals of two sessions his
10 name frequently occurs.  Some of the entries appear to
indicate that he so far overcame his timidity as to make
speeches.  Nor is this by any means improbable ; for the
Irish House of Commons was a far less formidable audience
than the English House ; and many tongues which were
tied by fear in the greater assembly became fluent in the
smaller.  Gerard Hamilton, for example, who, from fear
of losing the fame gained by his single speech, sat mute
at Westminster during forty years, spoke with great effect
at Dublin when he was Secretary to Lord Halifax.

20    While Addison was in Ireland, an event occurred to which
he owes his high and permanent rank among British writers.
As yet his fame rested on performances which, though
highly respectable, were not built for duration, and which
would, if he had produced nothing else, have now been
almost forgotten, on some excellent Latin verses, on some
English verses which occasionally rose above mediocrity,
and on a book of travels, agreeably written, but not indicating any extraordinary powers of mind.  These works
showed him to be a man of taste, sense, and learning.  The
30 time had come when he was to prove himself a man of
genius, and to enrich our literature with compositions which
will live as long as the English language.

In the spring of 1709 Steele formed a literary project, of
which he was far indeed from forseeing the consequences.
Periodical papers had during many years been published in
London.  Most of these were political ; but in some of them

questions of morality, taste, and love casuistry had been discussed. The literary merit of these works was small indeed; and even their names are now known only to the curious.

Steele had been appointed Gazetteer by Sunderland, at the request, it is said, of Addison, and thus had access to foreign intelligence earlier and more authentic than was in those times within the reach of an ordinary newswriter. This circumstance seems to have suggested to him the scheme of publishing a periodical paper on a new plan. It 10 was to appear on the days on which the post left London for the country, which were, in that generation, the Tuesdays, Thursdays, and Saturdays. It was to contain the foreign news, accounts of theatrical representations, and the literary gossip of Will's and of the Grecian. It was also to contain remarks on the fashionable topics of the day, compliments to beauties, pasquinades on noted sharpers, and criticisms on popular preachers. The aim of Steele does not appear to have been at first higher than this. He was not ill qualified to conduct the work which he had planned. 20 His public intelligence he drew from the best sources. He knew the town, and had paid dear for his knowledge. He had read much more than the dissipated men of that time were in the habit of reading. He was a rake among scholars, and a scholar among rakes. His style was easy and not incorrect; and, though his wit and humour were of no high order, his gay animal spirits imparted to his compositions an air of vivacity which ordinary readers could hardly distinguish from comic genius. His writings have been well compared to those light wines which, though deficient in 30 body and flavour, are yet a pleasant small drink, if not kept too long, or carried too far.

Isaac Bickerstaff, Esquire, Astrologer, was an imaginary person, almost as well known in that age as Mr. Paul Pry or Mr. Samuel Pickwick in ours. Swift had assumed the name of Bickerstaff in a satirical pamphlet against Partridge, the maker of almanacks. Partridge had been fool enough to publish a furious reply. Bickerstaff had rejoined in a second pamphlet still more diverting than the first. All the wits had combined to keep up the joke, and the town was long in convulsions of laughter. Steele determined to employ the name which this controversy had made popular ; and, in 1709, it was announced that Isaac Bickerstaff, Esquire, Astrologer, was about to publish a paper called the Tatler.

Addison had not been consulted about this scheme : but 10 as soon as he heard of it, he determined to give his assistance. The effect of that assistance cannot be better described than in Steele's own words. "I fared," he said, "like a distressed prince who calls in a powerful neighbour to his aid. I was undone by my auxiliary. When I had once called him in, I could not subsist without dependence on him." "The paper," he says elsewhere, "was advanced indeed. It was raised to a greater thing than I intended it."

It is probable that Addison, when he sent across St. George's Channel his first contributions to the Tatler, had no 20 notion of the extent and variety of his own powers. He was the possessor of a vast mine, rich with a hundred ores. But he had been acquainted only with the least precious part of his treasures, and had hitherto contented himself with producing sometimes copper and sometimes lead, intermingled with a little silver. All at once, and by mere accident, he had lighted on an inexhaustible vein of the finest gold.

The mere choice and arrangement of his words would have sufficed to make his essays classical. For never, not even by Dryden, not even by Temple, had the English 30 language been written with such sweetness, grace, and facility. But this was the smallest part of Addison's praise. Had he clothed his thoughts in the half French style of Horace Walpole, or in the half Latin style of Dr. Johnson, or in the half German jargon of the present day, his genius would have triumphed over all faults of manner. As a moral satirist he stands unrivalled. If ever the best Tatlers

and Spectators were equalled in their own kind, we should
be inclined to guess that it must have been by the lost
comedies of Menander.

In wit, properly so called, Addison was not inferior to
Cowley or Butler. No single ode of Cowley contains so
many happy analogies as are crowded into the lines to Sir
Godfrey Kneller; and we would undertake to collect from
the Spectators as great a number of ingenious illustrations
as can be found in Hudibras. The still higher faculty of
invention Addison possessed in still larger measure. The 10
numerous fictions, generally original, often wild and gro-
tesque, but always singularly graceful and happy, which are
found in his essays, fully entitle him to the rank of a great
poet, a rank to which his metrical compositions give him no
claim. As an observer of life, of manners, of all the shades
of human character, he stands in the first class. And what
he observed he had the art of communicating in two widely
different ways. He could describe virtues, vices, habits,
whims, as well as Clarendon. But he could do something
better. He could call human beings into existence, and 20
make them exhibit themselves. If we wish to find anything
more vivid than Addison's best portraits, we must go either
to Shakspeare or to Cervantes.

But what shall we say of Addison's humour, of his sense
of the ludicrous, of his power of awakening that sense in
others, and of drawing mirth from incidents which occur
every day, and from little peculiarities of temper and
manner, such as may be found in every man? We feel the
charm : we give ourselves up to it : but we strive in vain to
analyse it.                                                    30

Perhaps the best way of describing Addison's peculiar
pleasantry is to compare it with the pleasantry of some
other great satirists. The three most eminent masters of
the art of ridicule, during the eighteenth century, were, we
conceive, Addison, Swift, and Voltaire. Which of the three
had the greatest power of moving laughter may be ques-

tioned. But each of them, within his own domain, was supreme.

Voltaire is the prince of buffoons. His merriment is without disguise or restraint. He gambols; he grins; he shakes his sides; he points the finger; he turns up the nose; he shoots out the tongue. The manner of Swift is the very opposite to this. He moves laughter, but never joins in it. He appears in his works such as he appeared in society. All the company are convulsed with merriment, while the
10 Dean, the author of all the mirth, preserves an invincible gravity, and even sourness of aspect, and gives utterance to the most eccentric and ludicrous fancies, with the air of a man reading the commination service.

The manner of Addison is as remote from that of Swift as from that of Voltaire. He neither laughs out like the French wit, nor, like the Irish wit, throws a double portion of severity into his countenance while laughing inwardly; but preserves a look peculiarly his own, a look of demure serenity, disturbed only by an arch sparkle of the eye, an
20 almost imperceptible elevation of the brow, an almost imperceptible curl of the lip. His tone is never that either of a Jack Pudding or of a Cynic. It is that of a gentleman, in whom the quickest sense of the ridiculous is constantly tempered by good nature and good breeding.

We own that the humour of Addison is, in our opinion, of a more delicious flavour than the humour of either Swift or Voltaire. Thus much, at least, is certain, that both Swift and Voltaire have been successfully mimicked, and that no man has yet been able to mimic Addison. The letter of the
30 Abbé Coyer to Pansophe is Voltaire all over, and imposed, during a long time, on the Academicians of Paris. There are passages in Arbuthnot's satirical works which we, at least, cannot distinguish from Swift's best writing. But of the many eminent men who have made Addison their model, though several have copied his mere diction with happy effect, none has been able to catch the tone of his pleasantry.

In the World, in the Connoisseur, in the Mirror, in the Lounger, there are numerous papers written in obvious imitation of his Tatlers and Spectators. Most of those papers have some merit ; many are very lively and amusing ; but there is not a single one which could be passed off as Addison's on a critic of the smallest perspicacity.

But that which chiefly distinguishes Addison from Swift, ∨ from Voltaire, from almost all the other great masters of ridicule, is the grace, the nobleness, the moral purity, which we find even in his merriment. Severity, gradually hardening 10 and darkening into misanthropy, characterizes the works of Swift. The nature of Voltaire was, indeed, not inhuman ; but he venerated nothing. Neither in the masterpieces of art nor in the purest examples of virtue, neither in the Great First Cause nor in the awful enigma of the grave, could he see any thing but subjects for drollery. The more solemn and august the theme, the more monkey-like was his grimacing and chattering. The mirth of Swift is the mirth of Mephistophiles ; the mirth of Voltaire is the mirth of Puck. If, as Soame Jenyns oddly imagined, a portion of 20 the happiness of Seraphim and just men made perfect be derived from an exquisite perception of the ludicrous, their mirth must surely be none other than the mirth of Addison ; a mirth consistent with tender compassion for all that is frail, and with profound reverence for all that is sublime. Nothing great, nothing amiable, no moral duty, no doctrine of natural or revealed religion, has ever been associated by Addison with any degrading idea. His humanity is without a parallel in literary history. The highest proof of virtue is to possess boundless power without abusing it. No kind of 30 power is more formidable than the power of making men ridiculous ; and that power Addison possessed in boundless measure. How grossly that power was abused by Swift and by Voltaire is well known. But of Addison it may be confidently affirmed that he has blackened no man's character, nay, that it would be difficult, if not impossible, to find in

all the volumes which he has left us a single taunt which
can be called ungenerous or unkind. Yet he had detractors,
whose malignity might have seemed to justify as terrible a
revenge as that which men, not superior to him in genius,
wreaked on Bettesworth and on Franc de Pompignan. He
was a politician ; he was the best writer of his party ; he
lived in times of fierce excitement, in times when persons of
high character and station stooped to scurrility such as is
now practised only by the basest of mankind. Yet no pro-
10 vocation and no example could induce him to return railing
for railing.

Of the service which his Essays rendered to morality it
is difficult to speak too highly. It is true that, when the
Tatler appeared, that age of outrageous profaneness and
licentiousness which followed the Restoration had passed
away. Jeremy Collier had shamed the theatres into something which, compared with the excesses of Etherege and
Wycherley, might be called decency. Yet there still lingered
in the public mind a pernicious notion that there was some
20 connection between genius and profligacy, between the
domestic virtues and the sullen formality of the Puritans.
That error it is the glory of Addison to have dispelled. He
taught the nation that the faith and the morality of Hale
and Tillotson might be found in company with wit more
sparkling than the wit of Congreve, and with humour richer
than the humour of Vanbrugh. So effectually, indeed, did
he retort on vice the mockery which had recently been
directed against virtue, that, since his time, the open violation of decency has always been considered among us as
30 the mark of a fool. And this revolution, the greatest and
most salutary ever effected by any satirist, he accomplished,
be it remembered, without writing one personal lampoon.

In the early contributions of Addison to the Tatler his
peculiar powers were not fully exhibited. Yet from the
first, his superiority to all his coadjutors was evident. Some
of his later Tatlers are fully equal to any thing that he ever

wrote. Among the portraits, we most admire Tom Folio,
Ned Softly, and the Political Upholsterer. The proceedings
of the Court of Honour, the Thermometer of Zeal, the story
of the Frozen Words, the Memoirs of the Shilling, are excellent specimens of that ingenious and lively species of
fiction in which Addison excelled all men. There is one
still better paper of the same class. But though that paper,
a hundred and thirty-three years ago, was probably thought
as edifying as one of Smalridge's sermons, we dare not indicate it to the squeamish readers of the nineteenth century.    10

During the session of Parliament which commenced in
November 1709, and which the impeachment of Sacheverell
has made memorable, Addison appears to have resided in
London. The Tatler was now more popular than any
periodical paper had ever been ; and his connection with it
was generally known. It was not known, however, that
almost every thing good in the Tatler was his. The truth is,
that the fifty or sixty numbers which we owe to him were
not merely the best, but so decidedly the best that any five
of them are more valuable than all the two hundred numbers 20
in which he had no share.

He required, at this time, all the solace which he could derive from literary success. The Queen had always disliked
the Whigs. She had during some years disliked the Marlborough family. But, reigning by a disputed title, she
could not venture directly to oppose herself to a majority of
both Houses of Parliament ; and, engaged as she was in a war
on the event of which her own Crown was staked, she could
not venture to disgrace a great and successful general. But
at length, in the year 1710, the causes which had restrained 30
her from showing her aversion to the Low Church party
ceased to operate. The trial of Sacheverell produced an
outbreak of public feeling scarcely less violent than the out-
breaks which we can ourselves remember in 1820, and in
1831. The country gentlemen, the country clergymen, the
rabble of the towns, were all, for once, on the same side. It

was clear that, if a general election took place before the excitement abated, the Tories would have a majority. The services of Marlborough had been so splendid that they were no longer necessary. The Queen's throne was secure from all attack on the part of Lewis. Indeed, it seemed much more likely that the English and German armies would divide the spoils of Versailles and Marli than that a Marshal of France would bring back the Pretender to St. James's. The Queen, acting by the advice of Harley, determined to dismiss her
10 servants. In June the change commenced. Sunderland was the first who fell. The Tories exulted over his fall. The Whigs tried, during a few weeks, to persuade themselves that her Majesty had acted only from personal dislike to the Secretary, and that she meditated no further alteration. But, early in August, Godolphin was surprised by a letter from Anne, which directed him to break his white staff. Even after this event, the irresolution or dissimulation of Harley kept up the hopes of the Whigs during another month ; and then the ruin became rapid and violent. The
20 Parliament was dissolved. The Ministers were turned out. The Tories were called to office. The tide of popularity ran violently in favour of the High Church party. That party, feeble in the late House of Commons, was now irresistible. The power which the Tories had thus suddenly acquired, they used with blind and stupid ferocity. The howl which the whole pack set up for prey and for blood appalled even him who had roused and unchained them. When, at this distance of time, we calmly review the conduct of the discarded ministers, we cannot but feel a movement of indigna-
30 tion at the injustice with which they were treated. No body of men had ever administered the government with more energy, ability, and moderation ; and their success had been proportioned to their wisdom. They had saved Holland and Germany. They had humbled France. They had, as it seemed, all but torn Spain from the House of Bourbon. They had made England the first power in Europe. At

home they had united England and Scotland. They had respected the rights of conscience and the liberty of the subject. They retired, leaving their country at the height of prosperity and glory. And yet they were pursued to their retreat by such a roar of obloquy as was never raised against the government which threw away thirteen colonies, or against the government which sent a gallant army to perish in the ditches of Walcheren.

None of the Whigs suffered more in the general wreck than Addison. He had just sustained some heavy pecuniary 10 losses, of the nature of which we are imperfectly informed, when his Secretaryship was taken from him. He had reason to believe that he should also be deprived of the small Irish office which he held by patent. He had just resigned his Fellowship. It seems probable that he had already ventured to raise his eyes to a great lady, and that, while his political friends were in power, and while his own fortunes were rising, he had been, in the phrase of the romances which were then fashionable, permitted to hope. But Mr. Addison the ingenious writer, and Mr. Addison the chief 20 Secretary, were, in her ladyship's opinion, two very different persons. All these calamities united, however, could not disturb the serene cheerfulness of a mind conscious of innocence, and rich in its own wealth. He told his friends, with smiling resignation, that they ought to admire his philosophy, that he had lost at once his fortune, his place, his fellowship, and his mistress, that he must think of turning tutor again, and yet that his spirits were as good as ever.

He had one consolation. Of the unpopularity which his friends had incurred, he had no share. Such was the esteem 30 with which he was regarded that, while the most violent measures were taken for the purpose of forcing Tory members on Whig corporations, he was returned to Parliament without even a contest. Swift, who was now in London, and who had already determined on quitting the Whigs, wrote to Stella in these remarkable words : "The Tories carry it among the new members six to one. Mr. Addison's election has passed easy and undisputed ; and I believe if he had a mind to be king, he would hardly be refused."

The good will with which the Tories regarded Addison is the more honourable to him, because it had not been purchased by any concession on his part. During the general election he published a political Journal, entitled the Whig Examiner. Of that Journal it may be sufficient to say that Johnson, in spite of his strong political prejudices, pro-
10 nounced it to be superior in wit to any of Swift's writings on the other side. When it ceased to appear, Swift, in a letter to Stella, expressed his exultation at the death of so formidable an antagonist. "He might well rejoice," says Johnson, "at the death of that which he could not have killed." "On no occasion," he adds, "was the genius of Addison more vigorously exerted, and on none did the superiority of his powers more evidently appear."

The only use which Addison appears to have made of the favour with which he was regarded by the Tories was to
20 save some of his friends from the general ruin of the Whig party. He felt himself to be in a situation which made it his duty to take a decided part in politics. But the case of Steele and of Ambrose Phillipps was different. For Phillipps, Addison even condescended to solicit, with what success we have not ascertained. Steele held two places. He was Gazetteer, and he was also a Commissioner of Stamps. The Gazette was taken from him. But he was suffered to retain his place in the Stamp Office, on an implied understanding that he should not be active against the new government ;
30 and he was, during more than two years, induced by Addison to observe this armistice with tolerable fidelity.

Isaac Bickerstaff accordingly became silent upon politics, and the article of news, which had once formed about one third of his paper, altogether disappeared. The Tatler had completely changed its character. It was now nothing but a series of essays on books, morals, and manners. Steele

therefore resolved to bring it to a close, and to commence a
new work on an improved plan. It was announced that
this new work would be published daily. The undertaking
was generally regarded as bold, or rather rash ; but the
event amply justified the confidence with which Steele relied
on the fertility of Addison's genius. On the second of
January 1711, appeared the last Tatler. At the beginning
of March following appeared the first of an incomparable
series of papers, containing observations on life and literature
by an imaginary Spectator.                                        10

The Spectator himself was conceived and drawn by Addison ; and it is not easy to doubt that the portrait was meant
to be in some features a likeness of the painter. The Spectator is a gentleman who, after passing a studious youth at
the university, has travelled on classic ground, and has bestowed much attention on curious points of antiquity. He
has, on his return, fixed his residence in London, and has
observed all the forms of life which are to be found in that
great city, has daily listened to the wits of Will's, has
smoked with the philosophers of the Grecian, and has 20
mingled with the parsons at Child's, and with the politicians
at the St. James's. In the morning, he often listens to the
hum of the Exchange ; in the evening, his face is constantly
to be seen in the pit of Drury Lane theatre. But an insurmountable bashfulness prevents him from opening his
mouth, except in a small circle of intimate friends.

These friends were first sketched by Steele. Four of the
club, the templar, the clergyman, the soldier, and the merchant, were uninteresting figures, fit only for a background.
But the other two, an old country baronet and an old town 30
rake, though not delineated with a very delicate pencil, had
some good strokes. Addison took the rude outlines into his
own hands, retouched them, coloured them, and is in truth
the creator of the Sir Roger de Coverley and the Will
Honeycomb with whom we are all familiar.

The plan of the Spectator must be allowed to be both

original and eminently happy.   Every valuable essay in the
series may be read with pleasure separately ; yet the five or
six hundred essays form a whole, and a whole which has the
interest of a novel.   It must be remembered, too, that at
that time no novel, giving a lively and powerful picture of
the common life and manners of England, had appeared.
Richardson was working as a compositor.   Fielding was
robbing birds' nests.   Smollett was not yet born.   The
narrative, therefore, which connects together the Spectator's
10 Essays, gave to our ancestors their first taste of an exquisite
and untried pleasure.   That narrative was indeed constructed
with no art or labour.   The events were such events as occur
every day.   Sir Roger comes up to town to see Eugenio, as
the worthy baronet always calls Prince Eugene, goes with
the Spectator on the water to Spring Gardens, walks among
the tombs in the Abbey, and is frightened by the Mohawks,
but conquers his apprehension so far as to go to the theatre
when the Distressed Mother is acted.   The Spectator pays a
visit in the summer to Coverley Hall, is charmed with the
20 old house, the old butler, and the old chaplain, eats a jack
caught by Will Wimble, rides to the assizes, and hears a
point of law discussed by Tom Touchy.   At last a letter from
the honest butler brings to the club the news that Sir Roger
is dead.   Will Honeycomb marries and reforms at sixty.
The club breaks up; and the Spectator resigns his functions.
Such events can hardly be said to form a plot ; yet they are
related with such truth, such grace, such wit, such humour,
such pathos, such knowledge of the human heart, such knowledge of the ways of the world, that they charm us on the
30 hundredth perusal.   We have not the least doubt that if
Addison had written a novel, on an extensive plan, it would
have been superior to any that we possess.   As it is, he is
entitled to be considered not only as the greatest of the
English essayists, but as the forerunner of the great English
novelists.
  We say this of Addison alone ; for Addison is the Spec-

tator. About three sevenths of the work are his ; and it is
no exaggeration to say, that his worst essay is as good as
the best essay of any of his coadjutors. His best essays
approach near to absolute perfection ; nor is their excellence
more wonderful than their variety. His invention never
seems to flag ; nor is he ever under the necessity of repeating
himself, or of wearing out a subject. There are no dregs in
his wine. He regales us after the fashion of that prodigal
nabob who held that there was only one good glass in a
bottle. As soon as we have tasted the first sparkling foam 10
of a jest, it is withdrawn, and a fresh draught of nectar is at
our lips. On the Monday we have an allegory as lively and
ingenious as Lucian's Auction of Lives ; on the Tuesday an
Eastern apologue, as richly coloured as the Tales of Scherezade ; on the Wednesday, a character described with the
skill of La Bruyere ; on the Thursday, a scene from common
life, equal to the best chapters in the Vicar of Wakefield; on
the Friday, some sly Horatian pleasantry on fashionable
follies, on hoops, patches, or puppet shows ; and on the
Saturday a religious meditation, which will bear a compari- 20
son with the finest passages in Massillon.

It is dangerous to select where there is so much that deserves the highest praise. We will venture, however, to say,
that any person who wishes to form a just notion of the extent and variety of Addison's powers, will do well to read at
one sitting the following papers, the two Visits to the Abbey,
the Visit to the Exchange, the Journal of the Retired Citizen,
the Vision of Mirza, the Transmigrations of Pug the Monkey,
and the Death of Sir Roger de Coverley.

The least valuable of Addison's contributions to the Spec- 30
tator are, in the judgment of our age, his critical papers.
Yet his critical papers are always luminous, and often
ingenious. The very worst of them must be regarded as
creditable to him, when the character of the school in which
he had been trained is fairly considered. The best of them
were much too good for his readers. In truth, he was not

so far behind our generation as he was before his own. No
essays in the Spectator were more censured and derided than
those in which he raised his voice against the contempt with
which our fine old ballads were regarded, and showed the
scoffers that the same gold which, burnished and polished,
gives lustre to the Æneid and the Odes of Horace, is mingled
with the rude dross of Chevy Chace.

It is not strange that the success of the Spectator should
have been such as no similar work has ever obtained. The
10 number of copies daily distributed was at first three
thousand. It subsequently increased, and had risen to near
four thousand when the stamp tax was imposed. That tax
was fatal to a crowd of journals. The Spectator, however,
stood its ground, doubled its price, and, though its circulation
fell off, still yielded a large revenue both to the state and to
the authors. For particular papers, the demand was immense; of some, it is said, twenty thousand copies were
required. But this was not all. To have the Spectator
served up every morning with the bohea and rolls, was a
20 luxury for the few. The majority were content to wait till
essays enough had appeared to form a volume. Ten thousand copies of each volume were immediately taken off, and
new editions were called for. It must be remembered, that
the population of England was then hardly a third of what
it now is. The number of Englishmen who were in the
habit of reading, was probably not a sixth of what it now is.
A shopkeeper or a farmer who found any pleasure in literature, was a rarity. Nay, there was doubtless more than one
knight of the shire whose country seat did not contain ten
30 books, receipt books and books on farriery included. In
these circumstances, the sale of the Spectator must be considered as indicating a popularity quite as great as that of
the most successful works of Sir Walter Scott and Mr.
Dickens in our own time.

At the close of 1712 the Spectator ceased to appear. It
was probably felt that the shortfaced gentleman and his club

had been long enough before the town ; and that it was time to withdraw them, and to replace them by a new set of characters. In a few weeks the first number of the Guardian was published. But the Guardian was unfortunate both in its birth and in its death. It began in dulness, and disappeared in a tempest of faction. The original plan was bad. Addison contributed nothing till sixty-six numbers had appeared ; and it was then impossible to make the Guardian what the Spectator had been. Nestor Ironside and the Miss Lizards were people to whom even he could 10 impart no interest. He could only furnish some excellent little essays, both serious and comic ; and this he did.

Why Addison gave no assistance to the Guardian, during the first two months of its existence, is a question which has puzzled the editors and biographers, but which seems to us to admit of a very easy solution. He was then engaged in bringing his Cato on the stage.

The first four acts of this drama had been lying in his desk since his return from Italy. His modest and sensitive nature shrank from the risk of a public and shameful 20 failure ; and, though all who saw the manuscript were loud in praise, some thought it possible that an audience might become impatient even of very good rhetoric, and advised Addison to print the play without hazarding a representation. At length, after many fits of apprehension, the poet yielded to the urgency of his political friends, who hoped that the public would discover some analogy between the followers of Cæsar and the Tories, between Sempronius and the apostate Whigs, between Cato, struggling to the last for the liberties of Rome, and the band of patriots who still 30 stood firm round Halifax and Wharton.

Addison gave the play to the managers of Drury Lane theatre, without stipulating for any advantage to himself. They, therefore, thought themselves bound to spare no cost in scenery and dresses. The decorations, it is true, would not have pleased the skilful eye of Mr. Macready. Juba's

waistcoat blazed with gold lace ; Marcia's hoop was worthy
of a Duchess on the birthday ; and Cato wore a wig worth
fifty guineas. The prologue was written by Pope, and is
undoubtedly a dignified and spirited composition. The part
of the hero was excellently played by Booth. Steele undertook to pack a house. The boxes were in a blaze with the
stars of the Peers in Opposition. The Pit was crowded with
attentive and friendly listeners from the Inns of Court and
the literary coffeehouses. Sir Gilbert Heathcote, Governor
10 of the Bank of England, was at the head of a powerful body
of auxiliaries from the city, warm men and true Whigs, but
better known at Jonathan's and Garraway's than in the
haunts of wits and critics.

These precautions were quite superfluous. The Tories, as
a rule, regarded Addison with no unkind feelings. Nor was
it for their interest, professing, as they did, profound reverence for law and prescription, and abhorrence both of
popular insurrections and of standing armies, to appropriate to
themselves reflections thrown on the great military chief and
20 demagogue, who, with the support of the legions and of the
common people, subverted all the ancient institutions of his
country. Accordingly, every shout that was raised by the
members of the Kit Cat was echoed by the High Churchmen
of the October ; and the curtain at length fell amidst
thunders of unanimous applause.

The delight and admiration of the town were described
by the Guardian in terms which we might attribute to
partiality, were it not that the Examiner, the organ of the
Ministry, held similar language. The Tories, indeed, found
30 much to sneer at in the conduct of their opponents. Steele
had on this, as on other occasions, shown more zeal than
taste or judgment. The honest citizens who marched under
the orders of Sir Gibby, as he was facetiously called, probably
knew better when to buy and when to sell stock than when
to clap and when to hiss at a play, and incurred some
ridicule by making the hypocritical Sempronius their favour-

ite, and by giving to his insincere rants louder plaudits than they bestowed on the temperate eloquence of Cato. Wharton, too, who had the incredible effrontery to applaud the lines about flying from prosperous vice and from the power of impious men to a private station, did not escape the sarcasms of those who justly thought that he could fly from nothing more vicious or impious than himself. The epilogue, which was written by Garth, a zealous Whig, was severely and not unreasonably censured as ignoble and out of place. But Addison was described, even by the bitterest Tory writers, 10 as a gentleman of wit and virtue, in whose friendship many persons of both parties were happy, and whose name ought not to be mixed up with factious squabbles.

Of the jests by which the triumph of the Whig party was disturbed, the most severe and happy was Bolingbroke's. Between two acts, he sent for Booth to his box, and presented him, before the whole theatre, with a purse of fifty guineas for defending the cause of liberty so well against a perpetual Dictator. This was a pungent allusion to the attempt which Marlborough had made, not long before his fall, to obtain a 20 patent creating him Captain General for life.

It was April; and in April, a hundred and thirty years ago, the London season was thought to be far advanced. During a whole month, however, Cato was performed to overflowing houses, and brought into the treasury of the theatre twice the gains of an ordinary spring. In the summer the Drury Lane company went down to the Act at Oxford, and there, before an audience which retained an affectionate remembrance of Addison's accomplishments and virtues, his tragedy was acted during several days. The 30 gownsmen began to besiege the theatre in the forenoon, and by one in the afternoon all the seats were filled.

About the merits of the piece which had so extraordinary an effect, the public, we suppose, has made up its mind. To compare it with the masterpieces of the Attic stage, with the great English dramas of the time of Elizabeth, or even with

the productions of Schiller's manhood, would be absurd indeed.  Yet it contains excellent dialogue and declamation,
and, among plays fashioned on the French model, must be
allowed to rank high ; not indeed with Athalie, or Saul ; but,
we think, not below Cinna, and certainly above any other
English tragedy of the same school, above many of the plays
of Corneille, above many of the plays of Voltaire and Alfieri,
and above some plays of Racine.  Be this as it may, we have
little doubt that Cato did as much as the Tatlers, Spectators,
10 and Freeholders united, to raise Addison's fame among his
contemporaries.

The modesty and good nature of the successful dramatist
had tamed even the malignity of faction.  But literary envy,
it should seem, is a fiercer passion than party spirit.  It was
by a zealous Whig that the fiercest attack on the Whig
tragedy was made.  John Dennis published Remarks on
Cato, which were written with some acuteness and with much
coarseness and asperity.  Addison neither defended himself
nor retaliated.  On many points he had an excellent defence ;
20 and nothing would have been easier than to retaliate ; for
Dennis had written bad odes, bad tragedies, bad comedies :
he had, moreover, a larger share than most men of those
infirmities and eccentricities which excite laughter ; and
Addison's power of turning either an absurd book or an
absurd man into ridicule was unrivalled.  Addison, however,
serenely conscious of his superiority, looked with pity on his
assailant, whose temper, naturally irritable and gloomy, had
been soured by want, by controversy, and by literary
failures.

30    But among the young candidates for Addison's favour
there was one distinguished by talents from the rest, and
distinguished, we fear, not less by malignity and insincerity.
Pope was only twenty-five.  But his powers had expanded to
their full maturity ; and his best poem, the Rape of the Lock,
had recently been published.  Of his genius, Addison had
always expressed high admiration.  But Addison had early

discerned, what might indeed have been discerned by an eye
less penetrating than his, that the diminutive, crooked, sickly
boy was eager to revenge himself on society for the unkindness of nature.  In the Spectator, the Essay on Criticism had
been praised with cordial warmth ; but a gentle hint had
been added, that the writer of so excellent a poem would
have done well to avoid ill-natured personalities.  Pope,
though evidently more galled by the censure than gratified
by the praise, returned thanks for the admonition, and
promised to profit by it.  The two writers continued to ex- 10
change civilities, counsel, and small good offices.  Addison
publicly extolled Pope's miscellaneous pieces ; and Pope
furnished Addison with a prologue.  This did not last long.
Pope hated Dennis, whom he had injured without provocation.  The appearance of the Remarks on Cato gave the
irritable poet an opportunity of venting his malice under the
show of friendship ; and such an opportunity could not but
be welcome to a nature which was implacable in enmity, and
which always preferred the tortuous to the straight path.
He published, accordingly, the Narrative of the Frenzy of 20
John Dennis.  But Pope had mistaken his powers.  He was
a great master of invective and sarcasm : he could dissect a
character in terse and sonorous couplets, brilliant with an-
tithesis : but of dramatic talent he was altogether destitute.
If he had written a lampoon on Dennis, such as that on
Atticus, or that on Sporus, the old grumbler would have been
crushed.  But Pope writing dialogue resembled—to borrow
Horace's imagery and his own—a wolf, which, instead of
biting, should take to kicking, or a monkey which should try
to sting.  The Narrative is utterly contemptible.  Of argu- 30
ment there is not even the show ; and the jests are such as,
if they were introduced into a farce, would call forth the
hisses of the shilling gallery.  Dennis raves about the drama ;
and the nurse thinks that he is calling for a dram.  "There is,"
he cries, "no peripetia in the tragedy, no change of fortune,
no change at all."  "Pray, good Sir, be not angry," says the

E

old woman; "I'll fetch change." This is not exactly the pleasantry of Addison.

There can be no doubt that Addison saw through this officious zeal, and felt himself deeply aggrieved by it. So foolish and spiteful a pamphlet could do him no good, and, if he were thought to have any hand in it, must do him harm. Gifted with incomparable powers of ridicule, he had never, even in self defence, used those powers inhumanly or uncourteously; and he was not disposed to let others make his fame and his
10 interest a pretext under which they might commit outrages from which he had himself constantly abstained. He accordingly declared that he had no concern in the narrative, that he disapproved of it, and that if he answered the remarks, he would answer them like a gentleman; and he took care to communicate this to Dennis. Pope was bitterly mortified; and to this transaction we are inclined to ascribe the hatred with which he ever after regarded Addison.

In September 1713 the Guardian ceased to appear. Steele had gone mad about politics. A general election had just
20 taken place. he had been chosen member for Stockbridge; and he fully expected to play a first part in Parliament. The immense success of the Tatler and Spectator had turned his head. He had been the editor of both those papers, and was not aware how entirely they owed their influence and popularity to the genius of his friend. His spirits, always violent, were now excited by vanity, ambition, and faction, to such a pitch that he every day committed some offence against good sense and good taste. All the discreet and moderate members of his own party regretted and condemned
30 his folly. "I am in a thousand troubles," Addison wrote, "about poor Dick, and wish that his zeal for the public may not be ruinous to himself. But he has sent me word that he is determined to go on, and that any advice I may give him in this particular will have no weight with him."

Steele set up a political paper called the Englishman, which, as it was not supported by contributions from Addi-

son, completely failed. By this work, by some other writings
of the same kind, and by the airs which he gave himself at
the first meeting of the new Parliament, he made the Tories
so angry that they determined to expel him. The Whigs
stood by him gallantly, but were unable to save him. The
vote of expulsion was regarded by all dispassionate men as a
tyrannical exercise of the power of the majority. But Steele's
violence and folly, though they by no means justified the
steps which his enemies took, had completely disgusted his
friends ; nor did he ever regain the place which he had held 10
in the public estimation.

Addison about this time conceived the design of adding
an eighth volume to the Spectator. In June 1714 the first
number of the new series appeared, and during about six
months three papers were published weekly. Nothing can
be more striking than the contrast between the Englishman
and the eighth volume of the Spectator, between Steele without Addison and Addison without Steele. The Englishman
is forgotten ; the eighth volume of the Spectator contains,
perhaps, the finest essays, both serious and playful, in the 20
English language.

Before this volume was completed, the death of Anne produced an entire change in the administration of public affairs.
The blow fell suddenly. It found the Tory party distracted
by internal feuds, and unprepared for any great effort. Harley had just been disgraced. Bolingbroke, it was supposed,
would be the chief minister. But the Queen was on her
deathbed before the white staff had been given, and her last
public act was to deliver it with a feeble hand to the Duke
of Shrewsbury. The emergency produced a coalition between 30
all sections of public men who were attached to the Protestant succession. George the First was proclaimed without
opposition. A Council, in which the leading Whigs had seats,
took the direction of affairs till the new King should arrive.
The first act of the Lord Justices was to appoint Addison
their secretary.

There is an idle tradition that he was directed to prepare
a letter to the King, that he could not satisfy himself as to
the style of this composition, and that the Lords Justices
called in a clerk who at once did what was wanted.  It is
not strange that a story so flattering to mediocrity should
be popular; and we are sorry to deprive dunces of their
consolation.  But the truth must be told.  It was well
observed by Sir James Mackintosh, whose knowledge of
these times was unequalled, that Addison never, in any
10 official document, affected wit or eloquence, and that his
despatches are, without exception, remarkable for unpre-
tending simplicity.  Every body who knows with what ease
Addison's finest essays were produced must be convinced
that, if well turned phrases had been wanted, he would have
had no difficulty in finding them.  We are, however, inclined to believe, that the story is not absolutely without a
foundation.  It may well be that Addison did not know, till
he had consulted experienced clerks who remembered the
times when William the Third was absent on the continent,
20 in what form a letter from the Council of Regency to the
King ought to be drawn.  We think it very likely that the
ablest statesmen of our time, Lord John Russell, Sir Robert
Peel, Lord Palmerston, for example, would, in similar
circumstances, be found quite as ignorant.  Every office has
some little mysteries which the dullest man may learn with
a little attention, and which the greatest man cannot
possibly know by intuition.  One paper must be signed by
the chief of the department; another by his deputy : to a
third the royal sign manual is necessary.  One communi-
30 cation is to be registered, and another is not.  One sentence
must be in black ink, and another in red ink.  If the ablest
Secretary for Ireland were moved to the India Board, if the
ablest President of the India Board were moved to the War
Office, he would require instruction on points like these; and
we do not doubt that Addison required such instruction when
he became, for the first time, Secretary to the Lords Justices.

George the First took possession of his kingdom without opposition. A new ministry was formed, and a new Parliament favourable to the Whigs chosen. Sunderland was appointed Lord Lieutenant of Ireland ; and Addison again went to Dublin as Chief Secretary.

At Dublin Swift resided ; and there was much speculation about the way in which the Dean and the Secretary would behave towards each other. The relations which existed between these remarkable men form an interesting and pleasing portion of literary history. They had early attached 10 themselves to the same political party and to the same patrons. While Anne's Whig ministry was in power, the visits of Swift to London and the official residence of Addison in Ireland had given them opportunities of knowing each other. They were the two shrewdest observers of their age. But their observations on each other had led them to favourable conclusions. Swift did full justice to the rare powers of conversation which were latent under the bashful deportment of Addison. Addison, on the other hand, discerned much good nature under the severe look and 20 manner of Swift ; and, indeed, the Swift of 1708 and the Swift of 1738 were two very different men.

But the paths of the two friends diverged widely. The Whig statesmen loaded Addison with solid benefits. They praised Swift, asked him to dinner, and did nothing more for him. His profession laid them under a difficulty. In the state they could not promote him ; and they had reason to fear that, by bestowing preferment in the church on the ' author of the Tale of a Tub, they might give scandal to the public, which had no high opinion of their orthodoxy. He 30 did not make fair allowance for the difficulties which prevented Halifax and Somers from serving him, thought himself an ill used man, sacrificed honour and consistency to revenge, joined the Tories, and became their most formidable champion. He soon found, however, that his old friends were less to blame than he had supposed. The dislike with

which the Queen and the heads of the Church regarded him
was insurmountable ; and it was with the greatest difficulty
that he obtained an ecclesiastical dignity of no great value,
on condition of fixing his residence in a country which he
detested.

Difference of political opinion had produced, not indeed a
quarrel, but a coolness between Swift and Addison. They at
length ceased altogether to see each other. Yet there was
between them a tacit compact like that between the heredi-
10 tary guests in the Iliad.

> Ἔγχεα δ' ἀλλήλων ἀλεώμεθα καὶ δι' ὁμίλου·
> Πολλοὶ μὲν γὰρ ἐμοὶ Τρῶες κλειτοί τ' ἐπίκουροι,
> Κτείνειν, ὅν κε θεός γε πόρῃ καὶ ποσσὶ κιχείω,
> πολλοὶ δ' αὖ σοὶ Ἀχαιοί, ἐναίρεμεν, ὅν κε δύνηαι.

It is not strange that Addison, who calumniated and
insulted nobody, should not have calumniated or insulted
Swift. But it is remarkable that Swift, to whom neither
genius nor virtue was sacred, and who generally seemed to
find, like most other renegades, a peculiar pleasure in attack-
20 ing old friends, should have shown so much respect and
tenderness to Addison.

Fortune had now changed. The accession of the House of
Hanover had secured in England the liberties of the people,
and in Ireland the dominion of the Protestant caste. To
that caste Swift was more odious than any other man. He
was hooted and even pelted in the streets of Dublin ; and
could not venture to ride along the strand for his health
without the attendance of armed servants. Many whom he
had formerly served now libelled and insulted him. At this
30 time Addison arrived. He had been advised not to show
the smallest civility to the Dean of St. Patrick's. He had
answered, with admirable spirit, that it might be necessary
for men whose fidelity to their party was suspected, to hold
no intercourse with political opponents ; but that one who
had been a steady Whig in the worst times might venture,

when the good cause was triumphant, to shake hands with
an old friend who was one of the vanquished Tories.  His
kindness was soothing to the proud and cruelly wounded
spirit of Swift; and the two great satirists resumed their
habits of friendly intercourse.

Those associates of Addison whose political opinions agreed
with his shared his good fortune.  He took Tickell with
him to Ireland.  He procured for Budgell a lucrative place
in the same kingdom.  Ambrose Phillipps was provided for
in England.   Steele had injured himself so much by his 10
eccentricity and perverseness that he obtained but a very
small part of what he thought his due.  He was, however,
knighted; he had a place in the household; and he subsequently received other marks of favour from the court.

Addison did not remain long in Ireland.   In 1715 he
quitted his secretaryship for a seat at the Board of Trade.
In the same year his comedy of the Drummer was brought
on the stage.   The name of the author was not announced;
the piece was coldly received; and some critics have
expressed a doubt whether it were really Addison's.   To us 20
the evidence, both external and internal, seems decisive.   It
is not in Addison's best manner; but it contains numerous
passages which no other writer known to us could have
produced.   It was again performed after Addison's death,
and, being known to be his, was loudly applauded.

Towards the close of the year 1715, while the Rebellion
was still raging in Scotland, Addison published the first
number of a paper called the Freeholder.  Among his
political works the Freeholder is entitled to the first place.
Even in the Spectator there are few serious papers nobler 30
than the character of his friend Lord Somers, and certainly
no satirical papers superior to those in which the Tory Fox-
hunter is introduced.  This character is the original of
Squire Western, and is drawn with all Fielding's force, and
with a delicacy of which Fielding was altogether destitute.
As none of Addison's works exhibit stronger marks of his

genius than the Freeholder, so none does more honour to his
moral character. It is difficult to extol too highly the candour and humanity of a political writer whom even the excitement of civil war cannot hurry into unseemly violence.
Oxford, it is well known, was then the stronghold of Toryism.
The High Street had been repeatedly lined with bayonets in
order to keep down the disaffected gownsmen ; and traitors
pursued by the messengers of the Government had been concealed in the garrets of several colleges. Yet the admonition
10 which, even under such circumstances, Addison addressed to
the University, is singularly gentle, respectful, and even
affectionate. Indeed, he could not find it in his heart to deal
harshly even with imaginary persons. His foxhunter, though
ignorant, stupid, and violent, is at heart a good fellow, and is
at last reclaimed by the clemency of the King. Steele was
dissatisfied with his friend's moderation, and, though he
acknowledged that the Freeholder was excellently written,
complained that the ministry played on a lute when it was
necessary to blow the trumpet. He accordingly determined
20 to execute a flourish after his own fashion, and tried to rouse
the public spirit of the nation by means of a paper called the
Town Talk, which is now as utterly forgotten as his Englishman, as his Crisis, as his Letter to the Bailiff of Stockbridge,
as his Reader, in short, as everything that he wrote without
the help of Addison.

In the same year in which the Drummer was acted, and in
which the first numbers of the Freeholder appeared, the
estrangement of Pope and Addison became complete. Addison had from the first seen that Pope was false and malevo-
30 lent. Pope had discovered that Addison was jealous. The
discovery was made in a strange manner. Pope had written
the Rape of the Lock, in two cantos, without supernatural
machinery. These two cantos had been loudly applauded,
and by none more loudly than by Addison. Then Pope
thought of the Sylphs and Gnomes, Ariel, Momentilla, Crispissa and Umbriel and resolved to interweave the Rosicru-

cian mythology with the original fabric. He asked Addison's
advice. Addison said that the poem as it stood was a delicious little thing, and entreated Pope not to run the risk of
marring what was so excellent in trying to mend it. Pope
afterwards declared that this insidious counsel first opened
his eyes to the baseness of him who gave it.

Now there can be no doubt that Pope's plan was most
ingenious, and that he afterwards executed it with great
skill and success. But does it necessarily follow that Addison's advice was bad? And if Addison's advice was 10
bad, does it necessarily follow that it was given from
bad motives? If a friend were to ask us whether we
would advise him to risk his all in a lottery of which the
chances were ten to one against him, we should do our best
to dissuade him from running such a risk. Even if he were
so lucky as to get the thirty thousand pound prize, we should
not admit that we had counselled him ill; and we should
certainly think it the height of injustice in him to accuse us
of having been actuated by malice. We think Addison's
advice good advice. It rested on a sound principle, the 20
result of long and wide experience. The general rule undoubtedly is that, when a successful work of imagination
has been produced, it should not be recast. We cannot at
this moment call to mind a single instance in which this
rule has been transgressed with happy effect, except the
instance of the Rape of the Lock. Tasso recast his Jerusalem. Akenside recast his Pleasures of the Imagination, and
his Epistle to Curio. Pope himself, emboldened no doubt by
the success with which he had expanded and remodelled the
Rape of the Lock, made the same experiment on the Dunciad. 30
All these attempts failed. Who was to foresee that Pope
would, once in his life, be able to do what he could not himself do twice, and what nobody else has ever done?

Addison's advice was good. But had it been bad, why
should we pronounce it dishonest? Scott tells us that one of
his best friends predicted the failure of Waverley. Herder

adjured Goethe not to take so unpromising a subject as
Faust.  Hume tried to dissuade Robertson from writing the
History of Charles the Fifth.  Nay, Pope himself was one of
those who prophesied that Cato would never succeed on the
stage, and advised Addison to print it without risking a representation.  But Scott, Goethe, Robertson, Addison, had
the good sense and generosity to give their advisers credit
for the best intentions.  Pope's heart was not of the same
kind with theirs.

10    In 1715, while he was engaged in translating the Iliad, he
met Addison at a coffeehouse.  Phillipps and Budgell were
there ; but their sovereign got rid of them, and asked Pope
to dine with him alone.  After dinner, Addison said that he
lay under a difficulty which he wished to explain.  "Tickell,"
he said, "translated some time ago the first book of the Iliad.
I have promised to look it over and correct it.  I cannot
therefore ask to see yours; for that would be double dealing."
Pope made a civil reply, and begged that his second book
might have the advantage of Addison's revision.  Addison
20  readily agreed, looked over the second book, and sent it back
with warm commendations.

Tickell's version of the first book appeared soon after this
conversation.  In the preface, all rivalry was earnestly dis-
claimed.  Tickell declared that he should not go on with the
Iliad.  That enterprise he should leave to powers which he
admitted to be superior to his own.  His only view, he said,
in publishing this specimen was to bespeak the favour of the
public to a translation of the Odyssey, in which he had made
some progress.

30    Addison, and Addison's devoted followers, pronounced
both the versions good, but maintained that Tickell's had
more of the original.  The town gave a decided preference to
Pope's.  We do not think it worth while to settle such a
question of precedence.  Neither of the rivals can be said to
have translated the Iliad, unless, indeed, the word translation
be used in the sense which it bears in the Midsummer

Night's Dream.  When Bottom makes his appearance with
an ass's head instead of his own, Peter Quince exclaims,
" Bless thee !  Bottom, bless thee !  thou art translated."  In
this sense, undoubtedly, the readers of either Pope or Tickell
may very properly exclaim, " Bless thee !  Homer ; thou art
translated indeed."

Our readers will, we hope, agree with us in thinking that
no man in Addison's situation could have acted more fairly
and kindly, both towards Pope, and towards Tickell, than he
appears to have done.  But an odious suspicion had sprung  10
up in the mind of Pope.  He fancied, and he soon firmly believed, that there was a deep conspiracy against his fame and
his fortunes.  The work on which he had staked his reputation was to be depreciated.  The subscription, on which
rested his hopes of a competence, was to be defeated.  With
this view Addison had made a rival translation : Tickell had
consented to father it ; and the wits of Button's had united
to puff it.

Is there any external evidence to support this grave accusation ?  The answer is short.  There is absolutely none.  20

Was there any internal evidence which proved Addison to
be the author of this version ?  Was it a work which Tickell
was incapable of producing ?  Surely not.  Tickell was a
Fellow of a College at Oxford, and must be supposed to have
been able to construe the Iliad ; and he was a better versifier
than his friend.  We are not aware that Pope pretended to
have discovered any turns of expression peculiar to Addison.
Had such turns of expression been discovered, they would be
sufficiently accounted for by supposing Addison to have corrected his friend's lines, as he owned that he had done.  30

Is there any thing in the character of the accused persons
which makes the accusation probable ?  We answer confidently—nothing.  Tickell was long after this time described       /
by Pope himself as a very fair and worthy man.  Addison
had been, during many years, before the public.  Literary
rivals, political opponents, had kept their eyes on him.  But

neither envy nor faction, in their utmost rage, had ever
imputed to him a single deviation from the laws of honour
and of social morality.   Had he been indeed a man meanly
jealous of fame, and capable of stooping to base and wicked
arts for the purpose of injuring his competitors, would his
vices have remained latent so long?   He was a writer of
tragedy: had he ever injured Rowe?   He was a writer of
comedy : had he not done ample justice to Congreve, and
given valuable help to Steele?   He was a pamphleteer :
10 have not his good nature and generosity been acknowledged
by Swift, his rival in fame and his adversary in politics?

That Tickell should have been guilty of a villany seems to
us highly improbable.   That Addison should have been
guilty of a villany seems to us highly improbable.   But that
these two men should have conspired together to commit a
villany seems to us improbable in a tenfold degree.   All that
is known to us of their intercourse tends to prove, that it
was not the intercourse of two accomplices in crime.   These
are some of the lines in which Tickell poured forth his
20 sorrow over the coffin of Addison :

> " Or dost thou warn poor mortals left behind,
>   A task well suited to thy gentle mind ?
>   Oh, if sometimes thy spotless form descend,
>   To me thine aid, thou guardian genius, lend.
>   When rage misguides me, or when fear alarms,
>   When pain distresses, or when pleasure charms,
>   In silent whisperings purer thoughts impart,
>   And turn from ill a frail and feeble heart ;
>   Lead through the paths thy virtue trod before,
> 30    Till bliss shall join, nor death can part us more."

In what words, we should like to know, did this guardian
genius invite his pupil to join in a plan such as the Editor
of the Satirist would hardly dare to propose to the Editor of
the Age ?

We do not accuse Pope of bringing an accusation which he
knew to be false.   We have not the smallest doubt that he

believed it to be true; and the evidence on which he believed
it he found in his own bad heart.   His own life was one long
series of tricks, as mean and as malicious as that of which he
suspected Addison and Tickell.   He was all stiletto and
mask.   To injure, to insult, and to save himself from the
consequences of injury and insult by lying and equivocating,
was the habit of his life.   He published a lampoon on the
Duke of Chandos ; he was taxed with it ; and he lied and
equivocated.   He published a lampoon on Aaron Hill ; he
was taxed with it ; and he lied and equivocated.   He 10
published a still fouler lampoon on Lady Mary Wortley
Montague ; he was taxed with it ; and he lied with more
than usual effrontery and vehemence.   He puffed himself
and abused his enemies under feigned names.   He robbed
himself of his own letters, and then raised the hue and cry
after them.   Besides his frauds of malignity, of fear, of
interest, and of vanity, there were frauds which he seems to
have committed from love of fraud alone.   He had a habit
of stratagem, a pleasure in outwitting all who came near
him.   Whatever his object might be, the indirect road to it 20
was that which he preferred.   For Bolingbroke, Pope undoubtedly felt as much love and veneration as it was in his
nature to feel for any human being.   Yet Pope was scarcely
dead when it was discovered that, from no motive except the
mere love of artifice, he had been guilty of an act of gross
perfidy to Bolingbroke.

Nothing was more natural than that such a man as this
should attribute to others that which he felt within himself.
A plain, probable, coherent explanation is frankly given to
him.   He is certain that it is all a romance.   A line of 30
conduct scrupulously fair, and even friendly, is pursued
towards him.   He is convinced that it is merely a cover for
a vile intrigue by which he is to be disgraced and ruined.
It is vain to ask him for proofs.   He has none, and wants
none, except those which he carries in his own bosom.

Whether Pope's malignity at length provoked Addison to

retaliate for the first and last time, cannot now be known
with certainty.  We have only Pope's story, which runs
thus.  A pamphlet appeared containing some reflections
which stung Pope to the quick.  What those reflections
were, and whether they were reflections of which he had a
right to complain, we have now no means of deciding.  The
Earl of Warwick, a foolish and vicious lad, who regarded
Addison with the feelings with which such lads generally
regard their best friends, told Pope, truly or falsely, that
10 this pamphlet had been written by Addison's direction.
When we consider what a tendency stories have to grow,
in passing even from one honest man to another honest
man, and when we consider that to the name of honest
man neither Pope nor the Earl of Warwick had a claim,
we are not disposed to attach much importance to this
anecdote.

It is certain, however, that Pope was furious.  He had
already sketched the character of Atticus in prose.  In his
anger he turned this prose into the brilliant and energetic
20 lines which every body knows by heart, or ought to know by
heart, and sent them to Addison.  One charge which Pope
has enforced with great skill is probably not without foundation.  Addison was, we are inclined to believe, too fond of
presiding over a circle of humble friends.  Of the other
imputations which these famous lines are intended to convey,
scarcely one has ever been proved to be just, and some are
certainly false.  That Addison was not in the habit of
"damning with faint praise" appears from innumerable
passages in his writings, and from none more than from
30 those in which he mentions Pope.  And it is not merely
unjust, but ridiculous, to describe a man who made the
fortune of almost every one of his intimate friends, as "so
obliging that he ne'er obliged."

That Addison felt the sting of Pope's satire keenly, we
cannot doubt.  That he was conscious of one of the weaknesses with which he was reproached, is highly probable.  But

his heart, we firmly believe, acquitted him of the gravest part of the accusation. He acted like himself. As a satirist he was, at his own weapons, more than Pope's match ; and he would have been at no loss for topics. A distorted and diseased body, tenanted by a yet more distorted and diseased mind ; spite and envy thinly disguised by sentiments as benevolent and noble as those which Sir Peter Teazle admired in Mr. Joseph Surface ; a feeble sickly licentious- ness ; an odious love of filthy and noisome images ; these were things which a genius less powerful than that to which 10 we owe the Spectator could easily have held up to the mirth and hatred of mankind. Addison had, moreover, at his command other means of vengeance which a bad man would not have scrupled to use. He was powerful in the state. Pope was a Catholic ; and, in those times, a minister would have found it easy to harass the most innocent Catholic by innumerable petty vexations. Pope, near twenty years later, said that "through the lenity of the government alone he could live with comfort." "Consider," he exclaimed, "the injury that a man of high rank and credit may do to a 20 private person, under penal laws and many other disadvan- tages." It is pleasing to reflect that the only revenge which Addison took was to insert in the Freeholder a warm encomium on the translation of the Iliad, and to exhort all lovers of learning to put down their names as subscribers. There could be no doubt, he said, from the specimens already published, that the masterly hand of Pope would do as much for Homer as Dryden had done for Virgil. From that time to the end of his life, he always treated Pope, by Pope's own acknowledgment, with justice. Friendship was, of course, 30 at an end.

One reason which induced the Earl of Warwick to play the ignominious part of talebearer on this occasion, may have been his dislike of the marriage which was about to take place between his mother and Addison. The Countess Dowager, a daughter of the old and honourable family of

the Middletons of Chirk, a family which, in any country
but ours, would be called noble, resided at Holland House.
Addison had, during some years, occupied at Chelsea, a
small dwelling, once the abode of Nell Gwynn.  Chelsea is
now a district of London, and Holland House may be called
a town residence.  But, in the days of Anne and George the
First, milkmaids and sportsmen wandered between green
hedges and over fields bright with daisies, from Kensington
almost to the shore of the Thames.  Addison and Lady
10 Warwick were country neighbours, and became intimate
friends.  The great wit and scholar tried to allure the young
Lord from the fashionable amusements of beating watch-
men, breaking windows, and rolling women in hogsheads
down Holborn Hill, to the study of letters and the practice
of virtue.  These well meant exertions did little good, however, either to the disciple or to the master.  Lord Warwick
grew up a rake ; and Addison fell in love.  The mature
beauty of the Countess has been celebrated by poets in
language which, after a very large allowance has been made
20 for flattery, would lead us to believe that she was a fine
woman ; and her rank doubtless heightened her attractions.
The courtship was long.  The hopes of the lover appear to
have risen and fallen with the fortunes of his party.  His
attachment was at length matter of such notoriety that,
when he visited Ireland for the last time, Rowe addressed
some consolatory verses to the Chloe of Holland House.  It
strikes us as a little strange that, in these verses, Addison
should be called Lycidas, a name of singularly evil omen for
a swain just about to cross St. George's Channel.
30    At length Chloe capitulated.  Addison was indeed able to
treat with her on equal terms.  He had reason to expect
preferment even higher than that which he had attained.
He had inherited the fortune of a brother who died Governor
of Madras.  He had purchased an estate in Warwickshire,
and had been welcomed to his domain in very tolerable verse
by one of the neighbouring squires, the poetical foxhunter,

William Somervile. In August 1716, the newspapers announced that Joseph Addison, Esquire, famous for many excellent works both in verse and prose, had espoused the Countess Dowager of Warwick.

He now fixed his abode at Holland House, a house which can boast of a greater number of inmates distinguished in political and literary history than any other private dwelling in England. His portrait still hangs there. The features are pleasing ; the complexion is remarkably fair ; but, in the expression, we trace rather the gentleness of his disposition 10 than the force and keenness of his intellect.

Not long after his marriage he reached the height of civil greatness. The Whig Government had, during some time, been torn by internal dissensions. Lord Townshend led one section of the Cabinet, Lord Sunderland the other. At length, in the spring of 1717, Sunderland triumphed. Townshend retired from office, and was accompanied by Walpole and Cowper. Sunderland proceeded to reconstruct the Ministry ; and Addison was appointed Secretary of State. It is certain that the Seals were pressed upon him, 20 and were at first declined by him. Men equally versed in official business might easily have been found ; and his colleagues knew that they could not expect assistance from him in debate. He owed his elevation to his popularity, to his stainless probity, and to his literary fame.

But scarcely had Addison entered the Cabinet when his health began to fail. From one serious attack he recovered in the autumn; and his recovery was celebrated in Latin verses, worthy of his own pen, by Vincent Bourne, who was then at Trinity College, Cambridge. A relapse soon took 30 place ; and, in the following spring, Addison was prevented by a severe asthma from discharging the duties of his post. He resigned it, and was succeeded by his friend Craggs, a young man whose natural parts, though little improved by cultivation, were quick and showy, whose graceful person and winning manners had made him generally acceptable in

F

society, and who, if he had lived, would probably have been
the most formidable of all the rivals of Walpole.

As yet there was no Joseph Hume. The Ministers, therefore, were able to bestow on Addison a retiring pension of
fifteen hundred pounds a-year. In what form this pension
was given we are not told by the biographers, and have not
time to inquire. But it is certain that Addison did not
vacate his seat in the House of Commons.

Rest of mind and body seem to have re-established his
10 health; and he thanked God, with cheerful piety, for having
set him free both from his office and from his asthma. Many
years seemed to be before him, and he meditated many
works, a tragedy on the death of Socrates, a translation of
the Psalms, a treatise on the evidences of Christianity. Of
this last performance, a part, which we could well spare, has
come down to us.

But the fatal complaint soon returned, and gradually prevailed against all the resources of medicine. It is melancholy
to think that the last months of such a life should have been
20 overclouded both by domestic and by political vexations. A
tradition which began early, which has been generally
received, and to which we have nothing to oppose, has
represented his wife as an arrogant and imperious woman.
It is said that, till his health failed him, he was glad to
escape from the Countess Dowager and her magnificent
diningroom, blazing with the gilded devices of the House of
Rich, to some tavern where he could enjoy a laugh, a talk
about Virgil and Boileau, and a bottle of claret, with the
friends of his happier days. All those friends, however,
30 were not left to him. Sir Richard Steele had been gradually
estranged by various causes. He considered himself as one
who, in evil times, had braved martyrdom for his political
principles, and demanded, when the Whig party was
triumphant, a large compensation for what he had suffered
when it was militant. The Whig leaders took a very
different view of his claims. They thought that he had, by

his own petulance and folly, brought them as well as himself
into trouble, and though they did not absolutely neglect
him, doled out favours to him with a sparing hand. It was
natural that he should be angry with them, and especially
angry with Addison. But what above all seems to have
disturbed Sir Richard, was the elevation of Tickell, who, at
thirty, was made by Addison Undersecretary of State ; while
the Editor of the Tatler and Spectator, the author of the Crisis,
the member for Stockbridge who had been persecuted for firm
adherence to the House of Hanover, was, at near fifty, forced, 10
after many solicitations and complaints, to content himself
with a share in the patent of Drury Lane theatre. Steele himself says, in his celebrated letter to Congreve, that Addison, by
his preference of Tickell, " incurred the warmest resentment
of other gentlemen ;" and every thing seems to indicate that,
of those resentful gentlemen, Steele was himself one.

While poor Sir Richard was brooding over what he considered as Addison's unkindness, a new cause of quarrel
arose  The Whig party, already divided against itself, was
rent by a new schism. The celebrated Bill for limiting the 20
number of Peers had been brought in. The proud Duke of
Somerset, first in rank of all the nobles whose religion permitted them to sit in Parliament, was the ostensible author
of the measure. But it was supported, and, in truth, devised
by the Prime Minister.

We are satisfied that the Bill was most pernicious ; and
we fear that the motives which induced Sunderland to frame
it were not honourable to him. But we cannot deny that it
was supported by many of the best and wisest men of that
age  Nor was this strange. The royal prerogative had, 30
within the memory of the generation then in the vigour of
life, been so grossly abused, that it was still regarded with a
jealousy which, when the peculiar situation of the House of
Brunswick is considered, may perhaps be called immoderate.
The particular prerogative of creating peers had, in the
opinion of the Whigs, been grossly abused by Queen Anne's

last ministry ; and even the Tories admitted that her
Majesty, in swamping, as it has since been called, the Upper
House, had done what only an extreme case could justify.
The theory of the English constitution, according to many
high authorities, was that three independent powers, the
sovereign, the nobility, and the commons, ought constantly
to act as checks on each other.  If this theory were sound,
it seemed to follow that to put one of these powers under
the absolute control of the other two, was absurd.  But if the
10 number of peers were unlimited, it could not well be denied
that the Upper House was under the absolute control of the
Crown and the Commons, and was indebted only to their moderation for any power which it might be suffered to retain.

Steele took part with the Opposition, Addison with the
Ministers.  Steele, in a paper called the Plebeian, vehemently
attacked the bill.  Sunderland called for help on Addison,
and Addison obeyed the call.  In a paper called the Old
Whig, he answered, and indeed refuted, Steele's arguments.
It seems to us that the premises of both the controversialists
20 were unsound, that, on those premises, Addison reasoned
well and Steele ill, and that consequently Addison brought
out a false conclusion while Steele blundered upon the truth.
In style, in wit, and in politeness, Addison maintained his
superiority, though the Old Whig is by no means one of his
happiest performances.

At first, both the anonymous opponents observed the laws
of propriety.  But at length Steele so far forgot himself as
to throw an odious imputation on the morals of the chiefs of
the administration.  Addison replied with severity, but, in
30 our opinion, with less severity than was due to so grave an
offence against morality and decorum; nor did he, in his just
anger, forget for a moment the laws of good taste and good
breeding.  One calumny which has been often repeated,
and never yet contradicted, it is our duty to expose.  It is
asserted in the Biographia Britannica that Addison desig-
nated Steele as "little Dicky."  This assertion was repeated

by Johnson, who had never seen the Old Whig, and was
therefore excusable. It has also been repeated by Miss
Aikin, who has seen the Old Whig, and for whom therefore
there is less excuse. Now, it is true that the words "little
Dicky" occur in the Old Whig, and that Steele's name was
Richard. It is equally true that the words "little Isaac"
occur in the Duenna, and that Newton's name was Isaac.
But we confidently affirm that Addison's little Dicky had no
more to do with Steele, than Sheridan's little Isaac with
Newton. If we apply the words "little Dicky" to Steele, 10
we deprive a very lively and ingenious passage, not only of
all its wit, but of all its meaning. Little Dicky was the
nickname of Henry Norris, an actor of remarkably small
stature, but of great humour, who played the usurer Gomez,
then a most popular part, in Dryden's Spanish Friar.

The merited reproof which Steele had received, though
softened by some kind and courteous expressions, galled him
bitterly. He replied with little force and great acrimony ;
but no rejoinder appeared. Addison was fast hastening to
his grave ; and had, we may well suppose, little disposition 20
to prosecute a quarrel with an old friend. His complaint
had terminated in dropsy. He bore up long and manfully.
But at length he abandoned all hope, dismissed his physicians,
and calmly prepared himself to die.

His works he entrusted to the care of Tickell, and dedicated them a very few days before his death to Craggs, in
a letter written with the sweet and graceful eloquence of
a Saturday's Spectator. In this, his last composition, he
alluded to his approaching end in words so manly, so cheerful, and so tender, that it is difficult to read them without 30
tears. At the same time he earnestly recommended the
interests of Tickell to the care of Craggs.

Within a few hours of the time at which this dedication
was written, Addison sent to beg Gay, who was then living
by his wits about town, to come to Holland House. Gay
went, and was received with great kindness. To his amaze-

ment his forgiveness was implored by the dying man. Poor Gay, the most goodnatured and simple of mankind, could not imagine what he had to forgive. There was, however, some wrong, the remembrance of which weighed on Addison's mind, and which he declared himself anxious to repair. He was in a state of extreme exhaustion ; and the parting was doubtless a friendly one on both sides. Gay supposed that some plan to serve him had been in agitation at Court, and had been frustrated by Addison's influence. Nor is this 10 improbable. Gay had paid assiduous court to the royal family. But in the Queen's days he had been the eulogist of Bolingbroke, and was still connected with many Tories. It is not strange that Addison, while heated by conflict, should have thought himself justified in obstructing the preferment of one whom he might regard as a political enemy. Neither is it strange that, when reviewing his whole life, and earnestly scrutinising all his motives, he should think that he had acted an unkind and ungenerous part, in using his power against a distressed man of letters, 20 who was as harmless, and as helpless as a child.

One inference may be drawn from this anecdote. It appears that Addison, on his deathbed, called himself to a strict account, and was not at ease till he had asked pardon for an injury which it was not even suspected that he had committed, for an injury which would have caused disquiet only to a very tender conscience. Is it not then reasonable to infer that, if he had really been guilty of forming a base conspiracy against the fame and fortunes of a rival, he would have expressed some remorse for so serious a crime ? But it is unnecessary 30 to multiply arguments and evidence for the defence, when there is neither argument nor evidence for the accusation.

The last moments of Addison were perfectly serene. His interview with his son-in-law is universally known. "See," he said, "how a Christian can die." The piety of Addison was, in truth, of a singularly cheerful character. The feeling which predominates in all his devotional writings is gratitude.

God was to him the allwise and allpowerful friend who had
watched over his cradle with more than maternal tenderness ;
who had listened to his cries before they could form themselves in prayer ; who had preserved his youth from the
snares of vice ; who had made his cup run over with worldly
blessings ; who had doubled the value of those blessings, by
bestowing a thankful heart to enjoy them, and dear friends
to partake them ; who had rebuked the waves of the Ligurian
gulf, had purified the autumnal air of the Campagna, and
had restrained the avalanches of Mont Cenis.  Of the Psalms, 10
his favourite was that which represents the Ruler of all
things under the endearing image of a shepherd, whose
crook guides the flock safe, through gloomy and desolate
glens, to meadows well watered and rich with herbage.  On
that goodness to which he ascribed all the happiness of his
life, he relied in the hour of death with the love which casteth
out fear.  He died on the seventeenth of June 1719.  He had
just entered on his forty-eighth year.

His body lay in state in the Jerusalem Chamber, and was
borne thence to the Abbey at dead of night.  The choir sang 20
a funeral hymn.  Bishop Atterbury, one of those Tories
who had loved and honoured the most accomplished of the
Whigs, met the corpse, and led the procession by torchlight,
round the shrine of Saint Edward and the graves of the
Plantagenets, to the Chapel of Henry the Seventh.  On the
north side of that Chapel, in the vault of the House of
Albemarle, the coffin of Addison lies next to the coffin of
Montague.  Yet a few months ; and the same mourners
passed again along the same aisle.  The same sad anthem was
again chanted.  The same vault was again opened ; and the 30
coffin of Craggs was placed close to the coffin of Addison.

Many tributes were paid to the memory of Addison ; but
one alone is now remembered.  Tickell bewailed his friend
in an elegy which would do honour to the greatest name in
our literature, and which unites the energy and magnificence
of Dryden to the tenderness and purity of Cowper.  This

fine poem was prefixed to a superb edition of Addison's works, which was published, in 1721, by subscription. The names of the subscribers proved how widely his fame had been spread. That his countrymen should be eager to possess his writings, even in a costly form, is not wonderful. But it is wonderful that, though English literature was then little studied on the continent, Spanish Grandees, Italian Prelates, Marshals of France, should be found in the list. Among the most remarkable names are those of the Queen of
10 Sweden, of Prince Eugene, of the Grand Duke of Tuscany, of the Dukes of Parma, Modena, and Guastalla, of the Doge of Genoa, of the Regent Orleans, and of Cardinal Dubois. We ought to add that this edition, though eminently beautiful, is in some important points defective; nor, indeed, do we yet possess a complete collection of Addison's writings.

It is strange that neither his opulent and noble widow, nor any of his powerful and attached friends, should have thought of placing even a simple tablet, inscribed with his name, on the walls of the Abbey. It was not till three
20 generations had laughed and wept over his pages that the omission was supplied by the public veneration. At length, in our own time, his image, skilfully graven, appeared in the Poet's Corner. It represents him, as we can conceive him, clad in his dressing gown, and freed from his wig, stepping from his parlour at Chelsea into his trim little garden, with the account of the Everlasting Club, or the Loves of Hilpa and Shalum, just finished for the next day's Spectator, in his hand. Such a mark of national respect was due to the unsullied statesman, to the accomplished scholar, to the
30 master of pure English eloquence, to the consummate painter of life and manners. It was due, above all, to the great satirist, who alone knew how to use ridicule without abusing it, who, without inflicting a wound, effected a great social reform, and who reconciled wit and virtue, after a long and disastrous separation, during which wit had been led astray by profligacy and virtue by fanaticism.

# NOTES.

**Page 1.** *Title.* **Lucy Aikin** (1781-1864) was the daughter of John Aikin, a distinguished physician and man of letters. She was born at Warrington. She resided with her parents at Yarmouth and Stoke-Newington till the death of her father in 1822, when she removed to Hampstead, where, with the exception of a short interval at Wimbledon, she spent the remainder of her life. Miss Aikin was in early life a diligent student of French, Italian, and Latin ; and at the youthful age of seventeen began to contribute articles to magazines and reviews. In 1810 appeared her first considerable work, *Epistles on Women exemplifying their character and condition in various ages and nations ; with Miscellaneous Poems ;* and in 1814 she wrote her only work of fiction, entitled *Lorimer, a Tale.* These were her earlier works, but her reputation was gained entirely by her historical works, published between 1818 and 1843, viz. *Memoirs of the Court of Queen Elizabeth* (1818); *Memoirs of the Court of King James the First* (1822); *Memoirs of the Court of King Charles the First* (1833) ; *The Life of Joseph Addison* (1843). The last of these books, which contains many letters of Addison never before published, is the subject of this essay by Macaulay.

She wrote also a life of her father and of her aunt, Miss Barbauld, and many minor pieces. Her conversational powers were remarkable, and she was a graceful and graphic letter-writer. Her letters to her relatives and intimate friends show her relish of society, and are full of mother wit and lively anecdotes of distinguished and literary persons. She maintained for sixteen years (1826-1842) a graver correspondence with Rev. Dr. Channing, of Boston, on religion, philosophy, politics, and literature.

In religion Miss Aikin was a Unitarian, and she pronounces "our Church Establishment the most systematically servile in Christendom." In politics Miss Aikin was a supporter of the Whig aristocracy, with a generous love of liberty, but with cultivated tastes that precluded sympathy with democracy. In discussing the first Reform Bill, she defines radicalism as "the supremacy of the rude and selfish and ignorant many."

l. 2. **franchises** is used here in a comprehensive sense to include freedom, irresponsibility, immunity, privilege : it is synonymous with *immunities* in l. 18, and with *privileges* in l. 21, *infra*.

l. 12. **the courteous Knight**, Rogero (or Ruggiero). See next note.

l. 13. **Bradamante**, the sister of Rinaldo, in Ariosto's *Orlando Furioso* and Boiardo's *Orlando Inamorato*. She is a Christian, but loves Rogero (or Ruggiero), a Saracen knight, and, after incredible adventures, in which her prowess, assisted by her enchanted spear, is equal to that of a knight, she marries him after he has been baptized.

l. 15. **Balisarda**, Rogero's sword, made by a sorceress, capable of cutting through enchanted substances.

l. 20. **Memoirs of the Reign of James the First**, published by Miss Aikin in 1822. See Lucy Aikin, *supra*.

**Page 2**, l. 5. **dunce** (an application of the name of John Duns Scotus, the celebrated scholastic theologian called "Doctor subtilis," the subtle doctor, who died in 1308).
1. The personal name of Duns, used attrib. Duns man, a disciple or follower of Duns Scotus, a Scotist, a Schoolman : hence a subtle, sophistical reasoner.
2. A copy of the works of Duns Scotus : a comment or gloss by or after the manner of Scotus.
3. A disciple or adherent of Duns Scotus, a Dunsman or Scotist : a hair-splitting reasoner, a cavilling sophist.
4. One whose study of books has left him dull and stupid or has imparted no liberal education : a dull pedant.
5. One who shows no capacity for learning: a dull-witted stupid person : a dullard, blockhead.    (Murray's *English Dictionary*.)

l. 7. **Laputan flapper.**    Laputa was the flying island inhabited by scientific quacks, and visited by Gulliver in his "travels." These dreamy philosophers were so absorbed in their speculations that they employed attendants called "flappers" to flap them on the mouth and ears with a blown bladder when their attention was to be called off from "high things" to vulgar mundane matters (Swift).

l. 10. **Miss Aikin's book has disappointed us** etc.    In defence of Miss Aikin we may quote from the London *Athenaeum* : "Miss Aikin has not left a stone unturned that her monument to one of our most polished writers and complete minds may be fair, upright, and symmetrical.    Her book contains the first complete life of Addison ever put forth.    As a literary biography it is a

model ; and its pages are besides enriched by many hitherto un-
published letters of Addison."

In a letter dated April 19, 1843, Macaulay writes thus : "Dear
Napier,—You may count on an article from me on Miss Aikin's
*Life of Addison*. Longman sent me the sheets as they were
printed. I own that I am greatly disappointed. There are, to
be sure, some charming letters by Addison which have never yet
been published ; but Miss Aikin's narrative is dull, shallow, and
inaccurate. Either she has fallen off greatly since she wrote her
former works, or I have become much more acute since I read
them. By the bye, I have an odd story to tell you. I was vexed
at observing, in a very hasty perusal of the sheets, a great number
of blunders, any of which singly was discreditable, and all of
which united were certain to be fatal to the book. To give
a few specimens, the lady called Evelyn 'Sir John Evelyn';
transferred Christ Church from Oxford to Cambridge ; confounded Robert, Earl of Sunderland, James the Second's minister,
with his son Charles, Earl of Sunderland, George the First's
minister ; confounded Charles Montague, Earl of Halifax, with
George Savile, Marquis of Halifax ; called the Marquis of Hertford 'Earl of Hertford,' and so forth. I pointed the grossest
blunders out to Longmans, and advised him to point them out
to her without mentioning me. He did so. The poor woman
could not deny that my remarks were just ; but she railed most
bitterly both at the publishers and at the Mr. Nobody who had
had the insolence to find any blemish in her writings. At first
she suspected Sedgwick. She now knows that she was wrong in
that conjecture, but I do not think that she has detected me.
This, you will say, is but a bad return to me for going out of my
way to save her book from utter ruin. I am glad to learn that,
with all her anger, she has had the sense to cancel some sheets
in consequence of Mr. Nobody's criticism."

Again on June 15, 1843, he writes : "Dear Napier,—I mistrust
my own judgment of what I write so much that I shall not be
at all surprised if both you and the public think my paper on
Addison a failure : but I own that I am partial to it. . . . I
am truly vexed to find Miss Aikin's book so very bad that it is
impossible for us, with due regard to our own character, to
praise. All that I can do is to speak civilly of her writings
generally, and to express regret that she should have been
nodding. I have found, I will venture to say, not less than
forty gross blunders as to matters of fact in the first volume.
Of these I may, perhaps, point out eight or ten as courteously
as the case may bear. Yet it goes much against my feelings
to censure any woman, even with the greatest lenity. My
taste and Croker's are by no means the same. I shall not
again undertake to review any lady's book till I know how it
is executed."

l. 18. **Shakspeare and Raleigh,** an allusion to the *Memoirs of the Court of Queen Elizabeth,* published by Miss Aikin in 1818. See Lucy Aikin, *supra*.

l. 19. **Congreve and Prior,** two writers of the days of William and Mary and Anne, contemporaries of Addison. William Congreve was a dramatist (1670-1729). His chief plays were *Love for Love; The Mourning Bride,* and *The Way of the World.* (See also p. 52, l. 25, *infra,* and Note.) Matthew Prior (1664-1721) was a poet and diplomatist; he wrote with Charles Montague *The City Mouse and the Country Mouse;* he assisted in the negotiation of the Peace of Ryswick (1697) and of the Treaty of Utrecht (1711).

l. 20. **ruffs,** a kind of frill, formerly much worn by both sexes. So called from its uneven surface; the root appears in Icel. *rjúfa,* to break, rip up, break a hole in; A.S. *reáfan,* to reave, from √*rúp,* to break (Skeat).

**peaked beards,** beards trimmed to a point, as was fashionable in the court of Elizabeth.

**Theobald's,** a hamlet in Hertfordshire, situated on the New River, about four miles from Chipping Barnet, noted as the favourite residence of James I., who had here a magnificent seat and gardens, originally built by Lord Treasurer Burleigh.

l. 21. **Steenkirks,** a cant term for a neckcloth, a kind of military cravat of black silk; probably first worn at the battle of Steenkirk, Aug. 2, 1692.

**periwig** is the Dutch form of *peruke* (F. *perruque,* Ital. *parrucca,* Span. *peluca,* Lat. *pilus,* hair), an artificial head of hair.

l. 22. **Hampton,** a village of Middlesex, about twelve miles south-west of London. The royal palace of Hampton Court is about one mile from the village. The original palace was built by Cardinal Wolsey; additions were made by Henry VIII. and Sir C. Wren. Here resided successively Henry VIII., James I., Charles I., Cromwell, William III., Anne, and, lastly, George II.

**Page 3, l. 1. one who has been sleeping a hundred and twenty years in Westminster Abbey.** Addison died and was buried in Westminster Abbey in 1719; this essay was written in 1843.

l. 3. **that abject idolatry** etc., the so-called *lues Boswelliana,* against which Macaulay inveighs in his essay on *Croker's Edition of Boswell's Life of Johnson.* See pp. 21-26 and Appendix in this series.

l. 10. **heroic poems hardly equal to Parnell's.** Thomas Parnell (1679-1718) was an intimate friend of Swift, Addison, Steele and others. "As a poet, Parnell's work is marked by sweetness, refined sensibility, musical and fluent versification, and high moral tone. ... Pope, his junior by nine years, gave him much good advice. ... The best of his poems are, *The Hermit*, *The Fairy Tale*, *The Night Piece on Death*, *The Hymn to Contentment*, and *Hesiod, or the Rise of Woman*" (*Dictionary of National Biography*).

l. 11. **criticism as superficial as Dr. Blair's.** Hugh Blair (1718-1800), divine and critic, was born in Edinburgh, and was one of the distinguished literary circle which flourished at Edinburgh throughout the century. He was a member with Hume, A. Carlyle, Adam Ferguson, Adam Smith, Robertson, and others of the famous Poker Club. Blair encouraged MacPherson to publish the *Fragments of Ancient Poetry*, and eulogized their merits with more zeal than discretion in *A Critical Dissertation on the Poems of Ossian, the Son of Fingal* (1763). His lectures on the same subject expressed the canons of taste of the time in which Addison, Pope, and Swift are recognized as the sole models of English style, and are feeble in thought, though written with a certain elegance of manner (Leslie Stephen).

l. 12. **a tragedy not very much better than Dr. Johnson's.** Addison's tragedy was entitled *Cato*, Johnson's was *Irene*.

l. 21. **Button's** coffee-house succeeded Will's as the resort of the wits. Button was an old servant of Addison's or Lady Warwick's, who set up his coffee-house under Addison's patronage, about 1711, on the south side of Russell Street, Covent Garden. A lion's head and paws, serving as the letter-box for literary communications, was placed in front of the building, and the editor of the *Guardian* says, "What the lion swallows I shall digest for the use of the public."

l. 27. **the phrase of the old anatomists, sound in the noble parts** etc. In Dunglison's *New Dictionary of Medical Science* we find "*noble parts of the body*, the vital parts, as the heart, liver, lungs, brain" etc. By the old alchemists the noble were distinguished from the base metals, gold and silver from iron and lead etc., so by the old anatomists the parts of the body were divided into noble and base, the brain, heart etc., being regarded as noble, and the stomach, entrails etc., as base viscera.

**Page 4**, l. 4. **Biographia Britannica**, or the lives of the most eminent persons who have flourished in Great Britain and Ireland from the earliest ages down to the present times (1747).

l. 8. **lampoon** (F. *lampon*, a lampoon, orig. a drinking song; O.F. *lapper*, A.S. *lapian*, to lap, drink), a sarcastic writing aimed at a person's character, habits, or actions: a personal satire, humorous abuse in writing.

l. 11. **the liturgy of the fallen Church**, the services of the Established Church of England as opposed to those of the Presbyterians

Independents, and other sects of Nonconformists in the days of the Commonwealth.

l. 12. **the Wild of Sussex.** Does Macaulay mean the Weald of Sussex, a wooded tract fringed and engirt with uplands? "The centre of the county (Sussex) is occupied by a woodland tract denominated the Weald (Saxon, *weald*, a forest). It extends from the Downs, to which it runs parallel, to the Surrey Hills. Once this tract was an immense forest called by the Britons *Coit Andred*, and by the Saxons *Andredes Weald*, inhabited only by hogs and deer ; but it has been gradually cleared and brought into cultivation. According to the Saxon chronicle this wood was ' in length, east and west, 120 miles or longer, and 30 miles broad ' ; the Weald of Sussex now contains about 425,000 acres, and measures from 5 to 10 miles in breadth, and 30 to 40 miles in length " (Extracts from *Imperial Cyclopaedia*).

l. 13. **After the restoration** of Charles II. in 1660.

l. 14. **Dunkirk** was ceded to Cromwell after Blake's victory over the Spanish fleet at Vera Cruz in 1657, but it was sold by Charles II. in 1661 to Louis XIV., King of France.

ll. 16, 17. **Tangier ... Infanta Catharine.** In his *History*, chap. ii., Macaulay writes, "the fortress of Tangier, which was part of the dower of Queen Catharine, was repaired and kept up at an enormous charge. ... It involved us in inglorious, unprofitable, and interminable wars with tribes of half savage Mussulmans ; and it was situated in a climate singularly unfavourable to the health and vigour of the English race."

ll. 30, 31. **a Doctor of Divinity, Archdeacon of Salisbury, and Dean of Lichfield.** In a note to Thackeray's *English Humourists* Lancelot Addison is said to have been "Dean of Lichfield and Archdeacon of Coventry"; in the *Biographia Britannica* this is explained thus: "Dr. Addison was collated to the Archdeaconry of Coventry on the 8th of December, 1684, and held it with his deanery in commendam."

l. 32. **the Revolution** of 1688, when James II. fled and abdicated in favour of William of Orange.

l. 34. **the Convocation of 1689** rejected the scheme of the Latitudinarians for such modifications of the Prayer-book as would render possible a return of the Nonconformists, and a Comprehension Bill, which was introduced into Parliament, failed to pass, in spite of the king's strenuous support (Green's *History*). Macaulay gives an account of this convocation in chap. xiv. of his *History*.

    **the liberal policy of William and Tillotson.** Tillotson was noted for his enlightened piety. He was Archbishop at the time when William attempted to partially admit Dissenters to civil equality by a repeal of the Corporation Act. This attempt was fruitless, but the passing of a Toleration Act in 1689 practically established freedom of worship.

**Page 5, l. 2. schools in his father's neighbourhood,** *i.e.* at Amesbury, at Salisbury, and at Lichfield.

**l. 4. Charter House,** see p. 43, l. 24, *infra,* and note.

**l. 7. a barring out.** Dr. Johnson writes thus of Addison's life at Lichfield School : " Of this interval his biographers have given no account, and I know it only from a story of a *barring out,* told me, when I was a boy, by Andrew Corbet of Shropshire, who had heard it from Mr. Pigot, his uncle. The practice of *barring out* was a savage licence practised in many schools to the end of the last century, by which the boys, when the periodical vacation drew near, growing petulant at the approach of liberty, some days before the time of regular recess, took possession of the school, of which they barred the doors, and bade their master defiance from the windows. ... The master, when Pigot was a school-boy, was *barred out* at Lichfield ; and the whole operation, as he said, was planned and conducted by Addison."

**l. 8. he ran away from school** etc. This adventure is said to have taken place at Amesbury, where he was first sent to school, his master being one Nash.

**l. 29** etc. **That great and opulent corporation had been treated by James** etc. See Macaulay's *History,* chap. viii.

**l. 30. his Chancellor,** Jeffreys.

**l. 33. the prosecution of the Bishops.** Seven prelates—viz. Sancroft, the Archbishop of Canterbury, Lloyd, Bishop of St. Asaph, Turner of Ely, Lake of Chichester, Kerr of Bath and Wells, White of Peterborough, and Trelawney of Bristol—refused to read the Declaration of Indulgence (1688), and were brought to trial, but acquitted, to the joy of almost all the nation.

**l. 35. A president, duly elected,** John Hough. See p. 18, l. 11, *infra.*

**l. 36. a Papist** etc., Anthony Farmer.

**Page 6, l. 19. Demy,** a foundation scholar at Magdalen College, Oxford, so called because their allowance or "commons" was originally half that of a Fellow. The Latin form is 'semi-communarius' (Murray's *Eng. Dictionary*).

**l. 22. his favourite walk.** " Passing to the rear of Magdalene College on the left there opens a park filled with very ancient and noble trees, making that 'chequered shade' upon the short and verdant grass which poets love to talk about ; while here and there are groups of deer standing up or lying down with an air of satisfaction and contentment belonging to creatures occupying their native possessions. Then turning to the right you enter a tasteful iron gate and over a slight bridge upon a walk, which, extending some distance to the left, turns abruptly to the right, when it stretches along the Cherwell, and makes the circuit of the meadow. The trees throw a perpetual shade overhead, and the Cherwell keeps up a tinkling and gurgling melody beside you. Here a rustic mill catches the eye, there the towers of some of the colleges appear, half concealed by the intervening trees. Left and right by the walk are the brightest meadows : further off are views of the richly cultivated country. And this is Addison's walk " (Tappan's *Step from the New World to the Old*).

l. 24. **Cherwell**, a river rising in south-west of Northampton-shire, about three miles from the source of the Nene, and flowing south through Oxfordshire, past Banbury to the Thames, which it joins on the left bank at Oxford.

**Page 7**, l. 3. **Lucretius** (about B.C. 95-51), a Roman philo-sophical poet, author of *de Rerum Natura*.

**Catullus** (about B.C. 87-47), a Roman poet ; he wrote, in different styles and metres, lyrics, elegies, and epigrams.

**Claudian**, the last of the Latin classic poets ; he flourished under Theodosius and his sons, Arcadius and Honorius, and died probably about 408 A.D.

l. 4. **Prudentius**, the earliest of the Christian poets of any celebrity, was born A.D. 348. His poems possess little merit, and are chiefly remarkable for the impurity of their Latinity, and for their disregard of the laws of prosody.

l. 10. **Buchanan**, George (1506-1582), a distinguished scholar, poet, and historian of Scotland ; tutor of Montaigne, Professor of Latin at Bordeaux, and in 1547 at Coimbra; he was imprisoned by the Inquisition, and one of the penalties imposed on him was a translation of the Psalms into Latin, a task which he accom-plished with great success. He subsequently became classical tutor to Mary Queen of Scots. In his later years he wrote *A History of Scotland* and a treatise *de Jure Regni apud Scotos*.

**Milton** was perhaps the most accomplished Latin scholar of his day.

ll. 19-23. **His knowledge of Greek ... was less than that which many lads now carry away every year from Eton and Rugby.** Macaulay's school-boy has become proverbial. Cf. essay on *Boswell's Life of Johnson*, p. 24, ll. 10, 11, and note in this series. Mr. Courthope criticizes this passage thus : "That Addison was not a scholar of the class of Bentley or Porson may be readily admitted. But many scattered allusions in his works prove that his acquaintance with the Greek poets of every period, if cursory, was wide and intelligent ; he was sufficiently master of the language thoroughly to understand the spirit of what he read : he undertook while at Oxford a translation of

Herodotus, and one of the papers in the *Spectator* is a direct imitation of a *jeu d'esprit* of Lucian's. The Eton or Rugby boy who, in these days, with a normal appetite for cricket and football, acquired an equal knowledge of Greek literature, would certainly be somewhat of a prodigy."

ll. 28, 29. **Notes which Addison appended to his version of the second and third books of the Metamorphoses.** The *Metamorphoses* was written by Ovid, and is a collection of such fables as involved a transformation from the creation to the time of Julius Caesar ; thus Chaos is changed into the four elements, Daphne into a laurel, Io into a cow, Actaeon into a stag, Caesar into a comet, etc., etc.

l. 33. **Virgil,** the great Roman poet, author of the *Eclogues, Georgics,* and *Æneid* (B.C. 70-19).

**Statius** (A.D. 61-96) wrote *Silvae, Thebais,* and *Achilleis.*

**Claudian,** see p. 7, l. 3, *supra,* and note.

**Page 8, l. 1. the story of Pentheus in the third book of Metamorphoses.** It is related that Pentheus got upon a tree for the purpose of seeing in secret the revelry of the Bacchantes ; he was discovered by them, and torn in pieces.

l. 3. **Ovid** (B.C. 43-18), a Roman poet, wrote *Epistolae Heroidum, Ars Amatoris, Metamorphoses, Fasti, Tristia* etc.

**Ovid was indebted for that story to Euripides and Theocritus.** The fate of Pentheus is the subject of the *Bacchae* of Euripides, and of the 26*th Idyll* of Theocritus.

l. 12. **Ausonius,** a Roman poet (about A.D. 310-390), wrote *Epigrammata, Parentalia, Epitaphia Heroum, Idyllia* etc.

**Manilius,** a Roman poet of uncertain date, conjectured to have lived in the time of Augustus ; he wrote an astrological poem entitled *Astronomia.*

**Cicero,** the great orator, statesman, and philosopher of Rome (B.C. 106-143). Macaulay's advice to students of Latin was "Soak your mind with Cicero."

l. 14. **poetaster,** an inferior poet.

l. 18. **Apennines,** a chain of mountains, a continuation of the maritime Alps, which runs through Italy from north to south, and forms the backbone of the Peninsula.

l. 19. **Hannibal,** on his way into Italy crossed the Alps by the pass of the Little St. Bernard, called in antiquity the Graian Alps, thence he marched by the valley of the Aosta to the plains of the Po.

l. 20. **Polybius** (about B.C. 204-122) wrote a *History,* the first part of which comprised a period of 35 years, beginning with the second Punic war and the Social war in Greece, and ending with the downfall of the Macedonian dynasty in 168 B.C.

l. 21. **Livy** (B.C. 59-A.D. 17) wrote a History of Rome, *Annales*, from the foundation of the city to the death of Drusus, B.C. 9, in 142 books, of which 35 are extant. The third decade (Books **xxi.-xxx.**), which is entire, treats of the period from B.C. 219-201, and contains a full account of the second Punic war.

l. 22. **Silius Italicus** (A.D. 25-97), a Roman poet; his chief work is *Punica*, an heroic poem in 17 books, giving an account of the second Punic war from the capture of Saguntum to the triumph of Scipio Africanus.

**Rubicon**, a small river in Italy falling into the Adriatic, a little north of Ariminum; in the Republican period it formed the boundary between Gallia Cisalpina and Italy proper. Caesar's crossing this river at the head of his army was *ipso facto* a declaration of war against the Republic.

l. 23. **Plutarch**, the biographer and philosopher, was studying philosophy as a young man in A.D. 66. His great work is his *Parallel Lives* (βίοι παράλληλοι) of Greeks and Romans; there are 46 lives arranged in pairs; each pair contains a Greek and a Roman, *e.g.* Theseus and Romulus; Pericles and Q. Fabius Maximus; Alexander and Caesar, etc., etc.

l. 24. **the commentaries** of Caesar, distinguished for clearness, conciseness, and purity of Latin.

**letters to Atticus** (*Epistolarum ad T. Pomponium Atticum, Libri* xvi.), a series of 396 epistles written by Cicero to Atticus between the years B.C. 68 and 44.

l. 27. **Lucan** (A.D. 39-65) wrote various poems, but his only extant work is the *Pharsalia*.

l. 30. **Pindar** (about B.C. 522-442), the great lyric poet of Greece, wrote ἐπινίκια (triumphal odes), προσόδια (songs for processions), παρθένεια (songs of maidens), ὑπορχήματα (mimic dancing songs), σκόλια (drinking songs), θρῆνοι (dirges), and ἐγκώμια (panegyrics on princes).

**Callimachus**, an Alexandrine grammarian and poet, who flourished about B.C. 260-240, is said to have written 800 works in prose and verse; but only 6 *Hymns* and 72 *Epigrams* and a few fragments of his *Elegies* are extant.

**the Attic dramatists**, Aeschylus, Sophocles, and Euripides.

l. 32. **Horace** (B.C. 65-68) wrote *Odes, Satires, Epodes, Epistles*, and the *Ars Poetica*.

**Juvenal**, the great Roman satirist, flourished about 70 to 100.

**Statius.** See p. 7, l. 33, *supra.*

**Ovid.** See p. 8, l. 3, *supra.*

**l. 33. the Treatise on Medals,** more correctly *Dialogues upon the Usefulness of Ancient Medals.*

**Page 9, l. 10. Essay on the Evidences of Christianity,** entitled *Of the Christian Religion,* was a work entrusted by Addison to Tickell on his death-bed, and first published in the edition of 1721. It is unfinished, and can be regarded only as a rough draft of a more extensive work.

**l. 16. the Cock-Lane ghost.** See Boswell, pp. 137-8 (sub anno 1762) and p. 458 (sub anno 1778), also Macaulay's essay on *Boswell's Life of Johnson* and note in this series.

**l. 17. Ireland's Vortigern.** William Henry Ireland presented to his father, Samuel Ireland, a play in blank verse, entitled *Vortigern and Rowena;* the son represented this play to be Shakespeare's autograph. Sheridan produced *Vortigern* at Drury Lane on 2nd April, 1796—Kemble wished to fix the previous night, "All Fools' Day," for the event—it was simply laughed off the stage, and the forgery was afterwards admitted.

**l. 18. the Thundering Legion.** According to the legend, the Roman legion which overcame the Marcomanni in 179 is so called because a thunderstorm was sent in answer to the prayers of certain Christians ; this storm relieved the thirst of the legion. But this is a mere legend of no historic value ; the legion was so-called at least a century before the reign of Aurelius, probably because it bore on its shields or ensigns a representation of Jupiter Tonans, Jupiter the Thunderer.

**l. 19. Tiberius moved the senate to admit Jesus among the gods.** Addison writes as follows : "Tertullian, who wrote his apology about fifty years after Justin, doubtless referred to the same record when he tells the governor of Rome that the Emperor Tiberius, having received an account out of Palestine in Syria of the divine Person who had appeared in that country, paid him a particular regard, and threatened to punish any one who should accuse the Christians ; nay, that the emperor would have adopted him among the deities whom they worshipped, had not the senate refused to come into his proposal."

**l. 20. Agbarus,** or Abgarus, is a name common to many rulers of Edessa, the capital of the district of Osrhoëne in Mesopotamia. Of these rulers, one is supposed by Eusebius to have been the author of a letter written to Christ, which he found in a church at Edessa, and translated from the Syriac. The letter is believed to be spurious.

**l. 28. Herodotus** (B.C. 484-405 about), a Greek historian, and the father of history, was born at Halicarnassus ; he travelled much in Europe, Asia, and Africa, and probably wrote his history when he was at an advanced age, at Thurii.

l. 31. **Boyle**, the Hon. Charles (1676-1731), produced in 1695, at the suggestion of Dr. Henry Aldrich, then dean of Christ Church, Oxford, a new edition of the *Letters of Phalaris;* in answer to this Bentley wrote his *Dissertation on the Letters of Phalaris;* Boyle replied with *A Short Account of Dr. Bentley by way of Index* appended to the second edition of his book ; this was a joint performance, in which Francis Atterbury, afterwards Bishop of Rochester, took the chief part, and was probably assisted by George Smalridge, Anthony Alsop, John and Robert Freind ; hence Macaulay's scathing sarcasm, "Boyle is remembered chiefly as the nominal author of the worst book on Greek history and philology that was ever printed ; and this book, bad as it is, Boyle was unable to produce without help."

l. 32. **Blackmore**, Sir Richard (d. 1729), a physician and voluminous but unattractive writer in verse and prose, was born at Corsham, in Wiltshire, educated at Westminster School and St. Edmund's Hall, Oxford, and admitted fellow of the Royal College of Physicians in 1687.   Besides medical treatises he wrote heroic and epic poems, essays, histories, and theological dissertations ; few men, in fact, have written so much and been read so little. We do not know much of "his attainments in the ancient tongues" ; but after leaving the University, his necessities compelled him to adopt temporarily the profession of a schoolmaster, and he was taunted by his enemies thus :

"By nature form'd, by want a pedant made,
Blackmore at first set up the whipping trade,
Next quack commenced ; then fierce with pride he swore
That toothache, gripes, and corns should be no more.
In vain his drugs, as well as birch, he tried,
His boys grew blockheads and his patients died."

**Page 10, l. 2. aphorism** (Gr. ἀφορισμός, a distinction, a definition from ἀφορίζειν. From "the aphorisms of Hippocrates" transferred to other sententious statements of the principles of physical science, and at length to statements of principles generally).
1. A definition, a concise statement of a principle in any science.
2. Any principle or precept expressed in few words ; a short pithy sentence containing a truth of general import, a maxim.

**apophthegm**, or apothegm (Gr. ἀπόφθεγμα, something clearly spoken, a terse saying, from ἀποφθέγγεσθαι, to speak one's opinion clearly, from ἀπό, forth, and φθέγγεσθαι, to utter a sound, speak). A terse, pointed saying, embodying an important truth in few words ; a pithy or sententious maxim (Murray's *Dictionary*).

l. 10. **Bentley**, Richard (1662-1742), was born at Oulton, near Wakefield, in the West Riding of Yorkshire ; he was educated at Wakefield School and St. John's College, Cambridge.  He subsequently became Master of Trinity College and Vice-Chancellor of Cambridge University. His scholarship, his range and grasp of knowledge, his historical and literary criticism, as well as his verbal criticism, were unrivalled, and his influence cannot easily be measured. His chief works are *The Boyle Lectures*, *Fragments of Callimachus*, *The Dissertation on the Epistles of Phalaris*, also editions of *Horace*, *Terence*, *Manilius*, *Homer*, and *Paradise Lost*. (In the "English Men of Letters Series" there is an excellent account of Bentley by Professor R. C. Jebb.)

l. 20. **lines on the Barometer.** These are in Latin and entitled *Barometri descriptio*.

**lines on the Bowling Green** are in Latin and entitled *Sphaeristerium*.

l. 21. **Dissertation on the Epistles of Phalaris** was written between March, 1698, and the end of that year; it was published early in 1699. *The Epistles of Phalaris* are a collection of 148 letters—many of them only a few lines long—written in Attic Greek of that artificial kind which begins to appear about the time of Augustus. They are first mentioned by a Greek writer, Stobaeus, who flourished about 480 A.D. They belong to the class of literature produced in the first five centuries of the Christian era.

But all we really know about Phalaris is, that he was a legendary hero of Sicily, and that his name had become a proverb for horrible cruelty as early as about 500 B.C.

Bentley proves beyond dispute in his Dissertation that these letters are spurious, and could not have been written by Phalaris.

It is only fair to Boyle to point out that it was not he, but Sir W. Temple, that had asserted the genuineness of these letters; Boyle, on the contrary, expressed his doubt about them, but owned that he was "afraid of being undeceived." For a full account of this dispute, read Monk's *Life of Bentley*, De Quincey's *Essay on Bentley*, and the last few pages of Macaulay's *Essay on Temple*.

l. 22. **hieroglyphic** (Gr. ἱερός, sacred, and γλύφειν, to hollow out, engrave, carve, write in incised characters), symbolical or picture writing.

**obelisk**, a tall tapering pillar. (Gr. ὀβελίσκος, lit. a small spit, hence a thin pointed pillar ; dimin. of ὀβελός, a spit.)

l. 25. **the Battle of the Cranes and Pygmies,** ΠΤΓΜΑΙΟ-ΓΕΡΑΝΟΜΑΧΙΑ *sive Proelium inter Pygmaeos et Grues commissum*.

l. 28. **Swift,** Jonathan (1667-1745), Dean of St. Patrick's, wrote *The Battle of the Books*, *Tale of a Tub*, *Letters to M. B. Drapier*, *Travels of Samuel Gulliver*, *A History of the four last years of Queen Anne*, and other miscellaneous prose and poetical works, Sir Walter Scott and Johnson both allow to Swift the attribute

of originality; "Perhaps," says Johnson, "no author has
borrowed so little, or has so well maintained his claim to be considered as original."

l. 32. **Voyage to Lilliput**, one of the incidents of Gulliver's
travels. Lilliput was the country of the pygmies called
Lilliputians to whom Gulliver was a giant.

**Page 11, l. 3** etc. **Jamque acies** etc., these mock-heroic lines
might be translated thus, "Now between the battle lines the
leader of the Pygmies stalks erect, with awful pomp and stately
gait; in giant stature he surpasses all, and towers as high as half
a finger nail."

ll. 7-10. **The Latin poems ... Drury-Lane Theatre.** Cf. the
following extracts from Thos. Tickell's preface to Addison's
works, "He first distinguished himself by his Latin compositions,
published in the Musae Anglicanae, and was admitted as one of
the best authors since the Augustan age in the two Universities
and the greatest part of Europe, before he was talked of as a
poet in town. . . . Our country owes it to him that the
famous Monsieur Boileau first conceived an opinion of the English
genius for poetry by perusing the present he made him of the
Musae Anglicanae."

l. 13. **complimentary lines to Dryden.** Cf. Tickell, "The
first English performance made public by him is a short copy of
verses to Mr. Dryden with a view particularly to his translations." This copy of verses was written from Magdalen
College, Oxon. June 2, 1693.

l. 19. **Congreve**, see p. 2, l. 19, *supra* and *infra*.

l. 20. **Charles Montague** (1661-1715) was a poet and a patron of
poets; he wrote *Verses on the Death of King Charles II.*, in 1685,
and in partnership with Prior, *The Country Mouse and the City
Mouse*, in 1687. He held many high offices in the State; he was
at different times Chancellor of the Exchequer (1694), First
Commissioner of the Treasury and one of the Lords Justices (1698),
Auditor of the Exchequer (1699), and was raised to the peerage
as Earl of Halifax in 1700. As a poet he has been praised ex-
travagantly by Addison in his *Account of the Greatest English
Poets*, written in 1694. Dr. Johnson and Cibber estimated his
merits more correctly, while Pope and Swift vented their spleen
in severe satire on the noble poet.

l. 24. **a translation of part of the fourth Georgic.** Addison's
title of this work is *A Translation of all Virgil's Fourth Georgic,
except the story of Aristaeus*. Tickell writes as follows: "This
(the copy of verses to Mr. Dryden) was soon followed by a
version of the fourth Georgic of Virgil, of which Mr. Dryden
makes honourable mention in the postscript of his own translation of all Virgil's works; wherein I have often wondered that

he did not at the same time acknowledge his obligation to Mr.
Addison for giving him the Essay upon the Georgics prefixed
to Mr. Dryden's translation."

l. 25. **Lines to King William**, entitled *A Poem to His Majesty,
presented to the Lord Keeper;* these lines to the King are pre-
faced with twenty-eight lines of fulsome flattery to the Right
Honourable Sir John Somers, Lord Keeper of the Great Seal.

l. 29. **the Newdigate prize**, a prize for English verse founded
by Sir Rodger Newdigate. "The prize is of the annual value
of £21, and is confined to those undergraduate members of the
University of Oxford who have not exceeded four years from
their matriculation" (*Oxford University Calendar*).

l. 30. **the Seatonian prize**. "The Rev. Thomas Seaton, M.A.,
Fellow of Clare College, bequeathed to the University in 1741
the rents of his Kislingbury estate, now producing clear £40 per
annum, to be given yearly to that Master of Arts who shall
write the best English poem on a Sacred Subject" (*Cambridge
University Calendar*).

**The heroic couplet** is a rhyming couplet consisting of two
decasyllabic iambic lines, *e.g.*:

"Awake, my St. John! leave all meaner things
To low ambition, and the pride of kings."

l. 35. **distich** (Gr. δίστιχον, distich, couplet, from δι and στίχος,
row, line of verse), a couple of lines of verse, usually making
complete sense, and (in modern poetry) rhyming, a couplet.

**Page 12, l. 5. Pope**, Alexander (1688-1744), wrote *Essay on
Criticism, Rape of the Lock*, translations of Homer's *Iliad* and
*Odyssey*, the *Dunciad, Essay on Man*, and many other works.
Most of his poems are written in heroic couplets. See p. 11,
l. 30, *supra*.

l. 7. **Pastorals**, poems descriptive of shepherds and their occu-
pations, or of a country life; an idyll, a bucolic (Lat. *pastor*, a
shepherd, *pastus*, perf. part. of *pascere*, to feed, √*pa*, to feed).
Pope wrote his *Pastorals* in 1704, when he was only sixteen
years of age.

l. 11. **euphony**, a pleasing sound (Gr. εὐφωνία, εὔφωνος, sweet-
voiced; εὖ well, φωνή, voice, from √*bha*, to speak.

l. 14. **Rochester**, John Wilmot, Earl of (about 1647-1680), was
educated at Wadham College, Oxford, travelled in France and
Italy; distinguished himself in naval engagements against the
Dutch, and as a courtier was noted for his drunkenness, buf-
foonery, and poetry. Towards the end of his life, under the
influence of Bishop Burnet, he repented of his licentious life, and
on his death-bed commanded that his obscene and profane writings should be destroyed; but so far from his wishes being carried

out, an edition of his poems was published in the year of his death containing much that he never wrote. Bishop Burnet, Dr. Johnson, Pope, Hume, Aubrey, and others have criticised Rochester's works; Horace Walpole says concisely, "Lord Rochester's poems have much more obscenity than wit, more wit than poetry, more poetry than politeness." Aubrey says that he remembers hearing Andrew Marvel say that the Earl of Rochester was the only man in England that had the true vein of satire.

**Marvel,** Andrew (1620-1678), a native of Kingston upon Hull, Yorkshire, which he afterwards represented in Parliament, was educated at Trinity College, Cambridge. He was made, in 1657, assistant to Milton, who was then Latin Secretary to the Protector. Marvel spent much time, between 1661 and 1666, in Holland and Germany, and with Lord Carlyle, Ambassador Extraordinary to Russia, Sweden, and Denmark. He was not only a Member of Parliament, but also a political satirist. His best known works are, *The Rehearsal Transposed*, a satire against Samuel Parker, afterwards Bishop of Oxford; *Historical Essays on General Councils, Creeds etc., An Account of the Growth of Popery and Arbitrary Government in England*, and *Miscellaneous Poems*.

l. 15. **Oldham,** James (1653-1683), poet, was born at Shipton, in Gloucestershire, educated at Tetbury School and St. Edmund Hall, Oxford. He was patronised by the Earls of Rochester and Dorset, Sir Charles Sedley, and other wits, and was introduced to Dryden. He died when only thirty years of age. His poems consist of satires, pindarics, occasional copies of verses, and a great many translations from the classics. His satires won for him the name of the English Juvenal.

l. 16. **Ben Jonson** (about 1573-1637) wrote dramas, masques, poems, and miscellaneous prose, of which the following are some of the best known : *Every Man in his Humour, Every Man out of his Humour, Cynthia's Revels, Poetaster, Sejanus, Eastward Ho, Masque of Blackness, Volpone, Twelfth Night, Marriage Masques, Alchemist, Catiline, The Staple of News* etc. etc.

**Hoole,** John (1727-1803), translator of Tasso and Ariosto, held for many years the office of auditor in the India House. He was a friend of Dr. Johnson, and Boswell records several meetings at Hoole's House. Hoole attended Johnson in his last illness, and kept a diary of his visits.

Leslie Stephen says, "Hoole's translations are taken by Macaulay as typical specimens of the smooth decasyllable couplets of Pope's imitators. Scott, Southey, and Lamb, who ironically calls Hoole "the great boast and ornament of the India house," had anticipated Macaulay, and only Johnson's praise (see *Life of Waller*), and the sale of several editions, convince us that they were ever read."

Robert Southey writes, "that vile version of Hoole's ... the flat couplets of a rhymester like Hoole." Scott writes, "Mr. Hoole, the translator of Tasso and Ariosto, and in that capacity a noble translator of gold into lead.... He did exactly so many couplets day by day, neither more nor less; and habit had made it light to him, however heavy it might seem to the reader."

l. 21. **Brunel**, Isambard Kingdom (1806-1859), civil engineer, helped his father in his work at the Thames Tunnel. From his plans was constructed the suspension bridge across the river Avon, from Durdham Downs, Clifton, to the Leigh Woods. He was at different times of his life engineer to the Bristol Docks and the Great Western Railway; but his greatest fame was obtained in the construction of ocean-going steamers of dimensions larger than any previously known, and it was owing to his experiments that the screw propeller was adopted in the Navy. The largest ship built by him was the "Great Eastern." He invented also a machine for making pulley-blocks, to which Macaulay alludes here.

l. 25. **his translation of a celebrated passage in the Æneid,** viz. Bk. iv., ll. 178-183.

"Illam Terra parens, ira, irritata Deorum,
Extremam (ut perhibent) Coeo Enceladoque sororem ·
Progenuit; pedibus celerem et pernicibus alis;
Monstrum horrendum, ingens; cui quot sunt corpore plumae,
Tot vigiles oculi subter (mirabile dictu)
Tot linguae, totidem ora sonant, tot subrigit aures."

**Page 13, l. 2. Tasso,** Torquato (1544-1595), a celebrated Italian poet, wrote *Rinaldo*, *Aminta*, and the great epic, *La Gerusalemme Liberata*, describing the first Crusade. Concerning Hoole's translation of Tasso, see p. 12, l. 15, *supra*, and note.

l. 17. **clerk** (contr. from *cleric*, Lat. *clericus*, Gr. κληρικός, "of or pertaining to an inheritance," in later (Christian) use "of or belonging to the ecclesiastical or sacerdotal order"). The original sense was "a man in a religious order, cleric, clergyman." As the scholarship of the Middle Ages was practically limited to the clergy, and these performed all the writing, notarial, and secretarial work of the time, the name "clerk" came to be equivalent to "scholar," and especially applicable to a notary, secretary, recorder, accountant, or penman. The last has now come to be the ordinary sense, all the others being archaic, historical, formal, or contextual (Murray's *Dictionary*).

**Duke,** Richard (d. 1711), Prebendary of Gloucester, Fellow of Trinity College, Cambridge, was intimate with Otway, engaged with others in translations of Ovid and Juvenal, and wrote a number of poems and sermons. Dr. Johnson has written his life.

**Stepney**, George (1663-1707), was born in Westminster, educated at Westminster School and Trinity College, Cambridge. He acquired distinction as an envoy, was made one of the Commissioners of Trade in 1697. He wrote an *Epistle to Charles Montague, Esq., on his Majesty's Voyage to Holland* (1691), *A Poem*, dedicated to the memory of Queen Mary (1695). He contributed a *Translation from Ovid* to Jonson's *First Miscellany* (1684), and to the *Translation of Juvenal* by Dryden and others (1693), and was the author of some prose political pieces in *The Somers Tracts* etc. Dr. Johnson, in *Lives of the Poets*, styles Stepney "a very licentious translator," and finds in his original poems "little either of the grace of wit or the vigour of nature."

**Granville**, George, Viscount Lansdowne (1667-1735), was educated at Trinity College, Cambridge, where he took his M.A. degree at the early age of thirteen. He wrote poems, dramatic pieces, essays, and minor historical treatises, e.g. *The Gallants, Heroic Love, The Jew of Venice, A Letter from a Nobleman Abroad to his Friends in England, Letter to the Author of Reflections, Historical and Political*. Dr. Johnson has written his life. Horace Walpole sneers at him thus : " He imitated Waller ; but as that poet has been much excelled since, a faint copy of a faint master must strike still less." But both Dryden and Pope have praised him.

l. 18. **Walsh**, William, M.P. (1663-1707, about), was educated at Wadham College, Oxford ; was appointed Gentleman of the House to Queen Anne. He wrote *A Dialogue concerning Women; being a Defence of the Sex* (1691) ;—the preface is by Dryden ;— *Letters and Poems, Amorous and Gallant* (1692). These and other performances of his—epitaphs, elegies, odes, songs, etc.— were included in *The Works of the Minor Poets* (1749). Dr. Johnson has written his life. Dryden writes of him thus: " William Walsh of Abberley, Esq., who has so long honoured me with his friendship, and who, without flattery, is the best critic of our nation." Pope writes : " About fifteen I got acquainted with Mr. Walsh. He used to encourage me much"; and again :

"Such late was Walsh, the Muse's judge and friend,
Who justly knew to blame and to commend."

l. 26. **Dryden was now busied with Virgil**, his translation was published in 1697.

**(Dryden) obtained from Addison a critical preface to the Georgics** etc. Tickell remarks on Addison's " version of the fourth Georgic of Virgil, of which Mr. Dryden makes very

honourable mention in the postscript to his own translation of all
Virgil's works; wherein I have often wondered that he did not
at the same time acknowledge his obligation to Mr. Addison for
giving him the Essay upon the Georgics prefixed to Mr. Dryden's
translation."

**Page 14, ll. 9, 10. It is clear, from some expressions ... to take
orders.** These expressions occur at the end of Addison's
"Account of the Greatest English Poets" (1694):

" I've done at length ; and, now dear Friend, receive
The last poor present that my Muse can give,
I leave the Arts of poetry and verse
To them that practice 'em with more success.
Of greater truths I'll now prepare to tell,
And so at once, dear Friend and Muse, farewell."

l. 11. **Charles Montague.** See p. 11, l. 20, *supra*, and note.

l. 12. **verses well timed** etc., on the death of King Charles II.
(1685).

l. 16. **Dorset,** Charles Sackville, Earl of (1637-1706), was a great
favourite with the wits of the day. He wrote satires and songs ;
the best known is a song written at sea during the Dutch war,
1665, the night before an engagement, "To all you Ladies now
on Land," etc. Dr. Johnson praises him in his *Lives of the Poets*
as "a man whose elegance and judgment were universally confessed, and whose bounty to the learned and witty was generally
known." Dryden writes to Dorset : "I would instance your
Lordship in satire and Shakespeare in tragedy." Prior eulogizes
him thus : "There is a lustre in his verses like that of the sun in
Claude Lorraine's landscapes."

**Rochester.** See p. 12, l. 15, *supra*, and note.

l. 19. **Rasselas, prince of Abyssinia,** is the hero and title of a
tale by Johnson, published in 1759 ; chapter vi. contains a dissertation on the art of flying.

**Page 15, l. 2. Lord Chancellor Somers** (1650-1716), one of our
greatest statesmen, and also an author, was born at Worcester,
educated at the Middle Temple and Trinity College, Oxford, and
was called to the Bar in 1676 ; he was one of the counsels for the
Seven Bishops, 1688 ; he helped to prepare the Declaration of
Rights; he became Solicitor-General in 1689, Lord Keeper of the
Great Seal and Attorney-General in 1692, Lord Chancellor in
1697, and was raised to the Peerage as Baron Somers of Eves-
ham, in the County of Gloucester ; he was impeached by the
Tories, and acquitted in 1701 ; was President of the Royal
Society in 1702, and President of the Council for 1708-1710. In
1706 he drew up the plan for the union between England and
Scotland, and was chosen by Anne as one of the Commissioners
to carry it into execution. He died of apoplexy in 1716.

As an author he is best known for his legal and political publications; he produced also poetical versions of Ovid's epistles of Dido to Æneas, and of Ariadne to Theseus, and a translation of Plutarch's Life of Alcibiades.

l. 6. **The Revolution** of 1688.

l. 24. **At the present moment ... Poets,** *e.g.* Guizot, Thiers etc.

l. 33. **Somersets and Shrewsburies** are quoted here by Macaulay as types of an aristocracy of rank and wealth, as opposed to the Addisons and Priors, types of an aristocracy of intellect. The character of one Duke of Shrewsbury is sketched in this essay (p. 25, line 28 etc.), and allusion is made to "the proud Duke of Somerset" on p. 83, l. 21 etc.

**Page 16. l. 1. Both the great chiefs of the Ministry,** viz. Somers and Montague.

ll. 4, 5. **He had addressed ... to Somers,** viz. *The Poem to His Majesty.* See p. 11, l. 25, *supra,* and note.

l. 6. **and had dedicated to Montague ... Ryswick.** The title of this Latin poem is "*Pax Gulielmi auspiciis Europae reddita* 1697," and the dedication is as follows, "Honoratissimo viro Carolo Montagu armigero Scaccharii Cancellario, Aerarii Praefecto, Regi a Secretioribus consiliis etc."

The peace of Ryswick was concluded between England, France, Spain, and Holland, and signed by their representatives on 20th September, and by the Emperor of Germany on 30th October, 1697.

l. 17. **the Lord Chancellor,** Somers.

l. 20. **the Chancellor of the Exchequer,** Montague.

**Page 17, l. 3. Charles, Earl of Manchester,** succeeded Lord Jersey as ambassador extraordinary at the court of France. He arrived in Paris on 5th August, 1699. His principal function was to watch and, as far as possible, counteract the intrigues of the court of St. Germain, and accordingly on the death of James II. and the recognition of the Pretender by Louis XIV. he was re-called without leave-taking in September, 1701.

l. 5. **a toast.** (1) bread scorched before the fire. (O. Fr. *tostée.* Lat. *tosta,* fem. of *tostus,* perf. part. of *torrere,* to parch.) (2) A person whose health is drunk. It was formerly usual to put toasted bread in liquor. Shakes. *Merry Wives,* III. v. 3: "Go fetch me a cup of sack; put a toast in't." The story of the origin of the present use of the word is given in the *Tatler,* No. 24, June 4, 1709. "Many wits of the last age will assert that the word, in its present sense, was known among them in their youth, and had its rise from an accident at the town of Bath in the reign of King Charles II. It happened that, on a public day, a celebrated beauty of those times was in the Cross Bath, and one of the crowd of her admirers took a glass of the water in which the fair one stood, and drank her health to the company. There was in the place a gay fellow, half-fuddled, who offered to jump in, and swore, though he liked not the liquor, he would have the toast. He was opposed in his resolution, yet this whim gave foundation to the present honour which is done to the lady we mention in our liquors, who has ever since been called a toast." Whether the story be true or not, it may be seen that a toast, *i.e.* a health, easily took its name from being the usual accompaniment to liquor, especially in loving cups etc. (Skeat).

l. 8. **some lively lines written on the glasses of the Kit Cat Club** etc. Each member of the club was compelled to select a lady as his toast, and the verses which he composed in her honour were engraved on the wine-glasses belonging to the club. Addison's lines on the Countess of Manchester were as follows :

> "While haughty Gallia's dames, that spread
> O'er their pale cheeks an artful red,
> Beheld this beauteous stranger there,
> In native charms divinely fair,
> Confusion in their looks they showed,
> And with unborrowed blushes glowed."

**Kit Cat Club.** See p. 28, l. 6, *infra*, and note.

l. 11. **Versailles**, a city of the Department Seine-et-Oise, France, ten miles south-west of Paris. Here Louis XIV. built a palace, which was from 1680 to 1789 the residence of the kings of France.

l. 12. **Lewis the Fourteenth ... vices of his youth.** His chief vices were vanity, revenge, ambition, and perfidy ; his policy was the aggrandizement of France at the expense of his neighbours ; in gratifying this ambition he was absolutely without scruple ; his despotism, misgovernment, and persecution of the Huguenots sowed the seeds of the Revolution.

l. 17. **Racine**, John (1639-1699), a celebrated French poet and tragedian, wrote *Thébaide, Alexander, Andromaque, Britannicus, Phèdre, Esther, Athalie*, and other works.

l. 18. **Dacier was seeking for the Athanasian mysteries in Plato.** Andrew Dacier (1651-1722) was a learned French scholar, who, with his wife, produced the "Delphin" edition of the classics for the Dauphin. He translated *Horace*, the *Reflections of Marcus Antoninus, Aristotle's Poetics, Plato, Plutarch's Lives*, and the *Manual of Epictetus*.

l. 26. **Blois**, an ancient city, capital of the Department of Loir-et-Cher, France, on both sides of the Loire, about a hundred miles south-west of Paris.

l. 30. **an Abbé named Phillippeaux** supplied Joseph Spence with the following information : "Mr. Addison stayed above a year at Blois. He would rise as early as between two and three in summer, and lie abed till between eleven and twelve in the depth of winter. He was untalkative while here, and often thoughtful; sometimes so lost in thought that I have come into his room and have stayed five minutes there before he has known anything of it. He had his masters generally at supper with him, kept very little company beside, and had no amour whilst here that I know of, and I think I should have known it if he had had any."

l. 31. **Joseph Spence** (1699-1768) was born at Kingsclere, Hampshire, became Fellow] of New College, Oxford (1722), Rector of Birchanger, Essex (1728), was Professor of Poetry (1728-38), and Regius Professor of Modern History at Oxford (1742), Rector of Great Horwood, Bucks. (1742), Prebendary of Durham (1754), and was drowned at Byfleet, Surrey, in 1768. He was familiar with the wits and lords of his day, and travelled on the continent with Charles, Earl of Middleton (afterwards Duke of Dorset), 1730-1733, and with Henry, Earl of Lincoln (afterwards Duke of Newcastle), 1739-1742.

He was a friend of Pope, and wrote an *Essay on Pope's Translation of Homer's Odyssey;* he published also *Polymetis, Plain Matter of Fact, Observations, Anecdotes, and Characters of Books and Men* etc. etc.

**Page 18, l. 4. the Guardian,** a publication edited by Steele in 1713. It appeared daily, price one penny, and extended to 175 numbers. Steele wrote 82 papers and Addison 53. Letters from Blois appear in numbers 101 and 104.

l. 11. **Bishop Hough.** John Hough (1651-1743), the distinguished President of Magdalen College, Oxford (see p. 5, l. 35, *supra*) was subsequently made Bishop of Oxford, from whence he was removed to Lichfield and next to Worcester, where he died, honoured for his patriotism, piety, and munificence.

l. 12. **Malbranche,** or Malebranche, Nicholas (1638-1715), an earnest student of Descartes, whose philosophy he adopted and sought to explain in the interests of theology; he "postulated the Deity as the constant intermediate between our minds and the matter which surrounds them, and his system was received with great favour by those who desired to hold fast both to Descartes and to the Church " (J. P. Mahaffy). His works were numerous, and he is sometimes bracketed with Pascal as a profound reasoner of "the age of Louis XIV."

l. 13. **Boileau,** Nicholas (1636-1711), a famous French poet and satirist, received many marks of favour from Louis XIV. His *Art of Poetry* served in some degree as a model for Pope's *Essay on Criticism.*

l. 14. **Newton,** Sir Isaac (1642-1727), was distinguished as a natural philosopher, mathematician, astronomer, member of Parliament, and Warden of the Mint. He achieved many successes in science, and promulgated a new theory of light and colours. His grand discovery of the law of gravitation revolutionized the whole study of science. The Newtonian system was first published (in 1687) in his great work, the *Philosophiae Naturalis Principia Mathematica.*

l. 15. **Hobbes,** Thomas (1588-1679), a philosopher, published several works on politics and ethics, including *Human Nature, Leviathan, Liberty and Necessity, The Behemoth* etc.

l. 24. **Dryden,** John (1631-1700) was born at Aldwinkle, Northamptonshire, and educated at Westminster School and Trinity College, Cambridge. He was for a time Secretary to Sir Gilbert Pickering, one of Cromwell's Council, and wrote stanzas on the Protector's death ; but after the Restoration he became a staunch Royalist. His chief works are *Astræa Redux, The Duke of Guise, The Wild Gallant, Annus Mirabilis, Absalom and Achitophel, Religio Laici, The Hind and Panther, Alexander's Feast,* and a translation of *Virgil.*

l. 31. **Leicester Square,** a square in the west end of London. It has been the most popular resort of foreigners of the middle classes, especially of French visitors to London and émigrés. Till the present century the square was known as "Leicester Fields," and until the time of Charles II. continued to be unenclosed country. On what is the north side of the square Leicester House was built by Robert Sidney, Earl of Leicester, from whom it was rented by Elizabeth, Queen of Bohemia—"The Queen of Hearts"—who died there, Feb. 13, 1662. Frederick, Prince of Wales, resided there in 1737. Sir Joshua Reynolds, in 1760, went to reside at No. 47 Leicester Square. He took a forty-seven years' lease of this house, ...he added a gallery, painting-rooms for himself, his pupils, copyists, and drapery men—a considerable staff—and other conveniences. The father of George Morland, the painter, had previously occupied the house. The passage to Sir Joshua's painting-room remains intact ; but the painting-room has been transformed. (See *Life and Times of Sir Joshua Reynolds,* by C. R. Leslie, R.A., and Tom Taylor, M.A.)

**Sir Joshua** Reynolds, the greatest English portrait painter and first president of the Royal Academy (1723-1792). His works were very numerous ; about 700 have been engraved. The National Gallery possesses 23 of his works, of which we may mention the portrait of Admiral Keppel, Lord Heathfield, Lord Ligonier, Dr. Johnson, and himself ; and also the "Age of Innocence," the "Holy Family," and the "Infant Samuel." His house was the rendezvous of all the distinguished literary men of his time, *e.g.* Johnson, Boswell, Garrick, Burke, Gold-smith, Wharton, Burnet, and others.

**Streatham** Park was the residence of the Thrales; see Boswell, p. 439 (sub anno 1778), and p. 587 (sub anno 1782).

l. 32. **Mrs. Thrale.** Hector Lynch Salisbury (1741-1821), the daughter of John Salisbury of Bodville, Carnarvonshire, was married in 1763 to Henry Thrale, a brewer of Southwark, and M.P. for that borough. Soon after her marriage Johnson was introduced to her by Arthur Murphy in 1765. On the death of Mr. Thrale in 1781 she retired to Bath, where she was married in 1784 to Piozzi, an Italian music-master. With him she went to Florence, but on his death in 1809 she returned to England and died at Clifton, May 2, 1821. She was distinguished for her beauty and accomplishments. She was the authoress of *Anecdotes of the late Samuel Johnson, LL.D.*, *during the last twenty years of his Life* (1786), and *Letters to and from Dr. Johnson*. These publications are inferior in interest only to the work of Boswell. She wrote also *The Three Warnings*.

l. 33. **Lessing,** Gotthold Ephraim (1729-1781), an eminent German poet, biographer, archæologist, and dramatist. His *Letters on Literature* contributed to improve the taste of his countrymen. The tragedy, *Emilia Galotti*, is one of his most famous works.

l. 35. **Paradise Lost,** Milton's great epic poem, begun in 1642 and finished in 1658.

**Absalom and Ahitophel,** a poem by John Dryden, published in 1681, treating of the conspiracy to place the Duke of Monmouth, natural son to Charles II., on the throne.

l. 36. **Addison's Latin poems.** See p. 11, ll. 7-10, *supra*, and note.

**Page 19, l. 3. Johnson,** Dr. Samuel, the well-known lexico-grapher, biographer, dramatist, poet, novelist, and essayist (1709-1784); published *London, Vanity of Human Wishes, Irene, Dictionary of the English Language, Life of Richard Savage, Rasselas, A Visit to the Hebrides, Lives of the Poets*, the *Idler*, most of the *Rambler*, etc. His Life has been written by Towers, Hawkins, Boswell, Anderson, Russell, Carlyle, and Macaulay.

l. 4. **Nothing is better known of Boileau** etc. This passage occurs in Johnson's " Life of Addison," in *Lives of English Poets*.

l. 12. **caustic,** burning, corrosive, severe (Gr. καυστικός, burning, καίειν, fut., καύσω, to burn).

l. 20. **sycophant,** a servile flatterer (Gr. συκοφάντης); lit. a fig-shower, perhaps one who informs against persons exporting figs from Attica, or plundering sacred fig-trees : hence a common informer, slanderer, also a false adviser. "The literal significa-

tion is not found in any ancient writer, and is perhaps altogether
an invention" (Liddell and Scott). That is, the early history of
the word is lost, but this does not affect its obvious etymology;
it only affects the reason for it (Skeat).

l. 26. the Augustan age (B.C. 42-A.D. 14), the golden age of
Roman literature, made glorious by the works of Virgil, Horace,
Livy, Ovid, and others; Caesar and Cicero were just dead.

l. 29. Livy. See p. 8, l. 21, *supra*, and note.

l. 30. Pollio, C. Asinius (B.C. 76-A.D. 4), was of obscure origin,
but rose to the rank of Consul (B.C. 40), triumphed over the
Dalmatians, and rendered good service to Antony in the civil
wars. He afterwards lived on terms of familiarity with Augustus.
He won distinction both as an orator and as a historian of his
own times. He wrote also a Grecian history and Greek tragedies,
and founded a library at Rome for the public use.

l. 31. the inelegant idiom of the Po. Livy's "Patavinity"
was the reproach flung at him by the learned and critical
Pollio. This is mentioned by Quintilian, "Et in Tito Livio
mirae facundiae viro putet inesse Pollio Asinius quandam Pata-
vinitatem" (Quint. viii. 1). Quintilian, however, throws no light
on the nature of the taunt, which has given rise to a great
variety of conjectures. It has been said that the people of
Patavium (Livy's birthplace) were on Pompey's side, and that
the charge of Patavinity against the historian would, to followers
of Augustus, suggest a perverse political partiality. But this is
a far-fetched notion; and we may assume that what Pollio meant
by his criticism was what we should call a proneness to pro-
vincialism, an occasional use of words and phrases that would
not quite commend themselves to the most polished society of
Rome. If there was any such defect in Livy, it is altogether
beyond the perception of the best modern scholars; and it is
significant that Quintilian gives us no hint of it. It may be
supposed that Pollio's criticism was perhaps not well founded,
and that it may have been due to a love of carping, perhaps
also to a dislike of Livy, and a jealousy of his success and
popularity.

l. 33. Frederic the Great (1712-1786), king of Prussia, was a
great soldier and acute politician. His literary works include:
*Memoirs of the House of Brandenburg*, a poem on the *Art of War*,
*The History of his own Time*, and *The History of the Seven Years'
War*. All should read Carlyle's *Life and Times of Frederick the
Great*.

Page 20, l. 6. Erasmus, Desiderius (1467-1536), an illustrious
Dutch writer. He visited most of the cities of learning in his
day—Paris, Louvain, Turin, Bologna, Venice, Padua, Rome.
He resided in England, chiefly at Cambridge, from 1510 to 1514;

subsequently he went to Bâle, where he died.    His chief works are: *Adagia, De copia Verborum, De Ratione conscribendi Epistolas, Enchiridion militis Christiani, Praise of Folly, New Testament* (the first edition printed in Greek), *Epistles of Jerome, Colloquies, Ciceronians, Ecclesiastes, or the Manner of Preaching.*

**Frascatorius,** an eminent Italian poet, physician, philosopher, astronomer, mathematician, etc. ; was intimately acquainted with Pope Paul III., Cardinal Bembo, Julius Scaliger, and all the great men of his time.    He wrote a Latin poem entitled "Syphilis."    Scaliger ranked him next to Virgil.    He wrote also treatises on medicine and astronomy.

l. 8. **the Dissertation on India,** see note on Dr. Robertson, *infra.*

l. 9. **Dr. Robertson** (1721-1793), a Scotch divine and historian. His chief works are *History of Scotland during the reigns of Queen Mary and King James VI., History of the reign of Emperor Charles V., History of America,* and *An Historical Disquisition concerning the knowledge which the Ancients had of India etc. etc.*

**Sir Walter Scott,** poet, novelist, and miscellaneous writer (1771-1832), wrote *Lay of the Last Minstrel, Lady of the Lake, Marmion,* and other poems, also the *Waverley Novels, Tales of a Grandfather, Letters on Demonology and Witchcraft,* and many other works.

l. 12. **the noble alcaics of Gray.**    Thomas Gray (1716-1771) wrote *The Progress of Poesy* and *The Bard,* and other so-called Pindaric Odes in imitation of the poetry of the classical age ; his success has been criticised by many.    Mason wrote :

> "No more the Grecian Muse unrivall'd reigns ;
> To Britain let the nations homage pay :
> She boasts a Homer's fire in Milton's strains,
> A Pindar's rapture in the lyre of Gray."

Sir Archibald Alison writes, "Gray, whose burning thoughts had been condensed in words of more than classic beauty."    Dr. Johnson, on the other hand, is frigid and severe in his *Lives of English Poets.*    Neele, in his *Lectures on English Poetry* writes, "The lyrical crown of Gray was swept away at one fell swoop by the ruthless arm of Dr. Johnson.    That the doctor's celebrated critique was unduly severe must be admitted, but the stern censor had truth on his side nevertheless.    There is more of art than nature in Gray, more of recollection than invention, more of acquirement than genius.    If I may use a colloquial illustration, I should say that the marks of the tool are too evident on all that he does."    Macaulay is evidently one of Gray's admirers.

An *alcaic* is a verse consisting of two dactyls and two trochees.

l. 13. **the playful elegiacs of Vincent Bourne.**    The Latin poems of Vincent Bourne, an usher in Westminster School, have been greatly admired. Cowper, one of his pupils, wrote, "I love the memory of Vinny Bourne, I think him a better Latin poet than Tibullus, Propertius, Ausonius, or any of the writers in his way, except Ovid, and not at all inferior to him." Dr. Beattie thinks that Bourne's translations into Latin of the ballads of "Tweed-side," "William and Margaret," and of Rowe's "Despairing beside a clear stream," are in "sweetness of numbers and elegant expression at least equal to the originals, and scarce inferior to anything in Ovid or Tibullus."

*Elegiacs* are couplets of alternate hexameters and penta-meters.

l. 16 etc. **Ne croyez pas** etc., may be translated, 'Do not think, however, that I wish to find fault that way with the Latin verses which you have sent me from one of your distinguished scholars. I have found them very beautiful, and worthy of Vida or Sannazar, but not of Horace or Virgil.'

l. 19. **Vida**, Mark Jerome (1490-1566), a celebrated modern Latin poet, was born at Cremona, studied at Padua, Bologna, and Mantua, and while young was admitted into the congregation of the canons regular of St. Mark. He afterwards went to Rome and became a canon of St. John Lutheran. His talent for Latin poetry recommended him to Leo X., who gave him the priory of St. Silvester, near Tivoli. There he wrote his *Christiad*, and Clement VII., in recompense of his merit, bestowed on him in 1532 the bishopric of Alba, where he died.

**Sannazar**, or Sannazaro, Jacopo (1458-1530), an eminent Italian and Latin poet, was born at Naples; he was admitted to the train of King Ferdinand I. and the Princess Alfonso and Frederick; he accompanied them in several military expeditions. His most celebrated work is his *Arcadia*; his Latin poems consist of piscatory eclogues, elegies, epigrams, and a sacred poem, *De partu Virginis*.

l. 23. **Père Fraguier** (1666-1728), an able man of letters, was born at Paris; he joined the Jesuits in 1683, but left them in 1694, and, fixing his residence in Paris, was elected a member of the French Academy, and that of Inscriptions and Belles-lettres. He was a great admirer of Plato, whose philosophy he put into very elegant Latin verse in a piece entitled *Schola Platonica*. Besides Latin poems, he wrote in Latin prose three dissertations concerning Socrates, and various contributions to the memoirs of the Academy of Inscriptions.

**Catullus.** See p. 7, l. 3, *supra*, and note.

l. 31. **Quid numeris** etc., may be translated, "Why, oh Muse, do you bid me to lisp again in Latin numbers, born as I am far on this side the Alps from a Sicambrian sire?"

l. 31. **Sicamber.** The Sicambri or Sygambri were a German tribe, who dwelt originally north of the Ubii on the Rhine, from whence they spread towards the north as far as the Lippe; they crossed the Rhine, and laid waste part of the Roman territory in Gaul in B.C. 17.

l. 35. **Machinæ Gesticulantes.** Anglice, a puppet show; one of Addison's Latin poems.

**Page 21, l. 1. Gerano-Pygmæomachia.** Anglice, a fight be- tween the cranes and pigmies. See p. 10, l. 22; p. 11, l. 3, *supra*, and notes.

l. 15. **bombast** (a variant of *bombace*; O.F. *bombace*, cotton, cotton wadding; late Lat. *bombacem*, acc. of *bombax*, cotton, a corruption and transferred use of Lat. *bombyx*, silk. Gk. βόμβυξ, silkworm, silk). 1. The soft down of the cotton plant; raw cotton; cotton wool. 2. Cotton wool used as padding or stiffening for clothes. 3. Inflated or turgid language; high- sounding language on a trivial or commonplace subject; "fustian," "tall talk" (Murray).

**tinsel,** gaudy ornament, showy lustre. "Tinsell (dictum a Gall. *estincelle*, l. *scintilla*, a sparke). It signifieth with us a stuffe or cloth made partly of silk and partly of gold or silver, so-called because it glistereth and sparkleth like stones"— Minsheu, ed. 1627 [Minsheu's etymology is correct; the F. *estincelle* or *étincelle* lost its initial sound, just as did the F. *estiquet* or *étiquet*, which became *ticket* in English]. Lat. *scintilla*, a spark, which seems to have been mispronounced, as *stincilla*; cf. F. *brebis* from Lat. *vervecem*. *Scintilla* is dim. from a form *scinta*, a spark, not used, allied to Gk. σπινθήρ (= σκινθήρ), a spark, and perhaps allied to A.S. *scinan*, to shine (Skeat).

l. 23. **Dauphin** [F. *dauphin* (earlier *daulphin*, in 15th c. also *doffin*)= Pr. *dalfin*; pop. L. *dalphinus* for L. *delphinus* (ad. Gr. δελφίς, dolphin), whence Sp. *delfin*, It. *delphino*. In earlier use Eng. had *daulphin*, also *dolphyn*, -*in*, the same as the name of the fish: *dauphin* is after mod. F. since the 17th c.]. The title of the eldest son of the king of France from 1349 to 1830.

According to Littré, the name Dauphin, borne by the lords of the Viennois was a proper name, *Delphinus* (the same word as the name of the fish), whence the province subject to them was called Dauphiné. Humbert III., the last lord of Dauphiné, on ceding the province to Philip of Valois in 1349, made it a con- dition that the title should be perpetuated by being borne by the eldest son of the French king (Murray).

l. 21. **Charles, second of the name, King of Spain, died** in 1700 without issue; he willed his crown to Philip, Duke of Anjou, the younger son of Lewis the Dauphin, and grandson of Lewis

XIV. of France. At the end of the war of the Spanish Succession, Philip was left king, as Philip V. of Spain.

l. 23. **The King of France**, Lewis XIV.

l. 25. **the States General**, the Assembly of the United Provinces, which met at the Hague. See p. 28, l. 3, *infra*, and note.

**Page 22. l. 3. In December 1700.** Addison writes, "On the twelfth of December, 1699, I set out from Marseilles to Genoa etc." The error in the date is pointed out by Macaulay : "It is strange that Addison should, in the first line of his travels, have misdated his departure from Marseilles by a whole year, and still more strange that this slip of the pen, which throws the whole narrative into inextricable confusion, should have been repeated in a succession of editions, and never detected by Tickell or by Hurd."

l. 4. **the Ligurian coast**, on the north-west of Italy. It enjoys the mildest climate in the north of Italy, and one of the best on the Mediterranean.

l. 9. **capuchin** (from 16th c. F. *capuchin* (now *capucin*), allied to It. *capuccino*, fr. *capuccio, capuche*, hood), a friar of the Order of St. Francis, of the new rule of 1528. So called from the sharp-pointed capuche, adopted first in 1525, and confirmed to them by Pope Clement VII. in 1528.

l. 13. "**How are thy servants** ... *Spectator*, in No. 489, September 20, 1712. The Ode is as follows :

1.

How are thy servants blest ! O Lord,
How sure is their defence !
Eternal wisdom is their guide,
Their help Omnipotence.

2.

In foreign realms and lands remote,
Supported by Thy care ;
Through burning climes I pass'd unhurt,
And breathed in tainted air.

3.

Thy mercy sweeten'd every soil,
Made every region please ;
The hoary Alpine hills it warmed,
And smooth'd the Tyrrhene seas.

4.

Think, O my soul, devoutly think,
How, with affrighted eyes,
Thou saw'st the wide extended deep
In all its horrors rise !

**5.**
Confusion dwelt in ev'ry face,
  And fear in ev'ry heart,
When waves on waves, and gulfs in gulfs,
  O'ercame the pilot's art.

**6.**
Yet then from all my griefs, O Lord,
  Thy mercy set me free ;
Whilst in the confidence of prayer
  My soul took hold on Thee.

**7.**
For tho' in dreadful whirls we hung,
  High on the broken wave ;
I knew Thou wert not slow to hear,
  Nor impotent to save.

**8.**
The storm was laid, the winds retir'd,
  Obedient to Thy will ;
The sea that roar'd at Thy command,
  At Thy command was still.

**9.**
In midst of dangers, fears, and death,
  Thy goodness I'll adore ;
And praise Thee for Thy mercies past,
  And humbly hope for more.

**10.**
My life, if Thou preserv'st my life,
  Thy sacrifice shall be ;
And death, if death must be Thy doom,
  Shall join my soul to Thee.

l. 15. **Savona**, a seaport and city, twenty-two miles west by south of Genoa. Its cathedral dates from the 17th century.

l. 18. **Genoa**, a fortified seaport city of Italy at the head of the Gulf of Genoa, Mediterranean, seventy-nine miles south-east of Turin. In the older part of the city the streets are steep and very narrow. Among its principal edifices are the Doria, Pamfili, the Royal, Ducal, Brignole, Durazzo, Serra, Spinola, Balba, Pallavicini, and numerous other palaces, all rich in choice works of art ; the cathedral, a Saraceno-Gothic structure, and many other handsome churches.

**Doge** (F. *doge*, Venetian *doge*, Ital. *doce* = *duce*, Lat. *ducem* (*dux*), leader, duke). The title of the chief magistrate in the formerly existing republics of Venice and Genoa.

l. 19. **Book of Gold**, the Register of Nobles; the term is usually applied to "the peerage" of Venice rather than of Genoa.

l. 20. **He admired the narrow streets** etc. Addison writes, "The city itself makes the boldest show of any in the world. The houses are most of them painted on the outside, so that they look extremely gay and lively, besides that they are esteemed the highest in Europe and stand very thick together. The New-Street is a double range of palaces from one end to the other, built with an excellent fancy, and fit for the greatest princes to inhabit. I cannot, however, be reconciled to their manner of painting several of the Genoese houses. Figures, perspectives, or pieces of history are certainly very ornamental, as they are drawn on many of the walls, that would otherwise look too naked and uniform without them; but instead of these, one often sees the front of a palace covered with painted pillars of different orders. If these were so many true columns of marble set in their proper architecture, they would certainly very much adorn the places where they stand, but as they are now, they only show us that there is something wanting, and that the palace, which without these counterfeit pillars would be beautiful in its kind, might have been more perfect by the addition of such as are real. The front of the Villa Imperiale, at a middle distance from Genoa, without any of this paint upon it, consists of a Doric and Corinthian row of pillars, and is much the handsomest of any I saw there. The Duke of Doria's palace has the best outside of any in Genoa, as that of Durazzo is the best furnished within. There is one room in the first that is hung with tapestry, in which are wrought the figures of the great persons that the family has produced.... The churches are very fine, particularly that of the Annunciation, which looks wonderfully beautiful in the inside, all but one corner of it being covered with statues, gilding, and paint, etc., etc."

l. 24. **Milan**, a city in north Italy in a wide fertile plain on the little river Olona. The chief object of interest is the cathedral, a Gothic edifice of white marble, founded by Count Gian Galeazzo Visconti in 1386, and practically completed in 1805.

l. 26. **Lake Benacus**, a deep and rough lake in Gallia Transpadana, near Verona, through which the Mincius (Mincio) flows, now Lago di Garda.

l. 28. **Virgil** describes Benacus thus in *Georgic*, ii. 158:

"An mare, quod supra memorem, quodque alluit infra?
Anne lacus tantos? te, Lari maxime; teque
Fluctibus et fremitu assurgens, Benace, marino."

Addison quotes only the two last lines, and makes a slight change in them, thus:

"Adde lacus tantos, te, Lari etc., etc."

**Venice**, a fortified city and seaport of Italy, stands on some 120 islands on the lagoon of Venice; a vast shallow lake, which is separated from the Adriatic by a chain of low narrow islands.

l. 30. **Carnival** (It. *carnevale, carnovale* (whence French *carnaval*, Mid. Lat. (11th-12th c.) *carnelevarium, carnelevaria, carnilevamen.* These appear to originate in Lat. *carnem levare*, or It. *carne levare*, meaning " the putting away or removal of flesh (as food)," the name being originally proper to the eve of Ash-Wednesday).

l. The season immediately preceding Lent, devoted in Italy and other Roman Catholic countries to revelry and riotous amusement, Shrove-tide ; the festivity of this season (Murray).

l. 32. **the absurd dramatic pieces … Cato** etc.   Addison describes one of the diversions of the Carnival of Venice thus : "Operas are another great entertainment of this season.   The poetry of them is generally as exquisitely ill as the music is good. The arguments are often taken from some celebrated action of the ancient Greeks or Romans, which sometimes looks ridiculous enough. … The opera that was most in vogue during my stay at Venice was built on the following subject.   Cæsar and Scipio are rivals for Cato's daughter.   Cæsar's first words bid his soldiers fly, for the enemies are upon them.   'Si leva Cesare, e dice a Soldati. A la fuggo. A 'lo Scampo.' The daughter gives the preference to Cæsar, which is made the occasion of Cato's death.   Before he kills himself you see him withdrawn into his library, where, among his books, I observed the titles of Plutarch and Tasso.   After a short soliloquy he strikes himself with the dagger that he holds in his hand ; but being interrupted by one of his friends, he stabs him for his pains, and by the violence of the blow, unluckily breaks the dagger on one of his ribs, so that he is forced to dispatch himself by tearing up his first wound."

The student should note the absurdities and anachronisms in this scene, and should read Addison's version, his dedication to the Princess of Wales, the prologue by Mr. Pope, and the epilogue by Dr. Garth.

**Page 23, l. 3. Plutarch.**  See p. 8, l. 23, *supra*, and note. Plutarch flourished about A.D. 80, while Cato died B.C. 46.

**Tasso.**  See p. 13, l. 12, *supra*, and note.

l. 18. **San Marino**, one of the smallest and most ancient states in Europe, enclosed by the provinces Forli, Pesano, and Urbino, of the kingdom of Italy, situated nine miles south-west of Rimini.   Addison writes, "At twelve miles' distance from Rimini stands the little republic of St. Marino, which I could not forbear visiting, though it lies out of the common tour of travellers, and has excessively bad ways to it.   I shall here give a particular account of it, because I know of nobody else that has done it."   He then describes briefly its position, products, history, and government, concluding with these words, to which Macaulay draws attention : " Nothing, indeed, can be a greater

instance of the natural love that mankind has for liberty, and of
their aversion to an arbitrary government, than such a savage
mountain covered with people, and the Campania of Rome, which
lies in the same country, almost destitute of inhabitants."

l. 30. St. Peter's cathedral on the Vatican was begun in the
reign of Constantine the Great (first half of the fourth century),
but was entirely reconstructed from designs by Bramante,
Michel Angelo, and Maderna between 1506 and 1626.

the Pantheon, now the church of Santa Maria la Rotonda.

Page 24, l. 9. the Appian way. Appia via, a well-known high
road, begun by the Censor Appius Claudius Cæcus (about 313
B.C.), which started from the Porta Capena in Rome, and passed in
a direct line to the Albanian Mountains, and thence through the
Pontine Marshes to Capua ; and it was afterwards continued to
Brundusium, perhaps by Trajan.

l. 11. The lovely bay of Naples.

the awful mountain, Vesuvius.

l. 12. a farmhouse ... Herculaneum, and rows of vine ... Pompeii.
Herculaneum and Pompeii were buried by an eruption of
Vesuvius, 23rd to 26th August, 79, under cinders, scoriæ, and
lava, and remained so till 1748. Since 1860 the greater part of
Pompeii has been uncovered, whence it appears that it was enclosed by walls, entered by several gates, and had streets paved
with lava, terraced houses of two or three stories, with shops
and shop-signs still plainly visible, theatres, temples, baths, a
street of the tombs, a forum, prisons, and other public buildings.
Herculaneum was a town of Campania, situated on the sea
coast between Naples and Pompeii.

Herculaneum lay at the foot of Vesuvius ; its position was
discovered in 1711.

l. 14. Pæstum, a city of Lucania, formerly called Posidonia,
celebrated for its twice blowing roses: "biferique rosaria Paesti "
(Virg. Georg. iv. 119). Its modern name is Pesto, twenty-two
miles south-east of Salerno.

l. 18. Salvator Rosa (1615-1673), an eminent Italian painter,
was born near Naples. He excelled in painting combats, sea
pieces, and landscapes of romantic scenery with banditti. He
was also a musician, poet, architect, comic actor, and impro-
visatore. There is a landscape by him in the National Gallery.

l. 19. Vico, John Baptist (1668-1744), was born at Naples, and
became Professor of Rhetoric in that city. His principal work
is entitled Principles of a New Science, wherein he declared that
the history of mankind is regulated by laws as immutable as
those which govern the material world.

l. 21. ruined cities overgrown by the forests of Yucatan.
Yucatan is a peninsula of Central America, running out into the

Gulf of Mexico. Of these ruined cities Prescott writes, in his Appendix (Part I.) to the *Conquest of Mexico*, "But if the remains on the Mexican soil are so scanty, they multiply as we descend the south-eastern slope of the Cordilleras, traverse the rich valley of Oaxaca, and penetrate the slopes of Chiapa and Yucatan. In the midst of these lonely regions we meet with the ruins, recently discovered, of several ancient cities, Mitla, Palenque, and Itzalama or Uxmal, which argue a higher civilization than anything yet found on the American continent."

l. 22. **the tunnel of Posilipo,** which Addison calls "the grotto of Pausilypo." The entry to this tunnel or grotto was near the tomb of Virgil. Addison describes it thus, "If a man would form to himself a just idea of this place, he must fancy a vast rock undermined from one end to the other, and a highway running through it, near as long and as broad as the Mall in St. James's Park. This subterraneous passage is much mended since Seneca gave so bad a character of it. The entry at both ends is higher than the middle parts of it, and sinks by degrees, to fling in more light upon the rest. Towards the middle are two large funnels, bored through the roof of the grotto, to let in light and fresh air."

l. 24. **Capreæ,** an island in the Tyrrhene sea, near Campania; its modern name is Capri. Addison describes it thus: "This island stands as a vast mole, which seems to have been planted there on purpose to break the violence of the waves that run into the bay. It lies long-ways, almost in a parallel line to Naples. The excessive height of its rocks secures a great part of the bay from winds and waves, which enter again between the other end of this island and the promontory of Miseno.

l. 27. **the abuses of the government and the misery of the people.** The Neapolitans were in Addison's day under the rule of the Spaniards; Addison dwells at some length upon the griev-ances of the Neapolitans, who were oppressed, not only by their rulers, but also by their own countrymen, the clergy, the barons, and the lawyers; while high gabels were imposed on almost everything that could be eaten, drunk, or worn.

l. 28. **The great kingdom … to Philip the Fifth.** Spain had been bequeathed by Charles II. to Philip, Duke of Anjou, after-wards Philip V. See p. 21, l. 21, *supra*, and note.

l. 29. **Castile and Aragon,** two divisions of Spain, comprising together nearly the whole of the northern half of that country lying to the north of the river Guadiana and west of Catalonia and Valencia.

l. 36. **Jacobitism,** the principles of the Jacobites, *i.e.* of the adherents of James II. after his abdication, and of the subse-quent Pretenders of the Stuart line.

l. 36. **Freeholder**, a political periodical conducted by Addison and published twice a week. The first number appeared on Friday, Dec. 23, 1715; the last issue, No. 55, was on Friday, June 29, 1716.

**Page 25**, l. 1. **the Tory fox-hunter** etc. See No. 22 of the *Freeholder*, in which Addison describes a discourse with a country gentleman, in the course of which Addison asked him if he had ever travelled, and in reply "he told me he did not know what travelling was good for, but to teach a man to ride the great horse, to jabber French, and to talk against passive obedience; to which he added that he scarce ever knew a traveller in his life who had not forsook his principles and lost his hunting-seat" etc., etc.

ll. 4 and 5. **From Naples ... to Rome by sea ... Virgil had celebrated.** Addison writes: "I took a felucca at Naples to carry me to Rome, that I might not be forced to run over the same sights a second time ... As in my journey from Rome to Naples I had Horace for my guide, so I had the pleasure of seeing my voyage from Naples to Rome described by Virgil. It is, indeed, much easier to trace out the way Aeneas took than that of Horace, because Virgil has marked it out by capes, islands, and other parts of nature, which are not so subject to change or decay as are towns, cities, and the works of art.

**felucca** (It. *felu(c)ca*, Fr. *felouque*, Sp. *faluca*, Pg. *falua*, Mod. Arab. *falükah*, also *fulaikah*). Devic considers it to be of Arabic formation, cognate with Arab. *fulk*, ship, from root *falaka*, to be round. A small vessel propelled by oars or lateen sails, or both, used chiefly in the Mediterranean for coasting voyages.

l. 6. **the headland ... tomb of Misenus**, "Cape Misena ... the highest end of this promontory rises in the fashion of a sepulchre or monument, to those that survey it from the land, which perhaps might occasion Virgil's burying Misenus under it" (Addison).

**Misenus** was the companion and trumpeter of Aeneas, who was drowned and buried at Misenum, a promontory in Campania south of Cumae, said to be named after him.

" At pius Aeneas ingenti mole sepulcrum
  Imponit, suaque arma viro remumque tubamque
  Monte sub Aerio, qui nunc Misenus ab illo
  Dicitur, aeternumque tenet per saecula nomen."
                                    *Aen.* vi. 162 etc.

l. 9. **Circe**, a mythical sorceress, daughter of Helios (the sun), and Perse, lived, according to Homer, in the island of Aeaa. Ulysses tarried a whole year with her after she had changed several of his companions into swine.

l. 9. **Tiber** etc., the river upon which Rome was built. Addison writes : "Our next stage brought us to the mouth of the Tiber, into which we entered with some danger, the sea being generally pretty rough in the parts where the river rushes into it. The season of the year, the muddiness of the stream, with the many green trees hanging over it, put me in mind of the delightful image that Virgil has given us, when Aeneas took the first view of it.

> " Atque hic Aeneas ingentem ex aequore lucum
> Prospicit ; hunc inter fluvio Tiberinus amoeno,
> Verticibus rapidis, et multa flavus arena,
> In mare prorumpit ; variae circumque supraque
> Assuetae ripis volucres et fluminis alveo,
> Aethera mulcebant cantu, lucoque volabant.
> Flectere iter sociis terraeque advertere proras
> Imperat, et laetus fluvio succedit opaco."—*Aen.* vii. 29.

l. 12. **Ostia**, a seaport town in Latium, at the mouth of the Tiber.

**at Rome he remained** etc. This is an adaptation of Addison. "The places mentioned in this chapter (viz. Tivoli, Frescati, Palestrina, and Albano) were all of them formerly the cool retirements of the Romans, where they used to hide themselves among the woods and mountains during the excessive heats of their summer ; as Baja was the general winter rendezvous :

> " Jam terras volucremque polum fuga veris aquosi
> Laxat, et Icariis coelum latratibus urit.
> Ardua jam densae rarescunt moenia Romae :
> Hos Praeneste sacrum, nemus hos glaciale Dianae,
> Algidus aut horrens aut Tuscula protegit umbra,
> Tiburis hi lucos, Anienaque frigora captant."—*Sil.* iv. 1.

> " Albanos quoque Tusculosque colles
> Et quodcunque jacet sub orbe frigus.
> Fidenas veteres, brevesque Rubras,
> Et quod virgineo cruore gaudet
> Annae pomiferum Perennae."—*Mart.* lib. c. 23.

> " All shun the raging dog-star's sultry heat,
> And from the half-unpeopled town retreat ;
> Some hid in Nemi's gloomy forests lie,
> To Palaestrina some for shelter fly,
> Others to catch the breeze of breathing air,
> To Tusculum or Algido repair ;
> Or in moist Tivoli's retirements find
> A cooling shade and a refreshing wind."

l. 17 etc., **he, long after, poured forth in verse his gratitude** etc., see p. 22, l. 13, *supra*, and note.

**l. 25. Sienna…cathedral.** Sienna is a city of Tuscany, thirty-one miles south of Florence. Addison writes of the cathedral, "There is nothing in this city so extraordinary as the cathedral, which a man may view with pleasure after he has seen St. Peter's, though it is quite of another make, and can only be looked upon as one of the master-pieces of Gothic architecture" etc. He then proceeds to deplore the amount of money spent by our fore-fathers on Gothic cathedrals.

**l. 28. Duke of Shrewsbury.** At the early age of 28, Charles Talbot, Earl of Shrewsbury, became Secretary of State, in 1689. His talents, accomplishments, graceful manners, and bland temper made him generally popular ; but he lacked firmness and was inclined to a mild and moderate policy : finding his advice slighted, he in an evil hour entered into a secret engagement with the Jacobites in 1690, and thus committed a treason that threw a dark shade over all his remaining years. In 1693 he refused office in the government and retired into the country ; but in 1694 he was induced to accept the seals again, and for his com-pliance was rewarded with a dukedom and a garter. In 1696 Fenwick's confession exposed the correspondence with St. Ger-main's : Shrewsbury was forgiven by the King, but nothing would persuade the Duke to face the Parliament again, and he retired first to the Wolds in Gloucestershire and afterwards to Italy. (See Macaulay's History, "William and Mary," *passim*.) Addison does not mention the Duke of Shrewsbury in his "Remarks on Italy."

**Page 26, l. 4. the sculptures in the Museum, which he preferred even to those of the Vatican.** What is Macaulay's authority for this statement ? Addison writes, " Florence, for modern statues, I think excels even Rome, but these I shall pass over in silence that I may not transcribe out of others." And speaking of the Duke of Florence's new palace, he says, " I found in the court of this palace what I could not meet anywhere in Rome ; I mean an antique statue of Hercules lifting up Antaeus from the earth." But neither of these passages expresses a preference for the sculptures in the Museum over those in the Vatican. The most noted of the sculptures in the Museum at Florence are the Niobe group and Donatello's "Victorious David." Those of the Vatican include the Laocoon group, Apollo, Belvidere, and Torso of Hercules.

**l. 8. Eugene**, Francis, Prince of Savoy (1663-1736), was born in Paris but was banished by Louis XIV. to the Netherlands ; he went to Vienna and did good service for the Emperor against the Turks in Hungary. He subsequently (1701) won distinction in the " War of the Spanish Succession," and drove the French out of Italy (see note on Catinat, *infra*). He was associated in the command of the allied army with the Duke of Marlborough, and in 1704 had a large share in the famous victory of Blenheim.

l. 9. **Rhætian Alps**, or the Tyrolese Alps, from the St. Gothard to the Orteler by the pass of the Stalvio.

**Catinat**, Nicholas (1637-1712), a French Marshal, who in 1701 had the command of the army in Italy against Prince Eugene; his efforts were paralyzed by the want of funds, and meeting with several disasters he was forced to retreat.

**the rich plain of Lombardy**, composed of the north central part of the Po basin.

l. 10. **The faithless ruler of Savoy**. Victor Amadeus II. was made commander-in-chief of the Austrian troops sent against France in 1692, but was induced by bribes to go over to the side of Louis XIV.

l. 11. **Lewis the Fourteenth**.

l. 12. **Manchester**: see p. 17, l. 3, *supra*, and note.

l. 14. **the Grand Alliance against the House of Bourbon**, between the Emperor and the Dutch States-General (principally to prevent the union of the French and Spanish monarchies in one person) was signed at Vienna, 12th May, 1689; it was afterwards joined by England, Spain, and the Duke of Savoy.

l. 17. **Mont Cenis** (6835 ft.) gave its name to the pass over the Alps which was most used until the Mont Cenis tunnel was opened in 1871.

l. 19. **the road ... which now reminds the stranger of the power and genius of Napoleon.** In 1800 Napoleon crossed the Alps with his army: the left wing under Moncey (15,000 strong) was ordered to debouche by the way of St. Gothard. The corps of Thoreau (5,000 strong) took the direction of Mont Cenis: Napoleon reserved for the main body, consisting of 35,000, the gigantic task of surmounting with the artillery the huge barrier of the Great St. Bernard (Lockhart's *Life of Buonaparte*).

l. 21 etc. **To this journey Addison alluded in the ode** etc. : see p. 22, l. 13, *supra*, and note.

l. 25. **his Epistle to his friend Montague** etc. This Epistle was in English and translated into Italian by Signor Salvini, Professor of Greek at Florence. The English title is, "A Letter from Italy to the Right Honourable Charles, Lord Halifax, in the year MDCCI." The Italian title runs thus. "Littera scritta d'Italia al molto onorabile Carlo Conte Halifax dal Signore Giuseppe Addison d'anno MDCCI. In versi Inglesi, e tradotta in versi Toscani." Tickell writes: "The Letter from Italy" to my Lord Halifax may be considered as the text upon which the book of travels is a large comment, and has been esteemed by those that have a relish for antiquity as the most exquisite of his poetical performances.

l. 32. **the death of Dryden**, on May 1, 1700.

l. 33. **the publication of the Essay on Criticism**, by Alexander Pope in 1711.

l. 35. **Pope**, Alexander (1688-1744), was born in Lombard Street, London: he wrote his *Ode on Solitude* and *Pastorals* while still in his teens: his chief works were the *Essay on Criticism, Rape of the Lock,* translations of Homer's *Iliad* and *Odyssey,* the *Dunciad,* and *Essay on Man.*

**Parnell**, Thomas (1679-1718), Archdeacon of Clogher, and poet, wrote a satire on Dennis and Theobald called the *Life of Zoilus* ; other works by him are a *Life of Homer, A Fairy Tale, Batrachomyomachia* (the Battle of the Frogs and Mice, a transla- tion from Homer), *The Rise of Woman,* and some papers in the *Guardian* entitled *Visions.*

l. 36. **Prior**, Matthew (1664-1721), poet and wit of the reign of Queen Anne, published (with Mr. Montague, afterwards Lord Halifax) *The City Mouse and Country Mouse* in 1687, and the *Carmen Saeculare* in 1700. Johnson has given an account of him in *Lives of the Poets.* Thackeray, in his *English Humorists,* says, "Johnson speaks slightingly of his lyrics ; but with due deference to the Great Samuel, Prior's seem to me amongst the easiest, the richest, the most charmingly humorous of English lyrical poems."

**Page 27. l. 3. Halifax had now nothing to give** etc. In 1699 Halifax lost the leadership of the House of Commons, and re- signed the offices of Chancellor of the Exchequer and of First Lord of the Treasury. At the beginning of 1701 he took his seat in the House of Lords as Baron Halifax of Halifax, in the County of York. In the same year he was impeached on charges of corruption, and also of advising and promoting the Partition Treaty. But the House of Lords dismissed the impeachment for want of prosecution.

l. 12. **At Geneva** etc. Tickell writes : "Some time before the date of this letter (viz. to Stepney, dated November, 1702) Mr. Addison had designed to return to England, when he received advice from his friends that he was pitched upon to attend the army of Prince Eugene, who had just begun the war in Italy, as Secretary from His Majesty. But an account of the death of King William, which he met with at Geneva, put an end to that thought ; and as his hopes of advancement in his own country were fallen with the credit of his friends, who were out of power at the beginning of Her late Majesty's reign, he had leisure to make the tour of Germany on his way home."

l. 14. **Manchester.** See p. 17, l. 3, *supra,* and note,

l. 30. **He became tutor to a young English traveller**: who was this young traveller?  The Duke of Somerset wished Addison to be companion to his son, Lord Hertford, in his travels, but through a misunderstanding this proposition was not carried out.  See Mr. Courthope's *Life of Addison*, pp. 52-54, in "English Men of Letters" series.

l. 32. **his pleasing treatise on Medals** was entitled *Dialogues upon the Usefulness of Ancient Medals, especially in relation to the Latin and Greek Poets,* upon which Pope wrote *Verses occasioned by Mr. Addison's Treatise of Medals.*  The treatise was not published till 1726, about seven years after the author's death ; but Tickell says : "The book itself was begun to be cast into form at Vienna, as appears from a letter to Mr. Stepney, then Minister at that Court, dated in November, 1702."

**Page 28. l. 3. the United Provinces.**  The Seven Provinces of the Netherlands, that revolted successfully from Philip II. of Spain, the husband of our Queen Mary, joined together and prospered under the name of the United Provinces or Holland. Their Assembly was called the States-General.   See p. 21, l. 25, *supra*, and note.

l. 6. **Kit Cat Club**, formed about 1700, is said to have met first at an obscure house in Shire Lane.  The society consisted of thirty-nine distinguished noblemen and gentlemen zealously attached to the House of Hanover, among whom were the Dukes of Somerset, Richmond, Grafton, Devonshire, and Marlborough, and (after the accession of George I.) the Duke of Newcastle, the Earls of Dorset, Sunderland, Manchester, Wharton, and Kington, Lords Halifax and Somers, Sir Robert Walpole, Vanbrugh, Congreve, Grenville, Addison, Garth, Maynwaring, Stepney, and Walsh.

Steele, in No. 9 of the *Spectator*, after stating that "our modern celebrated clubs are founded on eating and drinking," adds "the Kit-Cat itself is said to have taken its original from a mutton-pie."  Malone, in his *Life of Dryden*, says "the club is supposed to have derived its name from Christopher Katt, a pastry cook, who kept the house where they dined, and excelled in making mutton pies, which always formed part of their bill of fare.  See also Boswell's *Life of Johnson* in this edition.

l. 19. **Lord Treasurer Godolphin.**  When the Tories returned to power at the end of William's reign Godolphin again became head of the Treasury (1700) ; and on the accession of Anne (1702) retained that post, and continued to be head of the Home Government during the next eight years.

l. 20. **Captain General Marlborough.**  At the close of William's reign Marlborough had the command of the English forces in Holland, and was appointed Ambassador Extraordinary to the States-General, who chose him Captain-General of their forces.

l. 35. **close** (Fr. *clos*, Lat. *clausum*).   1. An enclosed place, an enclosure.   2. In many senses more or less specific; as an enclosed field (now chiefly local in the English Midlands).   3. (*a*) An enclosure about or beside a building; a court, yard, quadrangle, etc.; (*b*) a farmyard (now in Kent, Sussex, Scotland); (*c*) the precinct of a cathedral: hence sometimes = the cathedral clergy (Murray's *Dictionary*).

**Page 29. l. 15. Canning**, George (1770-1827), entered Parliament in 1793, was Secretary for Foreign Affairs in 1807, and to him may be justly ascribed the line of British policy in Spain which destroyed the hopes of Napoleon, and led to his overthrow.   In 1816 he was President of the Board of Control, and in 1822 was again chosen as Secretary for Foreign Affairs.   He asserted the principle of non-interference in the internal affairs of foreign states; in home affairs he supported Catholic emancipation, free trade, etc.   In 1827 he was Prime Minister, but the Duke of Wellington, Lord Eldon, and Mr. Peel refused to serve under him.

l. 17. **Nottingham** etc.   With this passage compare the following from Green's *Short History of the English People*, p. 695. "In England itself the victory of Blenheim aided to bring about a great change in the political aspect of affairs.   With the progress of the struggle the Tory party had slowly drifted back again into its old antipathy to a Whig war. ... The bill against occasional conformity was steadily resisted by the Lords, and Marlborough's efforts to bend the Tory ministers to a support of the war were every day more fruitless.   The higher Tories, with Lord Nottingham at their head, who had thrown every obstacle they could in the way of its continuance, at last quitted office in 1704, and Marlborough replaced them by Tories of a more moderate stamp, who were still in favour of the war, by Robert Harley, who became Secretary of State, and Henry St. John, a man of splendid talents, who was named Secretary at War."

**Jersey**, one of the extreme Tories, he was dismissed from the Council along with Nottingham in 1704.

l. 18. **Lord Eldon** (1751-1838), was Solicitor-General in 1788, Attorney-General in 1793, Lord Chief-Justice in 1799, Lord Chancellor in 1801-1827, and in that capacity joined Wellington, Peel, and other strong Tories in refusing to serve in Canning's ministry.

**Lord Westmoreland**, or Westmorland, was one of the Tory ministry formed by Pitt in 1804.   He and Lord Eldon resigned office on the appointment of Canning as Prime Minister in 1827.

l. 21. **Somers.**   See p. 15, l. 2, *supra*, and note; also p. 16, l. 17.

I

**Halifax.** See p. 11, l. 20. **Charles Montague,** *supra*, and note; also p. 16, l. 20; p. 26, l. 25.

**Sunderland,** with Somers, Halifax, Wharton, and Russell formed the so-called "Junto," as leader of the Whig party. "Of these five members, Charles, Earl of Sunderland, son-in-law of Marlborough, was the youngest, and had also the reputation of being the most violent Whig. When the two ministers, Marlborough and Godolphin, were depending more and more upon the Whigs for support, the Junto stipulated that Sunderland should be made Secretary of State as the price of this support, and as a security that measures would not be introduced hostile to the principles of the Whigs...(the Queen, however, opposed this appointment), and Sunderland received another office in 1705, that of ambassador at Vienna. (See *Age of Anne*, by Edward E. Morris.) In 1717 Sunderland became First Lord of the Treasury, and in his ministry Addison was Secretary of State. (See *Essay on William Pitt, Earl of Chatham*, p. 291, and note.)

.**Cowper.** See p. 37, l. 5, *infra*, and note.

l. 28. **Blenheim,** a village in Bavaria, on the north bank of the Danube, near the little town of Hochstädt. Here Marlborough and Eugene, with a strange medley of an army, consisting of Englishmen, Dutchmen, Hanoverians, Danes, Wurtembergers, and Austrians, defeated the French and Bavarians under Marshal Tallard and the Elector; Tallard was taken prisoner.

l. 34. **the Act of Settlement** decided that the sovereign of England must be a Protestant; it was passed in 1702, whereby the succession to the crown after the death of William III. and Queen Anne without issue, was limited to Sophia, Electress of Hanover, grand-daughter of James I., and her heirs, being Protestants.

**Page 30. l. 4. Godolphin.** See p. 28, l. 19, *supra*; also *Essay on William Pitt, Earl of Chatham*, and note.

l. 17. **Think of two thousand gentlemen at least** etc. I have not succeeded in tracing the name of this absurd poem or of its author; if any of my readers should be more successful I hope that he or she will kindly let me know; perhaps it was an anonymous ballad.

l. 25. **Halifax.** See p. 29, l. 21, *supra*, and note.

l. 44. **the soft answer which turneth away wrath,** an adaptation of *Proverbs*, xv. 1, "A soft answer turneth away wrath."

**Page 31, l. 11. the Haymarket,** a street between Pall Mall and Piccadilly, and parallel to St. James's Street; it took its name from the market for hay and straw held there from Elizabeth's time to the beginning of this century.

l. 15. **Henry Boyle,** Lord Carleton (d. 1725), sat in Parliament for Tamworth from 1689 to 1690, for Cambridge University from

1692 to 1705, and for Westminster from 1705 to 1710. He was at various times a Lord of the Treasury, Chancellor of the Exchequer, Lord Treasurer of Ireland, and Secretary of State. The third volume of the *Spectator* was dedicated to him with the eulogy that among politicians no one had " made himself more friends and fewer enemies."

l. 20. **the poem** was entitled "The Campaign, a Poem ; to his Grace the Duke of Marlborough." It has been criticised by Wharton as a "Gazette in Rhyme."

l. 22. **the famous similitude of the Angel**, the paragraph containing the simile is certainly the finest in the poem :

> " But O, my muse, what numbers wilt thou find
> To sing the furious troops in battle joined !
> Methinks I hear the drum's tumultuous sound,
> The victor's shouts, and dying groans confound,
> The dreadful burst of cannon rend the skies,
> And all the thunder of the battle rise.
> 'Twas then great Marlbro's mighty soul was prov'd,
> That, in the shock of charging hosts unmov'd
> Amidst confusion, horror and despair,
> Examin'd all the dreadful scenes of war ;
> In peaceful thought the field of death survey'd,
> To fainting squadrons sent the timely aid,
> Inspir'd repuls'd battalions to engage,
> And taught the doubtful battle where to rage.
> So when an angel by divine command
> With rising tempests shakes a guilty land,
> Such as of late o'er pale Britannia's past,
> Calm and serene he drives the furious blast ;
> And pleas'd the Almighty's orders to perform
> Rides in the whirlwind and directs the storm."

l. 23. **Commissionership** of Appeals (in Excise), vacant by the removal of the famous Mr. Locke to the Council of Trade (Tickell).

l. 29. **the Epistle to Halifax.** See p. 26, l. 25, *supra*, and note.

l. 31. **the death of Dryden**, in 1700.

l. 32. **the dawn of Pope's genius.** Pope wrote his *Pastorals* in 1709, his *Essay on Criticism* in 1711.

l. 33. **The chief merit of the Campaign ... noticed by Johnson.** Johnson's words are, " the rejection and contempt of fiction is rational and manly."

l. 35. **The first great poet** etc., Homer, who lived about 900 B.C.

**Page 32, l. 13. Homer** etc. See in the *Iliad* his descriptions of Achilles, Ajax, Menelaus, Aeneas, Priam, Diomed, Hector, and others.

l. 16. **one of whom could with ease hurl rocks** etc., viz. Diomed, the son of Tydeus.

> ὁ δὲ χερμάδιον λάβε χειρὶ
> Τυδείδης, μέγα ἔργον, ὃ οὐ δύο γ' ἄνδρε φέροιεν,
> οἷοι νῦν βροτοί εἰσ'· ὁ δέ μιν 'ρέα πάλλε καὶ οἷος.
> —*Iliad*, v. 302 etc.

Translated by Lord Derby thus :

> " A rocky fragment then
> Tydides lifted up, a mighty mass,
> Which scarce two men could raise, as men are now :
> But he, unaided, lifted it with ease."

In *Iliad*, xx. 285 etc. we have the self-same feat ascribed to Aeneas.

l. 21. **Achilles** etc.   See *Iliad*, Bks. xx. and xxi.

l. 24. **Troy,** an ancient town of Phrygia, on the coast of Asia Minor, about nine miles south-south-east of the entrance to the Hellespont from the Aegean Sea.

**Lycia,** a country of Asia Minor between Caria and Pamphylia.

l. 25. **Scamander,** a river of Troas.

l. 27. **a shield and helmet of the best Sidonian fabric.** Sidon, one of the chief towns of Phoenicia, was famed in early times for its metal work.   See *Iliad*, xxiii. 741, and *Od.* xv. 118.

l. 28. **horses of Thessalian breed.** The horses of Thessaly were reputed the finest in Greece, hence the cavalry of Thessaly was very efficient, and the horse is the usual device on the coins of that country.

l. 32. **the Life-guardsman Shaw.** Jack Shaw (1789-1815) was a prize fighter of great stature and strength, who enlisted in the Life-guards. He lost his life at Waterloo after having performed prodigies of valour. He is said to have killed in that battle eight or ten Frenchmen with his own hand.

l. 34. **Mamelukes,** a body of Egyptian soldiers ; they were so powerful that the Sultans of Egypt were chosen from their ranks from 1254-1517.

l. 35. **Mourad Bey,** sometimes called the Egyptian Fabius, was regarded by Napoleon as the bravest, most active, and most dangerous of his enemies in Egypt. He distinguished himself at the battle of the Pyramids, and in several other engagements with Napoleon's generals in the Egyptian campaign of 1798-9. He died of the plague in 1801.

**Bey** (Osmanli, *bey*, prince, governor), a Turkish governor of a province or district ; also a title of rank.

**Page 33, l. 10. Silius Italicus.** See p. 8, l. 22, *supra*, and note.

l. 14. **Asdrubal,** or Hasdrubal, a son of Hamilcar, who crossed the Alps and entered Italy with reinforcements for his brother

Hannibal, but was met by the Consuls M. Livius Salinator and Claudius Nero near the Metaurus, where he was defeated and slain, B.C. 207.

l. 15. **the consul Nero.** See preceding note.

l. 17. **Fabius, Q.** Maximus, was Consul of Rome no less than four times, Dictator once, and was honoured with a triumph twice. It was through his skilful tactics, a masterly inactivity (from which he won the agnomen of Cunctator, the "delayer"), that Rome and Italy was saved from conquest by Hannibal.

ll. 17-19. **Thuris ... Morinus,** names of Carthaginian warriors.

l. 20. **Hannibal** (B.C. 247-183), the great Carthaginian, the terror of Rome, and one of the greatest generals the world has ever seen. Some of his chief exploits were the siege of Saguntum, the march over the Alps, victories at the Ticinus, at the Trebia, at Lacus Trasimenus, and at Cannae; but he was defeated by Scipio at Zama with great loss, and subsequently fled to Bithynia, where he took poison to avoid falling into the hands of the Romans.

ll. 20-21. **Perusinus and Telesinus,** names of Roman soldiers.

l. 25. **the Boyne,** a river which rises in the Bog of Allen, near Carbury, and flows north-east by Trim and Navan to Drogheda, and falls into the Irish Sea; about two and a half miles west of Drogheda an obelisk marks the site of the Battle of the Boyne, where William III. defeated James II. in 1690.

l. 27. **John Philips** (1676-1708) was a native of Bampton, Oxfordshire, and educated at Christ Church, Oxford; he published a poem in memory of Queen Anne in 1695, contributed his *Splendid Shilling,* a mock heroic poem in imitation of the verse of *Paradise Lost,* to a collection of poems printed in 1701; he published *Blenheim, a Poem,* in 1705 (from which Macaulay quotes an extract); *Cyder, a Poem in Two Books* in 1708; he wrote also an excellent Latin ode, *Ode ad Henricum St. John Armig,* dedicated to his patron, Lord Bolingbroke, in return for a present of wine and tobacco. Philips is the subject of one of Johnson's *Lives of the Poets.* Macaulay has a brief criticism of Philips in his *Critical and Historical Essays*; and from Campbell's specimens we may quote the following: "The fame of this poet (says the grave doctor of last century) will endure as long as Blenheim is remembered, or cider drunk in England. He might have added, as long as tobacco shall be smoked, for Philips has written more meritoriously about the Indian weed than about his native apple; and his muse appears to be more in her element in the smoke of the pipe than of the battle."

l. 28. **the battle of Blenheim.** See p. 29, l. 28, *supra,* and note.

l. 31. **Churchill,** the family name of the Duke of Marlborough. These lines are quoted from the poem entitled *Blenheim.*

**l. 32. Tallard.** See l. 28, *supra*, note on *Battle of Blenheim.*

**Page 34, l. 15. the famous comparison of Marlborough** etc. See p. 31, l. 22, *supra*, and note.

**l. 26. The great tempest** etc. Cf. this account with that in *Haydn's Dictionary of Dates.*

**l. 32. One Prelate ... Palace,** the Bishop of Bath and Wells. He and his wife were killed in bed in their palace in Somerset-shire, by the fall of a chimney during the memorable storm of 26th November, 1703.

**Page 35, ll. 6-7. The first effect ... disappointment.** Tickell writes: " It is not hard to conceive why this performance was at first but indifferently relished by the bulk of readers, who ex-pected an account, in a common way, of the customs and policies of the several governments in Italy, reflections upon the genius of the people, a map of the provinces, or a measure of their buildings. How were they disappointed when, instead of such particulars, they were presented only with a journal of poetical travels, with remarks on the present picture of the country, compared with the landskips drawn by classic authors etc. "

**l. 9. Victor Amadeus.** See p. 26, l. 10, *supra*, note on *the faithless ruler of Savoy.*

**l. 12. the war between the Trojans and Rutulians,** described by Virgil in *Aen.*, Bks. ix.-xii., where Virgil seems to use *Rutuli* convertibly with *Latini,* much as he makes the names of one of the Greek races stand for the whole army at Troy: see *Aen.* ix. 450, and notes thereon.

**l. 15. the gallantries of the Empress Faustina.** There were two empresses of this name, the wife of Antoninus Pius, and her daughter, the wife of Marcus Aurelius, both of them notorious for their licentiousness.

**l. 31. Dante,** Alighieri (1265-1321), the great Italian epic poet, author of the *Divina Commedia, Vita Nuova, Convito,* and *Canzoniere.*

**Petrarch** (1304-1374). His Italian name was Francesco Petrarca ; he was crowned poet laureate in 1341. His chief works are *Sonnetti, Canzoni ed Trionfi* (in praise of Laura), and some Latin treatises.

**Boccaccio,** Giovanni (1313-1375), the great friend of Petrarch : he wrote the *Decameron, A commentary on Dante's Inferno,* a life of its author, and much verse in Italian and Latin.

**Boiardo,** Matthew Maria (1430-1494), was born and educated at Ferrara ; he wrote *Orlando Innamorato,* a romantic poem which suggested to Ariosto his *Orlando Furioso.*

**Berni,** Francesco (1490-1536), an Italian poet, wrote satiric verses and extravaganzas entitled *Rimi Burleschi,* he revised or rather remodelled Boiardo's *Orlando Innamorato.*

**Lorenzo de' Medici** (1448-1492), surnamed "il Magnifico," was ruler of Florence after the suppression of the Pazzi, by whom his brother Giuliano was murdered ; he was a great patron of literature and wrote sonnets, canzoni, and lyric pieces in Italian, entitled *Stanze Bellissime, Rime Sacre, Poesie scelte* etc.

**Machiavelli,** Nicolo di Bernardo dei (1469-1527), was for many years secretary of the Republic of Florence, and distinguished for his political, historical, and other writings. His chief works are *Discorsi sulle Deche di Tito Livio* (Discourses upon Livy), *Arte della Guerra* (Art of War), *Istorie Fiorentino* (History of Florence), *Il Principe* (the Prince).

l. 32. **Ferrara,** a city of North Italy, twenty-seven miles north-of Bologna, was the residence of Ariosto and Tasso, and the birth-place of Savonarola. Addison's description is as follows: "At Ferrara I met nothing extraordinary. The town is very large but extremely thin of people. It has a citadel, and something like a fortification running round it, but so large that it requires more soldiers to defend it than the pope has in his whole dominions. The streets are as beautiful as any I have seen, in their length, breadth, and regularity. The Benedictines have the finest convent of the place. They showed us in the church Ariosto's monument ; his epitaph says he was 'Nobilitate generis atque animi clarus, in rebus publicis administrandis in regendis populis, in gravissimis et summis Pontificis legationibus prudentia, consilio eloquentia praestantissimus.' "

l. 33. **Ariosto,** Ludovico (1474-1533), the author of *Orlando Furioso,* wrote also seven satires, five comedies, many Italian and Latin poems, and a short prose tract entitled *Erbolato.*

**at Venice ... Tasso.** Addison writes thus: "I cannot forbear mentioning a custom at Venice which they tell me is particular to the common people of this country, of singing stanzas out of Tasso. They are set to a pretty solemn tune, and when one begins in any part of the poet, it is odds that he will be answered by somebody else that overhears him ; so that sometimes you have ten or a dozen in the neighbourhood of one another, taking verse after verse, and running on with the poem as far as their memories will carry them."

**Venice.** See p. 22, l. 28, *supra,* and note.

l. 34. **Tasso.** See p. 13, l. 2, *supra,* and note.

l. 35. **Valerius Flaccus** (died about 88), a poet of Padua in the time of Vespasian ; his chief work is the *Argonautica.*

l. 36. **Sidonius Apollinaris** (about 431-484), author of *Carmina* and *Epistolarum Libri IX.*, was bishop of Clermont in Auvergne in 472.

l. 36. **Ticin.** Addison writes : " Pavia is the Ticinum of the ancients, which took its name from the river Ticinus, which runs by it, and is now called the Tesin. This river falls into the Po, and is excessively rapid. The Bishop of Salisbury says that he ran down with the stream thirty miles in an hour, by the help of one rower. I do not know therefore why Silius Italicus has represented it as so very gentle and still a river in the beautiful description he has given of it.

"Caeruleas Ticinus aquas et stagna vadoso
 Perspicuus servat, turbari nescia, fundo,
 Ac nitidum viridi lente trahit amne liquorem ;
 Vix credas labi, ripis tam mitis opacis
 Argutos inter (volucrum certamina) cantus
 Somniferam ducit lucenti gurgite lympham."—Lib. 4.

"Smooth and untroubled the Ticinus flows,
 And through the crystal stream the shining bottom shows ;
 Scarce can the sight discover if it moves ;
 So wondrous slow amidst the shady groves,
 And tuneful birds that warble on its sides
 Within its gloomy banks the limpid liquor glides."

A poet of another nation would not have dwelt so long upon the clearness and transparency of the stream, but in Italy one seldom sees a river that is extremely bright and limpid, most of them falling down from the mountains, that make their waters very troubled and muddy, whereas the Tesin is only an outlet of that vast lake which the Italians now call the Lago Maggiore.

**Page 36, ll. 1, 2. The sulphurous stream of Albula ... Martial.** *Albula, ae,* or *Albulae, arum, sc. aquae,* several sulphur springs near Tibur, mentioned in Strabo and Pausanias, which were beneficial to invalids both for bathing and drinking. Only three now remain, which form three small lakes called Bagni di Tivoli.

Addison writes : " In our way to Tivoli I saw the rivulet of Salforata, formerly called Albula, and smelt the stench that arises from its waters some time before I saw them." Martial mentions this offensive smell in an epigram of the fourth book, as he does the rivulet itself in the first :

" Quod siccae redolet lacus lacunae,
 Crudaram nebulae quod Albularum."—Lib. iv., ep. iv.

" The drying marshes such a stench convey,
 Such the rank steams of reeking Albula."

" Itur ad Herculeae gelidas qua Tiburis arces,
 Canaque sulphureis Albula fumat aquis."—Lib. i., ep. v.

" As from high Rome to Tivoli you go,
 Where Albula's sulphureous waters flow."

**Martial** (about 41-104), a Roman poet, wrote fourteen books of *Epigrammata;* he was the friend of Juvenal, Quintilian, the younger Pliny, and the Emperor Domitian.

l. 3. **the illustrious dead of Santa Croce,** *sc.* Dante. This great poet was buried at Ravenna; but Florence has raised a monument to him in the church of Santa Croce, of which, probably, Macaulay was thinking.

l. 4. **Ravenna,** a city of Italy, formerly capital of the Romagna, in a marshy plain on the Montone, five miles from its port on the Adriatic.

**the Spectre Huntsman,** cf. Scott's *Wild Huntsman.*

l. 5. **Rimini,** the ancient Ariminum, a seaport city of central Italy, thirty-one miles south-east of Ravenna.

l. 6. **Francesca** da Rimini (d. 1285), daughter of Guido da Polenta, Lord of Ravenna; was married to Gianciotto Malatesta, Lord of Rimini. Her guilty love for her brother-in-law, Paolo, and her husband's revenge on them both, is the subject of a passage in Canto v. of Dante's *Inferno.*

l. 7. **Boileau-**Despréaux, Nicolas (1636-1711), a French poet, litterateur, and academician. His chief works are *Satires, Twelve Epistles, Epigrams, Art of Poetry,* and *Lutrin.* He was appointed joint historiographer with Racine.

l. 10. **Vincenzio Filicaja** (1642-1707), an elegant Italian poet; was senator of Florence, member of the Academies della Crusca and degli Arcadi, and was munificently patronized by Christina, Queen of Sweden. His works were chiefly patriotic sonnets, and odes celebrating the deliverance of Vienna, in 1683, from the Turks.

l. 12. **Somers.** See p. 15, l. 2, *supra,* and note.

l. 18. **tawdry,** showy, but without taste, gaudy. It was first used in the phrase "tawdry lace = a rustic necklace bought at St. Awdry's fair, held in the Isle of Ely (and elsewhere) on St. Awdry's Day, October 17." Awdry (or Audry) is a corruption of Etheldrida, the famous Saint who founded Ely Cathedral.

l. 19. **the lively Opera of Rosamond** was "inscribed to her Grace the Duchess of Marlborough."

l. 25. **heroic couplets to Pope.** See p. 11, l. 30, and p. 12, l. 5, *supra,* and notes.

**blank verse.** Verse that does not rhyme, each line usually consists of five iambic feet. Milton's *Paradise Lost* and *Paradise Regained* are examples of blank verse.

l. 26. **Rowe,** Nicholas (1673-1718) a dramatist, wrote *Jane Shore, The Fair Penitent* etc., and translated Lucan's *Pharsalia.*

l. 29. **Doctor Arne.** Thomas Augustine Arne (1710-1778) set Addison's *Rosamond* to music, and produced it in 1733 at the

theatre in Lincoln's Inn Fields; Arne's sister and younger
brother took parts in the play. He also set to music Milton's
*Comus* and Mallet's *Masques of Alfred*, in which "Rule Britannia" is introduced. He produced also operas entitled *Arta-
xerxes, Fairies, Love in a Village* etc., etc.

l. 33. **harpsichord**, an old harp-shaped instrument of music
(O.F. *harpechorde*, compounded of O.F. *harpe*, a harp, and *chorde*,
more commonly *corde*, a string).

**Page 37, l. 4. coalition** (in politics), an alliance for combined
action of distinct parties, persons, or states, without permanent
incorporation into one body.

l. 5. **Cowper**, William, first Earl of (1665-1723), the son of Sir
W. Cowper, a Hertfordshire baronet, was M.P. for the borough
of Hertford in 1695, and on the accession of Queen Anne was
made Queen's Counsel, and in 1705, Keeper of the Great Seal.
In 1706 he was appointed Lord High Chancellor; in 1717 he was
created an Earl; and in 1718 finally retired from office.

l. 6. **Somers**. See p. 15, l. 2, *supra*, and note.

**Halifax**. See p. 27, l. 3, *supra*, and note.

l. 12. **Sir Charles Hedges** was educated at Magdalen Hall and
Magdalen College, Oxford. In 1686 he was appointed Chancellor
and Vicar-General of Rochester, and soon after, Judge of the
High Court of Admiralty. In 1698 he was knighted, and served
in Parliament from 1701-1713. He was Secretary of State in
1700 under William III., and again, in 1702, under Anne. It
was he that drew up the much-debated Act of Abjuration. The
Tories made him Secretary of State; the Whigs prevailed on
Queen Anne to dismiss him from that office in 1706. He died in
1714.

Tickell writes of Addison: "His next advancement was to the
place of Under Secretary, which he held under Sir Charles
Hedges and the present Earl of Sunderland."

l. 13. **Charles, Earl of Sunderland**. This is the third earl of
that name (1675-1722). He married as his second wife a daughter
of Marlborough, and having fulfilled several diplomatic missions
was Secretary of State during the ascendency of the Whigs (1707-
1710). In 1715 he became Lord Privy Seal. Two years later he
was again Secretary of State, and was first Lord of the Treasury
from 1718 till the South Sea crash, when, though acquitted, he
was dismissed. (See also p. 29, l. 21, *supra*, and note.)

l. 17. **Harley**, Robert (1661-1724), was made Speaker of the
House of Commons in 1701, and was Secretary of State in 1708,
but was compelled to resign by Marlborough. He soon returned
to office with the Tories, as Chancellor of the Exchequer, in 1710,
and the Queen created him Earl of Oxford and Mortimer, and
Lord High Treasurer. He retained this office till a few days

before the death of Queen Anne in 1714. After the accession of George 1. he was impeached by the Whigs, and committed to the Tower for two years, then after a public trial, he was acquitted. After this he retired wholly from public business. He was a liberal encourager of literature, the patron of Pope and Swift, and a great collector of books. The Harleian collection of manuscripts in the British Museum was formed by him and his son Edward, who succeeded him. (See also Macaulay's "Essay on Boswell's Life of Johnson," in this series.)

l. 20. **the Duchess of Marlborough** (1660-1744) was all powerful at the accession of Queen Anne, but was supplanted by Abigail Hill in 1710, and compelled to give up her offices.

l. 21. **The Captain General**, the Duke of Marlborough. See p. 28, l. 20, *supra*, and note.

l. 27. **Sacheverell**, Henry (1672-1724), an English clergyman who was prosecuted in 1710 for some High Tory sermons preached at Derby and St. Paul's. The lightness of his sentence was regarded as a triumph by his party.

l. 31. **Somers**. See p. 15, l. 2, *supra*, and note.

l. 32. **Wharton**, Thomas, Marquis of (1640-1715), was a leading Whig politician under William III. and his successors, and was Lord-Lieutenant of Ireland for two years under Anne. He is said to have been the author of *Lillibullero*.

l. 33. **Malmsbury**, or Malmesbury, a municipal borough and market town in north-west division of Wiltshire. It returned two M.P.'s till 1832, and one till 1885, when it was disfranchised.

**Page 38**, l. 11. **chief Secretary for Ireland** under Wharton, who was Lord-Lieutenant of that country in 1709.

l. 14. **the heads of the great houses of Talbot, Russell, and Bentinck** are the Earl of Shrewsbury, the Earl of Russell, and the Duke of Portland respectively.

l. 16. **a post** etc., a secretaryship of state.

**Chatham**, William, Earl of. See Macaulay's essay on this statesman and orator.

**Fox**, Charles James (1749-1806), the third son of Henry Fox, and rival of the younger Pitt, was admittedly the finest orator of his time. Fox and Pitt were buried side by side. Scott writes thus in *Marmion* (Introduction):

> " Drop upon Fox's grave the tear,
> 'Twill trickle to his rival's bier :
> O'er Pitt's the mournful requiem sound,
> And Fox's shall the notes rebound."

l. 21. **the time when the Censorship of the Press ceased**, *i.e.* in 1695.

l. 22. **the time when parliamentary proceedings began to be freely reported,** *i.e.* about 1771.

l. 29. **the Conduct of the Allies** and of the late Ministry in beginning and carrying on the war, was the title of a political tract by Jonathan Swift, published ten days before the meeting of Parliament in December, 1711. Swift supports Harley, and discredits Godolphin by exhibiting the secret causes of affairs in England and the Continent.

l. 30. **the freeholder.** See p. 24, l. 36, *supra*, and note, and p. 64, l. 9, *infra*.

l. 36. **Antrim,** a county in the north-east of Ireland.

**Aberdeenshire,** a county on the east of Scotland.

**Page 39, l. 1. the pamphleteers** included in their numbers distinguished writers like Defoe, Addison, Steele, Swift, Bolingbroke, Somers, Atterbury, Prior, Pulteney, Dr. Shebbeare, Dr. Johnson, Edmund Burke.

l. 8. **triennial parliaments.** In the sixteenth year of Charles I., 1641, an Act was passed for holding parliaments once in three years at least. This Triennial Act was broken by the Long Parliament, and was repealed in 1664. Another Triennial Bill, passed in 1694, continued to be the statute law till the reign of George I., when it was repealed by the Septennial Act of 1716.

l. 10. **Mr. Pitt,** the Great Commoner, afterwards Earl of Chatham. See p. 38, l. 16, *supra*, and note.

**Mr. Fox.** See p. 38, l. 16, *supra*, and note.

l. 11. **Walpole,** Sir Robert, was Prime Minister of England twice, first, from 1715 to 1717 ; and when Sunderland was forced to resign after the bursting of the South Sea Bubble, Walpole was again made Premier (April, 1721), and held that office practically without a break for twenty-one years. His detractors dwell upon his inordinate love of power, and his systematic corruption ; while his admirers describe him as an able financier, a clever tactician in debate, a most serviceable minister to the House of Brunswick, and a firm friend of the Protestant succession. (See also Macaulay's " Boswell's Life of Johnson " in this series.) Thackeray, in his *Four Georges,* gives a sketch of this rough, unpolished, fox-hunting statesman. Macaulay describes his character in his " Essay on William Pitt, Earl of Chatham."

**Pulteney,** William, was born in 1682, and educated at Westminster School and Christ Church, Oxford. He began parliamentary life as a zealous Whig, but he was bitterly offended when, on the resignation of Carteret, Walpole neglected his claims, and made Newcastle Secretary of State. He then went into violent opposition, and joined Bolingbroke in conducting a paper called the *Craftsman,* which for years contained the

bitterest and ablest attacks on Walpole. On the resignation of
Walpole in 1742, Pulteney was created Earl of Bath, but from
that time his popularity and influence ceased. He became Prime
Minister in February, 1746, but was in office only two days. He
is said to have shortened his life by drinking, but we must
remember that hard drinking was the fashion of the day, and
that he nevertheless reached the good old age of 82 before he
died in 1764. (See also Macaulay's "Essay on William Pitt,
Earl of Chatham," and my notes.)

l. 17. **Grub Street**, a London street existing still but known
as Milton Street; it is in the parish of St. Giles, Cripplegate,
and runs from Fore Street to Chiswell Street. Johnson explains
it "As the name of a street in London much inhabited by writers
of small histories, dictionaries, and temporary poems." (See also
*Macaulay's Boswell's Life of Johnson* in this series.)

l. 20. **the Craftsman**, a periodical to which, among others,
Henry St. John, Viscount Bolingbroke, was a frequent contributor. See also l. 11, *supra*, note on Pulteney.

l. 25. **St. John**, Henry, after a brilliant career at Oxford,
entered Parliament as a Tory in 1701, and soon became a pro-
minent figure in his party. In course of time he became Secretary
at War, and Foreign Secretary, and received the title of Viscount
Bolingbroke. He was a Jacobite, and on the accession of the
Hanoverians he was dismissed from office and fled to France.
He was not only a statesman and orator but also a philosopher.
His chief works are : *Letters on the Study and Use of History,
Idea of a Patriot King*, and *Reflexions upon Exile.*" (See also note
on Bolingbroke, p. 63, l. 15, *infra*.)

l. 26. **Cowper.** See p. 37, l. 5, *supra*, and note.

l. 29. **Swift**, Jonathan (1667-1745), an Irish divine and writer,
friend of Sir W. Temple and of the Tory leaders of the reign of
Anne, conducted *The Examiner*, and wrote pamphlets in the
interest of the Tories ; in 1713 he became Dean of St. Patrick's.
His chief works are : *The Tale of a Tub, Gulliver's Travels, The
Drapier Letters, The Battle of the Books*, etc. (See also *Macaulay's
Boswell's Life of Johnson* in this series.)

l. 34. **cassock** (Fr. *casaque*, a long coat, sixteenth century) ;
in Littré (corresp. to Sp. and Pg. *casaca*, "a soldier's cassacke,
a frock, a horseman's coat," Minsheu), the military use is the
original, the ecclesiastical use appears to have arisen in English
in the seventeenth century (Murray).

**pudding sleeve**, a full sleeve, as a clergyman in full dress :
a phrase used by Swift himself.

**if he had not been encumbered by his cassock and his pudding
sleeves** means, therefore, if he had not been a clergyman.

**Page 40**, l. 21. **Nemesis, a** Greek goddess, who measured out to mortals happiness and misery ; in the Attic tragedians she appears as the goddess of Retribution, who brings down all immoderate good fortune, and checks the presumption that attends it, and is thus directly opposed to ὕβρις.

l. 29. **Mary Montague**, or Lady Mary Wortley Montague (1690-1762), was the daughter of the Duke of Kingston, and celebrated, even from her childhood, as Lady Mary Pierrepont, for her beauty and intellect : as a clever and beautiful child she was the pet and darling of the accomplished Whig society of the day, and a toast of the Kit-cat Club, when she was only eight years old. She married Mr. Edward Wortley Montague, whom she accompanied on his embassy to the court of Constantinople. She wrote letters, poems, and essays : she was the most brilliant letter-writer of this period : her letters are remarkable for their perfect style, precise judgment, and vivacious sarcasm.

l. 31. **The malignant Pope.** Lady Mary Wortley Montague calls him "the wicked wasp of Twickenham," and continues thus, "His lies affect me now no more. That man has a malignant and ungenerous heart ; and he is base enough to assume the mask of a moralist, in order to decry human nature, and to give a decent vent to his hatred of man and woman kind."

l. 33. **Swift.** See p. 39, l. 28, *supra*, and note.

l. 34. **Stella.** The poetical name bestowed by Dean Swift upon Miss Esther Johnson, whose tutor he was, and whom he married privately in 1716. Esther is perhaps akin to Gk. ἀστήρ, Lat. *Stella*, a star.

l. 35. **Steele**, Richard (1671-1729), dramatist and essayist, produced *The Christian Hero, The Funeral* or *Grief à la Mode, The Tender Husband, The Lying Lover, The Crisis* ; contributions to the *Tatler, Guardian*, and *Spectator* ; and several other works. He was "Governor of the Royal Company of Comedians, to which post, and to that of Surveyor of the Royal Stables at Hampton Court, and to the Commission of the Peace for Middlesex, and to the honour of Knighthood, Steele had been preferred soon after the accession of George I." (Thackeray's *Humorists*). His reputation as a writer procured him also the place of Commissioner of the Stamp office, which he resigned on being chosen M.P. for Stockbridge. But "he outlived his places, his schemes, his wife, his income, his health, and almost everything but his kind heart " (Thackeray's *English Humorists*).

**Page 41**, l. 2. **Terence**, or Publius Terentius Afer (B.C. 195-159), was a distinguished writer of Latin comedies : only six of his works are extant, viz. *Andria, Eunuchus, Heautontimorumenos, Phormio, Adelphi*, and *Hecyra*.

l. 3. **Catullus.** See p. 7, l. 3, *supra*, and note.

l. 5. **Young**, Edward (1684-1765), is described by Taine as "the author of *Night Thoughts*, a clergyman and courtier, who, having vainly attempted to enter Parliament, then to become a bishop, married, lost his wife and children, and made use of his misfortunes to write Meditations on Life, Death, Immortality, Time, Friendship, The Christian Triumph, Virtue's Apology, A Moral Survey of the Nocturnal Heavens, and many other similar pieces." The following are the titles of some of his works : *The Last Day, The Force of Religion or Vanquished Love, The Revenge, The Brothers, Ocean—an Ode, Busiris, King of Egypt* etc. (See also *Macaulay's Boswell's Life of Johnson* in this series.)

l. 16. "**assented with civil leer.**" An adaptation of

"Damn with faint praise, assent with civil leer,"

a line in Pope's *Epistle to Dr. Arbuthnot*, in the paragraph descriptive of Atticus (*i.e.* Addison).

l. 17. **coxcomb** [= cockscomb] : (1) a cap worn by a professional fool like a cock's comb in shape and colour (obs.); (2) a ludicrous appellation for the head (obs.); (3) a fool, simpleton (obs.), now a foolish, conceited, showy person, vain of his accomplishments, appearance, or dress ; a fop ; "a superficial pretender to knowledge or accomplishments" (J). (Murray's *Dict.*).

l. 19. **The Tatler**, or, "Lucubrations of Isaac Bickerstaff, Esq." A periodical publication started by Steele in 1709, and issued every Tuesday, Thursday, and Saturday. The first number was published on Tuesday, 12th April, 1709, the last number on 2nd January, 1711.

**Mr. Softly's sonnet.** See *Tatler*, No. 163.

l. 20. **the Spectator's dialogue ... lady Q—p—t—s.** See *Spectator*, Nos. 567 and 568.

l. 31. **St. Paul's in Covent Garden.** This church was built about the year 1633 by Inigo Jones at the expense of Francis, the fourth Earl of Bedford. In 1795 the interior was destroyed by fire, and restored at the expense of the parishioners. Here were buried many noted characters, Robert Carr, Earl of Somerset, the favourite of James I. ; Sir Peter Lely, the portrait painter ; Samuel Butler, the author of *Hudibras* ; W. Wycherley, Thomas Southerne, and Susannah Centlivre, the dramatists ; Robert Wilks, Thomas King, and Charles Macklin, the authors ; Grinling Gibbons, the sculptor and carver ; Dr. Arne, the musical composer ; and John Wolcot, the memorable Peter Pindar.

**Page 42,** l. 7. **peccadillo,** a small offence or sin. Diminutive of Sp. *peccado*, a sin ; Lat. *peccatum*, neuter of perf. part. *peccatus*, from *peccare*, to sin.

ll. 29-31. **veneration ... with which Johnson was regarded by Boswell, or Warburton by Hurd.** Boswell's affection, respect, and veneration for Johnson has been called "*lues Boswelliana.*" Macaulay's criticism of Boswell's character is too severe.    (See Appendix B to *Boswell's Life of Johnson* in this series.)   Richard Hurd, D.D., successively Bishop of Lichfield, and Coventry, and Worcester, edited in 1788 the works of William Warburton, Bishop of Gloucester.    Hurd was full of adulation for his brother bishop.

l. 32. **adulation,** flattery.    Lat. *adulari,* to flatter, fawn, to wag the tail as a dog does, which Curtius connects with *swal,* to wag, roll (cf. Skt. *val,* to wag, move to and fro ; Lat. *volvere,* to roll).   Fick identifies -*ul* in *adulari* with Gk. *ovpá,* a tail (Skeat).

l. 36. **coterie,** a set, company.    Littré connects it with O.Fr. *coterie, cotterie,* servile tenure ; *cottier,* a cottar, etc.    A *coterie* (Low Lat. *coteria*) was a tenure of land by cottars who clubbed together.

**Page 43,** l. 1. **Eustace Budgell** (1686-1737), a miscellaneous writer, was the son of Gilbert Budgell, D.D., of St. Thomas, Exeter, by his first wife, Mary, only daughter of Bishop Gulston of Bristol, whose sister was wife of Lancelot, and Mother of Joseph Addison.    Budgell was educated at Trinity College, Oxford.    He entered the Inner Temple and was called to the bar.    Addison, while secretary to Wharton, the Lord-Lieutenant of Ireland, made Budgell a clerk in his office.    He shared Addison's lodgings during the last years of Queen Anne, and took a considerable part in the *Spectator* ; 37 papers are ascribed to him.    Addison secured for Budgell several other lucrative appointments, and upon leaving Ireland in 1717 procured for him the place of Accountant General, worth £400 a year.    Budgell inherited in 1711 an estate of £950 a year encumbered with some debt, but subsequently was involved in great difficulties and vexatious lawsuits, which seem to have affected his brain.    He went from bad to worse, and in 1733 seems to have been party to the production of a fictitious will, by which the testator, Matthew Tindal, was said to give £2100, his manuscripts, and some property to Budgell.    It turned out that Tindal's whole property consisted of £1900 stock, but £1800 of this had been sold out and lent on bond to Budgell.    One of the bonds for £1000 had disappeared.    Budgell's character was hopelessly blasted, and on 4th May, 1737, he drove to Dorset Stairs, filled his pockets with stones, took a boat, plunged overboard, and was drowned.    He left a paper on his desk with these words, " What Cato did and Addison approved cannot be wrong."

l. 11. **gambler,** he lost £20,000, as he says, in the South Sea Bubble.

l. 12. **lampooner,** Budgell became a Grub Street author, and wrote pamphlets against Sunderland, Walpole, and others.

l. 17. **Ambrose Phillipps** (1671-1749), poet and dramatist, published *Pastorals* (ridiculed by Pope, who nicknamed him "Namby Pamby"), *A Poetical Letter from Copenhagen*, *Persian Tales*, *The Distrest Mother*, *The Briton*, and *Poems*. He was also editor for some time of the *Freethinker*. (See also *Macaulay's Boswell's Life of Johnson* in this series.)

l. 21. **Richard Steele**, see p. 40, l. 35, *supra*, and note.

**Thomas Tickell** was a poet and politician (1686-1740). He wrote *The Prospect of Peace*, *The Royal Progress*, *An Epistle to a Gentleman at Avignon*, *Verses on Cato*, *Kensington Gardens*, *Colin and Lucy*, and a translation of the first book of the *Iliad*. He contributed papers to the *Spectator* and also to the *Guardian*. He published a collected edition of Addison's works, and an elegy on his friend. (See also *Macaulay's Boswell's Life of Johnson*.)

l. 24. **the Charter House.** The Hospital of the Charter House was founded by Thomas Sutton in the reign of James I. In 1609 he procured " an Act of Parliament for the foundation of a Hospital and Free Grammar School at Hallingbury in Essex, but having subsequently purchased from the Earl of Suffolk the lately dissolved Charter House beside Smithfield, in Middlesex, he sought and obtained in the 9th of James I. certain letters patent which empowered him to found such Hospital and School in the Charter House." In 1872 the school was removed from Charter House Square to Godalming, Surrey.

l. 28. **the philosopher's stone.** The ancient alchemists thought that there was a substance which could convert all baser metals to gold ; this imaginary substance they named the philosopher's stone.

l. 36. **rake**, a wild, dissolute fellow. M.E. *rakel*, rash (corrupted into rake-hell). Cf. Swed. dial. *rakkela*, vagabond, connected with *rakkla*, to wander, rove, frequent form of *raka*, to run hastily (Skeat).

**swindler**, a cheat, one of our few loan words from High German. G. *schwindler*, an extravagant projector, a swindler. G. *schwindeln*, to be dizzy, act thoughtlessly, to cheat (Skeat).

**Page 44, l. 4. spunging-house**, or sponginghouse, the bailiff's house in which debtors were confined before they were taken to jail, or until they compounded with their creditors.

l. 14. **bailiff** (M.E. *baillif*, O.F. *baillif*, late Lat. *bajulivus*, prop. an adj. fr. *bajulus*, originally " carrier," afterwards " carrier on," manager, administrator).
1. One charged with public administrative authority in a certain district. (a) In England formerly applied to the king's officers generally, including sheriffs, mayors etc., nominated by him, but especially to the chief officer of a hundred ; still the

K

title of the chief magistrate of various towns, as the *High-bailiff of Westminster*, and of the keeper of some of the Royal castles, as the *Bailiff of Dover Castle*.  (*b*) Used as the English form of the title of various foreign magistrates : *e.g.* the French *bailli*, and German *landvogt*, also of the *bailly*, or first civil officer, in the Channel Islands, and formerly also of the Scotch *bailie*.

2.  An officer of justice under a sheriff, who executes writs and processes, distrains, and arrests : a warrant officer, pursuivant, or catchpoll (Murray's *Dictionary*).

l. 15.  **Savage**, Richard (1698-1743), poet and dramatist, noted for his genius, irregular and dissipated life, and consequent misery and privation.  He was the author of *Love in a Veil*, *The Bastard*, *The Wanderer*, *Sir Thomas Overbury*, and other works. Johnson published *The Life of Richard Savage* in 1744.  See also *Macaulay's Boswell's Life of Johnson* in this series.

l. 16.  **Steele**.  See p. 40, l. 35, *supra*, and note.

l. 26.  **Amelia**, a novel by Henry Fielding, published in 1751, of which we are told that Dr. Johnson " read it through without stopping."

l. 28.  **Booth**.  Lady Mary Wortley Montague wrote : " H. Fielding has given a true picture of himself and his first wife in the character of Mr. and Mrs. Booth, some compliments to his own figure excepted ; and I am persuaded some of the incidents he mentions are real matters of fact."    Thackeray says : " Amelia pleads for her husband, Will Booth ; Amelia pleads for her reckless, kindly old father, Harry Fielding.  To have invented that character is not only a triumph of art ; it is a good action.  They say it was in his own home Fielding knew her and loved her ; and from his own wife that he drew the most charming character in English fiction. ... Amelia is not perhaps a better story than Tom Jones, but it has the better ethics."

**Page 45, l. 6.  the Twelve Cæsars**.  Julius Caesar and the Emperors ; Augustus (B.C. 27) ; Tiberius (Claudius Nero), A.D. 14 ; Cains Caligula (37) ; Claudius I. (Tiberius Drusus), 41 ; Nero (Claudius), 54 ; Galba (Servius Sulpicius), 68 ; Otho (M. Salvius), 69 ; Vitellius (Aulus), 69 ; Vespasian (Titus Flavius), 69 ; Titus (Vespasian), 79 ; Domitian (Titus Flavius), 81.

**Bayle's Dictionary**, entitled *Dictionnaire Historique et Critique*, was first published in 1696.  The author, Pierre Bayle (1647-1706), was well versed in metaphysics, morals, theology, history, and politics.  Voltaire describes him as "the first of logicians and sceptics."    Bayle compares himself to Homer's cloud-compelling Jupiter.   "My talent," he says, "consists in raising doubts ; but they are only doubts."

l. 15.  **Tickell**.  See p. 43, l. 21, *supra*, and note.

l. 18. **Rosamond**, an opera inscribed to Her Grace the Duchess of Marlborough, was written while Addison was Under-Secretary to Sir Charles Hedges and the Earl of Sunderland (1706). See p. 36, l. 9, *supra*.

l. 22. **the rival bulls in Virgil.**   See *Georgic*, iii. 215 etc., and *Aeneid*, xii. 715 etc.

l. 23. **Wharton.**  See p. 37, l. 32, *supra*, and note.

l. 28. **patent.**  All grants of offices, honours, pensions, and particulars of individual and corporate privileges received from the Sovereign, and contained in charters or letters patent, that is, open letters, *litterae patentes*. They were so called because they are not sealed, but exposed to open view with the great seal pendent from the bottom, and were supposed to be of a public nature, and addressed to all the king's subjects.

l. 29. **Budgell.**  See p. 43, l. 1, *supra*, and note.

**Page 46**, l. 8. **Cavan**, capital of the County Cavan, the southernmost county of Ulster ; the town Cavan is seventy-two miles south-west of Belfast.

l. 16. **Gerard Hamilton** (1729-1796) was elected M.P. for Petersfield in 1754, and in the following year delivered the first and almost only speech he ever made in the British Parliament, from which he derived the nickname of "Single-Speech Hamilton." See *Macaulay's Boswell's Life of Johnson* and *Essay on Chatham.*

l. 25. **Latin verses**, viz. *Pax Gulielmi Auspiciis Europae reddita*, 1697 ; *Barometri descriptio*, *Pygmaeo-Geranomachia*, *Resurrectio delineata ad altare Col. Magd. Oxon.*, *Sphaeristerium*, *Ad D. D. Hannes insignissimum Medicum et poetam*, *Machinae gesticulantes*, *ad insignissimum virum D. Tho. Burnetum Sacrae theoriae telluris autorem.*

l. 26. **English verses** etc.   *A Poem to His Majesty ; Translations of Virgil, Horace, Ovid ; The Campaign* etc.

l. 27. **a book of travels.**   *Remarks on several parts of Italy* etc., in the years 1701, 1702, 1703.

l. 35. **Periodical papers** etc.  The first authentic English newspaper now known to exist is in the British Museum, entitled "The 23rd of May—The Weekly News from Italy, Germany etc.," published in 1622 by Nathaniel Butter, Nicholas Bourne, and Thomas Archer.  The names of other newspapers prior to the *Spectator* are *The Certain Newes of this Present Week, Diurnal occurrences, or the Heads of several Proceedings in both Houses of Parliament, Mercurius Britannicus, M. Pragmaticus, M. Politicus, M. Aulicus, The Public Intelligencer, The News, The Oxford Gazette*, which, with its twenty-fourth number became *The London Gazette*, and subsequently *The Gazette, The City Mercury,* or *Advertisements concerning Trade, Domestick Intelligence, The Universal Intelligence, The English Courant, The London Courant, The London Mercury, The Orange Gazette, The London Intelligence, The Harlem Courant, The Flying Post, Lloyd's News, Lloyd's List, The Country Gentleman's Courant, The Review.*

The first London daily paper was the *Postboy* (1695), it lasted for only four numbers ; the first successful daily newspaper was the *Daily Courant* (1703). (See *Encyclopaedia Britannica*, Article, " Newspapers.")

**Page 47, l. 5. Gazetteer,** publisher of news.

**l. 15. Will's,** a coffee-house in Russell Street, Covent Garden, the favourite meeting-place of men of letters. The paper from Will's criticized the current dramas, or contained a copy of verses from some author of repute, or a piece of general literary criticism (Courthope).

**the Grecian,** a coffee-house in Devereux Street in the Strand, the oldest in London, was the rendezvous of the learned Templars.

In *Tatler*, No. 1, the editor gives the following account of the contents of his paper : " All accounts of Gallantry, Pleasure, and Entertainment shall be under the article of White's chocolate-house ; Poetry under that of Will's coffee-house ; Learning under the title of Grecian ; Foreign and Domestic News you will have from St. James' coffee-house ; and what else I have to offer on any other subject shall be dated from my own apartment."

**l. 17. pasquinade,** a lampoon, satire. Formerly also *pasquil,* from F. *pasquille,* " a pas-quill " (Cot.). " F. *pasquin,* the name of an image or post in Rome whereon libels and defamatory rimes are fastened and fathered ; also a pasquill " (Cot.). It. *pasquino,* "a statue in Rome on which all libels are fathered " (Florio). Whence *pasquinata,* a libel, the original of F. *pasquinada.* " In the 16th century at the stall of a cobbler named *Pasquin* (Pasquino) at Rome, a number of idle persons used to assemble to listen to his pleasant sallies, and to relate little anecdotes in their turn, and indulge themselves in raillery at the expense of the passers-by. After the cobbler's death the statue of a gladiator was found near his stall, to which the people gave his name, and on which the wits of the time, secretly at night, affixed their lampoons " (Haydn, *Dict. of Dates*). " The statue still stands at the corner of the Palazzo Bracchi, near the Piazza Navona." Note in Gloss. to Bacon, *Adv. of Learning,* ed. Wright. (Skeat.)

**l. 24. rake.** See p. 43, l. 36, *supra,* and note.

**l. 33. Astrologer** (Gr. ἀστρολόγος, astronomer, prop. adj., telling the stars).

1. An observer of the stars, a practical astronomer. Obs.

(when astrologer and astronomer began to be differentiated, the relation between them was, at first, the converse of the present usage).

2. One who professes astrology in the modern sense : who pretends to judge of the influence of the stars upon human affairs (Murray).

l. 34. **Mr. Paul Pry**, the hero of a comedy by John Poole, who is described as " one of those idle, meddling fellows, who, having no employment themselves, are perpetually interfering in other people's affairs." The same author wrote *Little Peddlington and the Peddlingtonians* (1839). (See also *Macaulay's Boswell's Life of Johnston* in this series.)

**Mr. Samuel Pickwick**, the hero of the novel by Charles Dickens, published in 1836, entitled *The Posthumous Papers of the Pickwick Club*.

ll. 35, 36. **Swift ... Bickerstaff**. Swift derived the name Bickerstaff from a blacksmith's sign, and added Isaac as a humorous praenomen.

**Partridge**, an almanac-maker, who pretended to foretell the future.

**Page 48, l. 8. the Tatler.** See p. 41, l. 9, *supra*, and note.

l. 19. **St. George's Channel**, the sea between England and Ireland.

l. 29. **Dryden.** See p. 18, l. 24, *supra*, and note.

Dr. Johnson criticizes Dryden's characteristics thus : " To him we owe the improvement, perhaps the completion of our metre, the refinement of our language, and much of the correctness of our sentiments. By him we are taught 'sapere et fari,' to think naturally and express forcibly. ... What was said of Rome, adorned by Augustus, may be applied by an easy metaphor to English poetry embellished by Dryden : 'Lateritiam invenit, marneorcam reliquit' (He found it brick and left it marble)."

Edmond Malone collected and edited all Dryden's prose writings in 1800.

l. 29. **Temple**, Sir William, statesman and writer of letters, miscellanies, essays, etc. (1628-1698). See Macaulay's essay on *Memoirs of the Life, Works, and Correspondence of Sir William Temple*, by the Right Hon. Thomas Peregrine Courtenay.

l. 33. **Horace Walpole** (1717-1797), Earl of Oxford, youngest son of Sir Robert Walpole, was an antiquary and prolific writer. His chief works are : *The Castle of Otranto, The Mysterious Mother, Historic Doubts on the Life and Reign of Richard III., Memoirs of the Reign of George III.* etc., etc., and also *Letters*. For a criticism of his *Letters* etc., see Macaulay's *Essays*.

the half Latin style of Dr. Johnson.   See *Macaulay's Bos well's Life of Johnson*, p. 49 etc., in this series.

l. 34. the half German jargon of the present day, an allusion to the eccentric style of Carlyle, who had produced a translation of the *Wilhelm Meister* of Goethe (1824), *Life of Schiller* (1825), *Specimens of German Romance* (1827); he was also a frequent contributor to the *Edinburgh Review*: his articles to this review, many of which were on German subjects, became, as time went on, more and more markedly Carlylese in style, and peculiarly unlike the contributions of Macaulay to the same paper.

Page 49, l. 3. Menander (B.C. 342-201), an Athenian, the most distinguished poet of the New Comedy, was a pupil of Theophrastus, and an intimate friend of Epicurus; he wrote upwards of 100 comedies, of which only fragments are extant; we can form some idea of his works from those of Terence, who was little more than a translator of Menander, but the Latin imitations lacked the wit and elegance of the Greek originals.

l. 5. Cowley, Abraham, poet, dramatist, and essayist (1618-1667), wrote *Naufragium Joculare; Comoedia; Love's Riddle, a Pastoral Comedy; The Mistress; The Cutter of Coleman Street; The Wish; An Ode on Wit; The Davideis,* and other works. His prose works have been regarded as little less delightful than those of Montaigne.   Taine writes of him thus: "On this boundary line of a closing and dawning literature, a poet appeared, one of the most approved and illustrious of his time, Abraham Cowley, a precocious child, a reader and a versifier like Pope, and who, like Pope, having known passions less than books, busied himself less about things than about words. ... His prose is as easy and sensible as his poetry is contorted and unreasonable.   A polished man writing for polished men, pretty much as he would speak to them in a drawing-room—this I take to be the idea which they had for a good author in the seventeenth century.   It is the idea which Cowley's essays leave of his character; it is the kind of talent which the writers of the coming age take for their model; and he is the first of that grave and amiable group which, continued in Temple, reaches so far as to include Addison."

Butler, Samuel (1600-1680), wrote the burlesque poem, *Hudibras*, and other minor works.   *Hudibras* is a satire on the Puritans, especially the Presbyterians and Independents. "Butler," says Macaulay, "had as much wit and learning as Cowley, and knew, what Cowley never knew, how to use them. A great command of homely English distinguishes him still more from the other writers of the time."

"In general," says Hazlitt, "he ridicules not persons, but things, not a party, but their principles, which may belong, as time and occasion serve, to one set of solemn pretenders or

another. This he has done most effectually in every possible
way, and from every possible source, learned or unlearned. He
has exhausted the moods and figures of satire and sophistry.
His rhymes are as witty as his reasons."

ll. 6, 7. **the lines to Sir Godfrey Kneller** on his Picture of the
King (George I.) are as follows :

" Kneller, with silence and surprise
We see Britannia's monarch rise,
A godlike form, by thee display'd,
In all the force of light and shade ;
And, aw'd by thy delusive hand,
As in the presence-chamber stand.
  The magic of thy art calls forth
His secret soul and hidden worth,
His probity and mildness shows
His care of friends and scorn of foes :
In every stroke, in every line,
Does some exalted virtue shine,
And Albion's happiness we trace
Through all the features of his face.
  O may I live to hail the day,
When the glad nation shall survey
•Their sov'reign, through his wide command,
Passing in progress o'er the land !
Each heart shall bend, and every voice
In loud applauding shouts rejoice,
Whilst all his gracious aspect praise,
And crowds grow loyal as they gaze.
  The image on the medal placed,
With its bright round of titles grac'd,
And, stamp'd on British coins, shall live,
To richest ores the value give,
Or, wrought within the curious mould,
Shape and adorn the running gold.
To bear this form, the genial sun
Has daily, since his course begun,
Rejoic'd the metal to refine
And ripen'd the Peruvian mine.
  Thou, Kneller, long with noble pride,
The foremost of thy art, hast vied
With nature in a generous strife,
And touch'd the canvas into life.
Thy pencil has, by monarchs sought,
From reign to reign in ermine wrought,
And in their robes of state array'd,
The kings of half an age display'd.
  Here swarthy Charles appears, and there

His brother with dejected air :
Triumphant Nassau here we find,
And with him bright Maria joined :
There Anna, great as when she sent
Her armies through the continent,
Ere yet her hero was disgrac'd.
O may fam'd Brunswick be the last,
(Though heaven should with my wish agree,
And long preserve thy art with thee)
The last, the happiest British king,
Whom thou shalt paint, or I shall sing.
  Wise Phidias, thus his skill to prove,
Through many a god advanced to Jove,
And taught the polish'd rocks to shine
With airs and lineaments divine ;
Till Greece, amaz'd, and half afraid,
Th' assembled deities survey'd.
  Great Pan, who wont to chase the fair,
And lov'd the spreading oak, was there ;
Old Saturn too, with up-cast eyes,
Beheld his abdicated skies ;
And mighty Mars, for wars renown'd
In adamantine armour frown'd :
By him the childless goddess rose,    •
Minerva, studious to compose
Her twisted threads ; the web she strung,
And o'er a loom of marble hung :
Thetis, the troubled ocean's queen,
Match'd with a mortal, next was seen,
Reclining on a funeral urn,
Her short-lived darling son to mourn.
The last was he, whose thunder slew
The Titan race, a rebel crew,
That from a hundred hills ally'd
In impious leagues their king defy'd.
  This wonder of the sculptor's hand
Produced, his art was at a stand :
For who would hope new fame to raise,
Or risk his well-establish'd praise,
That, his high genius to approve,
Had drawn a George, or carv'd a Jove."

Sir Godfrey Kneller (1648-1723) was an eminent portrait painter,
patronized by Charles II., James II., William III., the Czar
Peter, Queen Anne, and George I.  Pope wrote the following
epitaph on his tomb in Westminster Abbey :

  Kneller, by Heaven, and not a master, taught,
  Whose Art was Nature, and whose pictures thought ;

Now for two ages having snatch'd from fate
Whate'er was beauteous, or whate'er was great
Lies crown'd with princes' honours, poets' lays,
Due to his merit, and brave thirst of praise.
   Living, great nature fear'd he might outvie
Her works; and dying, fears herself may die."

l. 19. **Clarendon,** Edward Hyde, Earl of (1608-1674), a staunch supporter of the Royalist cause during the Civil War and after the Restoration. His *History of Rebellion*, long regarded as a first-rate historical authority, has been proved to be not only a partial but a very inaccurate and untrustworthy narrative; but the dignity and liveliness of his style will ever rank Lord Clarendon among the great classical English prose-writers. He is excellent in the delineation of character, and these are the parts of his work most carefully elaborated. Macaulay says (in his Essay on *Lord Bacon*), "We suffer ourselves to be delighted by the keenness of Clarendon's observation, and by the sober majesty of his style, till we forget the oppressor and the bigot in the historian."

l. 23. **Cervantes,** de Saavedra, Miguel (1547-1616), began life as a page, afterwards entered the army, lost an arm at Lepanto, in 1571, and on his way home was captured by pirates who took him to Algiers; after five years he was ransomed and went to Madrid. He now devoted himself to literature; he wrote about 30 dramas and the immortal novel, *Don Quixote.*

l. 35. **Swift.** See p. 39, l. 28, *supra*, and note.

**Voltaire.** See p. 64, l. 7, *infra*, and note.

**Page 50,** l. 3. **buffoon** (Fr. *buffon, bouffon*, It. *buffone*, buffoon, fr. *buffa*, a jest, conn. with *buffare* to puff). Tommaseo and Bellini consider the sense of "jest" to be developed from that of "puff of wind," applied to anything light and frivolous: others *e.g.* Littré, refer it to the notion of puffing out the cheeks as a comic gesture (Murray's *Dictionary*).

1. A pantomime dance, obs.

2. A man whose profession is to make sport by low jests and antick postures" (J): a comic actor, clown; a jester, fool.

3. *transf.*, a low jester; "a man that practises indecent raillery" (J); a wag, a joker (implying contempt or disapprobation).

l. 13. **commination service.** A service used on the first day of Lent, denouncing God's anger and judgments against sinners.

l. 22. **Jack Pudding.** A buffoon that performs such tricks as swallowing yards of black-pudding etc. The word is compounded of Jack and pudding, just as a stage buffoon is called in French Jean-potage (John-potage), and in German Hans-wurst (John-sausage). See also *Spectator*, No. 47.

**Cynic** (Gr. κυνικός, dog-like, currish, churlish, cynic, fr. κύων, κυνός, dog).

1. One of a sect of philosophers in ancient Greece founded by Antisthenes, a pupil of Socrates, who were marked by an ostentatious contempt for ease, wealth, and the enjoyments of life; the most famous was Diogenes, a pupil of Antisthenes, who carried the principles of the sect to an extreme of asceticism.

2. A person disposed to rail or find fault; now usually one who shows a disposition to disbelieve in the sincerity or goodness of human motives and actions, and is wont to express this by sneers and sarcasms; a sneering fault-finder (Murray).

l. 30. **Abbé Coyer**, Gabriel Francis, wrote *A Life of Jean Sobreski, Moral Bagatelles, The Commercial Nobles, Travels in Italy, Holland* etc., *New Observations on England:* he died in 1782.

**Pansophe**, probably a name made up by Coyer, as Panurge was made by Rabelais.

l. 32. **Arbuthnot**, John, M.D. (1675-1735), was eminent as a physician, mathematician, and classical scholar. As a politician he was a staunch Tory, and with Swift became a member of the October Club, established in 1720 by Oxford, Bolingbroke, and their political and literary friends. He was also a member of the Scriblerus Club. He wrote *An Examination of Dr. Woodward's Account of the Deluge: An Essay on the Usefulness of Mathematical Learning; A Treatise concerning the Altercation or Scolding of the Ancients; The Art of Political Lying; Law is a Bottomless Pit, or the History of John Bull;* and other works. Dr. Johnson considered him "the first man among the eminent writers in Queen Anne's time." Swift said of him that "he has more wit than we all have; and more humanity than wit." Thackeray calls him "one of the wisest, wittiest, most accomplished, gentlest of mankind." Warton says, "It is known he gave numberless hints to Pope, Swift, and Gay, of some of the most striking parts of their works." Pope has given us his sentiments in his *Epistle to Dr. Arbuthnot.*

**Page 51, l. 1. the World.** A series of essays and sketches, edited by Edward Moore (1712-1752), some of which were contributed by Lord Chesterfield.

**the Connoisseur.** A periodical conducted by George Colman, the elder, and Bonnel Thornton, which began in January, 1754, and ended its career in 1756.

**the Mirror.** A literary paper, published on Tuesdays and Fridays in Edinburgh, from January 23, 1779, to May 27, 1780; it was edited by Henry Mackenzie, the novelist, assisted by contributions from George Home, clerk of the court of session; William, Lord Craig; Alexander, Lord Abercromby; William

M'Leod, Lord Bannatyne, Lord Cullen, Prof. Richardson, Lord Hailes, Lord Woodhouselee, Dr. Beattie, and others.

**the Lounger.** A weekly periodical published in Edinburgh from Saturday, February 5, 1785, to January 6, 1787, under the same editor, and with many of the same contributors as the *Mirror* had had.

l. 15. **the Great First Cause,** almost equivalent to Lucretius' "primordia rerum," Bk. i. 55 etc.

" Nam tibi de summa caeli ratione deumque
Disserere incipiam et rerum primordia pandam,
Unde omnis natura creet res auctet alatque
Quove eadem rursum natura perempta resolvat " etc.

l. 19. **Mephistophiles,** a devil in Goethe's *Faust,* next in rank to Satan; his character is that of a sneering, jeering, leering tempter.

l. 20. **Puck,** or Robin Goodfellow, the merry, mischievous sprite that plays a prominent part in *A Midsummer Night's Dream.*

**Soame Jenyns** (1704-1787), a poet and miscellaneous writer, was the author of *The Art of Dancing,* a poem ; *A Free Inquiry into the Nature and Origin of Evil,* and *A Review of the Internal Evidences of the Christian Religion.*

l. 21. **Seraphim.** An order of celestial beings, whom Isaiah beheld in vision standing above Jehovah as He sat upon His throne (*Is.* vi. 2). They are described as having each of them three pairs of wings, with one of which they covered their faces (a token of humility); with the second they covered their feet (a token of respect); while with the third they flew. They seem to have borne a general resemblance to the human figure, for they are represented as having a face, a voice, feet, and hands (ver. 6). Their occupation was twofold—to celebrate the praises of Jehovah's holiness and power (ver. 3), and to act as the medium of communication between heaven and earth (ver. 6).

The meaning of the word "seraph" is extremely doubtful; the only word which resembles it in the current Hebrew is *saraph,* "to burn," whence the idea of *brilliancy* has been extracted ; but it is objected that the Hebrew term never bears this secondary sense. Gesenius connects it with an Arabic term signifying *high* or *exalted* ; and this may be regarded as the generally received etymology.

**just men made perfect,** an adaptation of *Hebrews,* xii. 23, "the spirits of just men made perfect."

**Page 52, l. 5. Bettesworth,** an Irishman, satirized by Swift in *Miscellanies* : "On the Archbishop of Cashell and Bettesworth" and in "The Yahoo's Overthrow."

**Franc de Pompignan.** Jean Jacques de Franc, Marquess de Pompignan (1709-1784), was born at Montauban and brought up to the law; he became Advocate-General and afterwards first President of the Court of Aides at Montauban. He won distinction also as a poet, and in 1734 produced a tragedy entitled *Didon.* In 1764 he was admitted to the French Academy, and became an avowed opponent of the Encyclopaedists. He was, in consequence, satirized by Voltaire and others.

l. 16. **Jeremy Collier** (1650-1726), a non-juring bishop, published *A Short View of the Profaneness and Immorality of the English Stage,* and was answered by Congreve, Vanbrugh, Dennis, Dr. Drake, and others. The defence was weak, and the victory remained with Collier.

l. 17. **Etherege,** Sir George (1636-1689), dramatist and poet, wrote *The Comical Revenge, or Love in a Tub; She Would if she Could;* and *The Man of Mode, or Sir Fopling Flutter.* See also Macaulay's Essay on *The Comic Dramatists of the Restoration.*

l. 18. **Wycherley,** William (1640-1715), dramatist and poet, and a brilliant figure in the gay and profligate society of the day, wrote *Love in a Wood, The Gentleman Dancing Master, The Country Wife,* and *The Plain Dealer.* See also Macaulay's Essay on *The Comic Dramatists of the Restoration.*

l. 21. **the Puritans,** the name first given, it is said, about 1564, to persons that aimed at greater purity of doctrine, holiness of living, and stricter discipline than others. They withdrew from the Established Church, professing to follow the Word of God alone, and maintaining that the Church retained many human inventions and popish superstitions (Haydn's *Dictionary of Dates*).

l. 23. **Hale,** Sir Matthew (1609-1676), the celebrated Chief-Justice of the King's Bench in the reign of Charles II., wrote several works of a moral and religious character, e.g. *Contemplations, Moral and Divine; Pleas of the Crown;* and *The Nature of Religion.*

l. 24. **Tillotson,** John (1630-1694), Archbishop of Canterbury, was renowned as a parson, prelate, and preacher; his sermons were popular, and he set an excellent example of liberal charity and episcopal virtue. See also p. 4, l. 34, *supra,* and note.

l. 25. **Congreve.** See p. 2, l. 19, *supra,* and note. Hazlitt writes: "His style is inimitable, nay, perfect. It is the highest model of comic dialogue. Every sentence is replete with sense and satire, conveyed in the most polished and pointed terms. Every page presents a shower of brilliant conceits, is a tissue of epigrams in prose, is a new triumph of wit, a new conquest over dulness." See also Thackeray's *English Humorists,* Johnson's

*Lives of the Poets*, and Macaulay's Essay on *The Comic Dramatists of the Restoration*.

l. 26. **Vanbrugh,** Sir John (1666-1726), was distinguished as an architect and dramatist. The most remarkable specimens of architectural skill are Castle Howard and Blenheim. His epitaph runs thus :

> " Lie heavy on him, earth, for he
> Laid many heavy loads on thee."

His best known comedies are *The Relapse, The Provoked Wife, Æsop, The Confederacy, The False Friend.* He began *The Provoked Husband*, which was finished by Colley Cibber. His plays were "renowned for the well-sustained ease and spirit of the dialogue."

**Page 53, l. 1. Tom Folio,** a "broker in learning, employed to get together good editions, and stock the libraries of great men etc." See *Tatler*, No. 158.

l. 2. **Ned Softly,** "a very pretty poet, and a great admirer of easy lines etc." See *Tatler*, No. 163.

**the Political Upholsterer,** "the greatest newsmonger in our quarter etc." See *Tatler*, No. 155.

l. 3. **the Court of Honour.** See *Tatler*, No. 250.

**the Thermometer of Zeal,** or the church thermometer graduated thus from top to bottom : " Ignorance, Persecution, Wrath, Zeal, Church, Moderation, Lukewarmness, Infidelity, Ignorance. See *Tatler*, No. 220.

l. 4. **the Frozen Words.** See *Tatler*, No. 254.

**the Memoirs of the Shilling.** See *Tatler*, No. 249.

l. 9. **Smalridge, George** (1663-1719), was a schoolfellow of Addison at Lichfield, whence he was sent to Westminster School, thence to Christ Church, Oxford. Subsequently he became prebend of Flixton in Lichfield Cathedral. He was an intimate friend of Atterbury at school and at Oxford. In 1698 he was appointed minister of the new chapel (Broadway) Westminster. He won the reputation in London of being an excellent preacher, and in 1710 was made one of the Queen's chaplains. He was Canon of Christ Church when Atterbury was Dean, and when Atterbury became a Bishop, Smalridge succeeded to the Deanery. In 1714 he was promoted to the See of Bristol, and shortly afterwards was appointed Lord Almoner. Addison characterizes him as the most candid and agreeable of Bishops. In the *Tatler* (Nos. 73 and 114) Steele spoke of him ("Favonius") as "abounding in that kind of virtue and knowledge which makes religion beautiful." Macaulay's epithets are "humane and accomplished." After his death his widow published his *Sixty Sermons preached* *on several occasions.*  His portrait by Kneller is in Christ Church Hall.

l. 10. **squeamish**, scrupulously fastidious, over-nice (Scand. with Fr. suffix). [This is one of the cases in which initial *squ* is put for *sw*, cf. *squaime*, a swain, *squalteryn*, to swelter, M.E. *sweymous*, from M.E. *sweem*, "vertigo" or dizziness, or what we now call "swimming" in the head.]  The original sense is dizzy, as if from a swimming in the head, hence overcome with disgust or distaste, faint, expressing distaste at, and so over-nice, fastidious, squeamish (Skeat).

l. 12. **the impeachment of Sacheverell** for preaching in London before the Lord Mayor, and in Derby, at the assizes, two sermons, in which he attacked the Revolution, maintaining that resistance to a king was never justifiable, and declaring that the Church was in danger even in Her Majesty's reign.  He alluded to Godolphin under the nickname of "Volpone" or "the Fox." He was condemned by the House of Lords and suspended from preaching for three years.  The people, thinking him persecuted, took Sacheverell's side, and received him everywhere with enthusiasm.  (See also my notes on Macaulay's Essay on *The Earl of Chatham*, 93.)

l. 28. **event**, issue, result ; Lat. *eventus*, from *evenire* to come out, happen, result.

l. 31. **the Low Church party.**  Mr. Morris, in *The Age of Anne*, writes as follows: "The Tories were the Church party; those to whom the rites and doctrines of the Established Church were dear.  They were very hostile to Dissenters, and perhaps scarcely less hostile to the Roman Catholics.  The Whig party was in favour of toleration; to this party the Dissenters belonged (for they owed to it all the rights which they possessed), as well as those churchmen, who, preferring the doctrines of their own Church, yet considered other forms of government and modes of worship lawful.  Bishop Burnet tells us that in this reign the distinction between High and Low Church was first known, but, when he proceeds to explain it, we see that it is almost the same as the difference between Whigs and Tories."

l. 32-35. **outbreak of public feeling ... in 1820, and in 1831,** which resulted in the passing of the Reform Bill in 1832.

**Page 54**, l. 1. **general election,** an election of representatives throughout an entire country, to fill vacancies simultaneously created : opposed to a bye-election.

l. 5. **Lewis** the Fourteenth of France.

l. 7. **Versailles.**  See p. 17, l. 11, *supra*, and note.

**Marli,** or Marly-le-Roi, a town about 11½ miles west of Notre Dame, Paris, celebrated as the residence of Louis XIV.

l. 8. **the Pretender.** James Francis Edward Stuart, son of James II. and Mary of Modena, was born in 1688, the year of the Glorious Revolution. Lewis XIV. promised the exiled James upon his deathbed to recognize this young prince as King of England.

**St. James's** Palace, the only London palace of our sovereigns from the time of the fire at Whitehall, in the reign of William III., to the occupation of Buckingham Palace by her present Majesty.

l. 9. **Harley,** Robert. See p. 37, l. 17, *supra*, and note.

l. 10. **Sunderland.** See p. 37, l. 13, *supra*, and note.

l. 14. **Secretary,** the Earl of Sunderland.

l. 15. **Godolphin.** See p. 28, l. 19, and p. 30, l. 4, *supra*, and note.

l. 16. **white staff,** part of the insignia of his office.

l. 22. **the High Church party.** See p. 53, l. 31, *supra*, and note on the Low Church party.

ll. 33, 34. **They had saved Holland and Germany. They had humbled France,** by Marlborough's successful campaigns.

l. 35. **They had … torn Spain from the House of Bourbon,** by the exploits of Peterborough, the Earl of Galway, and General Stanhope.

**Page 55, l. 1. they had united England and Scotland** in 1707.

l. 6. **thirteen colonies,** viz. Massachusetts, Connecticut, New Hampshire, Rhode Island, New York, New Jersey, Pennsylvania, Maryland, Delaware, Virginia, North and South Carolina, and Georgia.

l. 8. **Walcheren,** an island at the mouth of the Scheldt, Holland. The unfortunate expedition of the British to this isle in 1809 consisted of 35 ships of the line and 200 smaller vessels, principally transports, and 40,000 land forces, the latter under the command of the Earl of Chatham, and the fleet under Sir Richard Strachan. Flushing was invested, bombarded, and taken; but nevertheless the expedition was a signal failure, owing to the want of vigorous action on the part of Lord Chatham; and in December he was compelled to return with as many of his troops as disease and an unhealthy climate had spared. The House of Commons instituted an inquiry, Chatham resigned his post of Master-General of the Ordnance to prevent greater disgrace; but the policy of Ministers in planning the expedition was approved.

ll. 13, 14. **the small Irish office which he held by patent,** that of keeper of the records in Bermingham's Tower, an Irish place bestowed on him by the Queen as a special mark of esteem, worth £400 a year.

patent, see p. 45, l. 28, *supra*, and note.

l. 15. **his Fellowship** at Queen's College, Oxford.

l. 16. **a great lady**, the Countess of Warwick.

l. 24. **He told his friends, with smiling resignation, that they ought to admire his philosophy** etc. He wrote to Wortley on 21st July, 1711: "I have within this twelvemonth lost a place of £2000 per annum, an estate in the Indies worth £14,000, and, what is worse than all the rest, my mistress. Hear this and wonder at my philosophy ! I find they are going to take away my Irish place from me too ; to which I must add that I have just resigned my fellowship, and that stocks sink every day."

l. 33. **he was returned to Parliament** by Malmesbury, which place he continued to represent till his death.

l. 34. **Swift**, see p. 39, l. 28, *supra*, and note.

l. 36. **Stella**, see p. 40, l. 34, *supra*, and note.

**Page 56, l. 7. the Whig Examiner**, this was started in opposition to the *Examiner* conducted by Swift. Only five numbers were published : No. 1 appeared on Thursday, Sept. 14, and No. 5 on Thursday, Oct. 12, 1710.

l. 23. **Steele**, see p. 40, l. 35, *supra*, and note.

**Ambrose Phillipps**, see p. 43, l. 17, *supra*, and note.

l. 26. **Gazetteer**, see p. 47, l. 5, *supra*, and note.

**Commissioner of Stamps**, see p. 40, l. 35, *supra*, and note on *Steele*.

l. 32. **Isaac Bickerstaff**, see p. 47, ll. 35, 36, and p. 41, l. 19, *supra*, and notes.

**Page 57, ll. 7, 8. At the beginning of March following**, the first number of the *Spectator* is dated Thursday, March 1, 1710-11.

l. 11. **The Spectator himself** etc., see *Spectator*, No. 1.

l. 19. **the wits of Will's**, see p. 47, l. 15, *supra*, and note.

l. 20. **the philosophers of the Grecian**, see p. 47, l. 15, *supra*, and note.

l. 21. **Child's** coffee-house was in St. Paul's Churchyard, and the resort of the clergy.

l. 22. **St. James's** coffee-house, in St. James's Street, was the haunt of statesmen and men of fashion, and at one time acquired an infamous notoriety for the ruinous gambling of its habitués. The Whigs resorted to St. James's, the Tories to the Cocoa Tree.

l. 23. **the Exchange**, see *Spectator*, No. 69. There have been no less than three Royal Exchanges. The first was built by Sir Thomas Gresham and opened by Elizabeth in 1571 ; it was destroyed by the Great Fire of London in 1666. The second building was destroyed by fire in 1838. The present building was erected in 1844.

l. 27. **These friends were first sketched by Steele** etc. Courthope criticises this passage thus: "This is a very misleading account of the matter. It implies that the characters in the *Spectator* were mere casual conceptions of Steele's: that Addison knew nothing about them till he saw Steele's rough draft: and that he, and he alone, is the creator of the finished character of Sir Roger de Coverley. But as a matter of fact, the character of Sir Roger is full of contradictions and inconsistencies, and the want of unity which it presents is easily explained by the fact that it is the work of four different hands. Sixteen papers on the subject were contributed by Addison, seven by Steele, three by Budgell, and one by Tickell. ... He was from the first intended to be a *type* of a country gentleman, just as much as Don Quixote was an imaginative representation of many Spanish gentlemen whose brains had been turned by the reading of romances. In both cases the type of character was so common and so truly conceived as to lend itself easily to the treatment of writers who approached it with various conceptions and very unequal degrees of skill. Any critic, therefore, who regards Sir Roger de Coverley as the abstract conception of a single mind is certain to misconceive the character" etc. etc.

l. 28. **the Templar** was a member of the Inner Temple. See *Spectator*, No. 2.

l. 30. **an old country baronet**, Sir Roger de Coverley.

**an old town rake**, Will Honeycomb.

**Page 58, l. 3. the five or six hundred essays**, the last number of the *Spectator* is No. 600, Wednesday, Sept. 29, 1714.

l. 7. **Richardson was working as a compositor.** Samuel Richardson (1689-1761), the novelist, was by trade a printer, and through the influence of Mr. Onslow, the Speaker, obtained the printing of the *Journals of the House of Commons*. In 1754 he was chosen Master of the Stationers' Company, and in 1760 he purchased a moiety of the patent of Law Printer to the King. He was far advanced in life, nearly fifty years of age, indeed, before he won fame as a writer. *Pamela* was published in 1740, *Clarissa Harlowe* in 1749, and *Sir Charles Grandison* in 1753.

**compositor**, one whose business it was to set up type for printing purposes; a type-setter.

ll. 7, 8. **Fielding was robbing birds' nests.** Henry Fielding was born in 1707, the *Spectator's* career was from 1710-11 to 1714; if this be taken literally, Fielding began robbing birds' nests at a very early age; probably the phrase is only equivalent to "Fielding was in his boyhood." He subsequently distinguished himself as a novelist, dramatist, and miscellaneous

L

writer. His principal works are: *The History of Jonathan Wild, Joseph Andrews, Tom Jones, Amelia, A Journey from this World to the Next, The Mock Doctor, Pasquin, Tragedy of Tragedies, The Wedding-Day* etc. Byron called Fielding "the prose Homer of human nature." Sir Walter Scott describes him as "the father of the English novel."

l. 8. **Smollett,** Tobias George (1721-1771), novelist and poet, wrote *The Tears of Caledonia; The Advice, a Satire; The Reproof, a Satire; The Adventures of Roderick Random; The Regicide, a Tragedy; The Adventures of Peregrine Pickle; The Adventures of Ferdinand, Count Fathom; A Compleat History of England; The Adventures of Humphrey Clinker,* and other works.

l. 13. **Sir Roger** de Coverley. See p. 57, l. 30, *supra,* and note.

**Eugenio,** *i.e.* Prince Eugene. See p. 26, l. 8, *supra,* and note; and *Spectator,* No. 269. Eugene visited England in 1717 to urge the Government to maintain the alliance against France and reinstate Marlborough.

l. 14. **Spring Gardens,** afterwards know as Vauxhall Gardens. The new Spring Gardens at Vauxhall are mentioned by Pepys 1665, Wycherley 1672, and in the *Spectator* 1711 (No. 383), as a place of great resort. These grounds were in 1859 sold for building purposes.

l. 15. **walks among the tombs in the Abbey.** See *Spectator,* No. 329.

**the Mohawks,** or Mohocks, a set of ruffians that infested the streets of London, and "made night hideous" by their lawless conduct. Their name was borrowed from the Indian Mohawks. See *Spectator,* Nos. 324, 335, 347.

ll. 17, 18. **the theatre where the Distressed Mother is acted.** See *Spectator,* No. 335.

**the Distressed Mother** was a play by Ambrose Phillipps (see p. 43, l. 17, *supra,* and note), founded on the *Andromaque* of Racine.

ll. 19, 20. **a visit in the summer to Coverley Hall ... old chaplain.** See *Spectator,* Nos. 106 etc.

l. 20. **eats a jack caught by Will Wimble.** See *Spectator,* No. 108. *Jack* is a familiar name for a small pike (fish) as distinct from a full-grown one.

**rides to the assizes ... Tom Touchy.** See *Spectator,* No. 122.

ll. 22-4. **a letter from the honest butler ... that Sir Roger is dead.** See *Spectator,* No. 517.

**Will Honeycomb marries** etc. See *Spectator,* No. 530.

l. 25. **The club breaks up** etc. See *Spectator,* Nos. 542, 549, 550 etc.

**Page 59, l. l, About three sevenths of the work are his** ; out of 635 Entire Papers, and 35 Letters and parts of Papers, total 670, Addison wrote 274 Entire Papers.

l. 9. **nabob**, an Indian prince, very rich man (Hindi-Arab). See Burke, speech on the *Nabob* of Arcot's debts. The word signifies "Deputy" or vice-roy, esp. applied to a governor of a province of the Mogul empire (Webster). Also *nabobb*, a nobleman. Hindi, *Nawwáb* (pl. of *náib*), vicegerents, deputies; vulg. *Nabob* (Bate's *Dict*.). But the word is merely borrowed from Arabic. Arab, *nawwáb*, a nabob, properly a plural form, signifying vicegerents, deputies; plural of *náib*, a vicegerent, lieutenant, deputy. Cf. Arab *nawb*, supplying the place of another (Skeat).

l. 13. **Lucian's Auction of Lives.** *Vitarum Auctio*, or Sale of the Philosophers, is an attack upon the ancient philosophers. The heads of the different sects are put up for sale, Hermes being the auctioneer.

**Lucian** was probably born about A.D. 120 at Samosata, the capital of Commagene in Syria. He spent much of his time travelling in Greece, Italy, and Gaul. His principal works were: *The Dialogues of the Gods, Jupiter Convicted, Jupiter the Tragedian, The Fisherman, The Banquet or the Lapithae, Nigrinus, Timon, Dialogues of the Dead, Icaro-Menippus*, and *Charon*.

l. 14. **Tales of Scherezade,** "The Arabian Nights." Scherezade, or Scheherezade, was the daughter of the Grand Vizier of the Indies. The sultan Schahriah, having discovered the infidelity of his sultana, resolved to marry a fresh wife every night and have her strangled at daybreak. Schcherazade entreated to become his wife, and so amused him with tales for a thousand and one nights that he revoked his cruel desire, bestowed his affection on his amiable and talented wife, and called her "the liberator of the sex."

**apologue** [a Fr. *apologue*, ad L. *apologus*, a Gk. ἀπόλογος, account, story, fable, from ἀπό and λόγος, speech]. An allegorical story intended to convey a useful lesson: a moral fable (applied more especially to a story in which the actors or speakers are taken from the brute creation or from inanimate nature).

l. 16. **La Bruyere,** John de (1644-1696), a French writer whom Bossuet employed as a teacher of history to the Duke of Burgundy. He was admitted a member of the French Academy. His *Characters in the Manner of Theophrastus* were drawn from real persons, and exposed the prevailing follies of his time.

l. 17. **the Vicar of Wakefield.** A novel by Oliver Goldsmith, published in 1766 (see Macaulay's *Boswell's Life of Johnson* in this series).

l. 18. **sly Horatian pleasantry,** an allusion to Horace's satires, which are characterized by a wit that is graceful, good-natured, pleasant, and full of common-sense.

l. 21. **Massillon,** Jean Baptiste (1663-1742), a famous French preacher, was appointed Bishop of Clermont in 1717. Louis XIV. once said to him : "Father, when I hear other preachers I go away much pleased with them ; but when I hear you I go away much displeased with myself."

l. 26. **the two Visits to the Abbey.** See *Spectator*, Nos. 26, 329.

l. 27. **the Visit to the Exchange.** See *Spectator*, No. 69.

**the Journal of the Retired Citizen.** See *Spectator*, No. 317.

l. 28. **the Vision of Mirza.** See *Spectator*, No. 159.

**the Transmigrations of Pug the Monkey.** See *Spectator*, No. 343.

l. 29. **the Death of Sir Roger de Coverley.** See *Spectator*, No. 517.

**Page 60, ll. 4-7. ballads ... Chevy Chace.** See *Spectator*, Nos. 70, 74.

l. 12. **stamp tax.** By 22 and 23 Car. II. (1670-1) duties were imposed on certain legal documents. In 1694 a duty was imposed on paper, vellum, and parchment. The stamp duty on newspapers was commenced in 1713, and every year added to the list of articles upon which stamp duty was made payable (Haydn's *Dict. of Dates*).

l. 19. **bohea** (Chinese *wu-i* (*shan*), the *wu-i* hills in north of Fukhien. Morrison gives "Bohea Tea, *wuicha*" (cha = tea), and Edkins says that the Fukhien dialect uses *b* for *w* or *v*).

*A.* Adj. of the wu-i hills, whence black tea was first brought to England, applied to all teas of similar quality grown elsewhere.

*B.* Subs. 1. = *Bohea-tea.* The name was given in the beginning of the eighteenth century to the finest kinds of black tea ; but the quality now known as "Bohea" is the lowest, being the last crop of the season (Murray).

l. 30. **farriery,** the art of the farrier : now = veterinary surgeon. *Farrier* (akin to O.F. *ferrier*, L. *ferrarius*, from *ferrum*, iron, in Med. L. often *ferrus* horseshoe), one who shoes horses, a shoeing smith ; hence one who treats the diseases of horses (Murray).

l. 33. **the most successful works of Sir Walter Scott and Mr. Dickens.** The sale of the early volumes of the Waverley Novels exceeded 35,000 in Scott's lifetime, and the sale of monthly numbers of the *Pickwick Papers* was upwards of 40,000 copies.

l. 35. **At the close of 1712 etc.** The last number of the *Spectator* is No. 600, published Wednesday, September 29, 1714 ; but No. 550 appeared December 1, 1712, and No. 556 appeared June 18, 1714. See below p. 67, l. 13 etc. and note.

l. 36. **the shortfaced gentleman,** the *Spectator*, No. 332, begins
" Dear Short Face " etc.

**Page 61, l. 3. In a few weeks the first number of the Guardian
was published.** This paper was edited by Steele, and began
Thursday, 12th March, 1713. It appeared daily, price one
penny, and extended to 175 numbers, of which Steele wrote 82
papers and Addison 53. Addison's first paper was No. 67.

l. 9. **Nestor Ironside,** the name assumed by Steele when, in the
character of an astrologer, he started the *Guardian*.

l. 10. **the Miss Lizards,** the daughters of Lady Lizard, described
as follows in the *Guardian* : " It is always the custom for one of
these young ladies to read while the others are at work ; so that
the learning of the family is not at all prejudicial to its manufac-
tures. I was mightily pleased the other day to find them all
busy in preserving several fruits of the season, with the Sparkler
in the midst of them reading over the *Plurality of the Worlds*.
It was very entertaining to me to see them dividing their speculations between jellies and stars, and making a sudden transition
from the sun to an apricot, or from the Copernican system to
the figure of a cheesecake " (No. 155).

l 17. **his Cato** " appeared in public in the year 1713, when the
greatest part of the last Act was added by the author to the
foregoing, which he had kept by him for many years. He took
up a design of writing a play upon this subject, when he was
very young, in the University, and even attempted something in
it then, tho' not a line as it now stands. The work was performed by him in his travels, and retouched in England, without any formal resolution of bringing it upon the stage till his
friends of the first quality and distinction prevailed with him to
put the last finishing to it, at a time when they thought the
doctrine of Liberty very reasonable " (Tickell).

ll. 28-31. **the followers of Cæsar** etc. The Dramatis Personae
were as follows :

MEN.

| | | |
|---|---|---|
| Cato, . . . . . . | . | Mr. Booth. |
| Lucius, a Senator, . | . | Mr. Keen. |
| Sempronius, a Senator, . | . | Mr. Mills. |
| Juba, Prince of Numidia, . | . | Mr. Wilks. |
| Syphax, General of the Numidians, | . | Mr. Cibber. |
| Portius, } Sons of Cato, { . | . | Mr. Powell. |
| Marcus, } . | . | Mr. Ryan. |
| Decius, Ambassador from Caesar, | . | Mr. Bowman. |

Mutineers, Guards etc. etc.

WOMEN.

| | | |
|---|---|---|
| Marcia, Daughter to Cato, . | . | Mrs. Oldfield. |
| Lucia, Daughter to Lucius, | . | Mrs. Porter. |

SCENE—A large hall in the Governor's Palace of Utica.

ll. 32-35. **Addison gave the play ... dresses.** "Addison appears to have behaved with great liberality to the actors, and, at Oxford, to have handed over to them all the profits of the first night's performance : while they, in return, Cibber tells us, thought themselves 'obliged to spare no pains in the proper decorations' of the piece" (Courthope).

l. 36. **Mr. Macready** (1793-1873), a celebrated actor and manager of Covent Garden and Drury Lane theatres. He acted at various times in most of the chief towns of the provinces, as well as in London, Paris, and America. On Macready's retirement from the stage in 1851, Tennyson wrote a sonnet containing these lines :

> " Thine is it, that our drama did not die,
> Nor flicker down to brainless pantomime,
> And those gilt gauds men-children swarm to see.
> Farewell, Macready : moral, grave, sublime,
> Our Shakespeare's bland and universal eye
> Dwells pleased, thro' twice a hundred years on thee."

**Page 62, l. 1. Marcia's hoop.** Hoop is a piece of whalebone or cane used for extending a petticoat ; a skirt with several hoops in it is sometimes called a crinoline. This style of dress was fashionable in Queen Anne's day.

l. 3. **The prologue was written by Pope,** and spoken by Mr. Wilks.

l. 9. **Sir Gilbert Heathcote** (1651 ?-1733), Lord Mayor of London, was born at Chesterfield of an ancient Derbyshire family, and was educated at Christ's College, Cambridge. He afterwards carried on business in St. Swithin's Lane as a merchant, trading in Spanish wines and in produce from Jamaica and India. He was one of the founders of the Bank of England, and in 1694 was elected by ballot one of its first Board of Directors, and on the dismissal of Sunderland from the Secretaryship in 1710 Heathcote, as governor of the Bank of England, headed a deputation to the queen to represent the injurious effects which any further changes in the ministry would have upon public credit. He held many municipal appointments, and in 1710 was elected Lord Mayor. He was M.P. for London in 1700-1710, in 1714 for Helston, Cornwall, in 1722 for New Lymington, and in 1727 for St. Germains, Cornwall. He was a staunch Whig, and used his influence with the merchants of London in support of Godolphin's administration. Despite his wealth Heathcote was noted for his parsimony. Pope characterizes him as "starting— from dreams of millions and three groats to pay" (*Dunc.* ii. 251). Again,

> " The grave Sir Gilbert holds it as a rule,
> That every man in want is either knave or fool."
> *Moral Essays*, Ep. iii. 101.

l. 10. **the Bank of England.** "The conception of the Bank originated with Paterson, a Scotchman, in 1691. Its small business was first transacted in the Mercer's Hall, then in the Grocer's Hall, and in 1734 was moved to the buildings which form the back of the present court towards Threadneedle Street. The modern buildings, covering nearly three acres, were designed in 1788 by Sir John Soane. ... The taxes are received, the interest of the National Debt paid, and the business of the Exchequer transacted at the Bank" (Hare, *Walks in London*).

l. 12. **Jonathan's,** a coffee-house in Cornhill, where the Stock Exchange was originally held, was the great scene of action in the South Sea Bubble of 1720.

**Garraway's,** a coffee-house in Exchange Alley, frequented by merchants and brokers.

l. 19. **the great military chief and demagogue,** C. Julius Caesar.

l. 23. **the Kit Cat.** See p. 28, l. 6, *supra,* and note.

l. 24. **the October** Club consisted of 150 Tory squires, members of Parliament, who met at the Bell Tavern in King Street, Westminster, and nourished their patriotism with October ale. (See also p. 28, l. 6, *supra,* note on *Kit Cat.*)

l. 27. **the Guardian.** See p. 61, l. 3, *supra,* and note.

l. 28. **the Examiner.** See p. 56, l. 17, *supra,* and note on *Whig Examiner.*

l. 33. **Sir Gibby,** Sir Gilbert Heathcote, governor of the Bank of England. See l. 9, *supra.*

l. 36. **the hypocritical Sempronius.** See list of dramatis personae, p. 61, l. 28, *supra.*

**Page 63, l. 1. rant,** violent language ; a Dutch word—O. Du. *ranten,* "*randen* or *ranten,* to dote or to be enraged" (Hexham). Cf. Low G. *randen,* to attack any one, to call out to one. Perhaps allied to O.H.G. *rázi,* M.H.G. *raeze,* wild, violent.

**plaudit,** applause (Lat.). The form *plaudit* is due to misreading Lat. *plaudite* as if it were an Eng. word in which the final *e* would naturally be considered as silent. Lat. *plaudite* means clap your hands : a cry addressed by the actors to the spectators requesting them to express satisfaction. It is imper. pl. of *plaudere,* to applaud, also spelt *plodere* (Skeat).

l. 2. **Wharton.** See p. 37, l. 32, *supra,* and note.

l. 7. **epilogue** (F. *epilogue,* Lat. *epilogus,* Gr. ἐπίλογος, the peroration of a speech, from ἐπὶ, in addition, and λόγος, a speech).
1. Rhet. The concluding part or peroration of a speech. Obs.
2. The concluding part of a literary work ; an appendix.
3. A speech or short poem addressed to the spectators by one of the actors after the conclusion of the play.

The epilogue to Cato was written by Dr. Garth and spoken by Mrs. Porter.

l. 8. **Garth**, Sir Samuel, physician and poet (about 1660-1719), wrote *The Dispensary*, *Claremont*, and a translation of the fourteenth and part of the fifteenth book of Ovid's *Metamorphoses*, besides the epilogue to Cato. See Johnson's *Lives of the Poets*. Thackeray, in his *Humorists*, speaks of "Garth the accomplished and benevolent, whom Steele has described so charmingly, of whom Codrington said that his character was all beauty, and whom Pope himself called the best of Christians without knowing it."

l. 15. **Bolingbroke**, Henry St. John, Viscount (1672-1751), entered Parliament in 1700, became Secretary of War in 1704, resigned his office in 1708, again formed part of the Ministry in 1710, and concluded the Peace of Utrecht. In 1712 he was created Viscount Bolingbroke, but, dissatisfied because he was not raised to an earldom, he quarrelled with his colleagues, effected the dismissal of Harley, and himself became Prime Minister. After the death of Queen Anne, the Whigs gained the ascendency. He, as a Tory, fled to France and became Secretary of State to James Edward, the Pretender. He was impeached and attainted, and it was not till 1723 that he was allowed to return to England. In 1725 his estates were restored to him, but he exerted all his talents against the Ministry until the fall of Sir Robert Walpole. He withdrew to France in 1735, but subsequently returned to England and died at Battersea in 1751. He was the intimate friend of Pope, Swift, and other authors of his time; and his own writings are distinguished for their easy, clear, and polished style. He wrote *A Dissertation upon Parties; Letters on the Spirit of Patriotism, or the Idea of a Patriot King*, and *On the State of Parties in the Reign of George I.; Letters on the Study of History*, and other works. It was to him that Pope addressed his *Essay on Man*.

l. 16. **Booth**. See list of dramatis personae, p. 61, l. 28, *supra*, and note.

l. 21. **patent**. See p. 45, l. 28, *supra*, and note.

l. 27. **the Act at Oxford**. In the Universities, *Act* is the name applied to a thesis publicly maintained by a candidate for a degree, or to show a student's proficiency. At Oxford the *Act* took place early in July. The graduates kept *Acts* or discussed theses on Saturday and Monday; on the intervening *Act Sunday* two of the new doctors of divinity preached *Act Sermons* before the University. The *Act* was last held after long interruption in 1733; in 1856 the name, with all that related to the ceremony, was removed from the Statute-book, and only survives in the appellation *Act Term* sometimes given to Trinity Term. At

Cambridge the name is still given to the thesis and accompany-
ing examination required for the obtainment of the Doctor's
Degree in Divinity, Law, and Medicine. (Murray's *Dictionary*.)

l. 35. **the masterpieces of the Attic stage**, the plays of Aeschylus, Sophocles, and Euripides.

l. 36. **the great English dramas of the time of Elizabeth**, the
plays of Shakespeare, Marlowe, Ben Jonson, Massinger, Beau-
mont and Fletcher, and others.

**Page 64, l. 1. Schiller**, Frederick (1759-1805), a celebrated
German poet and dramatist; "the productions of his manhood"
are *Wallenstein, Mary Stuart, The Maid of Orleans, The Bride of
Messina*, and *William Tell*.

l. 4. **Athalie**, a drama written by Racine at the request of
Madame de Maintenon, and published in 1691 : it is held by
some French critics to be the most perfect of his works.

**Saul**, a tragedy by Alfieri. See l. 7, *infra*, and note.

**Cinna**, produced in 1639, was, according to Voltaire, the
*chef d'œuvre* of Corneille. See l. 7, *infra*, and note.

l. 7. **Corneille**, Pierre (1606-1684), the father of French tragedy
and classic comedy; he wrote *Mélite, Clitandre, La Veuve, La
Galerie du Palais, La Suivante, La Place Royale, L'Illusion
Comique, Medea, Le Cid, Horace, Cinna, Polyeucte, Pompée, Le
Menteur*, and other works.

**Voltaire**, Francois Marie Arouet, called M. de (1694-1778),
produced works in almost every branch of literature, in poetry,
the drama, romance, history, philosophy, criticism, and even
science. His best known productions are his philosophical
novels (*Zadig, Candide, L'ingénu* etc.), his histories (*Siècle de
Louis XIV., Histoire de Charles XII.*), his correspondence,
satires, and poetical epistles, his tragedies (*Zaire, Alzire, Mérope,
Mahomet*, and *Rome sauvée*), and his epic poem, the *Henriade*.
He was also the chief contributor and leading spirit of the
*Encyclopedie*.

**Alfieri**, Vittorio (1749-1803), an Italian dramatist, published
his first drama, *Cleopatra*, in 1775. Thenceforward he was a
laborious student and dramatic author ; he composed fourteen
tragedies in seven years, studied Latin, and at the age of 48
made himself Master of Greek. Among his tragedies are *Saul,
Philip II., Antigone, Virginia, Agamemnon, Mary Stuart* etc.
He wrote also several poems and prose treatises.

l. 8. **Racine**, Jean Baptiste (1639-1699), a distinguished
dramatist, and friend of La Fontaine, Boileau, and Molière.
His chief works are the *Thebaide* or *Les Frères ennemis, Alex-
andre, Andromaque, Les Plaideurs, Bérénice, Bajazet, Mithri-
date, Iphigénie* (in the opinion of Voltaire the greatest work that
the French stage has produced), *Phèdre, Esther*, and *Athalie*.

**l. 9. Tatlers.**  See p. 41, l. 10, *supra*, and note.

**Spectators.**  See p. 57, l. 8 etc., *supra*, and notes, and p. 67, l. 13 etc., *infra*, and note.

**Freeholder**, a political periodical conducted by Addison, and published twice a week from Friday, December 23, 1715, to Friday, June 29, 1716.  It was undertaken at the time when the rebellion broke out in Scotland : Steele said of it that the ministry made use of a lute when they should have called for a trumpet.

**l. 14. it should seem**, we should say "it would seem."

l. 16.  **John Dennis** (1657-1734), dramatist and critic, wrote the following plays : *A Plot and no Plot, Renaldo and Armida, The Comical Gallant, Iphigenia, Liberty Asserted, Orpheus and Eurydice, Appius and Virginia* etc.  He wrote also critical essays on Milton, Congreve, Shakespeare, Addison, and Pope.  See also *English Men of Letters*, "Pope," pp. 44, 45.

l. 33.  **Pope was only twenty-five.**  Pope was born in 1688, and wrote the *Prologue to Cato* in 1713.

l. 34.  **the Rape of the Lock** was published in 1712.  See p. 72, l. 31, *infra*, and note.

**Page 65, ll. 2-4.  the diminutive, crooked, sickly boy ... the unkindness of nature.**  Pope inherited headaches from his mother and a crooked figure from his father. ... As the sickly, solitary, and precocious infant of elderly parents, we may guess that he was not a little spoilt, if only in the technical sense " (Leslie Stephen).

l. 4.  **the Essay on Criticism had been praised** etc.  See *Spectator*, No. 253, December 20, 1711.

l. 14.  **Pope hated Dennis, whom he had injured without provocation.**  " Pope had probably been a witness, perhaps more than a mere witness, to some passage of arms, in which Dennis lost his temper.  In more youthful impertinence he introduced an offensive touch in the *Essay on Criticism*.  It would be well, he said, if critics could advise authors freely,—

'But Appius reddens at each word you speak,
And stares tremendous with a threatening eye,
Like some fierce tyrant in old tapestry.'

The name Appius referred to Dennis's tragedy of Appius and Virginia" (Leslie Stephen).

l. 20.  **the Narrative of the Frenzy of John Dennis** " is written in that style of coarse personal satire of which Swift was a master, but for which Pope was very ill-fitted.  All his neatness of style seems to desert him when he tries this tone, and nothing is left but a brutal explosion of contemptuous hatred " (Leslie Stephen).

ll. 25, 26. **a lampoon such as that on Atticus**, which occurs in Pope's *Epistle to Dr. Arbuthnot.* See p. 41, l. 16, *supra*, and note; the lampoon is quoted at length in note on p. 78, l. 18, *infra.*

**that on Sporus.** In Pope's *Epistle to Dr. Arbuthnot* is the famous portrait of Lord John Hervey, son of the Earl of Bristol, and author of the *Memoirs of the Reign of George II.*

l. 28. **Horace's imagery and his own—a wolf, which, instead of biting takes to kicking, or a monkey which should try to sting.** An allusion to Horace, *Sat.* ii. i. 52, "Dente lupus, cornu taurus petit"; and ii. i. 53: "Nil faciet sceleris pia dextera: mirum Ut neque calce lupus quemquam, neque dente petit bos." Cf. Pope, *Sat.* ii. i. 85:

" Its proper pow'r to hurt, each creature feels ;
Bulls aim their horns, and Asses lift their heels ;
'Tis a Bear's talent not to kick, but hug ;
And no man wonders he's not stung by Pug."

l. 33. **the shilling gallery**, the cheapest seats in a theatre, that part of the house where you would expect to find the least educated, least refined, and least exacting audience.

l. 35. **peripetia**, Grk. περιπέτεια, *a turning right about*, i.e. *a sudden change, a revolution or reverse of fortune*, especially, *the sudden reversal of circumstances* on which the plot in a tragedy hinges, such as Oedipus' discovery of his parentage (Arist. *Poet.* ii. 1) (Liddell and Scott).

**Page 66, l. 18. In September 1713 the Guardian ceased to appear.** No. 167 appeared Tuesday, Sept. 12, 1713.

l. 20. **Stockbridge**, in Hampshire, eight miles west-north-west of Winchester. It was disfranchised in 1832.

l. 35. **the Englishman**, a political paper of extreme Whig views.

**Page 67, l. 13. In June 1714 the first number etc.** On Friday, June 18, 1714, appeared No. 556 of the Spectator.

l. 14. **during about six months**, No. 635 (the last) of the *Spectator* appeared, Monday, Dec. 20, 1714.

l. 15. **three papers were published weekly**, on Mondays, Wednesdays, and Fridays.

l. 22. **the death of Anne**, on August 21, 1714.

l. 25. **Harley.** See p. 37, l. 17, *supra*, and note.

l. 26. **Bolingbroke.** See p. 63, l. 15, *supra*, and note.

l. 28. **the white staff**, part of the insignia of office of the Lord High Treasurer.

l. 30. **the Duke of Shrewsbury.** See p. 25, l. 28, *supra*, and note. "Almost the last words that Queen Anne uttered were in giving to Shrewsbury the staff of Lord High Treasurer. 'Use it for the good of my people'" (Morris).

l. 36. **The first act of the Lords Justices was to appoint Addison their secretary.** "Upon the death of the late Queen, the Lords Justices, in whom the administration was lodged, appointed him (Addison) their Secretary" (Tickell).

Page 68, l. 6. **dunces.** See p. 2, l. 5, *supra*, and note.

l. 8. **Sir James Mackintosh,** statesman, historian, and miscellaneous writer (1765-1832), wrote *The Regency Question*; *Vindiciae Gallicae*; contributions to *The Monthly Review*; *On the Study of the Law of Nature and Nations*; a *History of England*; a *History of the Reformation in England* in 1688; *Life of Sir Thomas More,* and other works.

l. 22. **Lord John Russel** was leader of the Whigs and Prime Minister from 1846 to 1852; the chief work of his ministry was the carrying out of the policy of free trade into every department of British commerce.

**Sir Robert Peel** was the leader of the Tories and Prime Minister from Nov., 1834, to April, 1835; and again from Sept., 1841, to June, 1846.

l. 23. **Lord Palmerston** was Premier from Feb., 1855, to Feb., 1858. His was a Whig Ministry.

Page 69, ll. 3-5. **Sunderland** etc. "Soon after his Majesty's arrival in Great Britain, the Earl of Sunderland being constituted Lord Lieutenant of Ireland, Mr. Addison became a second time Secretary for the affairs of that kingdom, and was made one of the Lords-Commissioners of Trade, a little after his Lordship resigned the post of Lord Lieutenant" (Tickell).

l. 6. **At Dublin Swift resided** as Dean of St. Patrick; he was appointed to the Deanery in April, 1713.

l. 29. **the Tale of a Tub.** In this work Swift satirizes the corruptions of the Roman Catholic, Lutheran, and Calvinistic churches. The somewhat irreverent drollery of his work ruined his chance of preferment in the church; for the Archbishop of York, who had the ear of the Queen, asserted that the writer must be an infidel.

l. 36. **The dislike with which the Queen and the heads of the Church regarded him was insurmountable.** In his Essay on *Boswell's Life of Johnson,* Macaulay says, "Swift, but for the unconquerable prejudice of the Queen, would have been a bishop." Cf. Thackeray's *English Humorists,* "The Queen and the Bishops, and the world were right in mistrusting the religion of that man (Swift)."

Page 70, ll. 3-5. **an ecclesiastical dignity of no great value** etc., the deanery of St. Patrick's, which "was no great prize: he would have to pay £1000 for the house and fees, and thus, he says, it would be three years before he would be the richer for it; and, moreover, it involved what he already described as 'banishment' to a country which he hated" (Leslie Stephen).

l. 10. **Iliad** etc., the lines quoted are uttered by Diomed in Bk. vi., ll. 226-230. They are translated as follows by Lord Derby:

> " Then shun we, e'en amid the thickest fight,
> Each other's lance ; enough there are for me
> Of Trojans and their brave allies to kill,
> As heaven may aid me, and my speed of foot ;
> And Greeks enough there are for thee to slay,
> If so indeed thou canst."

l. 19. **Renegade**, or Renegado, an apostate, vagabond. (Span. *Renegado*, "an apostate" (Minsheu): lit. one who has denied the faith : p.p. of *renegar*, "to forsake the faith"; id. Low Lat. *renegare*, to deny again. It appears in M.E. as *renegat*, of which *runagate* is a corruption (Skeat).

**Page 71, l. 7. Tickell.** See p. 43, l. 21, *supra*, and note.

l. 8. **Budgell.** See p, 43, l. 1, *supra*, and note.

l. 9. **Ambrose Phillipps.** See p. 43, l. 17, *supra*, and note.

l. 10. **Steele.** See p. 40, l. 55, *supra*, and note.

l. 17. **the Drummer**, or "the Haunted House," a comedy produced at the Theatre Royal in Drury Lane in 1715, was founded on a tradition connected with Hurstmonceux House. It is not found in the edition of Addison's works in four volumes, published in 1721.

ll. 26-28. **Towards the close of the year 1715 ... Freeholder.** See p. 64, l. 10, *supra*, and note. Tickell writes : "The paper called the *Freeholder* was undertaken at the time when the rebellion broke out in Scotland."

l. 31. **the character of his friend Lord Somers**, in No. 39 of the *Freeholder*, is too long to be quoted here, but should be read and studied by all. At the beginning of the paper Addison quotes Lord Somers's motto, "Prodesse quam conspici," and shows how that nobleman made it his endeavour rather "to do worthy actions than to gain an illustrious character."

l. 32. **no satirical papers superior to those in which the Tory Fox-hunter is introduced**, viz. Nos. 22, 44, 47.

l. 34. **Squire Western**, a jovial, fox-hunting, country gentleman in Fielding's novel of *Tom Jones* : described by Sir Walter Scott as "an inimitable picture of ignorance, prejudice, irascibility, and rusticity, united with natural shrewdness, constitutional good humour, and an instinctive affection for his daughter."

l. 35. **Fielding.**  See p. 58, ll. 7, 8, *supra*, and note.

**Page 72, ll. 9-12. the admonition which...Addison addressed to the University etc.**  See *Freeholder*, No. 33.

l. 22. **Town Talk,** remembered only as the title of a paper by Steele.

**his Englishman.**  See p. 66, l. 35, *supra*, and note.

l. 23. **Crisis,** was published in 1714 to excite the apprehensions of the nation with regard to the Protestant succession.

**Letter to the Bailiff of Stockbridge, and his Reader.**  We may quote Macaulay's own words (p. 47, ll. 2-4, *supra*), "The literary merit of these works was small indeed; and even their names are now known only to the curious."  Steele wrote in the *Guardian* (No. 128), "The British nation expects the demolition of Dunkirk."  The *Examiner*, a Tory paper under the management of Swift, retorted by charging him with disloyalty.  Steele rejoined (22nd Sept., 1713) by a pamphlet entitled "The importance of Dunkirk considered," addressed to the Bailiff of Stockbridge, Hampshire, for which town in August he had been elected M.P.  *The Reader* was a short-lived paper begun by Steele in April, 1714, and dropped in May.  Addison contributed two papers, viz., Monday, April 16, 1714, and Wednesday, May 28, 1714.

l. 26. **In the same year etc.,** 1715.

l. 32. **the Rape of the Lock** is a mock-heroic poem by Pope, describing how Lord Petre stole a lock of hair from Miss Fermor.

**supernatural machinery,** composed of gods and goddesses, who, from the days of Homer, had attended to the fortunes of heroes.

ll. 35, 36. **The Sylphs and Gnomes, Ariel, Momentilla, Crispissa and Umbriel:** these are names of the aerial forms in *The Rape of the Lock*, which fluttered around the heroine Belinda.

**Sylph,** an imaginary being inhabiting the air.  See Pope's Introduction to *Rape of the Lock*.  Pope tells us that he took the account of the Rosicrucian philosophy and theory of spirits from a French book entitled *Le Compte de Gabalis*—Fr. *Sylphe*, the name given to one of the pretended genii of the air.  Gr. σίλφη, used by Aristotle, *Hist. Anim.* viii. 17. 8, to signify a kind of beetle or grub.  The other names of genii are gnomes, salamanders, and nymphs, dwelling in the earth, fire, and water respectively, and as all these names are Greek, we may be sure that sylph was meant to be Greek also (Skeat).

**Gnome,** a kind of sprite (*Fr. gnome,* a gnome).  It seems to be an adaptation of Gr. γνώμη, intelligence, from the notion that the intelligence of these spirits could reveal the secret treasures of the earth (Skeat).

**Rosicrucian mythology,** the Rosicrucians, a sect of mystical philosophers who appeared in Germany in the 14th century and again early in the 17th century, occasioned much controversy. *The Confessio Roseae Crucis*, 1615, is attributed to Valentine Andreas. They swore fidelity, promised secrecy, and wrote hieroglyphically, and affirmed that the ancient philosophers of Egypt, the Chaldeans, Magi of Persia, and Gymnosophists of the Indies taught the same doctrine (Haydn's *Dictionary of Dates*). The *Comte de Gabalis*, which furnished Pope with the machinery of the *Rape of the Lock*, was the work of a professed Rosicrucian.

Page 73, l. 1—page 74, l. 9. **He asked Addison's advice.** Mr. Taine, in his *History of English Literature*, writes thus : "Macaulay brings to the moral sciences that spirit of circumspection, that desire for certainty, and that instinct for truth which make up the practical mind, and which, from the time of Bacon, have constituted the scientific merit and power of his nation. If art and beauty lose by this, truth and certainty are gained; and no one, for instance, would blame our author for inserting the following demonstration in the life of Addison." He then quotes this passage, and continues: "What does the reader think of this dilemma and this double series of inductions? The demonstrations would not be more studied or vigorous if a physical law were in question."

l. 2. **a delicious little thing,** *merum sal.*

l. 26. **Tasso,** see p. 35, l. 34, *supra,* and note.

l. 27. **Akenside,** Mark (1721-1770), wrote *The Pleasures of Imagination* and some miscellaneous pieces. His life has been written by Dr. Johnson, Bucke, and Dyce. With regard to Akenside's recasting the *Pleasures of Imagination*, Johnson writes : "It is generally known to the readers of poetry that he intended to revise and augment this work, but died before he had completed his design. The reformed work, as he left it, and the additions which he had made are very properly retained in the late collection. He seems to have somewhat contracted his diffusion; but I know not whether he has gained in closeness what he has lost in splendour. In the additional book, the 'Tale of Solon' is too long."

l. 28. **Epistle to Curio.** Akenside "was impelled by his rage of patriotism to write a very acrimonious epistle to Pulteney, whom he stigmatizes, under the name of 'Curio,' as the betrayer of his country. ... Yet such was his love of lyricks that, having written with great vigour and poignancy his 'Epistle to Curio,' he transformed it afterwards into an ode disgraceful only to its author" (Johnson's *Lives of English Poets*).

l. 30. **made the same experiment on the Dunciad.** The first three books of the *Dunciad* appeared in May, 1728. The fourth book, or *New Dunciad*, as it was called, appeared in 1743. In the first three books Theobald was the King of the Dunces ; in the fourth book Theobald is degraded from the throne, and the crown is given to Colley Cibber.    Dr. Johnson mentions "the alterations which have been made in the *Dunciad,* not always for the better."

l. 30. **Waverley,** or " 'Tis Sixty Years Since," was Sir Walter Scott's first novel.    It appeared in 1814, but the first few chapters were written in 1805, and thrown aside in deference to the unfavourable opinion of certain of the author's friends.

**Herder,** Johann Gottfried von (1744-1803), a distinguished German author of great erudition.    He studied science, theology, philosophy, philology, natural and civil history, and politics. He was an intimate friend of Goethe, on whom he had a decided influence.    Goethe obtained for Herder the appointment of court preacher, general superintendent, and consistorial coun- sellor at Weimar.    Subsequently he became president of the high consistory, and was made a noble by the Elector of Bavaria. His chief works are *Fragments on the More Modern German Literature, Critical Words, Geist der Hebraischen Poesie,* and *Ideen zur Philosophie der Geschichte der Menschheit.*

**Page 74,** l. 1. **Goethe,** Johan Wolfgang von (1749-1831), the greatest modern poet and many-sided genius of Germany.    He studied, besides all branches of poetry, drawing, music, natural science, jurisprudence, theology, and philosophy.    His principal works are *Werther, Wilhelm Meister, Iphigenia, Egmont, Tasso,* and *Faust.*    He counted among his admirers and friends Herder, Schiller, and Napoleon.

l. 2. **Hume,** David (1711-1776), historian, philosopher, and miscellaneous writer, wrote a *Treatise of Human Nature ; Essays : Moral, Political, and Literary ; Enquiry concerning the Principles of Morals ;* and a *History of England.*

**Robertson,** William, D.D. (1721-1793), a Scottish historian, wrote a *History of Scotland, The History of the Reign of the Emperor Charles V., The History of America,* and *An Historical Disquisition concerning the Knowledge which the Ancients had of India.*    He was an intimate friend of David Hume and Dr. Johnson.    (See Boswell's *Life of Johnson.*)

l. 3. **Pope himself ... prophesied that Cato would never succeed on the stage etc.**    "When Mr. Addison," says Pope, "had finished his Cato, he brought it to me, desired to have my sincere opinion of it, and left it with me for three or four days.    I gave him my opinion of it sincerely, which was, 'that I thought he had better not act it, and that he would get reputation enough by only printing it.'    This I said as thinking the lines well written but the piece not theatrical enough.    Some time after Mr. Addison said, 'that his own opinion was the same with mine, but that some particular friends of his, whom he could not disoblige, insisted on its being acted" (Spence's *Anecdotes*). Cibber expressed a similar opinion as early as 1703, "Whatever spirit Mr. Addison had shown in his writing it, he doubted that he would never have courage enough to let his Cato stand the censure of an English audience; that it had only been the amusement of his leisure hours in Italy, and was never intended for the stage."

l. 10. **In 1715** etc. Pope's first volume of the *Iliad* appeared in 1715 (almost simultaneously with Tickell's version of the first *Iliad*): Pope's other volumes of the *Iliad* were published at intervals between 1715 and 1720.

l. 11. **at a coffeehouse, Button's.** See p, 75, l. 17, *infra*, and note.

**Phillipps.** See p. 43, l. 17, *supra*, and note.

**Budgell.** See p. 43, l. 1, *supra*, and note.

l. 12. **their sovereign,** Addison was the King of Button's, and surrounded by his "little senate," Budgell, Tickell, Carey, and Philips, he ruled supreme over the world of taste and letters.

**After dinner** etc. See Spence's *Anecdotes*.

l. 34. **Neither of the rivals can be said to have translated the Iliad.** Bentley's phrase, "A pretty poem, Mr. Pope, but you must not call it Homer," expresses the uniform view taken from the first by all who could read both (Leslie Stephen).

**Page 75, l. 1. Midsummer Night's Dream.** See Act iii. sc. 1, l. 121, where "translated"=changed.

l. 15. **The subscription, on which rested his hopes of a competence.** The subscribers paid a guinea a volume, and as 575 subscribers took 654 copies, Pope received altogether £5320 4s. at the regular price, whilst some royal and distinguished subscribers paid larger sums (Leslie Stephen).

l. 17. **Button's,** a coffee-house in Russell Street, Covent Garden, Addison's favourite resort.

l. 24. **Fellow of a College at Oxford,** Queen's College, Oxford.

l. 25. **able to construe the Iliad,** certainly as well as Pope. It has been suggested that the translations of Homer were consulted by Pope before the original. "Pope's ignorance of Greek," says Leslie Stephen—"an awkward qualification for a translator —is undeniable."

**Page 76, l. 7. Rowe,** Nicholas (1673-1718), poet-laureate and dramatist, wrote *The Ambitious Stepmother*, *Tamerlane*, *The Fair Penitent*, *Ulysses*, *The Royal Convert*, *The Biter*, *Jane Shore*, *Lady Jane Grey*, and a translation of Lucan's *Pharsalia*. See Johnson's *Lives of English Poets*.

l. 8. **Congreve**, William (1672-1729), a poet and dramatist, began life as a student at the Middle Temple, but abandoned the law for literature. His first comedy, *The Old Bachelor*, was produced in 1693. Other works by him are *Love for Love, The Double Dealer, The Mourning Bride, The Way of the World*, and *Poems.* See Thackeray's *English Humorists*, Johnson's *Lives of English Poets*, and Macaulay's *Essays.*

l. 9. **Steele.** See p. 40, l. 55, *supra*, and note.

**He was a pamphleteer**, *e.g.* he wrote an ingenious pamphlet on the signature of the Treaty of Utrecht, entitled *The late Trial and Conviction of Count Tariff.*

l. 11. **Swift.** See p. 10, l. 28, *supra*, and note.

l. 12. **Tickell.** See p. 43, l. 21, *supra*, and note.

l. 33. **the Editor of the Satirist.** The *Satirist* is mentioned in the *Penny Cyclopaedia* as a weekly paper in the year 1838. Sale, 2,971 ; advertisements, 86.

l. 34. **the Editor of the Age.** The *Age* is mentioned in *Penny Cyclopaedia* as a weekly London paper in the year 1838. Sale, 2,317 ; advertisements, 72. They appear to have been hostile organs, both of a libellous character.

**Page 77, l. 4. stiletto**, a small dagger. Ital. *stiletto*, "a little poniard." Florio, dimin. of *stilo*. O. Ital. *stillo*, now a gnomon (the index of a dial), formerly a dagger (Florio). Lat. *stilum*, acc. of *stilus*, a style, a pointed tool for engraving or writing.

l. 5. **mask**, a disguise for the face.

**The stiletto and mask** are the weapons of the stealthy assassin, of one that strikes and does not reveal himself.

ll. 7, 8. **a lampoon on the Duke of Chandos.** See Pope's *Moral Essays*, Epistle iv., l. 99 etc. "At Timon's villa let us pass a day" etc. This was "a description of Canons, the splendid seat of the Duke of Chandos. Chandos resented the attack, but Pope had not the courage to avow his meaning. He declared to Burlington (to whom the epistle was addressed) and to Chandos that he had not intended Canons, and tried to make peace by saying in another epistle (i., l. 54) that 'gracious Chandos is beloved at sight'" (Leslie Stephen). Johnson tells us that this exculpation was accepted by the duke "with great magnanimity, as by a man that accepted his excuse without believing his professions."

l. 9. **a lampoon on Aaron Hill** etc. Aaron Hill (1685-1750) was an ambitious and restless man ; he was a stage manager, a translator of Voltaire's *Merope*, and wrote no less than seventeen dramatic pieces, and was also, according to Dibdin, the projector of many schemes, *e.g.* for extracting oil from beech-nuts, for felling forests in the Highlands to provide timber for the navy, for cultivating Georgia and potash. Pope satirizes him thus in *Dunciad*, ii. 295 etc.:

> " The X essay'd ; scarce vanished out of sight,
> He buoys up instant and returns to light :
> He bears no token of the sabler streams,
> And mounts far off among the swans of Thames."

A note was appended applying the lines to Hill. Hill replied with a satire entitled *Tuneful Alexis;* he also wrote a note to Pope complaining of the passage in the *Dunciad*. Pope might have answered that the lines on the whole were complimentary, more complimentary, perhaps, than true ; but with his usual love of lying, Pope shuffled and said that he was not responsible for the notes, that "he would use his influence with the editors of the *Dunciad* to get the notes altered etc. etc." Hill was pacified by Pope's " pretty genteel equivocation."

l. 11. **Lampoon on Lady Mary Wortley Montague** etc. "The first of his *Imitations of Horace* appeared in 1733. It contained a couplet, too gross for quotation, making the most outrageous imputation upon the character of 'Sappho,'... an obvious name for the most famous of poetic ladies" (Leslie Stephen). The following passages

> "And at a Peer, or Peeress, shall I fret,
> Who starves a sister and forswears a debt?"
> 
> *Epilogue to Satires*, i. 111.

and

> "Where hapless Monsieur much complains at Paris
> Of wrongs from Duchesses and Lady Maries."
> 
> *Dunciad*, ii. 134.

contain allusions to Lady M. W. Montague and her sister, the Countess of Mar : the scandal that Lady Mary treated her sister hardly while the latter was out of her senses, and that she frightened a Frenchman of the name of Ruzemonde (who had entrusted her with a large sum of money to buy stock for him) out of England by threats of betraying her intrigue with him, is told in a letter from Horace Walpole to Sir H. Mann ; but Lord Wharncliffe states that the former accusation is unfounded, and the latter rests on a perversion of facts.

l. 14. **He robbed himself of his own letters.** For an account of this trickery, see *English Men of Letters*, "Pope," chapter vi., Correspondence.

l. 25. **an act of gross perfidy to Bolingbroke.** Pope had printed a whole edition (1500 copies) of *The Patriot King*, Bolingbroke's most polished work. The motive could have been nothing but a desire to preserve to posterity what Pope considered to be a monument worthy of the highest genius, and was so far complimentary to Bolingbroke. Bolingbroke, however, considered it as an act of gross treachery.  Pope had received the work on condition of keeping it strictly private, and showing it to only a few friends.  Moreover, he had corrected it, arranged it, and altered or omitted passages according to his own taste, which naturally did not suit the author's. ... Pope's behaviour is too much of a piece with previous underhand transactions, but scarcely deserves further condemnation (Leslie Stephen).

**Page 78, l. 7. The Earl of Warwick,** afterwards Addison's stepson.

**l. 18. He had already sketched the character of Atticus in prose,** in a letter to Craggs of July 15th, 1715.

**l. 19. the brilliant and energetic lines** etc.  Epistle to Arbuthnot, ll. 194-214, which are quoted at length, that, as Macaulay suggests, they may be learned by heart.

> "Peace to all such ! but were there One whose fires
> True Genius kindles, and fair Fame inspires ;
> Blest with each talent and each art to please,
> And born to write, converse, and live with ease ;
> Should such a man, too fond to rule alone,
> Bear, like the Turk, no brother near the throne.
> View him with scornful, yet with jealous eyes,
> And hate for arts that caus'd himself to rise ;
> Damn with faint praise, assent with civil leer,
> And without sneering, teach the rest to sneer ;
> Willing to wound, and yet afraid to strike,
> Just hint a fault, and hesitate dislike ;
> Alike reserv'd to blame, or to commend,
> A tim'rous foe, and a suspicious friend ;
> Dreading ev'n fools, by flatterers besieg'd,
> And so obliging, that he ne'er oblig'd ;
> Like Cato, give his little senate laws,
> And sit attentive to his own applause :
> While Wits and Templars ev'ry sentence raise,
> And wonder with a foolish face of praise ;—
> Who but must laugh, if such a man there be ?
> Who would not weep, if Atticus were he ?"

**Page 79, l. 7. Sir Peter Teazle,** a character in Sheridan's comedy of *The School for Scandal.*

**l. 8. Mr. Joseph Surface,** in Sheridan's *School for Scandal,* is a consummate hypocrite, and noted for his " sentiments."

**ll. 15-21. Pope was a Catholic... under penal laws and many other disadvantages.**  In 1700, in William III.'s reign, when England was still in mortal dread of the Restoration of the Stuarts and their religion, an Act was passed which punished the celebration of the Catholic worship as felony in a foreigner and as treason in a native; and by the same Act every Roman

Catholic was declared incapable of inheriting or purchasing land, unless he abjured his religion upon oath, and on his refusal his property was vested during his life in his next of kin, being a Protestant. He was also prohibited from sending his children abroad to be educated. These severe laws were enforced by proclamations and Acts of Parliament in the reigns of Queen Anne, George I., and George II. When the Pretender was expected in 1744, a proclamation, to which Pope thought it decent to pay obedience, forbade the appearance of Catholics within ten miles of London. And as Pope died on May 10th, 1744, he did not live to see the repeal of those obnoxious Acts, which were not only unworthy of the constitution of England, but a disgrace to humanity.

l. 23. **in the Freeholder a warm encomium on the translation of the Iliad.** See *Freeholder*, No. 40, Monday, May 7, 1715: "The illiterate among our countrymen may learn to judge from Dryden's Virgil of the most perfect epic performance; and those parts of Homer, which have already been published by Mr. Pope, give us reason to think that the Iliad will appear in English with as little disadvantage to that immortal poem."

l. 35. **The Countess Dowager** etc., viz. Charlotte, Countess of Warwick, daughter of Sir Thomas Myddleton of Chirk Castle, Denbighshire.

**Page 80, l. 1. Chirk** is a parish of Denbighshire, in Wales, about 5½ miles south-east of Llangollen.

l. 2. **Holland House,** an Elizabethan mansion in Kensington, about two miles west of the Metropolis, stands in a beautiful park. It was formerly the Manor House of Abbot's Kensington. Built in 1607 for Sir Walter Cope, it descended to his son-in-law, Henry Rich, first Earl of Holland, whence it was named Holland House. At a later date it was the headquarters of Sir Thomas Fairfax, and, as Macaulay writes (p. 81, *infra*), it "can boast of a greater number of inmates distinguished in political and literary history than any other private dwelling in England."

l. 3. **Chelsea,** a parliamentary borough and suburb of London. It is also noted for its hospital for superannuated soldiers, founded in the time of Charles II., and finished by Sir C. Wren in 1692.

l. 4. **Nell Gwynn** was at first an orange girl, and at one time gained her bread by singing from tavern to tavern; then she became the mistress of Hart and Lacy, the actors, afterwards of Lord Buckhurst, and finally of King Charles II. From her are sprung the Dukes of St. Alban's.

l. 25. **Rowe.** See p. 76, l. 7, *supra*, and note.

ll. 28, 29. **Lycidas ... St. George's Channel.** Lycidas is the name under which Milton eulogizes his friend and fellow-student,

Edward King. In the vacation of 1637 King sailed from Chester on a visit to his friends in Ireland, and was wrecked in St. George's Channel off the Welsh coast, and drowned.

l. 30. **Chloe** (Gr. χλόη, the first light green shoot of plants in spring, especially young green corn, grass, or foliage), a favourite name for a shepherdess or love-sick lass. Cf. Horace, *Od.* I. xxiii. 1 :

" Vitas hinnuleo me similis, Chloe."

It is here applied, in a bantering tone, to the Countess Dowager, a matron with a grown-up son, and described elsewhere (p. 82, *infra*) as " an imperious and arrogant woman."

l. 33. **a brother who died Governor of Madras**, this was Gulston, his second brother.

**Page 81. l. 1. William Somervile** (1677-1742) was educated at Winchester and New College, Oxford. At the latter place he obtained a fellowship, which he resigned on succeeding to his patrimonial estate, Edston, Warwickshire ; " he divided his time between his justiceship of the peace, his books, hounds, and bottle " (Allibone). The titles of his poems are *The Two Springs, The Chase, Field Sports*, and *Hobbinol, or The Rural Games*.

l. 14. **Lord Townshend** etc. See Macaulay's *Boswell's Life of Johnson*, p. 5, l. 22, and note, in this series: " Can Mr. Croker possibly be ignorant that Lord Townshend was made Secretary of State at the accession of George I. in 1714, that he continued to be Secretary of State till he was displaced by the intrigues of Sunderland and Stanhope at the close of 1716, and that he returned to the office of Secretary of State not in 1720 but in 1721 ? "

l. 15. **Lord Sunderland** etc. In 1717 Sunderland became First Lord of the Treasury. Stanhope received an earldom and became Secretary of State ; Addison was the other Secretary of State ; Aislabie was Chancellor of the Exchequer, and James Craggs, the Secretary of War. Sunderland resigned in 1721 and Walpole returned to power. Stanhope died suddenly in February, 1722, and was replaced as Secretary of State by Lord Townshend.

l. 18. **Walpole**, Sir Robert, Earl of Oxford (1676-1745), was Prime Minister of England twice, first from 1715 to 1717 ; and when Sunderland was forced to resign after the bursting of the South Sea Bubble, Walpole was again made Premier and held that office, practically without a break, for twenty-one years. (See Macaulay's *Boswell's Life of Johnson* in this series, p. 29, l. 23, and note.)

**Cowper.** See p. 37, l. 5, *supra*, and note.

l. 20. **the Seals**, part of the insignia of a Secretary of State.

l. 26. **the Cabinet,** a confidential committee of the Privy Council, selected to advise the sovereign in the discharge of those executive, legislative, and judicial duties which the constitution has reposed in him or her. Lord Sunderland, the leader of the first " homogeneous Ministry, chosen from the same party, representing the same sentiments, and bound together for common action by a sense of responsibility and loyalty to the party to which it belonged."

l. 29. **Vincent Bourne.** See p. 20, l. 13, *supra*, and note.

l. 33. **Craggs,** James (1685-1720), made a large fortune in the South Sea Bubble, and as Macaulay says (in *Essay on Earl of Chatham*), "was saved by a timely death" from a charge of peculation.  Yet Pope wrote his epitaph as follows :

" On James Craggs Esq.
In Westminister Abbey.

Jacobus Craggs
Regi Magnae Britanniae a secretis
Et consiliis sanctioribus,
Principis pariter ac populi Amor et deliciae
Vixit Titulis et Invidia major
Annos, heu paucos, XXXV
Ob. Feb. XVI. MDCCXX.

Statesman, yet Friend to Truth ! of Soul sincere,
In Action faithful, and in Honour clear !
Who broke no Promise, serv'd no private end ;
Who gained no Title, and who lost no Friend ;
Ennobled by Himself, by All approv'd ;
Prais'd, wept, and honour'd, by the Muse he lov'd."

**Page 82, l. 3. Joseph Hume** (1777-1835), an eminent statesman, who "became the self-elected guardian of the public purse, withstanding every abuse of the public money, by challenging and bringing to a direct vote every single item of public expenditure. ... Himself, as incorruptible as Aristides, he made it a special duty to hunt out and expose political corruption under whatever guise it lurked, and the whole army of place-hunters and jobbers found in him their most indefatigable and inexorable foe " (*Encyclopædia Britannica*).

l. 13. **Socrates** (B.C. 369-399), the great Athenian philosopher, talked, questioned, and discussed, not for pay, but from the love of truth and a sense of duty, and thus led the way to real knowledge.   He wrote no book, he founded no school nor system of philosophy, but counted among his pupils Alcibiades, Critias, Xenophon, and Plato.  For an account of his death see the last few chapters of Plato's *Apology.*

l. 14. **a treatise on the evidences of Christianity** etc.  "The scheme for the Treatise upon the Christian Religion was formed by the author about the end of Queen Anne's reign: at which time he carefully penned the ancient writings which furnish the materials for it.   His continual employment in business prevented him from executing it till he resigned his office of Secretary of State ; and his death put a period to it, when he had imperfectly performed only one half of the design, he having proposed, as appears from the introduction, to add the Jewish to the heathen testimonies for the truth of Christian history " (Tickell).

l. 25.  **the Countess Dowager.**  See p. 79, l. 35, *supra*, and note.

l. 27.  **the House of Rich,** the house of Warwick.   Rich was at one time the family name of Lord Warwick : in 1640, Robert Rich, Earl of Warwick, received from Witherings the patent of Postmaster.

l. 28.  **Virgil.**  See p. 7, l. 33, *supra*, and note.

**Boileau.**  See p. 18, l. 13, *supra*, and note.

l. 30.  **Sir Richard Steele.**  See p. 40, l. 55, *supra*, and note.

**Page 83, l. 6.  Tickell.**  See p. 43, l. 21, *supra*, and note.

l. 8.  **the Editor of the Tatler and Spectator, the author of the Crisis, the member for Stockbridge,** Sir Richard Steele.  See p. 40, l. 55, *supra*, and note.

l. 12.  **patent,** an official document conferring a privilege, so called because it was *open* (patens) to the inspection of all men.

l. 20.  **The celebrated Bill for limiting the number of Peers** etc. " Harley's creation of twelve Peers to ensure the sanction of the Lords to the Treaty of Utrecht showed that the Crown possessed a power of swamping the majority in the House of Peers.   In 1720, therefore, the Ministry introduced a bill, suggested, as was believed, by Sunderland, which professed to secure the liberty of the Upper House by limiting the power of the Crown in the creation of fresh Peers.   The number of Peers was permanently fixed at the number then sitting in the House ; and creations could only be made when vacancies occurred. ... The Bill, however, was strenuously opposed by Walpole " (Green's *History of the English People*).

l. 21.  The proud Duke of Somerset.  See p. 15, l. 32, *supra*, and note.   The Earl of Sunderland, as Prime Minister, usually has the credit of suggesting and framing this Peerage Bill.

l. 25.  **the Prime Minister,** the Earl of Sunderland.

**Page 84, l. 15.  the Plebeian,** "a Peerage Bill, introduced by Sunderland, the effect of which was to cause the sovereign to divest himself of his prerogative of creating fresh Peers, had been vehemently attacked by Steele in a pamphlet called *The Plebeian*, published March 14, 1719, which Addison undertook to answer in the *Old Whig* (March 19).   *The Plebeian* returned

to the attack with spirit and with acrimony in two numbers
published March 29th and 30th, and the *Old Whig* made a somewhat contemptuous reply on April 2nd. 'Every reader,' says
Johnson, 'surely must regret that these two illustrious friends,
after so many years passed in confidence and endearment, in
unity of interest, conformity of opinion, and fellowship of study
should finally part in acrimonious opposition. Such a controversy was "Bellum plusquam *civile*," as Lucan expresses it.
Why could not faction find other advocates? But among the
uncertainties of the human state we are doomed to number the
instability of friendship'" (Courthope).

l. 17. **the Old Whig.** See previous note.

l. 35. **the Biographia Britannica.** A dictionary of biography,
the second edition of which was edited by Dr. Andrew Kippis.
Five large folio volumes appeared in 1778-1779, bringing the
dictionary down to F, and the sixth was passing through the
press when Dr. Kippis died in 1795. The work is unfinished
still.

**Page 85, l. 1. by Johnson,** in his *Life of Addison.* See vol. x.,
p. 103 (Edition by Arthur Murphy). "*The Old Whig* answered
*The Plebeian*, and could not forbear some contempt of 'little
Dicky,' whose trade it was to write pamphlets.' Dicky, however, did not lose his settled veneration for his friend, etc. etc."

l. 3. **Miss Aikin.** See p. 1, *supra,* and note.

l. 7. **the Duenna,** a comic opera by Sheridan, produced at
Covent Garden in 1775.

l. 13. **Henry Norris** (died about 1733), an English actor, an
excellent comedian. He was the original Don Lopez (in *The
Wonder*) and Scrub. He had an odd squeaking voice, and was
called Jubilee Dicky from his successful impersonation of Dicky
in *The Trip to the Jubilee.* His sons announced themselves
later as "the sons of Jubilee Dicky," appearing to derive profit
from the name.

l. 15. **Dryden's Spanish Friar,** or the Double Discovery, produced in 1681, was written against the Roman Catholic priest-
hood.

l. 26. **dedicated them ... to Craggs,** in a letter etc., thus, "To
the Right Honourable James Craggs, Esq., His Majesty's
Principal Secretary of State.

"Dear Sir,—I cannot wish that any of my writings should last
longer than the memory of our Friendship, and therefore I thus
publickly bequeathe them to you in return for the many valuable
instances of your Affection. That they may come to you with
as little disadvantages as possible, I have left the care of them
to one, whom, by the experience of some years, I know well
qualified to answer my intentions. He has already the honour

and happiness of being under your protection ; and as he will very much stand in need of it, I cannot wish him better than that he may continue to deserve the favour and countenance of such a Patron.   I have no time to lay out in forming such compliments as would ill suit that familiarity between us, which was once my greatest pleasure, and will be my greatest honour hereafter.   Instead of them, accept of my hearty wishes, that the great reputation you have acquired so early may increase more and more ; and that you may long serve your country with those excellent talents and unblemished integrity which have so powerfully recommended you to the most gracious and amiable monarch that ever filled a throne.   May the frankness and generosity of your spirit continue to soften and subdue your enemies, and gain you many friends, if possible, as sincere as yourself.   When you have found such they cannot wish you more happiness than I, who am, with the greatest zeal, Dear Sir, Your most entirely Affectionate Friend and faithful Obedient Servant,

" June 4, 1719."                                                    J. ADDISON.

l. 34.  Gay, John (1688-1732), poet and dramatist, wrote *Rural Sports, The Shepherd's Week, The Wife of Bath, Beggar's Opera, What d'ye Call It, Three Hours after Marriage* (probably in conjunction with Pope and Arbuthnot), *The Captives*.  See Johnson's *Lives of English Poets,* Thackeray's *English Humorists,* and Macaulay's *Boswell's Life of Johnson* in this series.

Holland House.  See p. 80, l. 2, *supra,* and note.   This anecdote is told by Spence on the authority of Pope.

Page 86, l. 33.  His interview with his son-in-law etc.   From Young we learn that he asked to see the Earl of Warwick, and said to him, "See in what peace a Christian can die " ; words which are supposed to explain the allusion of the lines in Tickell's elegy :

" He taught us how to live and (oh ! too high
The price of knowledge) taught us how to die."
                              Extract from Courthope.

Page 87, l. 8.  who had rebuked the waves of the Ligurian gulf.  See p. 22, l. 4, *supra,* and note.

Had purified the autumnal air of the Campagna.  See p. 25, l. 12, *supra,* and note.

had restrained the avalanches of Mont Cenis.  See p. 26, l. 17, *supra,* and note.

l. 10.  Of the Psalms etc., viz. *Psalm* xxiii.

l. 19.  the Jerusalem chamber was the withdrawing room belonging to the Abbot's house at Westminster ; it still belongs to the Deanery.   The Jerusalem Chamber probably received its name from the subjects of the tapestries or paintings with which

it was decorated. It was here that Henry IV. was brought to
die when seized with illness in the Abbey on the eve of starting
for the Holy Land in 1413 (see the *Deanery Guide to Westminster
Abbey*).

l. 20. **the Abbey,** Westminster Abbey.

l. 21. **Bishop Atterbury** (1662-1732), was born at Milton Keynes
near Newport Pagnell, and was educated at Westminster School
and Christ Church, Oxford. In 1691 he took Holy Orders, and
adopted High Church principles ; he was chaplain in ordinary to
Queen Anne, Dean of Carlisle, preacher at the Rolls Chapel, a
Canon of Exeter, Dean of Christ Church, Bishop of Rochester,
and Dean of Westminster. His High Church principles were
well known ; and it is asserted that if a sufficient guard could be
obtained, he would proclaim the Pretender; at any rate, through
his sympathy with the Pretender, he involved himself in a "Bill
of Pains and Penalties," and died an exile in Paris. "With Pope
and Swift, and many of the principal literary characters of his day,
he was on terms of friendship, and was held in great esteem by his
associates as a man of great abilities and a skilful politician"
(Allibone).

l. 24. **the shrine of Saint Edward,** the chapel of Edward the
Confessor.

l. 26. **House of Albemarle.** In the south aisle of the chapel of
Henry VII. is a large and ostentatious monument (put up about
1717) to General George Monk, d. 1670, created Duke of Albemarle by Charles II., in whose restoration he played so prominent
a part.

l. 28. **Montague.** See p. 11, l. 20, *supra*, and note. Addison
was buried in front of Montague's monument. A slab of white
marble, with Tickell's epitaph in brass letters, marks the spot :

ADDISON.

" Ne'er to the chambers where the mighty rest,
Since their foundation came a nobler guest ;
Nor e'er was to the bowers of bliss conveyed
A fairer spirit, or more welcome shade.
Oh ! gone for ever ! take this long adieu,
And sleep in peace, next thy lov'd Montague.

l. 31. **Craggs.** See p. 81, l. 33, *supra*, and note.

l. 35. **the energy and magnificence of Dryden.** Cf. Campbell's
criticism of Dryden, "He is a writer of manly and elastic character. His strong judgment gave force as well as direction to a
flexible fancy ; and his harmony is generally the echo of solid
thoughts," etc., etc. Pope expressed his admiration thus : "He
could select from his (Dryden's) works better specimens of every
model of poetry than any other English writer could supply."

l. 36. **the tenderness and purity of Cowper.** Cf. Dr. Dibdin's estimate of Cowper : "The purity of his principles, the tenderness of his heart, his unaffected and zealous piety, his warmth of devotion (however tinctured at times with gloom and despondency), the delicacy and playfulness of his wit, and the singular felicity of his diction, all conspire by turns 'to win the wisest, warm the coldest heart.'"

**William Cowper** (1731-1800), wrote *Olney Hymns*, *John Gilpin*, *Lines to Mary Unwin*, and to his *Mother's Picture*, *The Task* etc.

**Page 88, l. 1. a superb edition**, in four vols. quarto.

l. 3. **The names of the subscribers** fill sixteen pages with two columns to a page.

l. 7. **Spanish Grandees**, *e.g.* Conde d' Ericeira (Portugal).

**Italian Prelates**, *e.g.* His Eminence the Cardinal de Guidice; Abbot Antonio Maria Salvini, Greek Professor at Florence; Abbé Muratori.

**Marshals of France**, *e.g.* Maréschal d'Estrées. His Royal Highness the Duke of Orleans, Regent of France.

l. 14. **in some important points defective**, *e.g.* it does not contain *The Drummer*, nor *The Old Whig*, nor *The Trial and Conviction of Count Tariff.*

l. 22. **in our own time**, in 1809 ; the statue is by Sir Richard Westmacott : and on the wall behind it, one on each side of it, are busts of Lord Macaulay and Thackeray. The following Latin inscription is engraved on the pedestal :

" Quisquis es, qui hoc marmor intueris,
   Venerare memoriam Josephi Addison,
      Quem fides Christiana,
      Quem virtus, bonique mores,
  Assiduum sibi vindicant patronum
      Cujus ingenium
Carminibus, scriptisque in omni genere exquisitis,
Quibus puri sermonis exemplum posteritati tradidit,
Rectique vivendi disciplinam scite exposuit
      Sacratum manet et manebit,
Sic enim argumenti gravitatem lepore,
Judici severitatem urbanitate temperavit,
Ut bonos erigeret, improvidos excitaret,
Improbos etiam delectatione quadam ad virtutem flecteret.

Natus erat A.D. MDCLXXII.
Auctisque paulatim fortunis
Ad summa reipublicae munera pervenit.
Excessit octavo et quadragesimo anno,
Britannorum decus et deliciae."

R. Westmacott, A.R.A., Sculptor.

It has been translated thus, "Whoever thou art, venerate the
memory of Joseph Addison, in whom Christian faith, virtue, and
good morals, found a continual patron ; whose genius was shown
in verse and every exquisite kind of writing ; who gave to
posterity the best examples of pure language, and the best rules
for living well, which remain and ever will remain sacred ; whose
weight of argument was tempered with wit, and accurate judgment with politeness, so that he encouraged the good and
reformed the improvident, tamed the wicked, and in some degree
made them in love with virtue. He was born in the year 1672,
and his fortune being increased gradually, arrived at length to
public honours. Died in the forty-eighth year of his age, the
honour and delight of the British nation."

l. 23. **Poet's Corner.** A part of the south transept of Westminster Abbey, in which are monuments to Chaucer, Spenser,
Shakespeare, Milton, Dryden, Goldsmith, and other poets.

l. 25. **Chelsea.** See p. 80, l. 3, *supra*, and note.

l. 26. **the Everlasting Club.** See *Spectator*, No. 72.

**the loves of Hilpa and Shalum.** See *Spectator*, Nos. 584
and 585.

# APPENDIX.

## ADDISON'S CHARACTER AND GENIUS.

This essay by Lord Macaulay should be compared with accounts by Johnson, Pope, Thackeray, Courthope, Stopford Brooke, and others. The following extracts will help us to understand Addison aright :

" His chief companions were Steele, Budgell, Philips, Carey, Davenant, and Colonel Brett. . . . Among these friends it was that Addison displayed the elegance of his colloquial accomplishments, which may easily be supposed such as Pope represents them. The remark of Mandeville, who, when he had passed an evening in his company, declared that he was a parson in a tyewig, can detract little from his character : he was always reserved to strangers, and was not incited to uncommon freedom by a character like that of Mandeville. . . . It was his practice, when he found any man invincibly wrong, to flatter his opinions by acquiescence, and sink him yet deeper in absurdity. . . . .

" He was a man in whose presence nothing reprehensible was out of danger : quick in discerning whatever was wrong or ridiculous, and not unwilling to expose it. 'There are,' says Steele, 'in his writings many oblique strokes upon some of the wittiest men of the age.' His delight was more to excite merriment than detestation : and he detects follies rather than crimes.

" If any judgment be made, from his books, of his moral character, nothing will be found but purity and excellence. Knowledge of mankind, indeed less extensive than that of Addison, will show, that to write, and to live, are very different. Many who praise virtue do no more than praise it. Yet it is reasonable to believe that Addison's professions and practice were at no great variance, since amidst that storm of faction in which most of his life was passed, though his station made him conspicuous, and his activity made him formidable, the character given him by his friends was never contradicted by his enemies ; of those, with whom interest or opinion united him, he had not only the esteem, but the kindness ; and of others, whom the violence of opposition drove against him, though he might lose the love, he retained the reverence.

"It is justly observed by Tickell, that he employed wit on the side of virtue and religion. He not only made the proper use of wit himself, but taught it to others : and from this time it has been generally subservient to the cause of reason and of truth. He has dissipated the prejudice that had long connected gaiety with vice, and easiness of manners with laxity of principles. He has restored virtue to its dignity, and taught innocence not to be ashamed. This is an elevation of character 'above all Greek, above all Roman fame.' No greater felicity can genius attain, than that of having purified intellectual pleasure, separated mirth from indecency, and wit from licentiousness ; of having taught a succession of writers to bring elegance and gaiety to the aid of goodness : and if I may use expressions yet more awful, of having 'turned many to righteousness.' . . .

"As a describer of life and manners, he must be allowed to stand perhaps the first of the first rank. His humour, which, as Steele observes, is peculiar to himself, is so happily diffused as to give the grace of novelty to domestic scenes and daily occurrences. He never 'outsteps the modesty of nature,' nor raises merriment or wonder by the violation of truth. His figures neither divert by distortion nor amaze by aggravation. He copies life with so much fidelity that he can be hardly said to invent : yet his exhibitions have an air so much original that it is difficult to suppose them not merely the product of imagination. As a teacher of wisdom, he may be confidently followed. His religion has nothing in it enthusiastick or superstitious : he appears neither weakly credulous, nor wantonly sceptical ; his morality is neither dangerously lax, nor impracticably rigid. All the enchantment of fancy, and all the cogency of argument are employed to recommend to the reader his real interest, the care of pleasing the Author of his being. . . .

"Whoever wishes to attain an English style, familiar but not coarse, and elegant but not ostentatious, must give his days and nights to the volumes of Addison."                    JOHNSON.

"We have seen in Swift a humorous philosopher, whose truth frightens one and whose laughter makes one melancholy. We have had in Congreve a humorous observer of another school, to whom the world seems to have no moral at all, and whose ghastly doctrine seems to be that we should eat, drink, and be merry when we can, and go to the deuce (if there be a deuce) when the time comes. We come now to a humour that flows from quite a different heart and spirit—a wit that makes us laugh and leaves us good and happy ; to one of the kindest benefactors that society has ever had, and I believe you have divined already that I am about to mention Addison's honoured name. From reading over his writings, and the biographies which we have of him, amongst which the famous article in the *Edinburgh Review* may be cited as a magnificent statue of the great writer and moralist of the last age, raised by the love and marvellous skill and genius of one of the most illustrious artists of our own ; looking at that calm, fair face and clear countenance—those chiselled features pure and cold—I can't but fancy that this great man, in this respect like him of whom we spoke in the last lecture (*i.e.* Swift), was also one of the lonely ones of the world. Such men have very few equals, and they don't herd with those. It is in the nature of such lords of intellect to be solitary—they are in the world, but not of it : and our minor struggles, brawls, successes pass under them. . . .

"He must have been one of the finest gentlemen the world ever saw ; at all moments of life serene and courteous, cheerful and calm. He could scarcely ever have had a degrading thought. He might have omitted a virtue or two, or many, but could not have had many faults committed for which he need blush or turn pale. When warmed into confidence, his conversation appears to have been so delightful that the greatest wits sat wrapt and charmed to listen to him. No man bore poverty and narrow fortune with a more lofty cheerfulness.

"Swift describes him over his cups, when Joseph yielded to a temptation which Jonathan resisted. Joseph was of a cold nature, and needed perhaps the fire of wine to warm his blood. If he was a parson, he wore a tye-wig, recollect. A better and more Christian man scarcely ever breathed than Joseph Addison. If he had not that little weakness of wine—why, we could scarcely have found fault with him, and could not have liked him as we do. . . . It is as a Tatler of small-talk, and a Spectator of mankind that we cherish and love him, and owe as much pleasure to him as to any human being that ever wrote. He came in that artificial age, and began to speak with his noble, natural voice. He came the gentle satirist, who hit no unfair blow ; the kind judge, who castigated only in smiling. While Swift went about, hanging and ruthless—a literary Jeffries,—in Addison's kind court only minor cases were tried ; only peccadilloes and small sins against society . . . every one of the little sinners brought before him is amusing, and he dismisses each with the pleasantest penalties, and the most charming words of admonition. . . . Commend me to this dear preacher without orders—this parson in the tye-wig. When this man looks from the world, whose weaknesses he describes so benevolently, up to the Heaven which shines over us all, I can hardly fancy a human face lighted up with a more serene rapture, a human intellect thrilling with a purer love and adoration than Joseph Addison's. . . . His sense of religion stirs through his whole being. In the fields, in the town ; looking at the birds in the trees ; at the children in the streets; in the morning, or in the moonlight; over his books in his own room; in a happy party at a country merry-making, or a town assembly, goodwill and peace to God's creatures, and love and awe of Him who made them, fill his pure heart, and shine from his kind face. If Swift's life was the most wretched, I think Addison's was one of the most enviable. A life prosperous and beautiful—a calm death—an immense fame and affection afterwards for his happy and spotless name."

THACKERAY.

"Addison was perfect good company with intimates, and had something more charming in his conversation than I ever knew in any other man; but with any mixture of strangers, and some-times only with one, he seemed to preserve his dignity much, with a stiff sort of silence." POPE, *Spence's Anecdotes.*

"It was my fate to be much with the wits; my father was acquainted with all of them. Addison was the best company in the world." LADY MARY WORTLEY MONTAGU.

"The characters he introduces, such as Sir Roger de Coverley, are finished studies after nature, and their talk is easy and dramatic. No humour is more fine and tender; and, like Chaucer's, it is never bitter. The style adds to the charm; in its varied cadence and subtle ease it has not been surpassed within its own peculiar sphere in England: and it seems to grow out of the subjects treated of. Addison's work was a great one, lightly done. The *Spectator,* the *Guardian,* and the *Freeholder,* in his hands, gave a better tone to manners, and hence to morals, and a gentler one to political and literary criticism. The essays published every Friday were chiefly on literary subjects, the Saturday essays chiefly on religious subjects. The former popu-larised literature, so that culture spread among the middle classes, and crept down to the country; the latter popularised religion. 'I have brought,' he says, 'philosophy out of closets and libraries, schools and colleges, to dwell in clubs and assem-blies, at tea-tables and in coffee-houses.'"

STOPFORD BROOKE.

"Addison's own disposition seems to have been of that rare and admirable sort which Hamlet praised in Horatio:

'Thou hast been
As one in suffering all that suffers nothing:
A man that Fortune's buffets and rewards
Has ta'en with equal thanks; and blessed are those
Whose blood and judgment are so well commingled
That they are not a pipe for Fortune's finger
To sound what stop she please.'

N

These lines fittingly describe the patient serenity and dignified
independence with which Addison worked his way, amid great
hardships and difficulties, to the highest position in the state;
but they have a yet more honourable application to the task he
performed of reconciling the social dissensions of his countrymen.
'The blood and judgment well commingled,' are visible in the
standard of conduct which he held up for Englishmen in his
writings, as well as in his use of the weapon of ridicule against
all aberrations from good breeding and common sense.  Those
only will estimate him at his true worth who will give, what
Johnson says is his due, 'their days and nights' to the study of
the *Spectator*."

COURTHOPE.

From Young we learn that, when Addison was dying, he asked
to see his wild stepson, the Earl of Warwick, and said to him:
"See in what peace a Christian can die."  But there is more to
be learned from this Christian's life than his death.

At the age of eleven he went to Charter House.  Mr. Courthope writes that "Charter House at that period was, after
Westminster, the best-known school in England, and here was
laid the foundation of that sound classical taste which perfected
the style of the essays in the *Spectator*."  Macaulay tries to prove
that Addison's classical acquirements were only superficial, and
asserts that "his knowledge of Greek, though doubtless such
as was, in his time, thought respectable at Oxford, was evidently
less than that which many lads now carry away every year from
Eton and Rugby."  Without going so far as Macaulay does in
depreciating Addison's knowledge of Greek, we are ready to grant
that Addison acquired a greater knowledge of Latin than of Greek
literature; and there can be no doubt that his proficiency in the
art of Latin composition (both prose and verse) did much to
form that easy dignity of style which few, if any, writers have
been able to imitate with success.

From the Charter House Addison passed, in 1687, at the early
age of fifteen, to Queen's College, Oxford; after spending two
years at that college, he was offered a Demyship at Magdalen
College, and subsequently became Fellow of Magdalen.  In 1699
he received from the crown a pension of £300 a year to enable
him to travel.  He went to France, and spent about eighteen
months in Blois and Paris studying the language.  In December,
1700, he set out for Italy, and spent nearly four years visiting
various cities in that country, in Switzerland, Germany, Austria,
and Holland.  During these travels he was educating his taste,
feeding his imagination, and noting the political life of the
countries through which he passed.

In March, 1702, William III. died, and Addison's travelling
pension ceased with the life of the sovereign that had granted it:
this caused Addison some pecuniary embarrassment.  The next

year his father died, and Addison returned to England in a state
of indigence. He thus experienced "the uses of adversity," without which no man's education is really complete.

Addison took lodgings up three pair of stairs, over a small shop in
the Haymarket ; and here it was that Henry Boyle, Chancellor of
the Exchequer (afterwards Lord Carleton), the emissary of Lord
Treasurer Godolphin, found Addison, and asked him to write a
poem to celebrate the victory of Blenheim. Addison accordingly
wrote *The Campaign*, and was rewarded with a Commissionership of Appeals in Excise.

This was only a stepping-stone to higher honours. From this
moment his success was assured. Supported by influential patrons
he became, in quick succession, Under-Secretary of State, M.P.
for Lostwithiel, for Malmesbury, and for Cavan, Chief Secretary
and Keeper of Records for Ireland, Commissioner for Trade and
Colonies, and finally, in 1717, Secretary of State. He performed
all his political duties with scrupulous integrity. But it is not as
a politician that we think of Addison now ; his statue stands not
among those of England's greatest statesmen, but among those of
her men of letters, in the Poet's corner. While he was passing
thus rapidly from one high office to another in the State, he was
writing poems and papers by means of which he was "the chief
Architect of Public Opinion in the eighteenth century."

He was a scholar, a statesman, a poet, an essay-writer, a
humourist, and a moralist of genuine, but not offensively ob-
trusive, religious feelings. In society, when among intimate and
congenial friends, his brilliant conversation was unequalled ;
"he was the best company in the world," said Lady Mary
Wortley Montagu, herself one of the most beautiful, accomplished and fascinating of women ; but among strangers he was
shy and reserved : this is not infrequently the case with men of
high culture and fine feelings. This shyness, amounting almost
to timidity, prevented him from taking an active part in Parliamentary debates ; but this timidity was not cowardice. He
could, and did, rebuke the faults and foibles of the greatest
and wittiest in the land. It requires a man of coarser fibre
than Addison to be combative in debate, or to bandy words in a
heated discussion. We can imagine the arch look, and eloquent
smile, with which he would acquiesce in the opinions of an opponent "invincibly wrong." That intemperate zeal in politics,
literature, art, or religion, that condescends to vulgar wrangling,
is contrary to all codes of courtesy and morals, and was absolutely distasteful to the dignified, generous, and amiable Addison,
"one of the finest gentlemen the world ever saw."

# CHRONOLOGICAL TABLE.

| Date. | Chief Events in Addison's Life. | Chief Works of some of Addison's Contemporaries. | Contemporary Events. |
|---|---|---|---|
| 1672 | Born on 1st May in the Rectory of Milston, near Amesbury in Wiltshire. | Dryden, *Marriage à la Mode.* | Second Declaration of Indulgence. Invasion of Holland by Louis XIV. Declaration of War by England upon Holland. Murder of De Witt. Election of William, Prince of Orange, at Stadtholder. |
| 1673 | | Sir William Temple, *Observations on the United Provinces of the Netherlands.* | Withdrawal of Declaration of Indulgence. Passing of the Test Act. Practical defeat of the English, and failure of the scheme for landing in Holland. |
| 1674 | | | Peace made with Holland. Milton died. |
| 1675 | His father was made Prebendary of Salisbury Cathedral, and Chaplain - in - Ordinary to the King. | Wycherley, *The Country Wife.* | |
| 1676 | | Etherege, *The Man of Mode, or Sir Fopling Flutter.* | Secret Treaty between Charles II. and Louis XIV. |
| 1677 | | Wycherley, *The Plain Dealer.* | William of Orange married to Princess Mary. |
| 1678 | | Butler, *Hudibras* (Pt. III.). Bunyan, *Pilgrim's Progress.* Tillotson, *Sermons.* | Forces raised and money voted by Parliament for War against France. Secret negotiations between Louis XIV. and Country Party, also between Charles and Louis. England withdraws from opposition to France. Treaty of Nimeguen. Titus Oates' deposition concerning Popish Plot. |

| Date. | Chief Events in Addison's Life. | Chief Works of some of Addison's Contemporaries. | Contemporary Events. |
|---|---|---|---|
| 1679 | | Burnet, *History of the Reformation of the Church of England* (Vol. I.). | Act for Licensing and for the Regulation of Printing (passed in 1662) expired. Habeas Corpus Act passed. Battle of Bothwell Bridge. |
| 1680 | | Otway, *The Orphan.* | The Exclusion Bill rejected by the Peers. |
| 1681 | | Dryden, *Absalom and Achitophel, The Medal.* | Strassburg seized. Luxemburg besieged by Louis XIV. |
| 1682 | | Dryden, *Mac-Flecknoe, Religio Laici.* Otway, *Venice Preserved.* Tillotson, *Sermons.* | Monmouth arrested at Stafford. |
| 1683 | His father was made Dean of Lichfield Addison went to Lichfield Grammar School for a short time. | | Discovery of the Rye-House Plot. |
| 1684 | Went to Charter House. | Bunyan, *Holy War.* | Flight of Monmouth to Holland. |
| 1685 | | | Death of Charles II. Accession of James II. Expedition of Argyll from Holland to Scotland, his failure and execution. Monmouth lands at Lyme, was defeated at Sedgmoor, captured and executed. The Bloody Assize. Revocation of the Edict of Nantes by Louis XIV. Flight of the Huguenots from France. James II. violates Test Act and claims dispensing power. |
| 1686 | | | Court of Ecclesiastical Commission established. |

| Date. | Chief Events in Addison's Life. | Chief Works of some of Addison's Contemporaries. | Contemporary Events. |
|---|---|---|---|
| 1687 | Left Charter House, entered Queen's Coll., Oxford. | Dryden, *The Hind and Panther.* Newton, *Principia Philosophiae Naturalis Mathematica.* Prior, *The City and Country Mouse.* | Declaration of Indulgence. James' attack upon the Universities. |
| 1688 | | | Declaration of Indulgence to be read in churches. Resistance and trial of the seven Bishops. William landed at Torbay. James escaped to France. |
| 1689 | Elected to a Demyship at Magdalen Coll., Oxford. | Locke, *Letter on Toleration.* | Declaration of Right. Proclamation of William and Mary as King and Queen. Grand Alliance between England, Holland, Spain, and Austria. James landed in Ireland. Siege of Londonderry. Passing of Mutiny Act and Toleration Act. The Bill of Rights. |
| 1690 | | Pepys, *Memoirs.* Locke, *Two Treatises on Government, Essay on the Human Understanding.* | Battle of the Boyne. |
| 1691 | | | Siege and capture of Limerick. |
| 1692 | | | Marlborough's plot to place Princess Anne on the throne. Massacre of Glencoe. Victory of La Hogue. Capture of Namur, and victory at Steenkirk by the French. |

| Date. | Chief Events in Addison's Life. | Chief Works of some of Addison's Contemporaries. | Contemporary Events. |
|---|---|---|---|
| 1693 | Took the degree of M.A. Wrote *Account of the Greatest English Poets, Verses to Dryden.* | Congreve, *The Old Bachelor, The Double Dealer.* Locke, *Thoughts concerning Education.* | Party Government advised by Lord Sunderland, and gradually adopted. |
| 1694 | *Translation of Fourth Book of Georgics, Essay on the Georgics.* | Tillotson, *Sermons.* | Triennial Bill passed. Death of Queen Mary. |
| 1695 | *Address to King William.* | Congreve, *Love for Love.* Locke, *The Reasonableness of Christianity, The Conduct of the Understanding.* | Siege and capture of Namur by William. |
| 1696 | | | Act for regulating Trials for Treason. Jacobite plots. |
| 1697 | *Verses on the Peace of Ryswick*(Latin). Probationary Fellow of Magdalen College. *Translation of the Second Book of Metamorphoses.* | Dryden, *Translation of Virgil, Alexander's Feast.* Congreve, *The Mourning Bride.* Vanbrugh, *The Relapse, The Provoked Wife.* | The Peace of Ryswick. |
| 1698 | Fellow of Magdalen College. | Jeremy Collier, *A Short View of the Profaneness and Immorality of the English Stage.* | First Partition Treaty to settle the question of the Spanish succession. |
| 1699 | Received from the Crown a travelling pension of £300 a year. *Pygmaeogerano-machia* (in *Musae Anglicanae*). In the summer he crossed over to France, he resided at Blois studying French. | Bentley, *Dissertation on the Epistles of Phalaris.* | Death of the Electoral Prince. |
| 1700 | He went to Paris; met Malebranche, Boileau, and others. In December set out from Marseilles to Genoa for a tour in Italy. | Dryden, *Fables.* Farquhar, *The Constant Couple.* Congreve, *The Way of the World.* Prior, *Carmen Seculare.* | Second Partition Treaty. Death of Charles II. of Spain. Outbreak of the War of the Spanish Succession. |

| Date. | Chief Events in Addison's Life. | Chief Works of some of Addison's Contemporaries. | Contemporary Events. |
|---|---|---|---|
| 1701 | In December he passed over Mont Cenis to Geneva (on the journey he wrote *Letter from Italy*), thence to Fribourg, Berne, Zurich, etc., etc. | Steele, *The Christian Hero*. | Grand Alliance between England, Holland, and the Emperor, joined subsequently by Prussia, Sweden, and the Palatinate. Death of James II. |
| 1702 | In the autumn he arrived in Vienna. On his way home passed through Germany and Holland; spent considerable time at Hamburg. Lost his pension. His father died. | Steele, *The Funeral or Grief à la Mode*. Clarendon, *History of the Great Rebellion*. | Death of William III. Accession of Anne. |
| 1703 | Corresponded with the Duke of Somerset about the tutorship of Lord Hertford, Somerset's son. Returned to England. Published *Remarks on Italy*. | Farquhar, *The Inconstant*. Rowe, *The Fair Penitent*. John Philips, *The Splendid Shilling*. Steele, *The Tender Husband*. | Queen Anne's Bounty. The great storm. |
| 1704 | Wrote *The Campaign*, and was rewarded with a Commissionership of Appeals in Excise. | Swift, *The Battle of the Books. Tale of a Tub*. Mandeville, *Æsop Dressed, or Fables writ in Familiar Verse*. | Battle of Blenheim. |
| 1705 | Attended Lord Halifax to the Court of Hanover. | John Philips, *Blenheim*. Pope, *Pastorals, Versions from Chaucer*. Temple, *Miscellanea*. | Regency Bill passed. |
| 1706 | Under-Secretary of State. *Rosamond* was performed on 2nd April. | Farquhar, *The Recruiting Officer*. | Battle of Ramilies. |
| 1707 | *The Present State of the War*. | Farquhar, *The Beaux' Stratagem*. | Act of Union with Scotland in operation. |
| 1708 | M.P. for Lostwithiel. | John Philips, *Cider*. | Battle of Oudenarde. |

| Date. | Chief Events in Addison's Life | Chief Works of some of Addison's Contemporaries. | Contemporary Events. |
|---|---|---|---|
| 170J | Chief-Secretary for Ireland (under Wharton), and Keeper of the Records. M.P. for Cavan. Wrote Papers in *The Tatler*. Friendship with Swift. | Ambrose Phillips, *Pastorals*. Steele published the firs number of *The Tatler*. | Battle of Malplaquet. |
| 1710 | M.P. for Malmesbury. In the Autumn lost Secretaryship and Keepership of the Records. Wrote *Whig-Examiner*. | Berkeley, *The Principles of Human Knowledge*. | Impeachment of Dr. Sacheverell. |
| 1711 | Last number of *The Tatler*. First number of *The Spectator*. Resigned Fellowship of Magdalen Coll. Bought estate of Bilton, near Rugby. | Pope, *Essay on Criticism*. Shaftesbury, *Characteristics of Men, Manners, Opinions, and Times*. | Occasional Conformity Act. |
| 1712 | Made Pope's acquaintance. Wrote essays in *The Guardian*. | Pope, *Rape of the Lock*. Ambrose Phillips, *The Distressed Mother*. Swift, *The Conduct of the Allies*. | Negotiations for peace opened at Utrecht. |
| 1713 | *Cato* was performed. *The late Trial and Conviction of Count Tariff*. Began *Evidences of the Christian Religion*. | Pope, *Windsor Forest*, *Ode to St. Cecilia's Day*. Gray, *The Wife of Bath*. Steele started *The Guardian*. | Treaty of Utrecht. |
| 1714 | Chief-Secretary for Ireland (under Sunderland). | Rowe, *Jane Shore*. Pope, *The Temple of Fame*. Gay, *What d'ye call it?* Mandeville, *The Fable of the Bees*. | Death of Queen Anne. Accession of George I. |
| 1715 | First number of *The Freeholder*. Rupture with Pope. | Pope, *Translation of Iliad* (Vol. I.). | Riot Act passed. The Jacobite Rebellion. Battle of Sheriffmuir. |
| 1716 | Commissioner for Trade and Colonies. Married to the Countess of Warwick. | Shaftesbury, *Letters by a Noble Lord to a Young Man at the University*. Lady Mary Wortley Montagu, *Town Eclogues*. | Flight of Pretender to France. |

| Date. | Chief Events in Addison's Life. | Chief Works of some of Addison's Contemporaries. | Contemporary Events. |
|---|---|---|---|
| 1717 | Secretary of State. | Pope, *Elegy on an Unfortunate Lady*, *Epistle from Eloisa to Abelard*. Pope and Gay, *Three Hours after Marriage*. | Triple Alliance between England, France, and Holland. |
| 1718 | Resigned Secretaryship of State. | | Quadruple Alliance between Great Britain, the Emperor, France, and Holland. |
| 1719 | Controversy between *The Old Whig* and *The Plebeian*. Died of asthma and dropsy on 17th July, at Holland House: was buried in Westminster Abbey. | Defoe, *Robinson Crusoe*. | Proposal of the Peerage Bill. |

Works published after his death, *Dialogues on Medals* (written during his tour in Germany), *The Drummer* (written probably about 1712), *Evidences of the Christian Religion* (left unfinished, begun in 1713).

# INDEX TO THE NOTES.

GLASGOW: PRINTED AT THE UNIVERSITY PRESS BY ROBERT MACLEHOSE AND CO.

www.ingramcontent.com/pod-product-compliance
Lightning Source LLC
Chambersburg PA
CBHW020609030726
47497CB00007B/2158